Praise for *Haunting Beauty*

"A complex, mysterious, and very satisfying story!"　　—Diana Gabaldon

"An intriguing, highly absorbing book that sucked me in and didn't let me go until its amazing conclusion. I was completely swept away by the mystery, the magical ambience, the vivid setting, and the chilling and original plot. A highly recommended must-read!"

　　　　　　　　　　　—Jennifer Ashley, *USA Today* bestselling author

"A dark and passionate romance with the literary brilliance of *The Time Traveler's Wife*."　　—Kathryne Kennedy, author of *Enchanting the Beast*

"Erin Quinn weaves a mystical tale of intrigue and seduction . . . The imagery is breathtaking and the prose is beautiful and authentic . . . You live the story, not just read it."　　—Calista Fox, author of *Object of Desire*

"Celtic fans will enjoy this trip into the Irish mists, which had plenty of legends and mystical visions. While the ghosts, evil books, and inherited capabilities are pretty standard, the way Quinn weaves them together is clever."　　　　　　　　　　　　　　　　—*Romantic Times*

"A complex story with lifelike characters, seductive passion, and . . . a wonderful dash of magical mystery. Vivid and breathtaking . . . *Haunting Beauty* is a book that you won't want to put down and leaves you breathless for more. The twists and turns Ms. Quinn throws you throughout the story suck you right in, right until the very end."

　　　　　　　　　　　　—*Night Owl* (Top Pick, 4 ½ stars)

"An intricately woven story where each day is touched by magic . . . Filled with fascinating characters, wonderful detail, and the beautiful scenery of Ireland. Readers will be drawn in right from the start. I would recommend this book to fans of paranormal romance that enjoy mystical elements and edge-of-your-seat suspense."　　　—*Darque Reviews*

Berkley Sensation titles by Erin Quinn

HAUNTING BEAUTY

HAUNTING WARRIOR

HAUNTING DESIRE

Haunting Desire

Erin Quinn

BERKLEY SENSATION, NEW YORK

THE BERKLEY PUBLISHING GROUP
Published by the Penguin Group
Penguin Group (USA) Inc.
375 Hudson Street, New York, New York 10014, USA
Penguin Group (Canada), 90 Eglinton Avenue East, Suite 700, Toronto, Ontario M4P 2Y3, Canada
(a division of Pearson Penguin Canada Inc.)
Penguin Books Ltd., 80 Strand, London WC2R 0RL, England
Penguin Group Ireland, 25 St. Stephen's Green, Dublin 2, Ireland (a division of Penguin Books Ltd.)
Penguin Group (Australia), 250 Camberwell Road, Camberwell, Victoria 3124, Australia
(a division of Pearson Australia Group Pty. Ltd.)
Penguin Books India Pvt. Ltd., 11 Community Centre, Panchsheel Park, New Delhi—110 017, India
Penguin Group (NZ), 67 Apollo Drive, Rosedale, Auckland 0632, New Zealand
(a division of Pearson New Zealand Ltd.)
Penguin Books (South Africa) (Pty.) Ltd., 24 Sturdee Avenue, Rosebank, Johannesburg 2196,
South Africa

Penguin Books Ltd., Registered Offices: 80 Strand, London WC2R 0RL, England

This book is an original publication of The Berkley Publishing Group.

Copyright © 2011 by Erin Grady.
Excerpt from *Haunting Embrace* by Erin Quinn copyright © by Erin Grady.
Cover illustration by Tony Mauro.
Cover design by George Long.
Interior text design by Tiffany Estreicher.

PRINTING HISTORY
Berkley Sensation trade paperback edition / April 2011

Library of Congress Cataloging-in-Publication Data

Quinn, Erin, 1963–
   Haunting desire / Erin Quinn.
      p.   cm.
   ISBN: 978-0-425-23895-0
   I. Title.
   PS3617.U5635H385   2011
   813'.6—dc22   2010054168

PRINTED IN THE UNITED STATES OF AMERICA

10 9 8 7 6 5 4 3 2 1

This one's for Judith Barker,
my favorite harpie,
who drew the dragon that looked like a dog
and stopped the insanity (if only for a moment).
You da bomb dot com, girlfriend.

Acknowledgments

It's a serious thing when an author can't find the words to express something, but I find myself in that boat as I try to thank Kate Seaver for all of her hard work in getting this book from my head to your hands. Special thanks also go to Paige Wheeler, who reminded me that breathing is never a bad thing and should be done in times of crisis.

Lynn Coulter and Kathryne Kennedy delivered insight, feedback, and a whole lot of TLC while I wrote this book. I am so lucky to have you for friends and I hope you know how much I appreciate all you do. Caroline Curran came through once more with words of wisdom on all things Irish. Any mistakes in that area are my own. Special thanks to Rebecca Goude Johnson, Julie Mahler, and Jodie Springer for their wonderful proofreading skills and feedback.

And I could not have survived this past year without the love and support of my family. My husband, daughters, and Mom and Dad—I thank you from the top, bottom, and gooey middle of my heart.

Chapter One

NOTHING was going the way Shealy had planned.

"Dad, be reasonable. I just—"

"*Reasonable*?" Donnell O'Leary demanded, his face turning an alarming shade of red.

They'd just finished dinner and were leaving the restaurant as he spoke, his outburst drawing the eyes of the other patrons. Shealy had known her dad wouldn't be happy about her plans, but she hadn't anticipated this. She eyed his coloring with dismay. He'd already had one heart attack—she didn't want to give him another.

"I've told you this before, Shealy," he said in a tight, angry voice. "There is nothing for you in Ireland. *Not one bleeding thing.* No reason to go back. Ever."

"I want to visit Mom's grave," she said calmly. "And I don't understand why that should upset you."

"Why would you care about seeing her grave?" he exclaimed, as if the idea were too bizarre to contemplate. "She's not even in it."

For a moment, his words robbed her of a response. She knew her mother's body wasn't in the grave—after the awful automobile accident, her body had never been found. But seven years had passed since her death, and Shealy needed closure that still hadn't come. It was so unlike her father, so insensitive of him not to understand that. She'd been in the hospital when they'd held the funeral services, and then her dad had packed them up and moved them to Arizona. She'd never even *seen* the place where her mother rested, in spirit if not in body.

But she didn't want to explain to him why she was so determined to go there now. She couldn't talk about the nightmares that chased her through the restless dark. Nightmares about her mother— horrible, gruesome dreams that told her that the time had come to face everything she'd tried to forget. She needed to move on and that meant going back first.

"It's not safe there," her father stubbornly continued as she stepped into the warm night air outside of the restaurant.

"Safe? Dad, Ireland is ten times safer than Phoenix. Their crime rate—"

"It's not safe for *you*, Shealy."

The sharpness of his tone held a bite that stopped her on the shadowed blacktop. Somewhere in the back of her mind a strange tickling sensation began, creeping down her spine, making her skin pucker despite the summer heat that still held tight to the evening.

"What's that supposed to mean?" she asked. "Why wouldn't it be safe for me?"

He avoided her eyes. "There are things you don't know, Shealy."

"So enlighten me."

"Things that should not be talked about, not in the open. Not at all."

Ah. Inside, she gave a sigh of relief and a mental eye roll as understanding hit her. For a minute there, he'd actually rattled her.

Donnell O'Leary was a conspiracy theorist to the depths of his wee Irish soul. He had issues and opinions about everything from underworld religion to common traffic laws. No doubt next he planned to spout about the Troubles or the Government or, God forbid, the Protestants.

"Dad, let's try to stay within the bounds of reality. I'm talking about a trip to a civilized country. Two weeks in the land of green and blarney. I'm not headed for Juárez, for God's sake. I'll be back before you even know I'm gone. I've already got my ticket. I'm going."

Donnell grabbed her arm as she moved past him and jerked her around to face him with a sudden violence that shocked her into silence. "Do you think I took you away from there on a whim? Do you think I'd have ripped us both up by the roots if I'd had a choice?"

For a moment, she could only stare at him, noting his color, the spark in his eyes that almost looked like panic. Frowning, she said, "You told me we moved because of the doctors. The specialists at Mayo Clinic that Dr. Campbell wanted me to see."

"Aye. And in part that's true. But there's more to it, things I've shielded from you. Things that are best left alone. Things you need to stay *away* from. Are you hearing me, girl? You are *not. Going. Back.*"

A gust of hot wind blew across the parking lot, chasing the echo of his anger. The restaurant had been packed when they'd arrived and they'd had to park in the back, by the trash. Now the lot was dark and deserted. The burned-out streetlight over their car left shadows creeping across the heated tar and whispering sounds rasping against the abruptly taut silence that followed.

She wanted to tell him to calm down. She was twenty-four years old and didn't need his permission, but an undefined feeling of threat prickled and poked at her. She opened her mouth to demand to know what these mysterious *things* he'd been protecting her from were, but an instinct as old as time silenced her and urged her toward the car. Pushing her to get out of the open.

"Let's—"

"Shhhh," he said. His eyes were wide, his expression frightened as he scanned the empty parking lot.

The air grated against them, lifting the hem of her skirt and blustering beneath it. It was hot—always hot in Arizona—but now that heat had weight and a dark, malevolent substance.

A trill of fear crept down her spine, but she didn't know what had scared her, why she suddenly had a sense of déjà vu that clenched her tight and terrified her.

"Get to the car," Donnell said, turning her and pulling her to the Toyota.

"What's going on?"

A sound—like a hundred nails running down a chalkboard, like a thousand knives scraping china, like millions of screams that went on unending—ripped through the oppressive quiet. The blistering cacophony surrounded them, an invisible wall that herded them into shadow and gloom.

"Dad, what is that?" she asked, gripping his hand, feeling the tremors coursing through his body. That tangible evidence of his alarm escalated her own. Her dad had weakened with illness, but remained one of the bravest men she'd ever known.

He tried to pull her toward the car, but the air felt strangely gelatinous, a membrane holding them captive in the small space they filled. Beyond the unseen barrier, the everyday world faded until there was only dusky night alive with that terrible sound. Shealy clapped her hands over her ears and so did Donnell, both of them turning in place, searching for an exit. Seeking an explanation.

Beneath her feet the asphalt began to rumble and shake. Pieces of the parking lot cracked, spidering like a shattered windshield. Was it an earthquake? A car alarm joined the melee, as if in response to her panicked thoughts. She grasped at a perverse sense of comfort the explanation brought. Earthquakes were real. Shadows that hemmed people in weren't.

But even as she thought it the darkness to her left split down the middle, like a huge piece of velvet ripped in two. She heard the sound of it tearing, felt her breath seize in her chest as she watched the fissure grow. Felt again that unfathomable sense of déjà vu. Through the rent in the night, she saw a rock wall shooting straight up, perpendicular to the earth. At its base was a huge stone plateau and on it stood a man and a teenage boy.

Mouth dry, Shealy saw the man suddenly look up, his golden brown eyes wide with shock. For an instant they stared at one another, Shealy and this man, and she felt the touch of that glance like she did the heat, the fear.

A queer sense of recognition staggered her.

There was no way she'd met this man before and then forgotten him. No possible way. He stood well over six feet, perhaps even six five. Tall and muscular, so perfectly sculpted the Greeks might have used him as the model of Atlas, holding the world on his shoulders. A wound seeped blood into the fabric of his open shirt and splattered the burnished skin of his tight, massive chest and muscular abdomen, but he stood tall and strong. And those eyes . . . those incredible eyes . . .

Who was he? Where was he?

Donnell muttered something that sounded like *Tier Nawn* and squeezed her hand tightly. She jerked her gaze from the man to her dad, saw the anger and . . . *recognition* in his face.

She'd barely had time to process that not only did Donnell see the man, but he recognized him, too, when a second section of darkness shredded to her right and through the gaping hole she saw another man, standing alone in a white room that gleamed with marble. Like a photonegative of the dark and powerful warrior to her left, this one had pale skin with blue eyes that blazed with rage and . . . *triumph.*

"Feck!" her father shouted and tried to put Shealy behind him, but the world shuddered violently, nearly knocking them off their feet. As if looking through windows, the two men caught sight of one another and the reaction was instantaneous. Murderous.

The one with the golden brown eyes lunged forward, exploding from the gash in the darkness like a demon. The pale man moved only seconds slower. In a heartbeat they stood in the swirling circle of confusion with Shealy and her dad trapped in the middle between them.

The blond man made a grab for Shealy, but her father blocked it. Enraged, he struck Donnell hard in the face, making him stagger back. Shealy's screams joined the chaos as she tried to get around her father and stop his attacker. Her dad was not as strong as he used to be—illness had withered away much of the brawn that he'd once worn so easily—but he seemed determined to keep her safe.

The pale man came at them again, but the dark one with the luminous golden eyes—the one her dad had called *Tier Nawn*—shoved the other man back, shouting something at him that Shealy couldn't understand. It felt like the world exploded, *im*ploded, ripping free of its moorings. Everything began to spin.

The ruptures in the darkness shrank, that gummy membrane surrounding them growing tighter, pinning them. And yet, the pale man strode forward easily, intent on Shealy. She didn't know why, didn't know how to evade him when the very air had become an enemy imprisoning her. *What, in God's name, did he want?*

Her father tried to stop him, but he gave Donnell a hard blow that sent him sprawling on the ground. She was still screaming, but she couldn't even hear her own voice over the roaring coming from beneath her feet, overhead, all around. His fingers reached for her throat and in his eyes she saw victory.

And then the other man slammed into them both, knocking the pale man away and falling on top of Shealy.

All the breath left her body as he crushed her beneath him. Her head hit hard against the asphalt. She saw stars, bright bursts of color, then black on black nothingness.

"Who?" she tried to ask. *Who are you?*

But the viscous cocoon caved in around them and Shealy felt a great suction pulling her. She cried out for her father, heard the echo of his voice as he shouted her name. She turned her head, saw him prone beside her, managed to get her hand out and touch her fingers to his just as the pale man, relentless and determined, crawled over Donnell's inert body to reach her. But in the same instant, a force she couldn't comprehend hauled her toward that great tear in the darkness, to that rocky cliff she'd glimpsed earlier.

The suctioning pressure grew until it felt like it would crush her, collapse her rib cage, and compress her skull, leaving her nothing more than flattened goo on the sizzling parking lot. The man on top of her tried to ease his weight, pushing up with massive arms. He was enormous, his muscles so sculpted they looked illusory. But the weight of him added to that grinding pressure left her in no doubt that every single inch of him was real. He had dirt smudged on his face, a bloody cut on his collarbone, and eyes that burned like whiskey. He stared into her face as if he might find answers there. If she hadn't been so scared, she might have saved him the trouble. Shealy O'Leary didn't have any answers.

Still he probed, grimacing as the air compressed, excruciating and unyielding. She stared into his eyes, feeling his ragged breath fan her face, the tremble of his arms as he fought an unwinnable battle with the agonizing pressure.

Who *was* this man?

The force bore down on them both and she clenched her eyes tight, knowing she'd probably never find out the answer because whatever was happening to her would likely kill them both. The man fought the weight of it, but his arms finally gave and he collapsed. His body covered her from head to toe, their faces side by side, his breath now a hot burst against her ear. The shrieking sounds rose to a crescendo, and then suddenly it felt as if they'd punched through the crust of asphalt and were falling. . . .

Chapter Two

"Christ's blood!" someone shouted.

Shealy turned her head sharply, sending jolts of agony to every nerve ending in her body. She was prone, spread out on something hard and uncomfortable. The teenage boy she'd glimpsed from the parking lot—the one she'd seen with the warrior through the rip in the darkness—stood beside her, looking down with an expression of horrified shock.

She tried to take a breath, to speak, but that crushing weight still pinned her and she couldn't draw in enough air to form words. In the same instant a handful of rapid, bewildering realizations hit her hard: the heaviness pressing down on her belonged to the dark warrior, sprawled over her body; the shadows and gloom had morphed into a bright and sunny day; the screeching noises had been replaced with what sounded like a pack of wild beasts fighting over a bloody bone; and—she craned her neck to search in every direction she could—she didn't see her father anywhere.

"Is my brother dead?" the boy demanded in a deep voice that was a pubescent contradiction to the youthful face. "Did y' kill him? I'll cut yer throat if y've harmed him, I swear I will."

The boy reached for a dagger when the man on top of her groaned and moved. Slowly he lifted his head from where it rested in the crook of her shoulder and neck. He looked disoriented, as confused as she was. Then those strange golden brown eyes met hers and the fog cleared, leaving them sharp and hot. He stared at her and the moment stretched out . . . unfurled . . . snapped.

Every cell in her body felt that look, felt the charge of electricity that hummed beneath the whiskey glow. Then the gaze moved from her eyes to her face, to the scars on her chin and throat, to the damaged shell of her ear. There were prying questions and hot awareness in every flick of its touch. Instinct made her want to cover her scars, turn her face away, but he'd trapped her with his unwavering perusal, pinned her with his big, heavy body.

As if suddenly realizing he was crushing her, he heaved himself up and off, rolling until he lay flat on his back beside her. Gratefully, Shealy sucked in a deep and painful breath. Somewhere nearby, the gnashing and snarling beasts she heard began to bay. It sounded like hundreds of them frothing for something. . . .

Where *was* she? Where had her dad gone? She gazed frantically in every direction but could see no sign of him.

The brilliant blue of the sky above hurt her eyes. The rocky, rough surface beneath her felt jagged in places. After a stunned moment, she surmised that she must be sprawled on the enormous flat stone she'd seen through the bizarre hole in the darkness. She remembered the feeling of being sucked in and then plunging through. . . .

She sat up suddenly, dizzy as the blood rushed from her head. "Where's my dad? What happened to him?" she said at the same time the boy asked, "Tiarnan, where did y' go? One minute y' were there and then . . ."

The man held up a hand to stop the questions and then stood on unsteady legs. For a moment he swayed, and Shealy watched anxiously. His shirt was stained with blood, his face gray and his hands raw. She remembered how he'd fought the pale man. Remembered how she'd felt that baffling sense of recognition.

"Where is my dad?" she asked again, more forcefully.

He ignored her question as he asked his own. "How did y' do it? How did y' pull me out?"

"Pull you . . . *Me*? I didn't do anything. You came out of . . . out of . . ." She flung her hands wide to indicate the great unknown that surrounded them. "Out of *here*. You came at me—at us. Not the other way around. I want to know where my dad went!"

Her voice rose with her panic, with her fear. The warrior watched her, silent but missing nothing. *Tier Nawn*, her father had called him, but the boy had given the pronunciation a softer lilt. *Tiarnan.*

"The old man was yer father?" he asked at last.

She nodded, hating that he'd said *was* instead of *is*. His words were shaped strangely, though, and she tried to tell herself he hadn't meant to use past tense. She had the perplexing sense that she shouldn't understand him at all, remembered how in the parking lot he'd shouted at the pale man and she'd been unable to decipher what he'd said.

The boy, Tiarnan's brother, said, "It must have been him that did it, then."

More confused by the moment, Shealy exclaimed, "That did *what*? What are you talking about? My father didn't *do* anything. That's what I'm telling you. You opened the darkness and then that other man—"

"Cathán," the warrior said. "He wanted y'."

Shealy stared at him, struck by the ring of unwanted truth in his words. She remembered how the pale man had charged her, knocked her father out of the way to get to her. If not for Tiarnan, he would have succeeded.

"I've never heard of Cathán. My dad and I were just walking to our car when you both attacked."

In two strides he stood in front of her and hunkered down so that his face was very close to hers. He balanced on the balls of his feet, agile, lethal, ready to pounce if she tried to flee. He lifted a hand and she flinched. Eyes narrowing with displeasure at that telling gesture, his long fingers curled against her chin and, he tilted her face so she could not avoid his eyes.

"I did not attack y', lass," he said darkly.

Shealy felt heat rise in her cheeks. No, he hadn't. In fact, he'd saved her from the pale man.

"But it's your fault I'm here," she managed to say, not sure at all if she spoke the truth. "You brought me."

Something flashed in those incredible eyes, something masculine and possessive, as if that simple statement—*you brought me*—had somehow made her his. She felt her mouth go dry, her heart begin to hammer.

"What is yer father's name? Tell me."

Bristling at his bossy tone, she mumbled, "Donnell. Donnell O'Leary."

"Leary," both he and his brother said at once, as if the name were a filthy profanity. He dropped his hand and stood abruptly.

"*O*'Leary," she corrected, more baffled by the moment.

Tiarnan said, "And did yer father take y' to the place I found y' so he could give y' to Cathán? Did he plan it?"

"Are you crazy?" she snapped. "No. That man *attacked* us. He hurt my father. Might have . . ."

She swallowed hard. She would not say what she thought. Her dad wasn't here, but that didn't mean the worst had happened. That didn't mean he wasn't someplace else—someplace safe. Someplace where wild beasts weren't howling like creatures of the night. She took a deep breath.

"My father would never have intentionally put me in harm's way," she said in a low voice.

Tiarnan studied her with such intensity she wanted to squirm. Then at last he said, "I believe y'."

She didn't know why she trusted him, why his belief in her mattered so much, but relief made her eyes sting and caught her off guard, taunting the weepy feeling swelling inside her. She stiffened her back, tried to focus her mind on anything but throwing herself into those strong-looking arms and bawling like a baby.

"Tiarnan," the boy said. "We're trapped and they've doubled since y' vanished. We've not time to sort this out now."

Shealy didn't need him to spell out what *they* were. She could hear them. The frenzied animals had grown more agitated at the sound of their voices, and their loud snarls finally seemed to register in Tiarnan's awareness. He strode to the edge of the stone tableau and looked down. The insanely snarling beasts must have been waiting just below, because their barks and growls escalated. Rabid. Echoing off the shale and slate, rebounding from the clear blue sky.

He cursed softly.

What in the hell was down there?

Shealy's body felt battered and torn, but she forced herself to stand. The boy glared at her, still holding his knife. The look in his eyes said he knew how to use it and he wouldn't hesitate.

Good to know.

Giving the bloodthirsty boy a wide berth, she hobbled to the edge of the flattened rock, taking in the landscape that crowded up to it. Harsh, unforgiving, drenched in green so lush it hurt her eyes, it stretched out, connecting the rocky crag looming behind her to the dark forest in the distance ahead. The browns and blacks of bark and boulders looked like violent scars in a drenched mosaic. The colors were too bright, *too stark* to be real.

And yet, without a doubt, it *was* real. Horrifyingly real.

She reached the edge and looked down.

Wolves, more than she could count, jockeyed and fought to climb onto the elevated table and reach them on top of the large flat rock. They were huge creatures with matted fur and bloody snouts. They jumped and nipped, snapping at one another, foaming at the mouth. With a cry, she stumbled back into something hard and unyielding. Arms came up around her, steadying her, holding her. She spun within them and found herself face to bare chest with the dark warrior.

She tilted her head, all too aware of the muscles and strength in that chest, all too aware of the man standing so close she could feel his heat. He smelled of leather and sweat and the fresh sea air.

Her gaze moved up the solid wall of muscle to the strong, square chin, the nose—crooked and scarred from breaking—the slashing dark brows arched over those amazing golden eyes, the long sooty lashes that framed them. His features were masculine and beautiful. A work of art in rough-hewn lines and forbidding tones. Compelling. Fascinating. *Dangerous.*

"Where are we?" she asked, surprised by the huskiness in her voice.

She felt his gaze on her scars again and automatically shook her head, letting her hair fall forward to hide them. He frowned at the gesture, rattling what little composure she had.

"We are in Fennore," he said.

Even his voice set off a tingle inside her.

"Ireland?" she asked. *Ireland? This?* "But . . . how . . . where . . . Are you saying this is the Isle of Fennore?"

She hated to even ask the question. The car accident that had killed her pregnant mother and nearly killed Shealy had occurred on the Isle of Fennore. She would never think of one without the other.

"No," he answered. "'Tis the black heart of Fennore. Inis Brandubh."

Brawn-doov. He made it sound almost musical, but she didn't know what it meant. Her Irish had never been good, and most of it had been forgotten in the years since she'd lived on American soil. *Inis* she recognized, though. That was *island.* So did he mean they were on Black Heart Island?

She gave Tiarnan a wary look, found him studying her again. His big hands were splayed over her waist, warm and disturbing, still holding her against his body. She should push him away, but something in the stillness of his grip, in the swirling gold and brown of his eyes stopped her. For a moment she felt the burn and churn of a conflict within him that she had no hope of understanding.

"Who are y'?" he asked at last.

"I'm Shealy," she said. "Shealy O'Leary."

"Leary," he muttered once more in a tone that held a confusing mix of accusation, confirmation, and resignation.

He released her, stepping back with a reluctance she couldn't miss. Her body swayed in protest, agreeing wholeheartedly that he should continue to hold her, to hold back her fears. As he turned, she caught another glimpse of emotion in those whiskey eyes. Regret and hunger, at war with one another.

"Who are *you*?" she asked when he began to pace like a caged lion, scanning the rocky cliff face behind them, then stalking to the other side of the stone plateau and staring out into the distance.

"I am Tiarnan."

As if that should explain everything.

"And this is my brother, Liam. We are prisoners here."

Prisoners? Shealy felt her jaw drop. "Why? Why are you prisoners?"

He flashed her a quick look. "*Why* is a pointless question and one neither of us can answer."

The ferocious wolves tracked him from the ground as he paced from edge to edge of the stone, jumping and yelping in vicious excitement. It suddenly dawned on her that Tiarnan was looking for a means to make their precarious perch defensible or a way to make their escape.

Good God, he thought those wolves would find a way up. Her realization came with a thousand grisly images that nearly made her swoon. She'd thought they were safe as long as they remained on their elevated perch.

Abandoning further questions, she spun and searched the same formidable rocks and vistas, seeing nothing that looked even close to an escape route. Worse, she saw that the rising slope behind them left their sanctuary uncertain at best. If those wolves were half as smart as the wolves she'd seen on the Discovery Channel, they'd find a way up the crag's face. She saw a point higher up where, if they reached it, they could leap over the gulf to the top of the stone plateau and get to their human prey.

Tiarnan examined the landscape with focused intensity. There were dark blotches in the shale that might have been caves, and he studied each silently. His shoulders were tight, his expression drawn. In his stance, in his steady weighing of odds, the considering glance at her, the pensive look at his brother . . . all of it gave her a flash of insight. This man was no stranger to dire circumstances. In that moment, he looked like someone accustomed to being the barrier between the life and death of those who depended on him. Accustomed to it and so weary of it. She saw it in every line of his body.

As if sensing her eyes on him, he looked up and once again pinned her with the heat of his gaze. It felt like he could see right through her to the vulnerability she fought so hard to hide. He might have saved her when the one he called Cathán had attacked, but she'd be a fool not to recognize danger in this man.

She broke away from the force of his stare and took a step back, searching for a way off this rock that didn't end with being eaten alive. On one side stood the forest that might offer shelter, but to get there they'd have to cross the wide open valley where there would be ample space for the pack to surround and kill them. That left the crag rising behind. The wall surged up ten or twelve feet before breaking down into boulders, then rocks that sloped and merged until they reached a high flat plain that looked like it stretched from rim to rim, as if the top of the mountain had been sliced cleanly off. On the other side she could hear the roar of the sea as it spewed and churned.

"We need to go up," Tiarnan said, pointing at the stone wall with its broken, jagged ledges and irregular protrusions.

Shealy saw only the impossibility of reaching it and the fear that even if they managed to get from this plateau to the top of the other, they wouldn't be able to escape. The wolves barked and growled incessantly as they circled below.

He went on calmly, as if life and death didn't hinge on his decision. "The caves won't help us—we'd just be exchanging one trap for another and if we're to die, I'd rather do it in the sea than be cornered in a dark hole. But if we could make it up that wee hill, there's a chance we could lose them."

"She won't be able to make the jump," Liam said, pointing an accusing finger at Shealy. "It's too far."

"She'll make it," Tiarnan said with a certainty that stunned her and almost made her believe him. But then she eyed the gap between the stone table and sheer rock wall—the jump he intended for her to make—and had to agree with Liam. Not only was the distance too far, they'd all need suction cups attached to their hands and feet to cling to the surface on the other side.

"We should leave her," Liam said, a scowl on his angel face. "She's not our problem."

"No," Tiarnan said. "She comes with us."

A soft breath escaped her. Flushing at the betraying sound she'd made, Shealy locked her knees to keep them from banging together. She didn't want to think of what would happen if these two males left her behind. She didn't want Tiarnan to know how grateful that one negative response had made her.

Tiarnan went on without glancing her way. "Her father opened the door, Liam. Do y' understand? For a moment, I escaped. If he's still alive, he'll be looking for her and when he finds her, he'll open it again. When that happens, y' and I are going through."

His words rolled over her, hard and flat. He wanted to use her like so many had before, and in doing so he would make sure she survived. He was wrong about her father, of course. Her father couldn't open any mystery door and free these two from this hellish place. Wrong to think that Donnell had anything to do with their current circumstances, but she didn't think it prudent to point that out now.

At that moment, one of the wolves scrambled up the sheer base of stone. The animal made it only a few feet and then pitched back, falling with a thud and yelp. But now others attempted it, their large paws gripping, claws spreading as they tried to scale the wall.

Beside her, Tiarnan rubbed the bloody wound at his shoulder and swayed on his feet but he didn't fall. She saw resolve on his face.

"There," he said, pointing to a jutting shelf that poked out a few feet up.

It didn't look very large or sturdy to Shealy, but from there they might be able to reach the lip between the massive boulders stacked on top of it and climb higher.

To get to the ledge, they would have to jump from the formation where the wolves had them trapped, across ten feet of bared fangs and bloodlust, catch the ridge just right, and then hope they could scramble up to the next level. It could be done. Possibly.

Tiarnan looked from his brother to her and back. Shealy knew he struggled to put parameters around their escape and form a plan that wasn't doomed. It was a lost cause, though. They had one way off this rock, and it didn't come with a safety net. Taking a deep breath, she stiffened her spine and raised her chin proudly. She'd never considered herself a weak or simpering woman. She was Irish, and Irish women did not bow to adversity, no matter how terrified they might be.

"They're coming, Tiarnan," Liam said.

He was right. The wolves surged up the crag, slipping, falling, fighting. But each attempt brought them closer to their goal, to the place in the shale where they, too, could make a critical leap.

The brothers exchanged a silent look, and she saw some decision reached.

Tiarnan pulled her forward then moved to stand at her back. From behind her he leveled his arm on her shoulder, pointing at what looked like a miniscule shelf. Numb, she realized that he intended for her to land there.

"Ye'll need power and speed in yer jump. Do not think about what yer doing. Just push yerself as far and fast as y' can."

Tiarnan waited for her nod and then came around to face her. She'd had years of practice hiding her feelings and now she was grateful for the mask that kept him from seeing the full extent of her terror. He searched her eyes for a silent moment. The brush of his warm fingers across her cheek startled her, but before she could speak, he'd turned away. Without a word he took a running step and leaped up over the chasm to the ledge, hitting hard, stumbling and then catching himself. Both Shealy and Liam watched with wide eyes and terror as the wolves snapped at his heels, fighting with each other as they tried to scale the wall to reach him.

Tiarnan caught his balance and inched to the side. Wrapping his fingers around a sharp flange, he leaned out, reaching. "Y' next, Leary."

Seeing how close it had been for him filled Shealy with dread. He was a warrior, big and strong and powerful. How could she possibly manage what he'd barely achieved?

"I don't think—"

"Don't think," he commanded.

Liam stepped back, clearing the way. "He's right. Just take a deep breath and run for it."

Realizing she still had on her high-heeled sandals, Shealy quickly bent to take them off and felt him watching with that gold, glittering gaze, looked up, and found herself ensnared in it. Turning, she threw her high heels over the edge and into the distance, grinning grimly as a few of the wolves took off after them.

"Now, Leary," Tiarnan ordered.

"It's Shealy," she corrected angrily as she faced the perilous chasm and Tiarnan, hand outstretched on the other side. "Shealy O'Leary."

Too terrified to do more than obey, she hiked up her dress and made a running jump for the other side.

Halfway across, she knew she wouldn't make it.

The certainty came with a wash of panic that made her skin hurt and her nerves burn. She flailed her arms and legs crazily, trying to use momentum, force of will, anything to breach the distance. Close, so very close, but not there.

Gravity sucked her down and she had only a second to read the terror in Tiarnan's eyes before she plunged. Below her the wolves frothed, snarled, and snapped. She felt teeth graze her ankle and then a hand locked over her arm and pulled. Her fall halted with a jerk that snapped her teeth and knocked a cry from her. Still scissoring her legs to keep the wolves from latching on, she felt her body move up an inch, then another. One of the bigger wolves found a break in the stones, raced up, and vaulted at her. Its body hit her hard and she felt the grip on her arm loosen, and then she slipped, screaming, twisting while its claws scored her flesh as it fell. Another wolf jumped from below and nipped at her but couldn't lock its powerful jaws on her thrashing leg. Above her Tiarnan and Liam shouted and Liam hurled rocks at the frenzied canines. She heard them yelp as they scattered.

Then Tiarnan's strong hands were towing her up again and he had her in his arms. She shook from head to toe and clung to him, feeling the pounding of his racing heart beneath her cheek. He held her tight, telling her she was safe. But it was a lie.

"They're coming," Liam shouted.

Tiarnan effortlessly swung Shealy around to the ledge behind him, and leaned out with a hand. "Come on, then. *Now.*"

Liam did as his brother had, stepping back for a running start then leaping off the edge with grace and power that catapulted him cleanly to the other side. Tiarnan caught his brother easily, his landing surer, softer than Tiarnan's had been—definitely less terrifying than Shealy's. Tiarnan hauled the boy up, and Liam used his brother's shoulder as a step to reach the next level.

The wolves had abandoned their efforts to reach the stone table and now found the break that allowed them to climb the rocky crag. They raced, slipping and sliding on the shale as they snaked between the boulders below, focused only on their prey above. Tiarnan pulled himself to the next ledge where Liam waited and then reached down for Shealy, hauling her up with one great motion. The sharp rocks cut Shealy's feet when she landed, but she didn't pause as she scrambled behind the boy and the man as they climbed, still feeling the graze of sharp teeth on her skin.

The wolves chased with speed and efficiency, gaining in numbers, getting closer until their snarls and yips felt like a hot breath bearing down on Shealy. And then suddenly Liam lay on his belly at the very top, looking down for Tiarnan, who hoisted Shealy up to him and onto the plateau before following.

They stopped for just a moment, the sound of their harsh breathing rising over the riotous sounds of the chasing pack. Ahead the rough terrain stretched flat for four or five hundred feet and then abruptly dropped to the churning sea. She could hear the crash and roar, smell the salt and brine.

"Keep moving," Tiarnan said, and both Liam and Shealy did as they were told, sprinting across the flattened peak. Shealy's lungs burned and her muscles quivered. Tiarnan grabbed her hand and pulled her faster until they reached the rim on the other side.

Just as she'd feared, they'd exchanged one peril for another. They stood at the edge of a plummeting cliff, and the only way down was another leap, this one from dizzying heights into the frigid sea. She stood above the churning waves, the roiling surf that slammed against rocks and sand, the certain death that such a fall would bring. She looked down at her bloodied legs and torn feet. Behind them, the wolves were gaining. They had seconds. Maybe less.

"We aim for there," Tiarnan said, pointing down to a surging tide pool between the stones. "The water looks deeper. The rocks are not so many."

She didn't see as many rocks either, but that didn't mean they weren't there, just below the surface. The three exchanged one silent glance, a good-bye, good luck. Shealy didn't know. The fear in Tiarnan's eyes was a living thing with jaws as great as those of the wolves. Not fear for himself, but for his brother. For her.

"Me first this time," Liam said, and without hesitation, he took the plunge.

Tiarnan reached for him as his body flew off the edge, as if he might stop him, as if there were a choice. Of course there wasn't. With a growl of frustration, he pulled Shealy close, gripping her hand tight in his. Behind them, the wolves had breached the edge of the plateau and raced, bodies stretched long and flat as they covered the distance in seconds.

"Be brave," Tiarnan urged.

With no time to think of what she did, Shealy leaped with him from the ledge, their hands still locked tight as they plummeted. One wolf followed them into the nothingness of the fall, snapping its jaws as they dropped, yowling as it realized what it had done. Shealy's scream tangled in her chest with her terror as she sailed down and down and down, anchored only by Tiarnan's strong grip. She heard a sickening thud as the wolf slammed into something hard and jutting, braced herself to do the same. But in the end, all she felt was the stabbing cold of icy water. All she knew was the darkness of its depths.

Chapter Three

TIARNAN hit the cold water and it felt like being skinned alive. The shock of it surpassed the heart-stopping plunge into the freezing waters. It took control of his mind, twisting it with panic and deadening his limbs until he felt like stone sinking hard and fast to the bottom of the ocean. His grip on Shealy's hand loosened, and the churning sea ripped them apart.

He opened his eyes in the cloudy depths, frantic, fearful. Battling the cold paralysis, he struggled for the surface. His lungs burning, he burst up out of the water and gulped in a wet breath of air, searching for the woman and his brother. No one answered when he called their names, no one else bobbed in the harsh waves.

He dove, dread pulsing in his blood even as the waters leached all the heat from him. A flash of white and pink caught the corner of his sight. Her dress, there, the Leary woman, with her eyes the color of coming storms. He kicked hard, caught her under her arms, and pulled her up to the surface. Her huge gasp made his heart stutter with relief. Still searching for a sign of Liam, he struggled against the deadly currents and made it to the rocky shore.

Shudders of cold wracked her body, and he hated to leave her even for a moment, but his brother was still out there and he had to find him.

"Go," she said through chattering teeth, somehow reading his mind. "I'm fine."

He hesitated only a moment. Numb from the cold, he dove back into the tide. Underwater, sounds became muffled moans and groans that drifted unerringly and eerily through the murk. He had no idea how long he'd been submerged in the dark waters, only that his lungs ached, his eyes stung, his skin burned with the icy cold, and he'd seen no sign of Liam. Still, he dove deeper, ignoring the danger in the bitter chill, the numbness cramping his muscles, draining him like a sieve.

Feeling helpless, hopeless, and desperate, he broke the surface with a gasp, shouting Liam's name, treading the choppy waters, spinning and searching for his brother's head bobbing among the waves. He heard Shealy calling to him, pointing at something from the shore and followed the line of her pale arm. There he was, face-down and floating away. It felt like forever to reach him, pull his face from the water. His skin had turned gray, his lips blue. He wasn't breathing.

Hooking his arm around Liam's chest, Tiarnan swam as hard as he could. And then Shealy waded out, taking his brother and dragging him in. As he pulled himself after, he saw her kneeling over Liam, ear to his chest. Frowning, she pulled open Liam's shirt and pressed hard above his heart with the heels of her joined hands. She counted, pumped again, then repeated the action. Then she plugged his nose, sealed his mouth with hers for a beat of one, two.

"What are y' doing?" he gasped.

"CPR," she said, hands at Liam's chest once more, then her mouth to his again. Twice, three times, and then . . .

Liam coughed, rolled to the side, and vomited what seemed like a pond's worth of gray-green water. Sucking great gulps of air, his brother flopped back against the beach. Alive. Suddenly too weak to do anything else, Tiarnan stretched out on the other side of him, shaking like a sapling in a stampede. They were alive. All of them. He hadn't believed it possible.

Shealy fussed over his brother for a few more minutes before she moved to Tiarnan's side, took his face between her small hands, and looked into his eyes. "Stay with me," she said.

He didn't know where she thought he might go. He couldn't feel his fingers or toes. She began rubbing his numb limbs, moving methodically from his shoulders to his arms, down to hands. He was too surprised to even speak when her brisk touch reached to his legs.

"We need a fire," she said. "We need to get warm."

He nodded, but when he tried to stand, he found that he couldn't do more than agree. He shook uncontrollably and the harder he tried to stop it, the more the trembling wracked his body.

Shealy jumped to her feet and scanned the rocky beach. Her pink and white dress hung limp and dripping, nearly transparent. Her skin puckered with cold, her breasts taut against the strange, wet material. He could clearly see the outline of them, her legs, the apex of her thighs. He almost laughed at the heated thoughts running through his frozen brain. He couldn't even stand and yet he pictured that gown coming off, imagined covering her body with his, pushing inside her heat. Possessing her.

He cleared his throat and tried again to stand. Failed. Embarrassed to be so weak in front of this woman, he growled low in his throat.

She gave him a startled glance. "You stay there," she ordered. "I'll gather up some driftwood. I hope you have matches."

He didn't know what *matches* were but thought he might be able to start a fire if she could find dry wood.

She scurried up the beach where driftwood had wedged into the stone. Some of it might be dry enough to light. She scooped up as many pieces as she could carry, giving him tantalizing glimpses of long creamy legs and silky thighs as she bent. He'd never seen clothing like she wore, and he alternated between wanting to cover her up before anyone else might glimpse her and stripping those sodden garments off.

Beside him, Liam coughed again. "Are we dead, then?" his brother asked. "And she's an angel come to torment us with what we'll never have?"

The sound of his brother's familiar voice gave Tiarnan the strength to sit. Above them, the wolves still circled and snarled, but they were smart enough to see disaster in the only way down and had given up hope of catching their prey. A few feet away in the foamy surf, one wolf lay dead, black lips pulled back around its sharp fangs, eyes open but sightless. Its body inched back and forth as the tide rolled in and out.

Shealy hurried to where he and Liam waited and dumped her pile of wood beside him. Moving like a gnarled old man, Tiarnan arranged the pieces and dug his flint from the pouch at his hips. In moments he had a spark and then a flame. He bent low to gently blow on it, felt Shealy's gaze fixed on his mouth, and another flame altogether burst to life inside him. She glanced up and caught his startled gaze. For a moment, he was lost in the silver sheen of her eyes. Her face turned red and she quickly looked away.

Before long he had a blazing fire snapping and sparking. As the three huddled around it, he glanced nervously at the sky. The sun blazed bright and high, but he knew it could move with startling speed and unpredictability. It might set in the next few minutes or the next few hours. They would warm themselves for a short time and then they must move on. They could not risk dark coming before they reached their encampment on the islet at the center of this forsaken island, where he and a few others had been cursed to live.

He pulled his shirt off and draped it near the fire to dry. He wanted to shuck his trews as well, but Shealy watched his every move and he feared he wouldn't be able to hide just what that silvery gaze did to him if he bared all. The salt water stung his open wounds, but it washed away the dirt and blood and healed as well, leaving his skin feeling tight and singed. Across the blazing fire, Shealy had drawn her knees up and pulled the skirt of her strange gown over them. He eyed the raw wounds on her legs and feet.

"Come here," he said to her.

"Why?"

"I want to look at that bite on yer leg."

She flinched, as if the mere mention of the wound made it more painful. Gingerly she rose and moved to his side. Liam watched with restless, wary eyes. He'd been raised in a time of war, had killed his first man before his tenth birthday. There were few Liam trusted, and his suspicion of this woman—whether or not she looked like an angel—felt palpable.

As soon as Shealy sat beside him, he pulled her legs into his lap, forcing her to brace her weight on her hands behind her. Gently he brushed the sand from her feet, grimacing at the angry, open gashes on them. She'd been forced to run with bare feet, but she hadn't complained once or lagged behind. She'd shown more courage and resilience than many men he'd known.

It roused a fierce need to protect her, this brave and mysterious woman who might be the first hope he'd had since the night he and Ruairi had ripped the pages from the Book of Fennore, and Tiarnan had been sucked into this place of nightmares with his brother.

But like Liam, he couldn't quite trust her. Cathán wanted her—no doubt for the same reason Tiarnan did. She could help them escape, and that made her invaluable.

When he touched her, though, it wasn't thoughts of using her to get to her father that filled his mind. Something about her woke a yearning he'd thought long dead. When he touched her, he wanted *more*. . . .

He shook his head, trying to banish the foolish hunger, but the feel of her silken skin, the light teasing scent of her flesh, soft and so blatantly female that it had made him want to bury his face in the crook between neck and shoulder and drown in it, would not be eased.

"Do you think those wolves have rabies?" she asked, watching him run his fingers over her satiny calf. Her skin felt like silk, and he thought of her legs twined with his own, hooked at his hip, holding him to her. . . .

She went on, "Some of them were foaming at the mouth. I read somewhere that that means rabies."

"There is much to fear in this place," he answered. "But we've all been bitten by the wolves at least once and none of us has yet sickened. I do not think they carry rabies."

"Whew. Well that's good," she said with a tremulous smile.

"The seawater washed yer bites clean. I think they'll heal fine."

She caught her lip between her teeth and nodded, watching his fingers as they trailed over her ankle, gentle on the place where the wolf had almost gotten ahold of her. His heart seized as he thought of those agonizing seconds when she'd dangled over the gulf with only his grip on her arm keeping her from certain death. He let out a deep and shaking breath and then moved to her instep, where the jagged stones had cut deep into her flesh.

She winced and he gentled his touch, barely brushing the tender arch before circling to the top where he let the warmth of his hands sink into her flesh. He could feel her gaze following each movement but he kept his head averted, afraid she'd see how much he wanted to enfold her in his arms, hold her close, and make her feel safe. It was a stupid desire. On Inis Brandubh, no place was safe.

"So tell me again what this horrible place is?" she asked, shivering as a damp breeze chased across the beach. Her hand trembled when she tugged a lock of hair forward to curl around her face, hiding the shell of her ear that looked to have been burned long ago and the fine network of pearly white scars on her chin and throat. He wanted to ask about those scars, but each time she caught him looking, a mask came over her features, locking him out. It was tangible, that slamming door.

Instead of prying, Tiarnan held her small foot in his big hands, noting that her toenails were painted a sunny pink that matched the flowers on her gown. He touched one and then another, marveling at the clarity of color, wondering what kind of dye she'd stained them with.

"Answer me, Tiarnan," she said, her voice husky.

The breathless sound of it heated his blood. He didn't want to talk about Inis Brandubh. Had his brother not been sitting on the other side of the fire, he thought he might not be talking at all.

"I do not know how to explain this place where we live."

"Hell, they call it," Liam offered.

"I can see why," she answered with a wry glance at his little brother.

"Y' know the Book of Fennore?" Tiarnan asked, hating to even speak its name.

Her look of surprise could not mask the recognition beneath it. She'd definitely heard of the Book, but the doubt in her expression contradicted that gleam.

"The Book of Fennore is a legend," she told him. "A myth."

"It's more than that," he said.

"My father thinks so, too. He wasted half of his life trying to find it. But you know what? He never did. Because it isn't real."

The vehemence in her words surprised him. "Yer father sought the Book of Fennore?"

She raised her brows in answer.

"Do y' know why he wanted it?"

"My dad has these twisted ideas. He said the Book of Fennore was some kind of legacy his family was supposed to guard, but they'd screwed up somewhere down the line and lost it. My grandfather was obsessed with finding it, too, but he couldn't either. Imagine that. He died alone and broke for his efforts."

Her bitter sarcasm confused him. The Book was no myth, though it was legendary.

Warily, he asked, "Is yer father a seer, then?" Seers were strange breeds that made him instinctively distrustful. The world of Fennore was so discordant that the very idea of a seer peering into the murky future unsettled him more than even this woman with her stormy eyes.

"You mean can he see the future? No. He's just an old man with a heart problem."

"But he did open"—*What had she called it?*—"the darkness. He opened the darkness and pulled me out, Shealy."

She shook her head, but frowned, obviously thinking back over those moments when Cathán had attacked.

Carefully Tiarnan chose his words. "This island that we're on now . . . is not an island at all. It's another world—a world that is connected to the Book of Fennore. We've been trapped here for a long time."

"How long?"

Flopping onto his back on the gritty beach and closing his eyes, Liam interjected, "A handful of minutes? A lifetime of years? Who knows."

At Shealy's look of consternation, Tiarnan tried to explain. "Time does not flow here like it does in the real world. The sun might rise and set in a blink of the eye or it might dally high in the sky for what feels like weeks on end. My brother was just a boy when we came; now he's almost a man and yet so many years could not have passed."

At least that's what he hoped. He couldn't bear to believe he'd been here that long.

"That's crazy," she said.

"Yes," he agreed.

Reluctantly, Tiarnan released her legs and reached for the shirt he'd set by the fire. It felt dry and warm. Gripping it on either side, he split it down the middle and began using the two pieces to wrap her battered feet. When they reached his shelter, he would find proper boots for her. He'd give her his own now, but he knew she'd never be able to keep them on her tiny feet and they would only trip her up and cause her to fall.

As he worked he spoke, describing the nightmare to which she'd come. "The seas surrounding Inis Brandubh are filled with creatures from the blackest nightmare. Creatures y' cannot imagine. The tides flow at unfathomable times. The treacherous currents defy any foolish attempt to breach the vast waters."

"There's no escape," Liam muttered, his voice sleepy.

No escape. *Until now.* Until this woman's father had opened the darkness. Where was he at this moment? Stumbling around Inis Brandubh, looking for his daughter? Perhaps already dead, killed by one of the monsters that called this world home? He closed his eyes, refusing to consider it. When Tiarnan had first seen him, he'd been struck immediately by a sense of familiarity that he didn't understand. He felt certain he'd seen the old man before, though he didn't know how that could be possible.

"What does this place have to do with the Book of Fennore?" Shealy asked.

"The Book of Fennore is not just a book. It is a vessel. A thing of power. Unfathomable power. And this world is a part of that."

He looked up into her widened eyes, watching with fascination as they moved like a stormy sky, layers of slate and silver, midnight blue and clouded white mixing with her confusion.

"Until I came here, I did not understand it either. Since then, I've come to imagine this world is inside the Book of Fennore in the same way that the heaven of Christianity is in the sky and hell is the brimstone beneath the earth's floor."

Her mouth formed a small *O* of comprehension, then her brows pulled in a frown. "How did *you* get here, Tiarnan?" she asked. "Is this your world? I mean, do you belong here?"

He might have laughed if her question hadn't cut so deeply into his heart. Did he belong here? Did he deserve this? His just rewards for a life of disappointment, of failure and betrayal?

"It's not my world," he said forcefully, knotting his shirt in place over her foot.

With her feet wrapped, he had no reason to keep her so near. He swung her legs from his lap, missing their warmth and weight instantly.

A strange impulse urged him to stop her from moving away, to pull her body against his and shelter her in his arms. Tiarnan balked at it, stunned by the intensity of the thought. He'd spent hardly any time in her presence, and yet he seemed aware of every breath she took. He feared that more time in her company would spur other yearnings, other feelings. He might start thinking he needed to protect her. A part of him already *wanted* to protect her. And in a land where danger lurked at every bend, where each day challenged him to stay alive—to keep his brother from harm—Tiarnan refused to let his thoughts about Shealy go any further.

He'd failed many before her. He was not strong enough to bear failing again.

"The Book of Fennore has been a curse on my family for all of my life, but I did not fully understand it until it sucked me in, like it did y'. I remember, just before it happened, three men came to see us. They were named Red Amir, Mahon Snakeface—Mahon had the markings of a viper tattooed on his face—and the last man was called Leary."

Shealy's eyes rounded. "That's why you keep calling me Leary, isn't it?"

He nodded. "Leary was a seer. He knew things before they happened." He cleared his throat and glanced away. "We did not get along."

Leary undermined all sense of control that Tiarnan had until he'd felt like a leaf tossed in the midst of a winter bluster. He'd made Tiarnan feel useless in the face of destiny.

"These men told us the story of the Book of Fennore," Tiarnan went on, fighting to keep his voice even, watching her shift, her skirt riding high on her thighs as she curled her legs beneath her.

"This is unbelievable," Shealy muttered, shaking her head.

Her gift of understatement struck him, and Tiarnan realized he was almost smiling. "It is worse than that, Shealy."

She returned his surprising almost-smile with a crooked grin that made something twist deep in his gut. She was beautiful, this woman. He looked away.

Clearing his throat, he went on. "These three men, they said that in the time of our ancestors, there was a Druid named Brandubh—"

"*Brawn-doov*," she repeated, drawing out the syllables.

"That's right. He was very powerful and valued by his king. There came a woman who also had powers. She had a book made of the most sacred hides and jewels, lined with silver smelted by hallowed fires and christened in blood."

"The Book of Fennore," she murmured, guessing correctly.

"It was a thing of power before it was ever used," Tiarnan

answered, pulling from his memory the exact words Red Amir had spoken when he'd told of it. "She cursed the Druid to spend eternity in a hell of her making, in the prison of the Book of Fennore. Here."

"Here?" she said and looked around, as if expecting Brandubh to appear. "You've seen him?"

"No. I do not know if he even exists anymore."

She leaned closer, scrutinizing him, trying to work out what he hadn't yet told her. Her dress met in a low dip over the swell of her breasts, and her position gave him a tantalizing view into that valley between them.

What would she do if he touched her? If he pulled her against him and kissed her?

What would *he* do, if she let him?

Across the fire he heard Liam give a soft snore and realized that his brother had fallen asleep. No one would know if he acted on the need that filled him, that made his skin feel painfully small and his craving for her touch too large to contain. But on the heels of that came another thought—why did this one woman have such an effect on him? Had she bewitched him? Wary, he looked away from her.

"I still don't get why *you're* here. Did you know this Druid? Did you piss off this Fennore woman?"

"No, lass. 'Twas long before my time."

"And what about the guy who attacked us? How does he fit in?"

"Cathán," Tiarnan said with a scowl. "He is here because of me. Because of what I tried to do to the Book of Fennore."

"What did you do?"

"I tried to destroy it."

"How?"

"I tried to hack it to pieces, but it would not cut. It is not a thing that could be burned either. I could not destroy it . . . but I managed to tear some of its pages free."

He looked at his hands and she moved closer to peer down at them, too. She took one of them in her own and stared at the scars on his palms and fingers, tracing her nail over them. He could still remember the razor bite of the pages as they'd fought the destruction, shredding Tiarnan's skin in defense.

"I cannot describe it, touching something that evil," he said, keeping his voice low so that Liam would not awaken, so that Shealy could not hear the tremor that ran through it. She sensed it, though, and looked up quickly, catching him by surprise. What did she see in his face? Terror? Guilt? *Shame?*

"It felt like all the bones in my body shattered, and then everything went white and the world rumbled. I remember falling and when I opened my eyes, I was here." He looked up, met her gaze, and said softly, "*In* the Book of Fennore."

Her mouth moved, but no words came out.

"I brought Liam with me, though I do not know how I did it. He'd been wounded and I feared I'd lose him, too. Perhaps that is why, or perhaps it is because of something greater than my puny thoughts."

"And Cathán? You brought him as well?"

"Evidently. We have all been trapped here since then. And I never thought I would escape. Until today."

"Until you saw me and my dad."

He nodded. "And Cathán."

Her eyes narrowed. "Where do you think Cathán is now?"

"I do not know. I search for him. I scour this island from shore to shore, hunting my enemy. But all I ever find are his monsters."

Angrily he pushed to his feet and paced a few steps away.

"In all of the legends, it was the Druid Brandubh who ruled the Book of Fennore. It was the Druid whose evil turned the purest heart black. The Druid destroyed anyone who touched the Book. But now Cathán controls all that power. He hones it, turns it into wolves that attack humans when there is game enough to feed a thousand wolves. He creates monsters that are so vile they cannot be described."

"Why?"

"Because he can? Because he wants me dead and is too much the coward to fight me like a man, to kill me himself. I believe he has put an end to the Druid and he is king of all that is wrong in this cursed land."

"That's why you attacked when you saw him tonight in the parking lot."

"He has evaded me at every turn, retreated to a place I cannot find. To see him, to have him so close and not end his life . . ."

"You protected me," she said.

"Aye."

He braced himself for another of her *whys?* But she was silent, eyeing him with a too-perceptive stare. "You think he was after my dad."

At his silence, her eyes widened as she heard what he did not say.

"You think my dad summoned Cathán? You think he arranged what happened? That he planned it?"

"Yer father opened the door."

"Yes, you keep saying that. But I'm telling you it isn't true. My dad looked for the Book of Fennore for years. *Years*, Tiarnan. He lost everything because of his obsession, just like his father. And I swear he wasn't hunting for it to use it, to tap into this power you say it has. He had these deluded ideas that he needed to hide it away, keep it safe from 'all of mankind.' Jesus, I can remember the fights he and Mom had over it. She thought he was crazy, fanatical. And he was. If he'd known how to *open doors* and find it, he would have done it a long time ago."

She believed what she said. He could see that, but he wasn't convinced she knew the truth. Power had corrupted many men. It had corrupted him, lured him to make decisions that had destroyed the things he valued most. The people he loved above all others.

The only certainty Tiarnan knew was that her father had opened the door and both Tiarnan and Cathán had done the impossible—escaped the world of Fennore if only for a few moments. Now Cathán had vanished once more, and he could only assume Shealy's father had gone with him. His gut told him Donnell O'Leary had not gone willingly. He'd fought Cathán, just as Tiarnan had. The circumstances of how he'd come to call Cathán were still undetermined, but if Donnell had been an unknown to Cathán before he'd opened the doors, he was no longer.

One thing seemed clear, though. Shealy's father had tried to protect his daughter. Wherever he might be now, he'd be trying to find her, and when he did, Tiarnan, his brother, and the others at his encampment would be by her side.

"It is time that we move," he said. "We don't want to be caught out here in the dark."

She frowned at him, trying to see beyond the mask he refused to let slip.

"I will take y' back to our encampment and then we will figure out how to find yer father, aye?"

"Aye," she agreed, but her eyes told him that he'd planted a seed of distrust within her. He tried to tell himself he was glad. He needed to keep his distance from her and everything he wanted when she was near.

With a deep breath, he settled reality around him once more. Longing for the touch of this woman was pointless. As long as they lived in the violent world of Fennore, longing for anything but escape would be a mistake.

Chapter Four

SHEALY walked at Tiarnan's side as they circled the rocky shore to a point where they could climb up and out of the cove. Her thoughts were as jumbled as the landslide of boulders tumbling into the sea. Watching for wolves or anything else that might jump out at them, Shealy kept quiet, but Tiarnan's words echoed in her head. Could it possibly be true, what he'd said? Was her father able to open a way into this world? Had he brought them here? Had he summoned the pale man, Cathán? If so, why?

Over the years since the accident, her father had rarely mentioned the Book of Fennore. She had assumed the tragedy that killed her pregnant mother and put Shealy in critical condition had been the catalyst to ending his obsession. Now she wondered ... had he merely hid it from her? Had he still been searching for the Book of Fennore? Had he found a way to *open the door* as Tiarnan called it?

She couldn't believe it, and yet, what about anything that had happened since they'd left the restaurant and crossed that dark parking lot could she believe? Her father had been consumed with finding the Book of Fennore to the point that her mother had begun to hate him for it. She'd planned on leaving Donnell, even though she'd been pregnant, but death had robbed her of the chance.

Shealy took a deep breath and pulled herself from that depressing slope. This wasn't the time or the place to dwell on the heartbreak she couldn't change. She had enough to worry about here and now. Like how fast the sun seemed to be racing to the horizon.

"This encampment of yours, is it far?" she asked in a low voice.

"Yes. We will be lucky to reach it before dark."

"Great," she said, eyeing every shadow with trepidation.

"We will be safe there."

"*Safe*? Is that really possible here?"

He shrugged. "The place I call *home* is set on an islet in the center of a rapid river. Y' can only reach it by crossing the water, and to do so is risky."

"Splendid."

"I know how to get there without dying, lass. But others would not be so lucky. That is what makes it secure."

"Sounds better by the minute."

He gave her a narrowed glance, gauging the sarcasm in her voice.

"How did you find this sanctuary?" she asked.

"Liam and I came upon it by chance when we were attacked by wolves—like what happened today. They chased us into the river. We thought we were either going to drown or be eaten, but there was a waterfall and the wolves wouldn't go over."

"But you did?"

"Not much of a choice," he said. "It was swim or die."

"I'm sensing a theme to life here."

His mouth quirked at that. "As luck would have it, we survived the falls and found an islet that is situated between the first and a second waterfall. The small one we went over and a larger one, farther down. We wouldn't have survived if we'd gone over that one."

Shealy eyed him, hearing the solemn note in his voice. He talked about life and death in the same way other men talked about fast cars and sporting events.

"So you live alone? Just you and Liam?" she asked, nodding at Liam's back. The boy walked ahead of them, easily scaling the rough terrain. Tiarnan lagged behind with her, mindful of her battered feet wrapped in the shirt off his back.

Which left his torso very bare. His skin looked like dark polished oak in the muted sunlight, displaying each rippling muscle of his back and chest, ribs and abdomen. She couldn't tell what genetic pool he pulled from—his skin color was burnished, but his eyes were light, tilted ever so slightly at the corners. He had silky black hair and high, sculpted cheekbones, a square chin. He seemed to be a seductive blend of many races. *The best of them all*, she thought with a flutter of agitation inside her. How many times had she caught herself staring at all that muscled flesh on the long walk across the treacherous island?

"There are others," he said, finally answering the question she'd nearly forgotten she'd asked. "Ye'll meet them soon enough."

"Did you bring them here, too? Like you did Cathán and Liam?"

He turned those whiskey eyes on her and in them she saw frustration, anger . . . shame. "Yes."

With that he grew quiet until they reached the enormous, raging river he called *Abhainn Mac Tíre*—Wolf River, he told her. The color of clouded jade, it roared like a great beast as it hurtled through a narrow canyon before exploding in a widened chute that snaked as far as she could see. She'd read somewhere that water of that color came from glaciers. As the sun dropped so did the temperatures, and she had no trouble imagining glacial cold in the higher elevations.

As she came to a stop beside Tiarnan, Shealy eyed the white rapids with foreboding. Did he mean for them to cross that? Surely not. But as she stood shivering on the bank, Liam caught something that dangled from a massive tree and pulled it down.

"What is that?" she asked.

"A *curragh*. A boat," he said without glancing her way.

Shealy's eyes widened. It didn't look like a boat. It looked like a saucer and about as sturdy as a toy. No way would that little thing hold up to the surging current of the racing river.

"Do not worry, lass," Tiarnan said in her ear, making her jump. "It'll keep y' dry enough."

"I don't believe you."

He shrugged and took the *curragh* from Liam, who promptly removed another from the branches of the tree where it hung suspended like some giant, deformed Christmas ornament. Liam removed a paddle from braces inside the boat, set it in the water, and climbed aboard. Moments later he zipped down the river.

"Come," Tiarnan urged, holding the other boat still so she could get in.

"I'm not a good swimmer," she said. "In case you didn't get that when I almost drowned earlier."

"'Tis a good thing we have the boat, then," he said with a serious expression.

"That is *not* a boat."

"It is all there is, lass. Worrying about it will not change it."

He was right and she knew it, but she still couldn't bring herself to get in the little round thing and let it carry her to what would certainly be a cold and wet death.

"You said there's a waterfall," she reminded him.

"Two," he said calmly. "One behind us and one ahead. We will be on land again before we reach the second."

"I—"

Evidently he'd had enough of her stalling because he tugged her hand, pulling her off balance and sending her stumbling into him.

Before she could right herself, he swept her up into his arms and stepped into the boat he'd held anchored with one foot.

"I don't think—"

"Don't think," he said for the second time that day.

And in the next instant he'd settled her on the bottom of the saucer and lowered his large frame behind her, shifting until she sat between his long legs as he maneuvered the paddle in the current.

His chest felt warm and solid on her back, and though she tried to keep her balance and not lean into him, the choppy ride made it a futile effort. At last she gave up and relaxed against him. The tight breath he released fanned the hair at her temples and made her think he'd been waiting for her to yield.

"I'll keep y' from harm," he murmured softly, and with the hard muscles of his chest and arms flexing around her, she almost believed him.

Night crept up and overtook them with an unnatural suddenness. One moment she was squinting as the sun glinted on the rapids and the next a veil of black had covered the world. Shadows on shadows shuddered and moaned as they swept by on the roaring river. With the night came freezing cold, and she welcomed the heat of the big man behind her. He maneuvered the boat with steady skill, keeping it level and afloat, but he couldn't prevent the spray from hitting them, and by the time she felt his thighs tightening as he used his weight to spin the *curragh* out of the fast current and into shallows that gave way to sandy beach, she was drenched.

Liam was already lifting his boat from the water and leaning it against a tree when Tiarnan stepped out of theirs and held it still so Shealy could follow. Through the gloom she saw the midnight shapes of what looked like huts perched on the small stretch of land. Torches burned at intervals and there seemed to be people moving about. As she took it all in, a young girl hurried up to where they stood. She had red hair and wore a pair of faded and torn blue jeans and a top that looked to be made of hide. The strange combination unsettled Shealy for reasons she couldn't even begin to comprehend.

The girl smiled at Liam. "Sure and wasn't I wondering when you would be back tonight," she said in a lilting Irish accent, moving closer to the adolescent boy. She looked to be nineteen or twenty to his fifteen or sixteen, but neither one of them seemed to care. Liam gave her a devil-may-care grin and whispered something in her ear. She laughed and the sound was filled with sexual promise.

Good grief, Shealy could almost smell the hormones cooking between the two of them.

"I've got a stew waiting if you want to come for a bite," she said. The invitation in her voice couldn't have been clearer if she'd been shedding clothing as she spoke.

"Is that so, sweet Sally?" he said, shooting Tiarnan a look of such masculine smugness that Shealy almost choked. She'd think twice before she thought of him as a boy again.

"Aye," Tiarnan said to that look. "I'll see y' in the morning."

Stunned, Shealy watched the two of them walk off together. The girl's laughter trailed behind them.

"Isn't he a little young for . . . you know."

Tiarnan's eyes held amusement as he glanced at Shealy. "No, I don't know. For what?"

"He's a minor. That's illegal in some places." *Like the USA, for one.* The girl—Sally—had to be at least eighteen, and Liam couldn't be old enough to drive in most states.

"Two people finding pleasure in one another is illegal where y' come from?" Tiarnan asked as he began walking in the other direction.

Shealy hurried to follow, not wanting to be left alone in the strange, thick darkness. "When one of them is a child it is."

"He's no child, Shealy. Not anymore."

Yes, she supposed he had a point. She'd seen the look in his eyes when he'd pulled his knife. He'd been prepared to kill her, and she had no doubt that if Tiarnan had been truly injured or—heaven forbid—*dead*, Liam would have struck first and wondered at the rightness of it later.

"I just think he's too young," she said. "He should wait."

"And what is it he should be waiting for?"

"Well, to grow up, for one," she said.

Tiarnan stopped so suddenly she bumped into his back. He turned and put his hands out to steady her as he gazed into her face. "This is Inis Brandubh, lass. It's made him a man beyond his years. Besides, he may not have the chance to grow up, and wouldn't it be a shame for him to miss the only enjoyment he's likely to ever get?"

His eyes glowed golden in the velvet night and she felt the heat of them as they skimmed her features and then moved lower, lingering on the arch of her throat, the dip of her neckline, the swell of her breasts. She swallowed hard and his mouth twitched, not quite a smile but something close. He looked like he might speak; perhaps suggest that his brother wasn't the only one old enough for pleasure. A hot, achy feeling settled low inside her, but a shuffling sound interrupted them.

Tiarnan's reflexes were instant. He turned, putting her behind him as he faced the dark.

"Just me. Jamie," a deep male voice with an American accent said. "I've been waiting for you to get back."

Shealy peered around Tiarnan's broad shoulders at the man who'd approached. He was easily as tall as Tiarnan, and brawn and muscle packed his frame. The two men might have been cleaved from the same stone, but the newcomer's skin color looked closer to ebony than oak. The whites of his eyes glowed in the dark skin surrounding them. He had short hair, shorn almost to the skull, and a military bearing that gave him a formidable appearance, but he flashed a bright and disarming smile.

"Who's that with you?" he asked, moving closer.

Shealy could feel the tension in Tiarnan's body as he answered. His hand came up behind him, curling around her thigh, keeping her from stepping out into the open. She didn't know if this man, Jamie, presented a danger or if Tiarnan had another motive for not wanting her to reveal herself. She didn't question him. Not here, in this night-drenched world.

"Is that Maggie?" Jamie said.

"No. This is Shealy. She is new."

"New?" the man exclaimed, and the smile vanished. "There hasn't been anyone new since . . ."

"I know. And I will tell y' all about her in the morning. It has been a . . . difficult day. I'm too tired to discuss it now."

Jamie narrowed his eyes. "Well, welcome, Shealy," he said, and held out a hand.

She hesitated for a moment, waiting for a signal from Tiarnan. With reluctance he gave it, pulling his fingers from where they rested on her thigh. She stepped out from behind him but only went far enough to lean forward and shake Jamie's hand and then tuck herself in beside Tiarnan's body. The moon peeked out for a moment, letting her see more of Jamie's features than simply eyes and teeth, but she didn't need the light to feel Jamie's curiosity as he studied her. She didn't like it. Too much of her life had been spent under the microscope to enjoy being examined.

"You look familiar," he said after a long moment.

"Do I?" she answered noncommittally. She got that a lot. The story of her reconstructive surgery after the accident had made her famous, in a wrong sort of way.

He nodded, still peering through the gloom with prying eyes.

At last he said, "Before you turn in, T, I wanted to warn you about something. We got us some new neighbors."

"And who would that be?" Tiarnan asked in a tone that held both hope and wariness.

Shealy grasped Tiarnan's arm and leaned into him, waiting for Jamie's answer. Maybe he'd seen her father. Maybe her dad was here, even now. She'd been fighting for her life since the darkness had split and Tiarnan charged out of it, but her father had been in her thoughts every step of the way. A part of her had held tight to the hope that she'd find him before night fell.

"Not who," Jamie said in a serious voice. *"What."*

Jamie paused, and Shealy let her forehead rest on Tiarnan's shoulder as disappointment washed over her. Not a person, then. Tiarnan's fingers brushed hers lightly and she realized with a jolt of surprise that in a very short time she'd come to find comfort in his touch.

Jamie went on. "It looked like a cross between an enormous dog and a giant bird. It had three heads and there was more than one of them. Like a pack or a flock. It was hard to tell how many there were, the way they moved."

Tiarnan sucked in a deep breath, and dread seeped into Shealy's cold body. He'd been fearless through everything they'd endured today—almost eaten by wolves, drowned in waters of ice. His brother had nearly *died* . . . and through it all Tiarnan had been a rock. But now he couldn't hide the shudder that went through him, and Shealy felt it down to her bones.

"Y' saw them yerself?" Tiarnan asked.

"Nah, Reyes and Zac spotted them."

"Where were these creatures seen?"

"Forest," Jamie said. "Almost in the foothills."

Tiarnan didn't hide his surprise when he asked, "Y' sent them that far?"

Jamie shrugged. "Something's brewing. You feel it, same as me."

Shealy stiffened at that. What was brewing? What did they feel?

Tiarnan said, "These monsters they saw, they're called *ellén tre-chend* and they are woven in history through tales of horror. It's said that once upon a time they laid Ireland to waste with their breath of fire. They may not be the size of dragons, but do not misjudge them. Dragons have mass to make them predictable."

He'd said dragons. *Twice.* Shealy tried to pretend he spoke hypothetically, but she knew he meant it literally. *Dragons.*

Unaware of the impact of his words, Tiarnan went on, "An *ellén trechend* is quick and deadly. They are to be feared."

Jamie snorted. "What the fuck don't we fear? Tell me that."

Shealy'd been on Inis Brandubh less than twenty-four hours and already she agreed.

"Did they attack yer people?" Tiarnan asked.

"Nope. Just watched. Looked like they were waiting."

Tiarnan scowled. She didn't have to see his face to feel his displeasure. Shealy was far from an expert on Inis Brandubh, but she could figure out that the coming of these creatures was very bad and had Tiarnan worried. Was it the timing? Their arrival on the same day as her father, if Tiarnan could be believed, opened the door to this world? Or was it something else? Something worse?

"Listen," Jamie said, "just wanted to give you a heads-up. Go get some grub, T. You look done in. I've got a patrol set, looking for trouble."

"Looking for it?" Tiarnan said. "It won't take them long to find it, not here."

"Roger that."

"Tell them to keep sharp. These creatures are smart as a man and as vicious as all the monsters of Inis Brandubh combined. Y' understand?"

Jamie nodded, his eyes shining and black in the night. Tiarnan gave the other man a weary nod, took Shealy's hand, and started walking again.

"What's going on, Tiarnan?" she asked as she fell in step with him. "You said Cathán had monsters that defy the imagination. What's so special about these ella whatevers?"

He made a soft sound in his throat. *"Ellén trechend."*

"Yeah, those."

"They are legendary, these creatures. Indestructible."

"Well, I'm pretty sure that dragons are, too."

"Not so. A dragon can be killed."

"Anything can be killed, Tiarnan."

"Aye, us included."

He did have a point, but it seemed a moot one given all that they faced. "Wasn't it you who said not to worry about what you can't change?"

He shot her a surprised glance.

"I'm just saying . . ."

He fell into a pensive silence after that, and she wondered what went on behind those amazing eyes of his. Was he brooding over the latest addition to this monstrous world? Or thinking of Jamie's words? *Something's brewing.* Was he searching for the relationship between the shifting climate of Inis Brandubh and Shealy's father? And more importantly, what would he do if he found a connection?

Chapter Five

TIARNAN felt entirely too nervous as he approached his shelter with Shealy at his side. He hadn't anticipated being alone with her at this moment. He'd thought his brother would be with him, a buffer to the tension worming through his gut. But only the two of them stood in a quiet that had become strangely intimate.

He lived on the farthest point on the shore in a hut barricaded by trees and bushes. It allowed him the illusion of privacy, of solitude. Now he cursed the seclusion. No good could come of being alone with this woman who already had him feeling like a drop of water on a sizzling stone.

He'd made the door to his hut narrow for defense purposes. The weakest point of the structure, he'd wanted it as small a target as possible and it was only wide enough for him to slip through if he turned sideways. Jamie, who came from a place called Detroit that existed somewhere in the distant future, had muttered about fire codes when he'd seen it and let Tiarnan know in no uncertain terms that he wouldn't be caught dead sleeping there. That worked out well for both of them, then. On the other side of the door, he'd built brackets and braces to reinforce it. It gave him a false sense of security and though he knew it wasn't real, it comforted him. *Sometimes.*

He held the door open for Shealy, stomach clenching as she went past him to enter. As if hearing his thoughts, she flashed him a silvery glance, scalding him with the shimmering awareness he saw in the depths of her eyes. She hesitated just inside, eyeing the place where he lived, where he slept, forcing him to touch her as he squeezed past.

Once inside, the room seemed surprisingly large with a high ceiling, giving even a big man like Tiarnan enough room to move around. A hole cut in the center of the blackened roof let smoke escape the fire from the pit directly below it. Using a skill he'd learned before his banishment to Inis Brandubh, Tiarnan had strung up a flue made of hide treated with clay that dangled from the hole in the roof to a round flange a few feet over the flames. The furnishings were sparse. He'd made beds of leather hide stretched across wooden frames for himself and his brother and positioned them perpendicular to one another in front of the fire, serving as both seats and a sleeping space. With the abundance of game on Inis Brandubh, he had plenty of furs to keep them warm at night.

His gaze settled on the beds and he realized Shealy stared at them, too.

"So," she said. "Is there a *sweet Sally* waiting for you to get home with a hot meal and a rubdown?"

"No," he said, flushing. "There is no one."

"Is that your choice or aren't there any other women here?"

There were, in fact, three unattached females on the island. The few others had found mates as soon as possible—it was not wise to be alone in this terrifying world. Each of the single women who remained had made their interest in Tiarnan apparent, but he refused to let any of them get close.

"It is my choice," he said, frowning at her, hoping to discourage further questions.

"Why?" she asked.

Of course she asked.

"When we first came," he said, "there were nearly a hundred of us."

"A hundred? How is that possible?"

He shook his head. "That is a foolish question, lass. Anything is possible."

"Were you all together—I mean, were they there with you when you tried to destroy the Book? When you came through?"

"No, yet all are connected to the Book in some way. They came from different times, like y'. Some from the future, some from the past. We have pieced together the theory that they were all near the cavern on the Isle of Fennore where it happened and the echoes of what I did to the Book sucked them in."

He could see her working through that, trying to understand how his tearing pages from the Book of Fennore had been like ripping a giant hole between the real world and this one. The reverberations of what he'd done had resonated through time, slashing through the layers of past, present, and future, and leaving a gaping maw to devour everything in its wake.

She caught her lip between her teeth and shook her head. He couldn't tell if she'd grasped the broader implications of it or if it had confounded her. He was too exhausted to trust his own judgment and from the looks of Shealy, she was, too. She swayed unsteadily on her feet.

He forced himself to keep his touch impersonal as he took her arm and led her to Liam's empty bed. "Sit," he said.

She caught the edge in his voice and gave him a startled glance. He still held her arm, and he couldn't quite make himself let go. Some obstinate piece of him, some part he'd thought long ago destroyed, urged him to hold on to her. Keep her close, no matter the cost.

He gave her a gentle push and she plopped onto Liam's bed, seeming very fragile. But she'd acted with astounding courage today. She'd not lagged in the chase of their lives, had no doubt saved Liam by breathing breath back into his lungs. She'd been terrified, ripped from the security of her own world and plunged into the horror of his. Everything that made him a man responded to the strength and femininity he saw in her even now. It roused a violent instinct in him—a need to protect—that very need he'd warned himself not to feel.

Cursing under his breath, he knelt and removed the tatters of his shirt from her feet before shifting to the cold fire and adding kindling. He struck his flint and in moments had a blaze going.

"You said *were*," she murmured. "You said there *were* nearly a hundred. How many are there now?"

"Twenty-six," he replied through the tightness in his chest.

He didn't turn around to see the shock on her face. He didn't have to.

"Most died in the first few weeks," he went on. "Before we found this islet. We lived on the run and we were too vulnerable."

His voice cracked, and he cleared his throat.

"Some simply gave up. They could not cope with the terrors of Inis Brandubh. They quit trying to survive."

He heard the leather straps of the bed creak and glanced over his shoulder. She pinned him with that stormy gaze, thunderclouds moving in the midnight shades.

"That's not your fault, Tiarnan. You can't save everyone, especially if they don't want to be saved."

He swallowed, fighting to keep his tone level, his emotions deep below the surface. "I didn't say it was."

"You didn't have to. You know what I thought the first moment I saw you? Before you even came out of the darkness?"

Dry-mouthed, he shook his head. He braced for what she would say, told himself it wouldn't matter if she saw the failings that were as much a part of him as the scars on his hands and the wounds in his heart.

"I thought you looked like you had the weight of the world on your shoulders. Atlas, I remember thinking. But you looked strong enough to carry it."

He could not speak. The flickering flames played against her ivory skin, bathing her in gold and shadow. She looked lovely, so earnest. So wrong about him.

"No one should have to carry that much, though," she continued. "That kind of burden will destroy you. And you can't blame yourself because those people gave up, or feel guilty because you didn't save the ones who didn't give up and died trying. I might have died today."

He couldn't stop his knee-jerk reaction to that, but she went on, oblivious to the pain she caused.

"Liam might have died, too. But it wouldn't have been your fault, even if we both did. I've only been here a day, but even I can see that there's no way to control what happens here. People live and people die, Tiarnan. It's the way of the world."

He opened his mouth to disagree, to tell her that the way of the world did not apply to Inis Brandubh, but she stopped him.

"*Any* world, Tiarnan."

It felt as if something deep inside him cracked open at her words, and he reached out, bracing himself against the edge of the fire pit. In her face he saw understanding and he realized that she, too, carried a weight too heavy to bear, one she thought she deserved to carry. He saw loss and guilt, and he wondered, what had been snatched from Shealy O'Leary that had left those shadows in her eyes?

She met his gaze, and the directness of his stare seemed to

unsettle her. She lifted a shaking hand to her hair, combed it forward to cover the side of her face in a gesture he'd seen many times that day. It was the scars she tried to hide, but there was more to it. He wanted to ask, but didn't.

The less he knew about her, the better.

Because the more he learned, the more he wanted to know.

"Quit staring at me," she said defensively. "I know I probably look like a sea monster, but it's been a rough day."

He *was* staring, but not for the reasons she seemed to think. Bruises on her cheek appeared as darker shadows in the murk, dirt smudged her face, and her hair lay tangled around her shoulders. But it was the flashing storm in her eyes that captivated him and made him unable to look away.

She crossed her arms beneath her breasts and rubbed her chilled flesh. Silently he stood and pulled a warm fur from the bed. He settled it over her shoulders, tucking it around her, letting his fingers linger against the soft skin of her throat. A slashing crescent-shaped scar hooked up from her throat to curl around her damaged ear, a wound that looked like it should have killed her. It merged with the smaller web of puckered white skin beneath her chin.

"Thank you," she said softly.

Without making her rise, he grabbed the base of Liam's bed and hauled it closer to the warm flames. She gripped the sides, holding on as her center of balance shifted. As soon as she stilled, Tiarnan moved away and crouched on the other side of the fire again, watching her.

"Are y' hungry, lass?" he asked.

When she nodded, he went to the shelves where he stored bread and dried venison. He filled a cup with cool water and brought it to her along with a plate of food before making his own. A simple meal, but they both ate it without complaint.

Finished, she asked, "Who is Maggie?"

He frowned, caught off guard by the question.

"Jamie asked if I was Maggie when he first caught sight of me."

"Oh. Just a woman."

"Your woman, Tiarnan?"

"I told y'. I do not have a woman."

She caught her lip at that and gave him a look from beneath her lashes that made his entire body feel suddenly tight and hot.

"Y' should sleep now," he said, standing quickly and taking a few steps away. "We both should."

Exhaustion sawed at his bones, yet he feared he would never manage to sleep with Shealy so close, when it felt as if every part of him was tuned to her every move.

She took a deep breath and nodded. "You're right. I'm so tired."

She slid between the furs on Liam's bed, watching him as he banked the fire and then climbed into his own. In the silence, he heard the soft sound of her breath, thought he could smell the sweet perfume of her scent.

Her silence had the weight of piled stones upon his chest. Then softly, her voice husky with fatigue and fear and something else that he dared not identify, she said, "Thank you for saving me, Tiarnan. Thank you for protecting me."

The gift of gratitude twisted inside him. She shouldn't thank him. If she did in fact remain on Inis Brandubh, she would learn that soon enough, and Tiarnan knew it would kill him to watch the disappointing knowledge fill those mist-and-cloud eyes.

For a little while there was quiet, but he lay tense, aware of the woman so close. Aware of her fear, her need to feel safe. He could give that to her, but at what cost? He might have saved her today, but what about tomorrow or the next day or the next? He'd seen too many die to allow himself to care for this woman.

She shifted again in the rough bed of furs. From the corner of his eye, he saw her sit up and turn to peer at him through the dark.

He braced himself not to stir or show any sign of wakefulness, but he waited, knowing what she would do. Feeling the pull of her need. Feeling the desire to give her what she wanted pulsing with his own heart.

Her movements were tentative, her breaths short and soft. She climbed from Liam's bed and hesitated at the side of his for just a moment. Then she pulled back his furs and slid her soft, feminine body next to his. He couldn't have stopped the groan in his throat if his life had depended on it.

It had been so, so long . . .

She settled next to him, and resigned to his torment, he pulled her into the bend of his body, molding her curves into his angles, her back snug to his chest as he sheltered her with his strong arms. She fit like she'd been made for him, and his hands gentled over her, caressing as they crossed her chest and held her. She smelled sweet and *good*, her beguiling female scent light and enthralling. All of it wrapped around him and made him feel something he hadn't for so many years.

Vital. Needed. Strong.

The tension in her vibrated against him, and he knew she felt the weight of his arousal pressing at her back. He willed her to fall asleep, to leave him alone in this purgatory of emotion.

But he prayed she would not.

Chapter Six

THE heat of Tiarnan's body blazed down Shealy's back, silken and hot through the thin fabric of her dress. He was aroused. She felt the weight and pressure of his erection against her, knew instinctively that he held on to his self-control by a very thin thread.

They'd both almost died last night . . . or today . . . or last year, if Tiarnan could be believed—and she thought he could. On a very visceral level, she sensed that Tiarnan was a man of truth and honor. If he said the sky was yellow, then yellow it would be. But right now, he wasn't saying anything. His breathing was strained, coming in short, hot bursts against her ear. The muscles in his arms bunched tight, but his hands were gentle where they held her, almost apologetic as they stroked.

Shealy didn't let herself dwell on anything that tried to crowd into her overloaded brain. At that moment, she needed to *feel*. She needed to know that however terrifying this place was, she, at least, was real.

Before she could change her mind, she turned in his arms, feeling him resist for just an instant as he tried to hold her still. Then she pressed against him, her dress twisted at her hips, her face level with his. For a long moment they stared at one another, searching the shadows that concealed their expressions, each seeking mercy, absolution perhaps.

He spoke with a deep murmur. "I don't think—"

"Don't think," she said against his mouth.

She caught a glimpse of pain in his golden brown eyes and for a panicked moment she thought he might reject her and pressed closer, letting him feel her body.

"Don't think, Tiarnan."

She ran her hands up his bare chest, reveling in the feel of him. He was hard, slabbed muscle beneath hot, silken skin. Every inch of him, strong and hewn. Her fingers slid up the column of his throat then back to tangle in his dark brown hair, twisting in it to bring his lips closer to hers. He made a sound in his throat that lit a fire deep inside her and then he pulled her tight against him with a groan, and that, too, fanned the inferno, as if her having him against his will made the forbidden moment that much sweeter.

His reluctance didn't extend to his body though, and he rolled, pulling her beneath the satisfying weight of him, crushing her in a way that screamed sex through every nerve ending. One massive thigh slid between her legs, and she arched up, rubbing against it, thrilling in the friction. He brushed his lips against hers, the kiss soft, and she opened to him, letting him know he was welcome wherever he might want to venture. The feel of his tongue, so hot and velvet, so foreign and somehow exotic in her mouth, made her moan and her fingers clench in his hair.

She kicked back the furs as her temperature spiked and she shivered at the quick breath of cold before his hands began to roam over her body, thumbs brushing against her nipples, dipping down her ribs to close over her hips, pulling her up and into the hard thrust of his pelvis. He caught the hem of her dress and yanked it up with an impatience that thrilled her. The zipper at her back thwarted his efforts, and she sat, turning so he could pull it down. For a moment he seemed distracted by the simple thing but then the two halves of her dress opened and he pushed them off her shoulders and bared her back to his hot mouth. When she turned again and he caught sight of her lacy bra, his mouth opened and his eyes glazed in a way that made her feel powerful, beautiful.

Then she was naked, beneath him once more, and the realization cut through the heat like a sharp blade, adding a new dimension to the blind groping, the desperate clinging. Tiarnan propped himself on his elbows, looking down the length of her body, gaze hot on her breasts, hungry on the rippled stretch of her ribs as they heaved with each heavy breath she sucked in.

She felt the stroking glance like a caress as it moved down to the place where their bodies pressed together. He stared at that point of flesh upon flesh and then his gaze moved to her face again. In those whiskey depths she saw something that spoke of wonder . . . and he smiled. His eyes crinkled at the corners and his lips parted to show white teeth, slightly crooked in a way that made that smile all the more sexy.

Shealy felt to her soul that she saw something rare, something as intimate as the touch of his hands on the softness of her breasts. That smile was a crack in his armor, a gift of his pleasure, and she answered it with a smile of her own, dragging her fingertips down the hard planes of his chest, over the rigid lines of his abdomen to that soft and vulnerable place just beneath his belly button. He had to lift his hips so she could tug at the laces that held his pants shut and he sucked in to give her access, never looking away from her face, never even glancing at the scars that marred the right side, the sickle-shaped wound on her throat, or the misshapen shell of her ear. It was as if he didn't see them . . . or more importantly, as if they were too inconsequential to matter.

Her fingers slipped under the loosened waist and she pushed his pants over his hips, feeling him sway from one side to the other so she could maneuver them past the hard arousal that sprang free and rested, velvety and heavy, on her stomach. The feel of it there, the knowledge of its purpose, of her own intent—all of it gathered like a hot, molten pool deep inside her body.

At last she closed her eyes, arching against him as she shut out that carnal male spark in his gaze. His mouth covered hers in a kiss that no longer felt gentle, no longer giving. It demanded, it took, and it punished in a way that Shealy craved. He didn't hurt her—it wasn't about that. It wasn't about dominance or pain. It was about forgetting every single thing but the texture, taste, and friction of their mouths as they moved against one another. They used teeth and tongues and lips to narrow the moment into just this, only this. The need to relinquish control and simply *feel* governed them both. His rough and scarred palms rasped against her throat, her breasts, squeezing, stroking, waking every erogenous zone she had.

His lips followed, open mouthed and wet-hot over her nipples, tonguing and teasing until she felt like they were hardwired to the ache growing below. At his mercy, she tried to curl her fingers around the hard length of him, but somehow he stayed just out of reach. While he was distracted by his play, she anchored her foot and pushed, rolling until she sat on top of him, straddled his hips, staring down at the bare expanse of his chest. The banked fire burnished him in shades of gold and bronze, casting his muscular form into something beyond beauty.

He had his own scars, battle wounds. Small rounded puckers of silky skin, long jagged slashes of pink-white, irregular depressions that spoke of flesh gouged out and excruciating pain. Two raw places appeared to be freshly stitched, yet he was perfect—it stole her breath just how perfect. His shape—from broad shoulders, heavy and strong, to arms that bunched and bulged to the slabs of his chest, hard and flat with nipples small and tight—pleased every part of her. She could have bounced a basketball off the ripped abs that narrowed and angled down to the dark trail of hair and the vee of hips beneath her.

His big hands circled her thighs and inched up until he raised her above him. She looked down between their bodies, watching as he shifted, and then slowly, God, so slowly, he entered her. Shealy threw back her head with a moan that came from the very center of her being. A moan that seemed to expand as she stretched over the thick length of hard heat. She sank back, meeting his thrust until he was buried deep inside her.

A quicksilver shiver went through her and she opened her eyes to find him watching her face, and for a moment she was embarrassed, wondering if her expression had revealed the way this felt, as if he'd stroked every cell in her body. She'd had sex before, and that's what she'd thought this would be. Sex. Hard, driving, forgettable. But in that look she realized what a part of her had known all along—nothing about this man would ever be forgettable.

And then he began to move, still holding her hips, her body astride his as he lifted her up each time he pulled back, watching her face for every nuance of pleasure because he knew, *he knew* he pleased her. The flash of pure masculine satisfaction on his face could not be mistaken any more than the answering purr in her throat could be denied. He felt that stiff coil of need in her, felt how each long stroke tightened it another notch, and the knowledge gratified him. She didn't need words to explain it because spiraling within him was the mate to the emotion; she was not alone in this seduction.

Every muscle in his body tensed with each thrust. Sweat glistened on his chest as he kept the strokes long and smooth when she knew he wanted to pound. He wanted to hammer her with his body until they felt like one. It seemed he took some pride in the measured control, as if he'd accomplished some great feat in bringing her to this fervor without allowing either one of them to spill over the edge.

She leaned down and kissed him, losing herself in the twin assault of his soft tongue and his hard thrusts. She relented willingly when he rolled her to her back and settled between her spread thighs, sliding deep with a satisfied groan that seemed to vibrate down to the very point where they were joined. Goose bumps broke out over his shoulders and back as he held himself still. He looked at her then, as if contrite for the pending loss of his iron control. But control wasn't what she wanted, not at any degree. She wanted abandon, she wanted wild, she wanted passion so great that it could not be reined in.

She rocked her hips against him, daring him to withstand the torture, feeling her own sense of power grow when she saw him surrender. He braced his arms on either side of her head and he drove into her, hard and relentless, without kisses, without words, and Shealy felt that tight, hot need grow and grow until it filled even the particles in the air and then snapped with a scream she muffled open-mouthed against his shoulder, letting it pulse with her release as she orgasmed once, then again in a long, lush wave as Tiarnan gave a low, guttural curse and came with her, pounding flesh and the scent of their sex so thick that it pushed her over again, until it was almost pain.

Hearts racing, they both stilled at last and lay for long moments in a boneless heap as the cold dried the sweat from their bodies and brought with it the chill of a moment taken and lost. Slowly Tiarnan eased his weight off of her, flushing as he looked into her eyes and then quickly away.

She could feel her own face getting hot as she reached for her tattered dress. She wanted a shower but she knew from her crude surroundings she wouldn't get one. Still, the scent of him, clean and male and seductive, clung to her skin with an intimacy that felt at once jarring and soothing. She'd known this man less than a day and yet a part of her felt as if she'd known him a lifetime. *There's a word for it*, she thought. People who became ensnared in their attraction in a time of extreme duress, but she couldn't remember it right now. Couldn't remember anything but the heat of his body and the dejection she felt now that it was gone.

She heard him behind her, the sound of his pants sliding over his hips and then more shuffling as he moved around. After a moment, he handed her a soft washcloth.

"There's water in the bowl," he said to her back.

Nodding, she held her dress in front of her as she cleaned up, aware of him waiting, watching. With her dress on, she felt better, but she couldn't manage the zipper. His warm fingers at her spine made her stiffen and melt in simultaneous reactions. As soon as he'd pulled it up, he moved away quickly.

"We should sleep," he said, his voice deep and stoic. And yet the throb of loss somewhere in his words quieted the tumultuous insecurities that hammered at her now.

She glanced back to catch a wary glimmer in eyes that just moments before had burned with heat. She approached the beds, looked at the one she assumed belonged to Liam and then at Tiarnan's. As awkward as she felt, she still didn't want to sleep alone. Silently she slipped between Tiarnan's furs, waiting tensely to see if he would join her. When the bed creaked beneath his weight, her eyes fluttered shut with relief.

He pulled her back into the hard curve of his body, covered them both, and said nothing. For a long time afterward, they both lay still and stiff until finally, painfully, Shealy succumbed to sleep.

Chapter Seven

A T first, Shealy didn't realize the screams came from outside. She thought another nightmare chased her through her sleep. Her own screams, perhaps, echoing as she leaped from the cliffs with the wolves snarling at her heels.

Then she felt the heated body next to her move, and instantly she awoke.

Tiarnan. She slept in Tiarnan's bed, his arms holding her tight. In a rush, her memory filled in all the missing pieces of where she was, what had happened . . . the sex that had touched and soothed something inside her even as it opened a chasm between them that gaped wide even now.

Another scream split the silence. This time she knew it hadn't come from her nightmares. The horror in the sound ruptured the remains of that fine bubble of slumber that tried to insulate them. Tiarnan was on his feet in an instant. Peering through the gloom of predawn, Shealy watched him from the warmth of the bed they'd shared as he pulled on boots and reached for a sword and an ax, gripping one in each hand as he strode to the door. He wore only his pants and all that bare flesh reminded her of how it had felt beneath her hands.

"What's happening?" she asked, her voice husky with sleep but her mind sharp and alert as she sat bolt upright.

More shrieks of terror had joined the others and now it seemed the darkness writhed with them.

One hand pushing open the door, Tiarnan glanced back and his eyes burned at the sight of her in his bed, no matter that the world around them seemed to be in a jarring panic. In that flashing second, a taut awareness stretched across the room, binding them in an inexplicable way. And then another shriek—a sound so piercing and discordant that it couldn't be human—broke the tenuous hold.

"Stay here," he said, turning sideways to get through the narrow doorway.

He disappeared in an instant, and Shealy sat stiff with fear as the chaos outside built into cacophony. She scrambled out of the cradle of warm furs and inched to the door. Smoke stained the air, singed the freshness with an acrid taint as unfamiliar as the screeching and screams. Whatever burned, it wasn't anything she'd ever smelled before.

What was out there?

She remembered nothing of the landscape that waited beyond Tiarnan's shelter. It had all been shifting shadows and lurking gloom when they'd arrived last night.

Carefully, she inched the door open and stared out at a sandy bank trailing into the black wrapper of predawn. They were at the point of the islet, where the river split and flowed fast around it on either side. She could smell its nearness, but she couldn't hear anything over the shouts and cries coming from every direction. If she'd wanted to run, she wouldn't have a clue which way to go.

Someone called orders, voice raised to be heard over the panic and mayhem that she couldn't see. Had the wolves returned? Through the instant terror the thought signaled, a sane voice told her no, that didn't fit. There were no howls or snarling growls, no triumphant barks over cornered prey. A wolf didn't make that strange bleating whine—strident yet droning. It echoed endlessly. What sounded like that? It couldn't be human—it sounded too loud, too alien.

Beneath her feet the earth quaked in a disjointed shudder. Shealy stepped back from the door, instinct urging her to hide, but there was nothing in the room but the two beds and a table. An image of her cowering under either flashed through her head, along with an inane memory of a storybook elephant trying to hide beneath a tiny mushroom.

Against the far wall sat a low shelf with an array of knives, a quiver full of arrows, and a bow propped nearby. She scurried over and picked up one of the heavy blades, wondering what she intended to do with it. She'd never even boned a chicken, for Chrissakes. She hefted it and then grabbed one of the arrows, finding some absurd comfort in the length of it. She'd never used a bow, didn't think now was the time to learn. But the glinting point at the end of the long shaft looked lethal and she felt better holding it.

A boom came from outside of the stone walls, as if a giant wrecking ball had swung into a structure like this one and brought it down. A loud clatter of rocks cascading, hurling through the gloom, followed instantly. Eyes wide, she stared, as if she had X-ray vision that could penetrate the walls and see what happened on the other side. That eerie screeching drone filled every molecule of air, and a hard, cold jolt went through Shealy's body.

What was out there?

Terrified, she backed away, never averting her eyes from the wall that separated her from whatever rampaged on the other side.

"Get behind it, *behind it!*" a man shouted.

Tiarnan. Already she recognized his voice. It sounded full of fear and rage.

Another *boom* reverberated through her body, and before she could react, a third thundering rumble shook the shelter, and suddenly rocks flew at her as the wall exploded inward. She screamed, stumbling as she tried to duck and protect her head from the hard round missiles bombarding her. The heavy knife tumbled to the floor, but somehow she kept hold of the arrow. She heard Tiarnan shouting again, but her ears rang and she was shaking so hard her teeth chattered, drowning out his words. An unearthly shriek sliced into her eardrums, making her think they'd ruptured. Arms above her head, she peered out and saw through the hole in the wall just what made that sound.

"Mother of God," she breathed.

The creature stood four, maybe five, feet tall and was equally broad across its massive shoulders. Like the American buffalo, she thought in some distant part of her mind. But the comparison ended there. The beast didn't have fur—instead silvery feathers covered it like armor. Thick legs extended from enormous, muscled shoulders and ended in pointed talons. Five sets of legs ranged down its long, thick body.

Fast. It would be very fast.

But that was not the most terrifying aspect of the creature. What chilled her blood and clenched at her heart rose up above the monstrous body and stared at her. The monster had three heads.

Three. Heads.

She understood at last. This was the creature Jamie had been talking about. *This* was the thing that had terrified Tiarnan. He'd said it was indestructible. Staring at it now, she believed him. A dim glimmer of dawn broke the black velvet of night, and she could see the horror of it clearly.

Each of its three heads was squared and heavy boned, like a

gigantic helmet, with a long flat brow and gigantic extended jaws that snapped, exposing double ridges of sharp triangular teeth. Its mouth opened so wide it could chomp a man with one bite, like a shark. The necks were long, and they gave the heads a mobility that was snakelike as they writhed amidst the people scattered and running in a panic. When they reared on their back legs, they towered over everyone. One set of eyes pinned her, unwavering while the other two heads turned and snapped at the fleeing people around it.

Men with weapons like Tiarnan's circled it fearlessly, with a steely focus that gave Shealy a moment's hope. But then from behind the bulky body with its centipede-like legs a fourth, fifth . . . *ninth* head appeared as the beasts clustered together.

They moved in a closely knitted unit, like a swarm of predatory insects. Huge, deadly vermin with ferocious eyes, beastly bodies, and tails that swung wildly, crashing into the shelters built in a circle, destroying them with the mass and weight of each blow. As she watched, one of them lowered its heads and charged into one of the huts, bringing it down in a shower of rock and dust. She saw terror-filled faces on the people who'd hidden inside before the jaws snapped up one of them and swallowed in a chomping gulp. The other two occupants were devoured before anything could be done to stop it.

Shealy stood frozen with shock, watching the unthinkable, still held in the cold stare of the monster directly in front of her. Nothing the imagination could conceive would rival the horror of it. One of the creatures jerked and three mouths opened, shooting streams of viscous fluid at a cluster of terrified women and children. The noxious liquid hit them and they cried in agony, spinning and running for the river but making it only a few steps before keeling over, skin rolling off them in great, slimy hunks. A scream had been building in Shealy's chest. Now it broke free as she stumbled, fumbling for the door behind her as she tried to back out without looking away from the beast watching her.

But the doorway was narrow and she still clutched the arrow in her hands, held across her body, both ends catching at the frame and barring her exit. She saw the problem, knew she had only to turn the arrow and she could escape, but her fingers were numb and the command to shift couldn't escape the clogging fear jamming the synapses in her brain.

The creature inhaled deeply, all three heads facing her now, all acting as one. Shealy felt her tattered dress flutter outward in the suction it created. It would spit those burning acids on her and she'd no longer have to worry about her scarred face because this monster would strip her of it forever. She was jabbering something, and Tiarnan shouted at her to move, to run. The words came through the dense sting of terror, heard but not understood. Felt, but not realized.

Then suddenly she gave a convulsive shake that swung the clutched arrow off kilter and fell through the open door behind her. She hit the ground with a *thud* that knocked the breath from her. The door slammed shut, momentarily breaking the hold those six eyes had on her. The taste of blood in her mouth, the jarring pain from the fall knocked her out of her trance, and she scrambled to her feet, running wildly away with no sense of direction or thought.

The creature gave another cawing screech that hacked and harvested the fear so thick in the air. The screams of terrified people surrounded Shealy as they raced in mindless clusters from the nightmare. But the tiny island on the river offered no shelter from the three-headed beasts. They spat their erosive fluids at them, and all around her people howled in pain and fell to the ground as it ate through their skin and immobilized them in a slow, torturous death.

Ahead of her, a woman stumbled, and the small child in her arms fell. In an instant the woman was snapped up by vicious jaws.

Shealy had only a glimpse of the woman's face, but it was enough to cut through her terror and slice her to the quick. A part of her mind fought what her eyes clearly saw, denying that it could be true. For a frozen moment their gazes met, clung, and Shealy saw in the woman's eyes the same astonished disbelief that must be in her own. It was over in a flash as the creature tossed its head and chomped its jaws on the woman's body, but there was no mistaking the grief, the love, the loss that had been packed into that look.

"*Mom?*" Shealy breathed.

"Run," the woman cried as teeth sliced through her. Blood sprayed her face but she choked out three last words. "Take her. *Run.*"

The voice went through Shealy like a bolt of lightning and she did as she was told, scooping up the toddler and clutching the warm little girl to her chest as she ran away from the beast with the others. She glanced back to see the woman who'd looked so much like her mother devoured with sickening speed, leaving Shealy doubting that she'd really seen the familiar features, that the voice had been the one from her memory, the one that once had sung to her and told her stories. The one that had whispered *I love you* each night before bedtime.

It couldn't be. . . .

They'd reached the edge of the island, and like sheep herded to a cliff, those in front plunged into the raging river. The current here was ferocious and loud, echoing with the sounds of the huge waterfall up ahead. From the shore, Shealy could almost feel the force of its pull.

"No!" someone shouted. "The fall will kill you, fools!"

She didn't know who spoke but she saw those who'd charged in being sucked away and hurled over a great wash of thundering white water. Shealy skidded to a stop at the river's edge and gasped at the flailing arms and legs that tried to fight the inevitable. In moments, they were gone.

The child in her arms cried piteously. Shealy looked into the little girl's face, numbed, stunned. The eyes that stared back at her held a silvery sheen and a rounded shape that Shealy knew all too well. They were the same eyes that stared back at her from her mirror every morning.

With a gasp, Shealy spun, facing the bloody ground where the woman who'd held this child had died, seeing again the shock on her face as her terrified eyes met Shealy's.

Oh. My. God . . . It couldn't be and yet . . .

The swarm of three-headed creatures droned around her, stopping her frantic thoughts. They had leveled every structure until it looked like a war zone. Less than a dozen men and a few strong women remained, and they circled the beasts as they spewed their death potion and snapped their shark jaws. She could see Tiarnan and Liam among them.

One of the beasts lifted on its rear legs and scanned the island while the others chomped and spat and swiped their great tails. In the blink of an eye, the monsters had cut the number of men and women in half.

They needed help. They needed a *miracle.*

Helplessly, she looked down at the child in her arms—into the eyes so like her own—and a great shudder went through her body. She felt a strange sense of reaching out, of sharing a kindred message that some ancient part of her mind understood while the rest of Shealy remained baffled. What she was thinking couldn't be.

It wasn't possible that the little girl she held could be who Shealy thought she was. Surely her mind was playing tricks on her and the woman she'd seen devoured seconds ago wasn't Shealy's mother . . . couldn't be her mother. Her mother was dead, her body washed out to sea. . . .

She covered the girl's face, turning it into her shoulder as the carnage went on. Her stomach heaved, but she fought it. She had to think. She had to do something. She'd lost the knife, but she still clutched the arrow in her hand. An arrow with no bow. A bubble of hysteria rose up in her just as a strange icy prickle puckered her skin from head to her bare feet.

The creature that had risen on hind legs spotted her.

Mouth dry, heart hammering, she looked into the cold, pitiless eyes and realized it had not found her by chance. It had been looking for her.

It made a sound in its stout throat, a chortling buzz that brought the other heads up and around. Frozen with fear, Shealy watched all nine of the three creatures' heads turn to face her. The moment stretched impossibly long, passed frightfully quick, and then the creatures *swarmed*. There was no other word for it. They didn't take flight and yet they came together like wasps, a black and gray cloud of motion bearing down on her. Taloned feet churned the dirt as they charged at Shealy.

She screamed. She knew it, but she couldn't hear herself over the strange cawing whine the monsters made. The little girl in her arms screamed, too, and their terror seemed to twine together, creating a bond that felt electric.

The air between them seemed to warp, like haze over heated asphalt. It made the distance between them and the monsters bend and flatten in alternating waves. One of the creature's heads stuck out in the lead, teeth flashing in a macabre smile. The child clung so tight that Shealy couldn't draw a breath. This was it. This thing—*things*— were going to eat her and the poor child she had no hope of saving.

From the corner of her eye, she saw a flash of color. Tiarnan, racing at the monster's side, his legs stretching to keep pace. He seemed somehow bigger, faster than the others who followed as he pulled his long sword over his head and brought it down on one of the writhing necks.

Yes, that's what they needed. Bigger. Faster. Stronger . . .

His blade bounced off the shiny feathers with a metallic clang. The creature didn't even slow down.

Like armor, Shealy thought, watching the swarm rush at her. It wasn't fair. Feathers should be soft. Pliable.

The air around her warped again, enveloping her and the child until it felt like the source must be coming from one of them. She looked down, met the little girl's wide eyes, and knew she was right. A charge of electric heat shot through them both and then it pushed outward, overpowering the piercing drone of the monsters. The power felt thick and soundless, like a solid force that flowed between invisible barriers, infusing the particles of air around them until it slowed the seconds. Shealy was dimly aware that tremors shook her and the child, tremors that came from deep inside and worked their way out like a great tidal wave bearing down on the shore.

The little girl in her arms twisted to face the doom racing toward them. Huge tears streamed down her face, but she pointed a finger at the creatures and cried, "No."

Tiarnan bellowed something at Shealy. She could see his mouth moving, the fear in his eyes as he stared at her, willing her to run. Yes, that's what he said. Run. *RUN.*

But there was nowhere to go. Couldn't he see that?

Behind Tiarnan, dawn lit the horizon and cast a dark shadow over the creatures, over Shealy who stood in their path. They were close, so close she could smell the dank and oily scent of them, could see the flecks of black and white in their steely feathers, feel the heat of their frenzy.

Feathers should be soft.

Still holding the child on her hip, Shealy shifted and brought the arrow she clutched up and out, a thin, useless weapon against the enemy of destruction. A shout broke through the fog of silence that had shielded her, and suddenly everything happened at a speed that defied comprehension.

A snarling rumble—deep and dark—rose from Tiarnan's mouth and he leaped in front of her, hitting the ground with powerful legs braced, turning with a grace that stole her breath. He snatched the arrow from her outstretched hand, shoving her away as he faced the monsters. She stumbled, still holding the child and unable to break her fall as she sailed backward.

Impossibly fast, Tiarnan plunged the arrow into the black eye of the nearest head, shoving it down into whatever brain compelled it, then in one fluid movement, he swung up with the huge sword clenched in his other hand, slamming the blade into the flesh beneath the chin of a second writhing head. Shealy braced for that clanging metallic ring but instead she heard the squelch of flesh, and then the severed head flew into the air and bounced to a stop at the river's edge just as she fell to the ground beside it. She stared into the flat black eyes.

Tiarnan's cry echoed loud and clear as he chopped and hacked, ax in one hand and sword in the other. He was covered in blood, moving so quickly that he dodged the lethal spray of one creature while slicing limbs and piercing the flesh of the others.

Something had changed, Shealy thought as she stumbled to her feet and dodged to the side, narrowly missing the crushing weight as a now headless creature toppled and crashed to the ground. After seeing that Tiarnan's blade cut through the armor that held them at bay, the four men left to fight beside him crowded in, going for eyes and legs, jumping away from the vicious swipe of a tail. The creatures howled their pain and panic, clearly confused by their failing defenses. The second monster lost its battle and went down with a shriek that felt like a million nails dragging across a sheet of steel. The other men closed in on it, but the animal fought ferociously and its snapping jaws bit into one attacker and cut the man in two before he could even cry out.

Only one of the creatures remained, and it fixed its gaze on Shealy.

It charged in a loping canter, trampling the fallen bodies of its brethren as it bared its teeth. Tiarnan's chest heaved as he ran it down, using his ax to anchor himself in its side and then swing up onto its back. He ran up the spine like he would a rocky hill then dropped astride it, swung his sword, and lobbed off one of the heads, spinning and taking another in an instant that shattered into microseconds of blood and violence. The beast tried to turn on Tiarnan, but he was too quick and it was injured. It staggered to the right, blood streaming from the stumps of its necks. Tiarnan balanced on its massive shoulders, pulled his sword high, and then brought it down with a force that cut through bone and gristle and severed the last head from the body.

The creature listed, lurching one direction then another, until its legs simply collapsed and it hit the ground with an echoing *boom*.

The sudden silence solidified in a golden hue as rays of sun pierced the trees and bathed the battlefield in radiance.

Tiarnan stood atop the corpse, king of the carnage. He looked larger than life, muscles bunched and quivering with power, skin gleaming with blood and gore—some his own, most the creatures'. He threw his head back and let loose a roar of fury and triumph. At his feet, the three surviving men who'd fought with him did the same. They roared at the rising sun. They roared at the ground soaked with blood.

They roared at death and at the life that had not been snatched away.

In her arms the child quieted, hiccupped, and then tucked her head beneath Shealy's chin.

As the deafening shouts of victory echoed around her, Shealy fell back against the solid earth and cried.

Chapter Eight

TIARNAN knelt beside Shealy's prone body, preparing himself to find that her heart no longer beat and her lungs had frozen in death. But when he touched the satin warmth of her cheek, her eyes fluttered open and captured him in the mists of a silvery storm.

"Yer alive," he said softly.

Her lashes were spiky and blood splattered her face and body. A child lay sprawled across her with arms tight around her neck. He recognized the little girl who'd been born on this islet. Her name was Ellie. She had a thumb stuck between her lips and she sucked furiously, eyes clenched tight.

Shealy sat up unsteadily and Tiarnan reached out to help her, but she flinched away, and her reaction stung him more than he wanted to admit. She hadn't flinched from him last night. He started to pull back, but then she threw her arm around his neck, curling herself into the hard planes of his body, and he found himself embracing both woman and child as a feeling of unbelievable wholeness washed over him.

Clearly, he'd lost his mind.

She was soft and pliant beneath his touch, and gently he soothed her, running his fingers through her hair, rubbing small circles against her back, remembering the way she'd arched into him last night. The way she'd welcomed him into her body, making him feel alive for the first time in what seemed a hundred years. He felt the damp heat of tears on his bare chest and he wished he wasn't covered in blood. He didn't want any part of the vile *ellén trechend* touching her. Yet the creatures had come for her. He knew it with a certainty that shook him. He'd seen how they fixed their black eyes on her and followed her across the islet.

Why? *Why?*

Had the monsters come to kill her or take her away? Were they sent or had they merely been stalking human prey? Yesterday Jamie said they'd been seen watching, spying. Tiarnan hadn't thought it possible that a creature so ghastly could possess enough intelligence for that, but this morning he'd seen it with his own eyes.

"T," Jamie said, standing behind him.

Tiarnan looked back to see the dark-skinned man bathed in the gold of sunrise and the blackened blood of their enemy. He was as torn and battered as Tiarnan, half dressed as if he, too, had been ripped from slumber by the beasts. But his eyes blazed with battle lust that had yet to dim. Behind him stood Zac—a big man who wore the look of a Northman—and Reyes, who had the dark eyes of the Spaniards, both wounded but alive. Liam leaned against a boulder not far behind. Tiarnan took a deep breath as relief washed over him at the sight of his brother. Then he scanned the devastation of their settlement for signs of life. Not a single dwelling remained erect. Nothing and no one moved in the soft breeze that seemed to mock the violence it rustled.

"Are there others?" Tiarnan asked, his throat hoarse from shouting, his voice raw.

Jamie shook his head. "Not even bodies to bury. Whatever it sprayed, it just ate them away. Nothing's left. We'll go downriver and see if anybody made it over Endless Falls, but I doubt it. There's no surviving that."

"What the fuck were those things?" Reyes said, horror and fear in his tone.

"*Ellén trechend*," Tiarnan replied softly. "They are creatures of the Gods."

"Creatures of hell, maybe," Jamie muttered.

"Fuck me," Zac said, shaking his head. "I didn't think we were going to win this one." His legs gave a suspicious wobble, and he sat suddenly, putting his head between his knees. "I couldn't get a shot at any of them. It was like they were wearing armor."

Jamie nodded in agreement. "I had a few clean blows, but my blade just bounced."

"How'd you get through it?" Reyes demanded, staring at Tiarnan. They all stared at Tiarnan.

He glanced down at Shealy, still confused about what had happened. He hadn't been able to pierce those ironlike feathers either. His sword had chinks in it from the effort. But Shealy, child in her arms, had stood in front of them as they bore down on her. She'd held out that useless arrow, as if that could stop a creature of that size and weight. But then he'd felt a shift—like a wave washing over him. Only there was no water, no dampness, and not a whisper of breeze. Still the air had shimmered, like sheer silk flapping between him and Shealy and the *ellén trechend*. When it was done, he'd sensed a change, sensed the creatures hesitate as if they, too, had felt it. He'd swung his sword and the creatures had bled.

"They wanted her," Jamie said, nodding at Shealy, who'd gone very still in Tiarnan's arms. "Why?"

Shealy pulled back a little and looked at Jamie with those big drenched eyes. But her head was up and her back straight. She shifted the child she held, putting a protective hand over the girl's white blonde hair and dipping her chin so that her own hair fell forward in that practiced gesture he'd seen last night. The silky puckers of her scars were barely noticeable, but she didn't like others to see them. That much was clear.

She caught him staring and lifted her chin higher, her eyes shuttered. She hadn't moved and yet he felt the chill of her withdrawal, just as he had last night when she'd turned away from him. Tiarnan had let it happen then, but now he tightened his arms, keeping her in place, refusing to let her move away.

"Who is she?" Zac asked.

"My name is Shealy O'Leary."

"I know who you are," Reyes said. "I've seen you on TV."

She nodded, but Tiarnan was confused. He didn't know what *TV* was, but he didn't like that Reyes had seen her there. Disconcerted by the power of his possessive feelings, he said nothing.

Zac and Jamie looked as if they'd suddenly solved a perplexing puzzle. "That's why you looked familiar last night," Jamie muttered. "Just when you think it can't get any fucking weirder." All three men wore an expression of awe and a bit of *knowing* that was far too personal. They all spoke in the same manner, shared a cadence in their language that struck him as similar. They could easily be from the same time and place. They might even have met one another there. For all Tiarnan knew, *TV* was a way of saying neighbors, friends . . . lovers.

Irritated at the anger that stirred, he glanced at Shealy again. Her expression had smoothed and not a flicker of emotion showed on it. She might have been cast from stone the way she stared back without actually focusing on any one of them. Tiarnan sensed selfpreservation in her every breath.

He didn't like being on the ground with the others towering over him. Without a word he stood, pulling Shealy and the child up with him and keeping her close to his side when she tried to move away.

In her arms, the child sniffled, and Shealy asked, "Do you know who this little girl is?"

"Ellie," Tiarnan said.

"Who is her mother?"

The men looked from one to another, none of them wanting to say it. What did it matter who her mother had been when now she was almost certainly dead?

Tiarnan cleared his throat. "Maggie. Her mother was Maggie."

"Maggie who?"

Tiarnan glanced around the circle again, looking for a sign that one of them knew. They shook their heads.

Jamie said, "Last names don't get used too much around here. I don't think anyone ever knew hers."

Shealy frowned, but went on with her questions. "When was Ellie born?"

"Not long after we came," Zac said, blue eyes framed with sorrow. "Maggie was pregnant when she got here. I had some field training in the service and that made me the closest thing to a doctor around. I helped deliver Ellie."

"Why do y' ask, Shealy?" Tiarnan said softly.

"My mother's name was Margret O'Leary. Everyone called her Maggie."

The silence that followed that statement was thick and uncomfortable. None of them knew quite what to say to that. It seemed irrelevant, her mother's name, given the devastation they'd only just survived that morning. But something in Shealy's stillness, in the intent way she looked at the child in her arms, made Tiarnan pause. Eyes narrowed, he glanced between Ellie and Shealy, suddenly noticing similarities in their features that he'd missed before.

Then Ellie looked up from Shealy's arms and pinned him with storm-cloud eyes.

"Maggie," he began, still too uncertain to voice the bigger question. "Y' knew her?"

Shealy's face was tight, her bottom lip caught between her teeth. When she released it to speak, Tiarnan noted that it trembled.

"My mom was killed—we *thought* she was killed—in a car accident seven years ago. She was pregnant when it happened." She looked back at Ellie, took a breath. "I saw Maggie right before the m-monster . . ." A painful pause, another deep breath. "Before the monster killed her. Maggie was my mother. I'm almost certain."

By Tiarnan's estimation, Ellie was not yet three years old, but time on Inis Brandubh didn't pass in the same way it did in the real world. Seven years out there might be a minute on Inis Brandubh. Seven years here might be eternity on the other side. There was no rhyme or reason to how it flowed and no way to measure it.

"This car accident you thought killed her?" Jamie asked, his usually gruff tone gentle. "It happened on the Isle of Fennore?"

"Yes. Our car went off the cliffs and into the sea. My father was able to escape and save me, but my mom was never found."

The men exchanged another weighted glance. As Tiarnan had told Shealy last night, all of the people who lived on this tiny islet could trace their coming to Inis Brandubh directly back to the Isle of Fennore. They'd each been there when the white light had blinded them, then sucked them in and spewed them out here.

Jamie looked at Tiarnan. "You found Shealy yesterday?"

Tiarnan nodded.

"Where?"

Before Tiarnan could answer, Shealy said, "In a parking lot outside of a restaurant in Arizona."

The shocked silence echoed like a great clap of thunder. Tiarnan counted one, two, three . . . and then everyone started talking at once. Tiarnan didn't know what a *parking lot* or *restaurant* or *Arizona* was, but he understood that the words were synonymous with Shealy's world, a world the other men had once shared.

"Wait a minute. Wait a goddamned minute," Jamie said, quieting the rumble. "Let me make sure I'm getting this straight. You"—he pointed at Tiarnan—"saw her"—the finger moved to Shealy—"*outside* of Inis Brandubh?"

Tiarnan glanced at Shealy, at her pale face and clouded eyes, and once more that unwelcome urge to protect her gripped him. He'd trusted these men with his life many times over and yet he didn't want to share with them anything about Shealy O'Leary. And that bothered him, greatly. In a short amount of time, Shealy had managed to alter his perception of his own world in more ways than he could believe.

"Yes," he said at last. "I was pulled through. Into her world."

Once again, the voices erupted, demanding, exclaiming, disbelieving.

Tiarnan held up his hand. "As was Cathán."

"Cathán?" Jamie shouted. "*Cathán?* How? And why the fuck would you come back if you were out?"

"I cannot tell y' how it happened. It was done in an instant. As for coming back, it was not my choice, but even if it was, I would not have left my brother and I would not have walked away from any of y' either."

Jamie laughed. "You really mean that, don't you, T?"

Frowning, Tiarnan nodded. Of course he meant it.

"Don't get me wrong," Jamie said, "I want out of here as bad as anyone, but if you get the chance again, you take it. All of you. This isn't the kind of place where you can afford to be a hero."

The truth of that settled heavily around them, and yet Tiarnan knew that Jamie would not have left any of them behind either, if there was a chance of them all getting out. In his arms, Shealy shifted, and he moved his hand to help support the weight of the child. Ellie was a wee thing, but then so was Shealy.

"So how did you get pulled through?" Zac asked.

"Shealy's father. He opened a doorway and released both me and Cathán from Inis Brandubh. I do not know how and I do not know why."

When they would have peppered Shealy with questions next, Tiarnan held up his hand again. "Shealy does not know either. She'd never heard of this place before she came."

"Well, where is her dad?" Jamie demanded.

"I do not know if Cathán pulled him into Inis Brandubh or if Shealy's father let Cathán loose in the real world. I only know that the door opened and I went through. When it closed again, both Shealy and I were back on this side and her father was gone."

Jamie shook his head. "But she said her mother . . . She said Maggie was her mother."

Tiarnan nodded, looking at the child whose resemblance to Shealy seemed more pronounced by the moment. "Perhaps it was why her father opened the door. To find her and the child."

"That doesn't make sense," Shealy said. "We thought my mom was dead and the baby—" Her voice cracked and she took a moment to steady it. "The baby wasn't even born when she . . . We had a funeral for them and everything."

Tiarnan pulled Shealy closer, trying to still the shivers that wracked her body. Shivers that had nothing to do with the cold and everything to do with shock. The child in her arms watched him with solemn eyes.

"What do y' remember about this day when yer . . ." He paused, trying to recall the words she'd used.

"Car. She was in a car accident, T," Jamie said. "Carts on wheels that go really fast."

Ah. He nodded. "When yer cart went over the cliffs. Did y' see the door open then?"

Shealy shook her head. "No, but I don't remember anything about it. I was hurt pretty bad in the accident. I almost died. I have memories of the moments just before but nothing during. Nothing until a few weeks after when I woke up in the hospital."

Zac shook his head, his eyes filled with sympathy. "I saw pictures of you on the news after it happened," he said. "You were in bad shape. They put you back together good as new, though, didn't they?"

She made a sound in her throat that wasn't quite laughter and certainly held little humor. It had a bitter note to it that confused Tiarnan even more. He wished he understood the strange undercurrents of her reactions, but there were too many unknowns for him. They used unfamiliar words and he knew he was missing the significance of those he did comprehend.

Reyes and Zac exchanged a weighted glance and then went back to staring at Shealy. Tiarnan didn't like the familiar way they let their eyes rove over her face, lingering on the scars for a brief moment before moving down the creamy arc of her throat, lower. Her gown was filthy, torn, and showing more flesh than before. He wanted to cover her up. He wanted to growl, like he had when he'd killed the three-headed creatures.

"She's what brought those monsters here," Jamie said.

Shealy stiffened. "I didn't bring them. How can you even suggest that?"

"They wanted you," Jamie insisted flatly.

She lowered her eyes at his words, and Tiarnan saw that she knew it was the truth. She'd felt their focus, their drive to have her. But the silvery gaze that lifted to his face was bewildered and frightened, not secretive. She didn't know anything about the *ellén trechend*. He would wager his life on it.

"Are you working for Cathán?" Jamie asked casually.

"She's not a spy," Tiarnan snapped.

"Let the lady answer for herself."

"I've never even seen him before. Never even heard his name before Tiarnan told me who he is," she said, lifting her chin, but still holding her head at that peculiar angle with her hair hiding much of her face.

"But your father knows him. And it's a given he's connected to this place."

"He searched for the Book of Fennore," Tiarnan told them, knowing they would find out eventually.

Jamie cursed beneath his breath. "Well there you go. So what are *you* looking for, Shealy O'Leary? You after the Book, too? You here to make some deals with Cathán? Because I don't believe in coincidences. I deal with facts and the fact is, you came and brought one hell of a disaster with you."

"I'm not after the Book," she said, incredulous. "That stupid Book almost got me killed. If my dad hadn't been looking for it, we never would have been on that island. My mother wouldn't have . . ." She trailed off and her gaze went to the blood-soaked ground where Maggie had fallen and then been eaten by the *ellén trechend*.

"Leave her alone," Tiarnan said in a dark voice. "She is just a woman who needs our help. And I believe her."

Jamie didn't back down. "I don't get in your business, T. But right now you need to think. In all the time we've been here, nothing like that has ever come to dinner, you hear me?"

Jamie flicked his hard gaze over Shealy, lingering on the child in her arms before skimming down and up again. Once more there was familiarity in that glance that made Tiarnan want to step in front of Shealy and hide her. It was ridiculous and unwarranted. Jamie had every right to question her presence. In his place, Tiarnan would do the same.

Shealy shifted, and the child in her arms clutched her reflexively. "Listen," she said. "I'd love to stand trial while you accuse me of making it rain monsters, but do you think we could sit down first? She's small, but she's heavy."

Perhaps it was the way Shealy's voice cracked with emotion as she spoke, perhaps it was how fragile she herself appeared, with bruises on her arms and legs and blood splattering her from head to toe. Maybe it was the child whose life she'd saved. Whatever the reason, the tension seemed to ebb, and Tiarnan exhaled softly.

Jamie nodded and then looked around, as if seeing the wreckage for the first time. "Look at this place. Not even a chair left."

"We going to rebuild?" Zac asked, staring grimly at the ruins.

No one answered. Tiarnan supposed no one knew. If the monsters they'd defeated heralded more of the same, what point would there be in rebuilding? They had wiped out an entire settlement, killed more than twenty people in a matter of minutes.

Jamie looked at Tiarnan. "You think there's more of those things out there?"

Tiarnan held his gaze. "There's more of everything out there, and y' know it yerself."

"Christ," Jamie said, looking with defeat at the remains of their homes.

Using his chin, Tiarnan pointed at a fallen tree beside the river. "Come, Shealy. Y' can sit there."

Jamie, Reyes, and Zac moved aside while Tiarnan led Shealy to the deadwood. Liam, who'd been unusually quiet during the discussion, followed behind. Tiarnan gave him a curious glance and noted the grief in his brother's eyes. Only then did he realize. *Sally.* Sally was gone. His little brother had been at war more than half of his young life and he'd learned to harden his heart to things that could break it. But Sally had slipped in as women tended to do and now she was dead.

Tiarnan swallowed hard, rearing away from that thought. He put a consoling hand on Liam's shoulder as he passed, and Liam gave him a jerky nod. But there were shadows in his eyes that had not been there before and Tiarnan mourned the addition.

As if sensing his thoughts, Shealy glanced at him over her shoulder. She looked exhausted and vulnerable, battered from the attack and the circumstances she could barely grasp. But in her rain-colored eyes he saw strength and courage. He tried to harden his heart against her, but somehow she'd cracked the armor he wore around it and left him defenseless.

He sat beside her on the log and waited for the others to take seats as well. They lowered themselves to the marshy earth in a loose circle and waited.

The river raged past them, the current mighty here and danger-ous. With the pull of Endless Falls less than three hundred feet downriver, this particular stretch was treacherous and impassable. Still, the steady thunder of rushing water seemed to calm them all, so long as no one looked in the other direction where the headless bodies of the monsters lay in bloody heaps and the ruins of their settlement littered every inch of the islet.

Shealy shifted the child in her arms, easing Ellie's weight onto her lap, gazing at the little girl's face with a poignant mixture of remorse and wonder. He felt the burn of her pain, could only imag-ine what she must feel, finding a mother she'd thought dead only to witness her brutal murder.

And now she held a sister she'd never known.

All the men waited until Shealy looked up, tilting her head to cover the side of her face with her hair. A part of him wanted to reach over and push it back and prove that she had nothing to hide, but he forced himself to sit still and wait.

"You said your father searched for the Book of Fennore," Jamie said, gently now that they'd calmed. "Why?"

She sighed and a flush spread up her throat. "He thought he was part of some ancient order," she told him. "His father believed the same thing. It was a family obsession, looking for it."

"What did he want from it?"

"Nothing. I mean, he was under the delusion that he was supposed to protect it. He called himself a Keeper. Said it was his duty to find the Book and put it where it couldn't be found, where the world would be safe from it. He sounded like a lunatic when he talked about it."

Jamie's eyes narrowed. "A Keeper."

"That's right." She frowned, noting his expression. "Why?"

Yes, Tiarnan wanted that answered as well. Something about the tension in Jamie's body set off alarms.

"But he never found the Book?" Jamie went on.

"No. And I'm not convinced that it was my dad who 'opened the door' as Tiarnan says. He's just a normal guy, my dad. And he quit looking for the Book after my mother . . ." She clenched her jaw and let out a pent-up breath. "After the accident, he quit looking. He moved us from Ireland to Arizona and he hasn't even mentioned it again."

"Why Arizona?" Zac asked.

"There was a specialist, a doctor there. Plus it's dry. At least those were the reasons he gave me. He said he was sick of the rain."

Tiarnan touched her arm. "Do you think he suspected your mother was here, Shealy?"

"No," she said. "God no. He thought she was dead. We both did."

Her eyes grew misty and she swallowed hard.

"I need to find him," she said.

"If he went back, if he's on the other side, you're SOL, sweetheart," Jamie said.

Shealy looked up, her eyes round.

"Unless T here knows what he's talking about and your dad really can open the door."

"I saw it. I stepped through it," Tiarnan said.

"Well, what about you?" Reyes asked suddenly.

As one they all looked at her, and Shealy pressed back against Tiarnan.

"What about Shealy?" Tiarnan asked.

"You saw what she did to those monsters," he answered. "She *changed* them."

"No," she said.

"You did," Jamie agreed. "They were like tanks. Nothing penetrated. Nothing stopped them. And then . . ."

"I felt a blast," Liam said, speaking for the first time. "It went right through me."

Zac and Reyes nodded. They'd felt it, too.

"It wasn't me," Shealy said.

Tiarnan watched her. Unable to stop himself, he brushed her hair away from her face and gently tucked it back, exposing the small patch of scars and the injured shell of her ear, wanting to press his lips to each tiny flaw even as a voice deep inside mocked him, told him he was digging his own grave. He need only look at the pain in his little brother's eyes to see the results of caring about someone in this place of violence. He needed to put distance between himself and Shealy O'Leary.

Shealy frowned at Tiarnan and flipped her hair out from behind her ear.

"I felt it, too, lass," he murmured. "It was a force, like a wind, and it came from y'."

"It wasn't me," she insisted. And then she looked down at the child dozing in her arms. "It was her. Ellie . . . my sister."

"She's just a baby." Jamie said what they were all thinking.

"She's old enough to be scared," Shealy answered softly. "And when those things were coming at us, she . . . did something. I felt it, too." In the silence that followed, each of them considered this and what it might mean. They'd never noticed anything unique about the cute little girl. She'd been doted upon by one and all and hadn't once exhibited any special abilities . . .

"So what now?" Jamie asked, and Tiarnan could not tell what went on behind the other man's dark eyes. He didn't know if Jamie believed Shealy or if he thought her lying.

"If my father's here, I need to look for him," Shealy said.

"You won't find him," Jamie responded. "Tell her Tiarnan."

Tiarnan took a deep breath, prepared to agree with Jamie—prepared to dash all Shealy's hopes that her father could be found. But something held him back. He'd been without hope for so long, he hardly knew what it felt like. But since seeing Shealy through that rip in the darkness, things had changed. *He'd* changed.

There was a reason why she'd come to this world. To him.

"There is a chance," Tiarnan said carefully. "I believe he will be looking for her."

"And what about Cathán?" Jamie asked.

"If finding Shealy's father brings Cathán into my reach, all the better. Cathán has taken everything I've ever cared about. I will finally be able to do what I've wanted to do for most of my life. I will kill him."

He'd said the words a hundred times or more, but now they rang with a finality that thrilled him.

"I hear you, my friend. We all want that," Jamie said, but he eyed Tiarnan with unmistakable reservation. "But this is not the time to air old grudges. Whatever those *things* were that came here tonight—Cathán sent them. You know it."

"All the more reason to hunt him down and be done with him once and for all," Tiarnan responded.

"We've been hunting him since we got here. What makes you think we'll find him now? What makes you think we can find anyone now?"

Tiarnan looked at Shealy again, remembering that wash of . . . *power* he'd felt go through him. It had been charged, like the air after a lightning strike. He didn't know what to call it . . . magic, perhaps. He only knew that it had changed the odds and allowed him to kill their foes.

Shealy said the power had come from the child, but Tiarnan wasn't convinced. Even if the child was the source of it, that only sparked another question within him. If Shealy's father had the power to open the door between the worlds, and her sister could change an indestructible monster into something that could be slain, then what power did Shealy have? What might she be able to do? Could she be the source of an even greater magic than what they'd felt this morning?

Choosing his words with care, he said, "Shealy's father can release us from this world, Jamie. He can help us all to leave this place. What risk is not worth that?"

For a moment, no one spoke. Reluctantly, Tiarnan went on, voicing words he wished he didn't have to say.

"There's more we need to consider. If Cathán has captured Shealy's father, he can use him to escape this world. If he has her father, we must free him before that happens."

"It could have happened already."

"I do not believe it."

"Why not?"

"Why would Cathán send the *ellén trechend* if he'd left this world behind?"

Jamie scowled. "That brings us to another important point. If Cathán can summon the wolves, the dragons, the *monsters* that were here today, we don't stand a chance against him. It's a miracle we're even alive. How in the hell do you think we're going to come out the winners in a battle with him?"

"We don't go to battle," Zac said into the drawn silence. Surprised, they all faced him. "We're not storming the gates, right? It's a rescue. When the military operates a rescue, they don't send the whole troop. They send a team that can move fast. Get in and out without being seen."

Beside him, Reyes nodded, but the look on Jamie's face was far from agreement. It might have been funny under other conditions, but now he looked like he might take that heavy blade he carried and start whacking. Zac and Reyes had been his to command since the beginning. That one of them would speak against him was not only unexpected, it was an offense.

Reyes looked between the two men with an unhappy expression. Obviously, he didn't want to take sides, but all of them could see he wouldn't have a choice. Not this time.

"I'm in," he said. "Tiarnan's right, no matter how we look at it. Her father is the one and only ticket out, and from my perspective it's either us on the train or its Cathán. I'm voting for us."

Jamie let out a deep breath. It defied his ability to grasp that in the space of one morning he'd fought three-headed creatures and had his authority challenged by subordinates who'd never questioned him before.

Tiarnan said, "Going after her father will be dangerous, and I do not ask y' to come. I only ask that y' don't try to stop me. The time has come for me to face my enemy once and for all. It is my battle. I will face it alone."

Jamie snorted. "Fuck you, T. That ain't happening." He looked at Reyes and Zac, shook his head again, and then put his hand out. Without hesitation, the other two men placed theirs on top of his. Liam moved from where he sat and added the weight of his hand to the pile.

It had been a long time since any man had offered to fight Tiarnan's battles. A long time since he'd felt man enough to take on his own demons. That simple gesture of trust that Jamie made filled Tiarnan with dread and hope in equal but warring doses. If ever there'd been a God to pray to, he prayed now that he did not fail them.

Feeling something hard swell in his chest, Tiarnan stepped forward. As he placed his hand over the others, he sensed the weight of Shealy's gaze on his face. He stared into her stormy eyes and felt as if she'd bared his soul. There in the clouded depths he saw compassion, understanding, commitment. And then, with a deep breath and a look of utter determination, Shealy O'Leary put her hand on top of them all.

"To Oz," she said softly.

Jamie laughed. "Yeah. Follow the fucking yellow brick road."

Tiarnan didn't know what that meant, but he saw the journey snake out ahead of them, twisted and dark with the unknown. And despite the years of failure that had scored his life to this point, despite the defeat that ate at him like a disease, he felt a glimmer of optimism. Maybe, just maybe this time he would succeed.

Maybe it was time for hope.

Chapter Nine

AFRAID couldn't come close to describing what Meaghan Bal-lagh felt.

She had no idea where she was, how she'd come to be there, or, more importantly, how the hell to find her way home. She'd been walking for about an hour, hoping something would look familiar, but the forest in which she'd found herself grew darker, more alien.

She paused, looked around hopelessly for a clue—a flashing neon sign that said "This Way, Meaghan" or bread crumbs—*anything*. But all she saw was more of the same cloistered shadows, thick with menace.

She pushed on, moving faster now. Branches tore at her clothes and whipped her face and bare arms, but now that she'd sped up, she couldn't bring herself to slow down. It was the kind of thing stupid teenagers did in the movies—running through unknown territory in blind terror. She'd never understood the rationale before.

Now she got it loud and clear.

Running gave the fear purpose.

She was glad for her jeans, thankful for the rubber-soled shoes on her feet. If she hadn't changed at the last minute, she'd be doing this sprint of terror in shorts and sandals. The forest thinned and ahead the trees ended abruptly. Beyond was open meadow stretching out as far as she could see. It was light out there, and her survival instincts warred at the beckoning sunshine. The darkness under the canopy of trees whispered with malevolence, playing on her fear of the dark that had plagued her since she was little. Sly and insidious, it tracked her fleeing footsteps.

Still, she couldn't bring herself to break from cover, couldn't convince her adrenaline-drenched system to slow down and think. She veered right, panic in the driver's seat. She didn't want to be caught out in the open.

The terrain grew rocky as she ran parallel to that taunting meadow, forcing the trees to grow at angles, slowing Meaghan despite the fear screaming *faster* in her head. Weaving between boulders and trunks, she strained to hear beyond the terror. Was she running from shadows? From the feeling of threat inside her own head? Or was something real out there?

She didn't know. Only her own labored breathing and pounding feet filled her ears, but beneath it she felt that malicious murmur that vibrated through the disturbed air and sent dread of a different kind through her.

The ground sloped, and soon she was climbing with her lungs on fire and her legs shaking from exertion. By degrees she rose, breaking from the confined grasp of the woods. Relief made her shudder. She didn't let herself look back as she hefted herself up another level. Only a scattering of trees managed to thrive in the stony foundation—enough to make her feel less exposed but not so many that they obstructed the view.

She crawled over a huge boulder, then the next and the next, each rise making her feel a little safer, convincing her that the terrifying presence she'd sensed hovering in the gloom of the trees had been her imagination kicked into overdrive.

At last the feeling of being tracked by unseen eyes eased. Finally she paused and glanced back. From her new vantage, she could see for miles in every direction. The tree line was a looming fortress behind her, fiendishly shadowed and tense with anticipation. The open meadow below and to her left spread out sparse and still in the distance.

With a gasp she leaned against a boulder, trying to catch her breath. Trying to understand where she was and how she'd gotten there. One minute she'd been in Ballyfionúir, combing the cavern beneath the restored castle where her family lived, searching for her half brother, Rory. It had taken a hefty shot of whiskey to talk herself into going down there. The cavern encapsulated every fear of darkness she'd ever had.

Even with the afternoon sun bathing it in gold, the cavern maintained an air of dank gloom and thick menace not unlike the forest from which she'd just emerged. Bad things had happened in that cavern, and Meaghan felt the shocked shiver of them suspended in the primeval air.

But the last time she'd seen Rory, he'd been headed for the cavern. He'd come home for Nana Colleen's funeral only to leave in the middle of the service, racing toward the cliffs that led down to it like something had called to him.

He needed to be alone, the other mourners whispered amongst themselves. *Overcome by emotion*, they agreed with sage nods.

She'd thought so, too, but that had been a week ago.

On the outside, Rory looked invincible, but she remembered when he was a teenager—even then haunted by his own personal nightmares. She'd worshiped him as a child and resented him when he'd gone off to America, leaving her behind. But she was grown up now and she knew that her half brother had a good heart and more than his share of pain.

She also knew that Rory was somehow connected to the mysteries surrounding the Book of Fennore. Talk of the Book and its elusive tie to her family had followed Meaghan her entire life. Ask any one of the MacGraths or the Ballaghs if it was fact or fantasy and they'd become fecking doorposts, acting like they didn't know what she meant. Meander down to the pub, though, and she'd get an earful of lore and fancy. For a girl like Meaghan whose curiosity had gotten her in trouble more times than not, the Book of Fennore became an irresistible lure.

After her grandmother's funeral service, when the mourners had turned to celebrating Nana's life by the pint, the family had searched for Rory. He wasn't in the cavern as they'd expected. Nor was he in the castle, or any of the pubs, or anywhere else for that matter. Not a soul had seen him since he'd run from the funeral. It was as if he'd simply vanished into thin air. Just vanished.

There'd been rumors about Rory's father—her mother's first husband, Cathán MacGrath—vanishing from the cavern beneath the ruins many years before. When she was little, Meaghan had asked her mother about it, but she'd only laughed and said it was a lie. Her first husband had disappeared all right, but not by any mystifying way. Meaghan's mother said he'd run off with another woman or been shot by an angry father who'd caught him dallying with his daughter. Nothing unsolved about that.

But with Rory gone, the story of Cathán seemed much more than rumor.

The Gardai had investigated, but found nothing to indicate foul play, no signs of struggle or illegal activity. Rory's duffel bag sat in his room, just as he'd left it, filled with nothing more lethal than his fresh and citrusy aftershave. He hadn't left the island by ferry and no one had taken him to the mainland in their boat. Garda Walsh had hinted that Rory might have fallen and been washed out to sea. It was a possibility that had also been assigned to his father, years ago.

Left with little choice, Meaghan and her family had begun to mourn yet another tragedy in their lives.

And then, a few days later, Meaghan had been cleaning up at the children's center that she and her half sister Danni operated and she'd seen the book of fairy tales lying open on the floor. There'd been a picture on one of the pages and across the top in big letters it read, "Ruairi of Fennore Commands the Sea."

The larger-than-life man poised atop the choppy waves in the picture, hands raised with power, was her half brother. Rory's face stared out at her from the portrait captured there—not his likeness, not someone similar. Impossible though it was, the depicted man was Rory, and Meaghan knew it down to her bones.

That very afternoon she'd gone to the cavern, swallowing her own monstrous fears, convinced she would find answers. In the alternating light made by the tide swelling at the mouth of the cave, blocking the sun then releasing it in steady surges, she'd felt the eerie stillness and the oppressive shadows. She'd sensed a tension, stretching tight, filling the void and vanquishing the steady roar of the sea. It had taken every ounce of grit she had not to turn and run.

The cave had gone black and silent and then light and sound exploded like a wartime detonation. For an instant, she thought she saw Rory with another man, right there in front of her. But the light had grown so bright, the rumble so loud that she'd closed her eyes and clapped her hands over her ears. The ground had shook, bringing rocks tumbling down around her. Her brother-in-law, who'd rebuilt the castle, always warned against going into the cavern. He'd said it wasn't safe. She thought how angry he'd be when they found her body in the rubble later.

And then just as suddenly as the shaking had begun, it stopped.

Meaghan opened her eyes to find she was no longer in that cavern. She was in a thick forest, alive with buzzing insects and the dark, swaying branches of unfamiliar trees. She couldn't recall the steps that had taken her from the cave to this wooded area. All she remembered was the cavern and then . . . this.

She wiped her brow and then looked around again. The rocky hills couldn't be called mountains, but they rose in a choppy range that played sentry to the soaring peaks behind them. There were gaping grottos speckled amongst the boulders that led into alcoves or tunnels. Casting a nervous glance at the sun, which seemed to have slipped across the sky at an alarming speed, Meaghan warily approached one of the shadowed depressions. The last thing she wanted was to go from the fire to the frying pan and startle some big, fast creature in its lair, but the thought of being caught out in the open when twilight leached the color from the sky terrified her more than the idea of entering one of the depressions of her own free will. With one last glance over her shoulder, she crept into the yawning black mouth and paused, ears straining for the slightest shift or shuffle.

A wide tunnel, long and curved, sloped down in front of her. Cautiously she followed it, monitoring the stretch of light spilling from the entrance, careful not to exceed its reach. She caught a whiff of smoke as she drew deeper in. It made no sense that a natural fire would be burning inside a tunnel, so that meant that someone had started it. Bolstered by the idea that she'd find someone else, refusing to let herself consider that someone being dangerous, she crept on. The farther she went, the darker it became, and now her fear grew with the shadows, making her want to cower and run with the same bipolar force.

She inched around a blind corner and found herself in a rounded, wide chamber lit by a small fire in the center. The flames flickered, dancing on the walls and animating shadows on the ceiling. There was an old man sitting beside the fire, and he looked up in surprise and stared at her. The sight of him was so unexpected, so out of place that Meaghan froze for a moment, certain he was an illusion.

"Who are you?" she asked, and her voice felt very loud in the silence.

She'd startled him, and he gave a muffled yelp as he jumped to his feet, staring at her like she might be an apparition that would vanish with a gust of wind. In a flashing instant she saw relief and then disappointment move across his face, like he'd been expecting, *hoping for*, someone else. Who he expected to meet in this godforsaken place, she had no idea. His lip was split and a nasty black eye gave him a piratical look, but he didn't seem aggressive or hostile in any way, nor did he seem disoriented or delusional.

"I am Donnell O'Leary," he answered in a tired voice. "Recently of the United States."

"Meaghan. Meaghan Ballagh, Ballyfionúir," she said softly.

"Ballagh," he repeated in a tone that made the hairs at her nape stand on end. "Of course. You've the look of your mother."

He couldn't have shocked her more if he'd sprouted horns and a pelt. "You know my mother?"

"No. But I've seen pictures."

"Where?" she demanded as images of an obsessed stalker flashed in her mind.

"The paper, when her husband disappeared."

Well that made sense. Her mother's first husband disappearing had caused quite a scandal on the Isle of Fennore. The old-timers still talked about the trouble they'd had keeping the tabloids from invading. She took another step closer to the warmth of the fire.

"What are you doing here?" she said, perching cautiously on a rock opposite where he sat.

"I was chased. By a wolf if you can believe such a thing. You?"

"A *wolf?*" Meaghan stared at him with her jaw dropped. "Where the feck are we?" she blurted.

"Now, that's the question," Donnell said with a sad shake of his head. "And one I'm not sure I can answer. I've been here for a day or two—I can't say if it's one or the other. It seems that the sun rises and sets unpredictably, but I know that's not possible."

"No, it's not," Meaghan said, eyeing him even as she thought of the sun, which had seemed to slip from the sky in double time.

"How did you get here?" he asked.

"I'm not really certain." Feeling foolish, she told him about going to the cavern and the blinding light that came before opening her eyes here. "It happened like that," and she snapped her fingers. The sound echoed unnaturally loud around them.

"The Isle of Fennore," he said darkly. "The last time I was there I was in an automobile accident. I lost my wife and almost lost my daughter, Shealy."

Meaghan frowned, his words stirring a memory inside her. And then her eyes widened. "O'Leary!" she exclaimed. "Your daughter is Shealy O'Leary?"

Donnell nodded, looking miserable. "You know her, then?"

"Only from the papers."

Shealy O'Leary was the spokesperson for a charitable organization that helped kids with correctable deformities. Her own amazing transformation from the mangled wreckage of the accident that had nearly killed her to the beautiful woman who'd graced magazine covers and appeared on commercials had made her famous worldwide. The media had followed her recovery like a reality television progam.

Donnell looked down and shook his head. "Just before that accident, something like what you described happening in the cavern . . . it happened to me. To us."

"What do you mean?"

"I saw a blinding light and felt the car jerk. I thought it was an earthquake, but then the car vanished and we were here."

"Here?" Meaghan said, confused. "In this cave?"

"No, Ms. Ballagh. Here in this world where time runs on its own clock."

Frowning, she shook her head. "I don't understand."

Donnell didn't appear to have heard her. "It was just for a moment," he said. "A blink of the eye. But what I saw . . . Terrible things, Ms. Ballagh."

Dry-mouthed, Meaghan tried not to ask, but she couldn't help it. "Like what?"

"Monsters," he whispered.

Monsters? She laughed. She couldn't help it. *Monsters.* But Donnell O'Leary's face held no humor.

"I don't blame you for not believing me. I wouldn't believe me either if I was sitting across the fire listening. But this is a dangerous place. Somehow my daughter and I ended up back in that car, sailing over the cliff and into the sea. But my wife, Maggie—she didn't come with us."

Meaghan frowned. "The papers said she died in the accident."

"What else would they say? That a bright light sucked her into an impossible world and killed her?"

It was just too queer, all of this, and suddenly she thought perhaps she *had* been struck by the falling stones. Perhaps she was in hospital getting pumped full of morphine or something that caused wild delusions just like this.

No, a voice of reason insisted. Dreams didn't have texture, and she could feel the chill in the air, the heat of the fire, the taste of fear in her mouth.

A silence fell between her and the old man as each of them contemplated their unbelievable circumstances. Then, faintly at first and louder as they drew closer, Meaghan heard voices. They echoed down the tunnel from outside.

People.

Meaghan jumped to her feet and moved through the winding corridor to investigate. Behind her, Donnell O'Leary followed.

They reached the mouth of the cave and down below they saw a gathering of men on horses. There were eight, maybe ten of them circled around another man on foot.

She thought of raising her arms and shouting to get their attention, but a small voice of caution made her crouch and watch first. The man without a horse was tall and handsome, dressed in a bizarrely formal white button-down shirt and creased black trousers. He might have just come from the office. He turned in place, eyeing the men who surrounded him, and Meaghan was surprised to see a clerical collar at his throat.

One of the mounted riders clicked his tongue and urged his horse forward. The tall man shifted to watch him, and Meaghan glimpsed his face. Beside her, Donnell sucked in a breath.

"'Tis Father Mahon. Kyle, I mean," Donnell said.

"You know *him, too*?" Meaghan asked.

He didn't look like any priest she'd ever met. He was too young and far too handsome, temptation in the flesh. She was certain that many a female had dreamed of sinning during his sermons.

"Aye, I know him well," Donnell said with a note of despair in his voice. "When I first met him, he was a deacon, planning on devoting his life to the church."

There was something in Donnell's tone that set alarms clanging in her already distressed mind.

"What is he doing here?"

But Donnell wasn't listening anymore. Uneasy, Meaghan glanced back to the gathering, noting a tension she'd missed before.

There was wariness on the priest's face and in the shuttered expressions the other men wore. The priest held his hands out at his sides, showing compliance. Meaghan couldn't tell if he was part of the group or a . . . prisoner.

Frowning at her own thoughts, she looked at the others and saw . . . good God, the others wore swords. *Swords.*

"Why are they so hostile?" Meaghan whispered. "He's a priest."

Donnell didn't answer and she glanced back at him to find a look of horror on his features.

"I've got to help him," Donnell said. "Lord above, what did I get him into?"

Without another word, he started climbing down the huge boulders, moving gingerly as he descended.

"Wait," Meaghan hissed. "Where are you going?"

Donnell paused, glancing up at her, and his foot dislodged some pebbles that rappelled down to where the men gathered. Alert, the riders began scanning the rocky hillside. They saw Donnell immediately and caught sight of Meaghan before she could duck and hide. The one who seemed in charge snapped his fingers and two others broke from the circle and dismounted, handing off their reins and starting to climb.

"Run, girl," Donnell said. "Run."

His words went through her like a shot of adrenaline, but now three other men had left their horses and began to climb, coming fast. There was no way to get down and past them. She had to go up, into the dark and winding passageways.

Donnell called out a greeting to the approaching men, told them he came in friendship, but his words did nothing to gentle the hands that grabbed him. With a last glance back, Meaghan scrambled back into the tunnel, racing down the winding corridor, past the fire, plunging into the darkness that was held tight in the confined space. Her fear tried to strangle her, writhing like a serpent beneath her skin. This dark was as shrouded and evil as the shade of the forest. She felt it brushing against her as she ran, teasing the hairs on her arms, blowing softly against her nape.

Echoing from behind her, she heard raised voices coming closer, gaining on her. Why were they chasing her? What did they want?

Her foot slid on gravel and she careened into the rock wall. Pain sliced through her shoulder, making her fingers go numb. Gasping, she turned at another tunnel that veered off to the right. In her head she tried to keep track of where she was going, afraid she'd get lost in the winding labyrinth, terrified of the grasping shadows and the malignant taint that permeated them. The voices behind pursued, getting closer, louder as the tunnel grew darker and narrower. She couldn't see anything and the air felt old and dank, as if it had been trapped for a million years.

Not good, not good at all.

Panic made her feel sluggish even as it boosted her energy and spurred her to go faster. Then suddenly she plowed full speed into a solid wall. The impact jarred every bone in her body and snapped her neck back as stars exploded behind her eyes. Her knees wobbled and then gave. She hit the floor hard just as the chasing footsteps reached her.

"Think this is the one he's looking for?" asked a man whose face she couldn't make out in the gloom.

"Would be a fine thing if it was," another answered.

The first man grabbed her roughly and jerked her to her feet. "You'll be coming with us, won't you now?"

"I don't think so," she said, and tried to yank her arm free of his grasp. But he was strong and not in the mood to play games.

She fought. She'd taken self-defense courses. She knew to go for eyes and groin, to stomp on insteps, elbow the solar plexus. Scream. She did all of that. She slammed her head hard into the nose of the man who caught hold of her again and was rewarded with his shout of pain and the hot spray of blood against her neck, which nearly made her vomit. She'd have to be Wonder Woman to come out of this the winner. She was nowhere close to that.

Cursing, the first man held her while the other gave her a cold look.

"Lights out, sweetheart," he said as he doubled up his fist and punched her hard in the face.

Chapter Ten

UNFATHOMABLE as it seemed, only a day ago Shealy's biggest fear was telling her father about her trip to Ireland. Now here she stood, on an island that couldn't be, in a world that didn't exist. And if that didn't stretch the bounds of reality enough, she held a sister who'd been buried, unborn, seven years ago. She still couldn't believe it—*any* of it. But not believing didn't equal *not real*. That left her two choices—curl up in a corner, plug her ears, close her eyes, and pretend she didn't know what went on beyond the radius of sensory perception; or deal with it.

Option one left the high risk of being devoured by something of the three-headed variety. And while option two had its merits, she'd learned the hard way that even though dealing with things she'd rather avoid wasn't easy and it certainly wasn't fun, it was usually quicker than ignoring them. Better to move on than to dwell in misery. That was her philosophy.

Yeah, that's why you still put your makeup on with a spatula, a snide voice in her head taunted.

Forcibly she shut it out and focused on the warm sleeping child she still held. *My sister . . .*

She had a sister—a little baby sister who needed her. How in the world could she hope to protect her in this nightmare?

Shaking her head, she glanced up and caught Tiarnan watching her with those whiskey-colored eyes. His gaze skimmed her face, seeming to peer into her soul. Just the sight of him stole the air from her lungs and forced everything from her brain except the memories of last night, when his touch had gone beyond physical. He'd turned her emotions into a knot that seemed to bind her tighter and tighter to him. Flushing hotly, she looked away, but it was not so easy to tune Tiarnan out. She remained painfully aware of his every move, his every breath and before long, the hard lines of his body, the broad shoulders, the muscled arms that had held her so gently . . . all of him drew her gaze once more.

Liam left to search for survivors downriver, but Jamie and the other two men still stood nearby, discussing their plans in low tones. Then Jamie let loose a few colorful and juicy curses that would have done many an Irishman proud, before turning to herd in his troop of two and set about gathering supplies from the wreckage. He'd committed to helping find her father, but he still had reservations about the wisdom of the journey, reservations about Shealy and what her role in all of this would prove to be. She didn't know how to convince him to trust her so she didn't try. She could only hope he'd figure things out on his own and not view her with suspicion each time that ebony gaze found her.

He'd taken two steps away when she noticed the tattoo on his left shoulder blade. Stunned, she simply stared as her brain stuttered with surprise, trying to explain yet another inexplicable thing.

Black ink connected three spirals without a visible beginning or end on his shoulder. A common enough symbol in Ireland; it was on ruins everywhere. But Jamie wasn't from Ireland, and Shealy knew that the symbol had a deeper meaning—one linked directly to the Book of Fennore.

"Where did you get that tattoo?" she asked, her question stopping him when he would have walked off. In her arms, Ellie shifted but did not wake.

Jamie frowned, glancing back at her with narrowed eyes . . .

"Detroit. Why?"

"My dad has the same one. Only his is on his chest."

Beside her, Tiarnan stiffened. Jamie took note of it before he crossed back to where they stood.

"My daddy had this tattoo and so did his daddy," he said. "It's a family thing."

Tiarnan cut his eyes from Jamie to Shealy. She sensed that he was making connections that she herself hadn't quite linked together yet. Still, by his expression, something wasn't adding up.

"My dad called it a 'family thing' as well," Shealy told them. "He said all the men had it. Of course, most of our family is dead, so really, he was the only one."

Jamie shifted his weight, scowling. "I'm the last in my family, too."

There was something important here, some critical piece of knowledge that went with this strange symbol both men wore. She felt the magnitude of it but couldn't quite pull it in and analyze just what it was. How did the tattoo link Jamie from Detroit to Donnell O'Leary of Ireland?

"What is your last name, Jamie?" Shealy asked softly.

"Redman."

It meant nothing to her but she hadn't expected that it would. Gaze fixed on the big, kind of scary-looking man, she asked, "How did *you* get here? I know about Tiarnan and Liam . . . but what were you doing on the Isle of Fennore?"

Jamie drew in a deep breath then slowly let it out. With the air of a man burdened with a terrible secret, he said, "My dad died when I was eight. Cancer. He fought it for years before it took him. I don't have any memories of him before he was sick. I'm not even sure that I remember what he looked like really, except for pictures."

Shealy could relate to that. She'd been seventeen when her mother had been snatched away—not by death, she now knew, but gone just the same. She remembered her clearly, and yet there were days when she had to dig out her photo album to make sure that she could still picture her features, the way her eyes had sparkled, the tilt of her smile. . . .

"He left a journal, though," Jamie went on in that serious tone.

Shealy watched him, feeling the revelation coming but still unsure of what it would reveal. Her dad kept a journal, too.

"My mom gave it to me a few years back. When I first read it, I thought he must have been crazy. Being sick had rotted his mind."

"Why?" she asked, although an idea had already begun to take shape.

"He wrote about the Book of Fennore."

"He thought he was a Keeper," she breathed.

"Yes."

"*What?*" Tiarnan exclaimed, stepping forward with an anger that startled them both. "Yer father was a *Keeper* and y' never thought to mention it?"

If possible for such a big, militant man, Jamie looked shame-faced. "I didn't believe it was true, T. Not until . . ." He nodded at Shealy.

"How could y' come to this world and doubt anything after that?" Tiarnan asked with obvious disbelief.

"The journal read like a lunatic had written it. He talked about evil entities and Druids and ceremonies to *seal the fucking Book* should it ever be opened. You'd have to see it with your own eyes to get what I'm talking about. It was crazy shit."

Tiarnan took a deep breath and let it out slowly. "Aye. I can see yer point."

"But you believed whatever it said enough to travel from Detroit to Ireland, to the Isle of Fennore?" Shealy insisted.

"I was stationed in the UK. Me, Zac, and Reyes. We got leave and hopped over. I just wanted to see it."

"Well that y' did," Tiarnan said with a wry glance.

Jamie shuffled his feet in a gesture so uncharacteristic that Shealy gaped at him. She said, "There's more, isn't there?"

"I can't believe I'm saying this but . . . Well in all that bullshit I read, there was something that stuck out. He said there were three Keepers. That's what the symbol stood for—the mark of a Keeper. He listed names. Leary was one of them."

"That makes sense," Shealy agreed.

"To who?" Jamie demanded.

"Last night Tiarnan told me of three men in his time who knew about the Book of Fennore."

"Leary, Red Amir, and Mahon Snakeface," Tiarnan said.

"Red Amir," Jamie said softly. "Redman."

Tiarnan paled at that but said nothing.

"Before our accident," Shealy said, "my dad was searching for other Keepers. I never knew their names, but I do know the men he sought were Irish, not soldiers from Detroit."

Jamie scratched his head, as if unsure which of the facts he'd just learned struck him as the most bizarre. Then at last he gave a shrug and a sour smile. "I'm all out of answers," he said, "I guess your dad and I will have a lot to talk about when we find him, though, won't we?"

With that he strode away, tension etched in every line of him. He was not a man who liked mystery. Shealy already understood that about him. His stringent rules must be the only thing that kept him sane in a place like this, where nothing made sense. Zac and

Reyes, the two other soldiers, went after him, ready to take orders, and Shealy let out a breath of relief when they were gone.

Tiarnan did not follow. For a moment they stood silent, wary as they eyed one another. Shealy was caught between the need to keep strict boundaries between them, and the desire to throw herself into his arms and let his kisses convince her that he could keep her safe. She didn't know how she could think of him as both a threat and a sanctuary, but she did and the flashing memories of the night before, of the intimacy that had caught her off guard and made what they did so much more than just sex only added to the confounding mix of her emotions. Her agitation filled the empty space between them and became a spiked barrier, keeping them apart.

The rules had changed, and *safe* was too nebulous a concept when she looked at all that hard muscle and those beautiful eyes. Yet he'd protected her—continued to protect her even as he undermined all her resolve and security. The men she'd known in the past had never made her feel this way—as if she'd offered free passage into her head when she'd let him into her body.

That enigmatic golden brown gaze moved over her face, and she knew he'd heard her thoughts and now the glow of them held something knowing, pleased, *possessive*. Disconcerted, she walked on stiff legs to the log where they'd sat earlier. Tiarnan moved quickly for such a large man and helped her ease to a sit without waking Ellie . . . her sister. It seemed she couldn't stop repeating that to herself. She had a sister. *A sister.*

"She looks like y'," he said.

"Not so much. Just the eyes. She looks a great deal like our mother, though." And once, before the accident, before the surgeries, Shealy had looked like her, too.

She ducked her chin, hiding the pain in her eyes, refusing to share that part of herself with him. Before he could pry into her secrets, she stopped him with a question of her own. "Why did you seem so surprised when Jamie said he and the others would come with us to find my father?"

A tiny flinch, then shutters came down over his eyes. He shook his head. "I wasn't."

"Liar. I saw your face."

Her bluntness shocked him—she saw that clearly and she wondered if he'd refuse to talk to her now. She'd seen that reaction in men before, the way they closed themselves up rather than share. But Tiaran surprised her once again. Slowly he lowered his big frame next to her and rested his elbows on his knees, hands dangling between them. For a moment, the quiet stretched tautly, but then at last he said, "Before Inis Brandubh, I was the leader of my people."

"Like, you were the captain or you were the king?"

His lips quirked. "My father was a king. I was just a man trying to walk in his footsteps."

Her mouth fell open. She'd been teasing when she'd said *king*, but Tiarnan spoke the word with a grave reverence that told her it was no joke.

"We were at war with Cathán, had been for many years, since I was Liam's age. Maybe younger," he went on, voice deep and solemn. "I made decisions that cost us dearly. Even my own brother lost faith and turned his back on me."

"Liam?" she said, stunned. She'd only seen absolute loyalty from Liam.

"No, lass. Not Liam. Eamonn. He was the next eldest, next in line should I die. He thought he knew better how to rule."

"Did he?" she asked and then wished she could call the words back as soon as they were out. He kept his eyes downcast but she felt the anguish move through him and it wounded her.

Looking at his linked hands, he shrugged, reseating that heavy weight he carried on those strong, broad shoulders.

"I cannot say if he would have made better choices. Perhaps. Perhaps not. I'll never know because he turned traitor rather than follow me."

"He betrayed you?" she blurted, wondering what kind of fool this Eamonn must have been to do such a thing. Look up *honor* and *courage* in the dictionary and Shealy was certain there'd be a picture of Tiarnan.

"Yes," he answered stoically. "He betrayed me."

The pain in his voice rasped against her sensitive nerves and incited a burst of anger at this unknown brother who had caused it. "If he's a traitor, then why are you still beating yourself up over what *he* thought?"

Tiarnan turned his head, meeting her steady gaze. "I'm not."

"Sure you are. You don't think you deserve their loyalty, Jamie and the rest, because your brother betrayed you. That's on him, Tiarnan. Not you. Obviously you deserve the faith that Jamie and the others have in you."

"Obviously?" he repeated, brows arching. "What makes y' say that?"

"You saved all of our lives today. I saw. You were *unbelievable*. You were like five men. And I swear you looked ten feet tall. If you hadn't come between me and that *thing* it would have done to me what it did to my mother."

Her voice cracked and she lowered her eyes to the sleeping girl in her arms.

"It would have killed us both. I've never met anyone like you before. If you made some wrong decisions in your past, then it's probably because there weren't any right ones to make."

"Look at me," he said so softly she almost didn't hear him.

Warily she lifted her gaze from Ellie and raised it to meet his, found herself captured by the golden sheen, the burning emotion behind their glow. Slowly, deliberately, he leaned in, never closing his eyes, never looking away. The moment seemed to stretch out unending as Shealy's heart raced to catch up with her pounding pulse.

He paused just before his mouth closed over hers, and Shealy found she couldn't breathe at all as she waited, yearning. In this world of peril, letting herself *feel* seemed the stupidest thing to do. And yet she leaned forward, bridging that gap between them.

At her surrender, he made a sound in his throat that burned her inside out. Only Ellie, still sleeping against her, kept her from throwing her arms around him and giving herself over to the sensations coiling tight in her stomach. He smelled of the wild wind and the dark mysteries of a man tested and proven. His taste was a sensory explosion, filled with color and velvet textures, passion and sizzling heat. He slid his fingers into her hair, cupping her head so he could deepen the kiss, his tongue soft and seductive, enticing her to open and let him in, reminding her of how his body had felt last night, heavy and hot beside her, silken steel above her, hard and demanding moving within her. . . .

She wanted him. More than she'd wanted anything in a very, very long time.

And that terrified her.

Reluctantly she pulled away, fighting her own desire as well as his. His eyes flashed with regret, yet his crooked smile promised another time, told her she would not always be able to run from this thing between them.

She thought he might say something, tell her what he thought, what he wanted. Tell her that she had thrown him as off balance as he had her. But all he said was, "While everyone is getting ready, y' should take the chance to wash the blood off. There's a pool on the eastern side y' can use."

He spoke in a cool voice, but those eyes were hot and they told her his thoughts had been traveling the same dangerous road as her own, and getting away from her was not the route they'd taken. Despite herself, she was pleased.

"The water's cold," he said calmly, his words contradicting the riot of heat inside her. "We used to have baths, but they were destroyed." He glanced past her at the rubble that littered the small islet. "Still, a cold wash will be better than nothing. Isn't that right, lass?"

She nodded, not even certain if they were talking about baths or something more important. He smiled again and her heart thumped in her chest.

"I think I'll go wash up as well." He glanced down at his blood-stained body and clothes and then at hers.

Blood, gore, and mud caked the sundress she'd worn to dinner with her father. More of the same splattered her arms and legs, her hair. She felt the stiffness of it on her chest and throat. Well, she supposed she didn't have to worry about the scars showing beneath all that, did she?

The foul muck covered Ellie as well. The only part of the toddler that the filth didn't layer was the thumb that she'd had jammed in her mouth since Shealy had scooped her up.

"Ellie," she said softly. The child woke with a start at her name and looked at Shealy with wide, shocked eyes. "Shhhh," she murmured. "It's okay. You're safe."

The little girl sat up and peered at Tiarnan. He smiled at her and touched her silky cheek with a finger.

"How does an ice-cold bath sound to you, little sister?" Shealy asked. "Sounds like heaven to me." Ellie stopped sucking her thumb for a moment and then squirmed until she got a tighter grip on Shealy, making it known that wherever Shealy went, Ellie would go, too. Something deep within her heart ached at the trusting, desperate gesture. Her sister had seen atrocities that an adult mind couldn't cope with. She'd been nearly eaten, orphaned, and now she was stuck with Shealy, who'd never even had a dog to care for. She knew next to nothing about children and zilch about young ones. But she would learn. She vowed she would take care of this small being with her big eyes and elfin features. But Ellie was defenseless, and Shealy shied from the enormity of the task. How could she protect her newfound little sister in this strange and terrifying place?

Tiarnan's eyes seemed to follow her every move, and again she felt like he'd tracked her thoughts.

"Y' saved her life," he said.

"I could have just as easily put her in more danger. You were right. Those things were after me. It was all so terrifying, I didn't even know what I was doing. It's lucky I didn't get her killed."

"Are y' always so hard on yerself, Shealy O'Leary?"

She caught her hand rising to cover her scars just as she noted his gaze trailing the movement. Blushing, she forced the hand to casually drop to her side and stared at him challengingly, daring him to say something. A part of her hoped he would. Just one wrong word, and then maybe she could gather her protective cloak around her once more and shut him out as she'd done to others before him. Put him at arm's length instead of feeling like he'd already slipped beneath her skin. She'd never felt so naked, so vulnerable as she did with this big warrior.

He said nothing, but he didn't lower his gaze either. He leaned forward again, brushed her hair back, exposing the scarred flesh of her cheek and the mangled shape of her ear. Dr. Campbell's frustrated face came to mind. *Just one more surgery*, he'd said, but the allergy to anesthesia had grown so severe that she'd almost died on the table during the last one. They'd had to quit before they finished, leaving her imperfect. Work of art, interrupted.

It took more will than it should have not to squirm as he slowly ran his gaze over her face, noting every imperfection with the same unflinching expression. She was used to people staring at her, but with Tiarnan, it was different. He made her feel stripped—and not in a good way. She didn't like being so exposed.

"What time will we be leaving?" she asked to distract him and then felt immediately stupid. This wasn't the kind of place where clocks marked the minutes.

Tiarnan ran the pad of his thumb over the crescent scar at her throat, and a shiver that had nothing to do with cold went through her. She knew he felt it, that sizzling awareness, and he brushed the silky flesh again before at last he glanced away from her scars and scanned the horizon.

"Soon," he said. "Soon."

Chapter Eleven

SHEALY held Ellie's hand as they followed Tiarnan to the other side of the islet where a small peninsula blocked the raging current and allowed a tiny pool to form. Trees offered privacy and the birds chirped merrily in the branches, oblivious to the carnage that had taken place here just that morning.

"Do not go out past that point," he warned, indicating the tail end of the jutting eddy. "The current is deep and fast and will suck y' in if y' venture any farther."

She didn't need to be told twice. She remembered those who'd fled into the river in the last moments before dawn. They'd been swept away in seconds.

He left her and Ellie with a rough bar of soap that smelled wonderfully like him and made her insides tense into a tight, slick coil with the memory of her face pressed against his skin, breathing that scent in, losing herself in it. . . . Trying to ignore her rampant thoughts, Shealy jabbered nonsense at Ellie as she stripped them both and stepped into the pool. The water was as cold as he'd promised, but it felt blissful to wash the blood and stench from her hair and body. Ellie gave a distressed cry when the chill hit her, but then she, too, seemed to surrender to the numbing tingle. The pool was shallow enough for Shealy to sit and Ellie to stand while they washed. When she waded out, she found Tiarnan had left them skins to dry with and clothes—at least some type of clothing—to wear. The garments were crude, but soft and clean.

The sun had risen, and after blotting the worst of the water from their bodies, Shealy wrapped one skin around her and spread the other out on the ground. She settled down beside Ellie, using fingers to comb through the snarled mess of the child's hair. Everything that had happened since the attack last night in the parking lot had kept her from dwelling on her father and where he might be, but now her fears crowded in and she worried about him. Where was he? Safe and dry back home? Not captured, not endangered at all?

She clung tight to the hope Tiarnan had given her when he'd said that their mysterious assailant, Cathán, would not have seen the need to send the monsters if he'd held her father prisoner. The fact that he'd launched an assault could only mean that her father was still at large.

God, she hoped that was true. A longing to be with her dad welled up inside her, so hot and strong that it brought tears to her eyes. What would he say when he saw Shealy again? When he met his other daughter for the first time? When he learned that his wife had given birth in this prehistoric hell and lived here all this time without them?

Seeing Shealy's distress, Ellie crawled into her lap and patted her arm. Laughing and crying at the same time, she held the child close, picturing her father's face. After the accident, he'd been like the walking dead. In one shattered moment, he'd lost the love of his life and the daughter he'd known. As if she'd been replaced by a changeling, Shealy had become a stranger. While the doctors reconstructed her face and body, guilt began to rebuild the person inside. She'd felt responsible for the accident, for the fight that had begun because of her thoughtless comment about the Book of Fennore.

Her stomach clenched, and it seemed the world tilted in a nasty, jarring roll. Shealy braced herself as Ellie clutched at her and the earth warbled like a blanket floating to the ground on pockets of uneven air, like it had the night the darkness ripped open and Tiarnan charged out. She had the sense of sailing, of falling, and then suddenly, plunging through something thick and warm, hot pudding that sucked at her and tried to wrench Ellie from her arms. She felt a spark—a supercharge of energy that seemed to come from within her and grow as it circled her sister, as if Ellie had somehow amplified it before it rebounded. She'd felt a similar sensation when the three-headed beasts had attacked, but then she'd been certain the rushing wave of energy had come from Ellie alone. Now it seemed to originate deep inside of Shealy. Frightened, she held on tight, fighting against the caging gel that sucked at them. Her eyes were sealed shut. She couldn't scream, couldn't breathe.

Her wildly thumping heart and Ellie's harsh breaths exhaled near her ear snuffed out the sound of the rushing river. Then slowly, as if from a great distance, she heard voices. Angry and raised, they were suddenly everywhere. Shealy tried to open her eyes and found them still sealed, and yet images appeared behind the lids and with them, the feeling of moving at warp speed while being strapped to a big, cushy cloud filled with feathers softer than a dream, a cloud that she sank deeper and deeper into until the world beyond jetted by like a blur. Then suddenly her eyes flew open and she stood in her dad's study—a room from their house in Ireland, where she'd grown up. Ellie clung to her tightly.

Her father paced the floor, talking to another man—someone she thought she should know, but he had his back turned to her and she didn't really care who he was. She only cared about her dad. Donnell looked different than he had the night before last, younger than she'd ever seen him, though fatigue pulled his face and dark shadows circled his eyes.

"How can you look at the evidence and not see it, Kyle?" he demanded, pointing at a satchel the other man wore over his neck and one shoulder. Shealy saw the corner of her father's journal poking from it. "Look again. Flip the pages and see what I've been telling you—"

He stopped abruptly and suddenly turned his head. His shocked gaze settled on Shealy. For a moment, they stared at each other in absolute silence. From the corner of her eye, she saw the other man turn as well, knew he, too, was staring at her.

"Daddy?" she said.

Donnell's mouth moved wordlessly and then he seemed to gather himself. "Shealy? God in heaven, is that you? Where are you, child?"

"I . . ." She glanced over her shoulder, saw the river of Inis Brandubh spread out like a ribbon waving behind her.

When she looked back at her father, he'd stepped closer. He was staring at the landscape beyond her, at the rampant river and the dark woods huddled on the other side of its banks. And then his gaze settled on Ellie and his eyes widened. She could feel the warmth of him, smell the Old Spice cologne that he'd never give up. There was stubble on his cheeks, but it had yet to go gray. In fact, there was no gray anywhere in his hair.

"Who's that in your arms?" he asked softly.

"My sister. Daddy, Mom is dead."

"Of course she's dead, honey. I told you that. She died in the accident."

"No. No she didn't. The monsters ate her."

Tears stung her eyes and made hot trails down her cheeks.

Donnell's face drained of all color. "Monsters? *Monsters?* Where are you, Shealy. *Where. Are. You?*"

"Inis Brandubh. I'm looking for you, Daddy."

"Looking for me? No, no my Shealy. You mustn't. Wherever you are, you must try to get home. Don't worry about me. Do you understand? I'm here at home, safe and sound, just waiting. You see that, don't you?"

She nodded, but there'd been a note of deceit in his voice. Yes, she could see that he was safe but he wasn't home—not where they lived now—and he looked so different. She heard someone calling her name and she glanced back impatiently.

"Who is that?" her dad asked.

"Tiarnan," she answered, and her father's eyes filled with fear. The other man in the room with him stepped closer, and she saw that he was a priest, recognized him at last. Father Mahon.

Mahon.

The name had never meant anything to her before, but now she realized that the name Mahon went with the three Keepers Tiarnan had told her about. The priest reached out, laid a hand on her shoulder as if to test the theory that she was real.

"Shealy," her father began urgently. "You have to—"

But whatever else he said, she couldn't hear because the study vanished as abruptly as it had appeared, taking with it her father and the priest. Instantly she was back in that world of gel and silence, clutching Ellie, feeling that current connecting them. They flew through the absolute quiet, sinking into the viscous cloud that held them. Then suddenly the sound of rushing water roared in her ears and Tiarnan's voice called her name again. She blinked her eyes, staring at the banks of the river while her stomach rolled.

"Oh my God," she said to Ellie. Her little sister stared back unflinching. "It was me. *I* opened the darkness."

"Shealy?" Tiarnan called again, concern heavy in his tone.

"Yeah, just a minute," she answered, her voice wavering with shock and emotion. *What just happened?* "We're getting dressed."

"Was it me all along? In the parking lot?" she breathed. Ellie didn't answer, of course. "Did you . . . did *you* see what just happened? Did you see my dad? *Our dad?* Could you see them?" Ellie nodded. Her eyes were round and wide, and deep within them lurked a knowing Shealy didn't understand. But there was too much chaos to sort through in her head.

How? How had it happened? She hadn't just returned to her world. She'd gone backward in time, to the past before tragedy had aged her father. How? Why? Was it a dream?

"Shealy, we're waiting for y'," Tiarnan said.

Quickly she stood, pulling on the tunic he'd left for her. She'd opened the mystical door Tiarnan had talked about. If she could figure out how she'd done it, she could help them all escape.

Suddenly another realization stole her breath. If they knew what she could do, would they help her find her father? Or would they simply wait for her to do it again? She had no control over when it happened, how it happened. Could she trust them with that knowledge? Any of them?

She heard them speaking nearby and forced her thoughts away. She'd keep this new information to herself for now and decide what and who to tell later.

The shapeless tunic Tiarnan had left for her was as large as a potato sack and hung to her knees. It had no sleeves and no form, but it was a vast improvement over her torn dress and smelled of Tiarnan in a way that seduced her senses and calmed her malaise. There was a leather cord she used to tie it at the waist, keeping it from feeling like a tent she might have to fight for mobility. A miniature version of the oversized tunic had been left for Ellie.

When Shealy emerged, she found the men, too, had washed and changed into fresh clothes and now waited to begin their journey. Liam stood beside his brother, looking drawn and somber. Only then did it occur to her that the girl he'd been with last night had died in the attack. Grief for the girl she'd hardly known swamped her. Tiarnan had been right—in this place, one shouldn't wait for the right time to embrace life because it might be snatched away in a flash. As if hearing her thoughts, Liam gave her a sad, lopsided smile.

They seemed to be waiting for her to do or say something, but she had no idea what. She still couldn't believe they'd all agreed to help her, and she feared that something in her expression would give away how shaken she felt.

"Ready?" Jamie asked.

With an uncertain shrug, she mumbled, "Yes. I'm ready."

Scrubbed squeaky clean, Shealy had to suppress the urge to hide her face from them. She settled with letting her hair fall forward to cover the scars. From the corner of her eye, she caught Tiarnan watching the gesture.

Jamie hung back as they all made their way to several small boats like the ones Tiarnan and Liam had used last night. Tiarnan dumped his pack in one of the round vessels, giving Liam a nod as his brother climbed in with them and pushed off.

"Won't he be pulled down to the waterfall?" she asked.

"Still don't trust me to keep y' safe, lass?" Tiarnan teased. "Do not fret. I know where the river can be crossed."

Of course he did. He lived here.

A moment later, Shealy found herself in another of the *curraghs* with Ellie clinging to her like a baby monkey. Tiarnan pushed the boat off the banks and then stepped in. She settled against him without waiting this time. He reached around to cradle the two of them against his chest, and for a moment, Shealy felt as if she'd come home. As if this was where she belonged—here, in the circle of this man's arms, no matter what danger they faced.

Tiarnan rowed, his muscles bunching as he fought the tow that wanted to drag them down and over the enormous falls that thundered in the distance. His legs braced against the edges of the saucer-shaped boat, thighs tightening as he used his weight and mass to keep them on track. She held on to the side with one hand and Ellie with the other, glad she had nothing in her stomach because the rocking would surely have brought it up. It took only a few minutes to reach the other side, but it felt longer and by the time he helped her step back onto solid ground, Ellie in her arms, she felt queasy.

"I told y' not to worry," he said, keeping her hand in his.

By some silent communication, they all fell in with Jamie leading, followed by Liam. Tiarnan, Shealy, and Ellie were in the middle and bringing up the end came Zac and Reyes. They trudged forward in silence, moving single file when needed.

Before the darkness of the forest swallowed them, Shealy looked back at the river and the ruined settlement they left behind. The hulking corpses of the monsters lay at the center, bathed in bright sunlight. A stench rose off them and rode the teasing breeze across the water. She wondered what other horrors awaited them on this quest—for certainly even she understood that they'd embarked on more than a rescue mission.

Ellie grew heavy in minutes, but her sister would not walk, nor would she allow Tiarnan to take her. She gave a panicked scream when Jamie, Reyes, or Zac came near. She'd only allow Liam to hold her. He lifted her from Shealy's grasp and blew a raspberry on her belly. The little girl didn't laugh, but she did put her arms around Liam's neck and let him carry her.

With each step they took, the world around them changed. The trees banded together, tangling branches high overhead until they blotted out every ray of sun with a canopy of leaves and twigs that rustled and cracked in the quiet. No birds sang out, no squirrels chattered from their limbs here. On the forest floor, vines seemed to grow as they watched, writhing over dirt as black as oil. Brambles lay innocently over pitted nooks and crannies that grabbed and sucked, tripping the unwary, intent on twisting ankles and breaking bones. Deadwood skimmed beneath the surface like silent crocodiles at home in their swamp of nettles that tore at skin.

She'd be lying if she didn't admit to feeling a menace in their growth. They wanted to hurt the trespassers, and the fact that they were plants didn't negate their power to do it.

"We tried to clear a way, when we first got here," Jamie said, falling back to walk just ahead of them. "Me, Zac, and Reyes came out here and hacked away all the vines, trying to make a trail through the woods."

Shealy looked around, seeing no sign of even the smallest path. Behind them, Zac made a sound of disgust.

"Why'd you stop?" Shealy asked.

"By the time we'd made it fifty feet in, everything had grown back," Jamie said flatly. "You couldn't even tell where we'd been."

She could see it in her mind, the barren path, the creeping vines filling it in as fast as the men could clear it.

"Don't ever turn your back on Inis Brandubh, Shealy," Jamie said, picking up his pace. "You never know what's going to sprout up behind you."

She told herself her guilty conscience made that sound like a threat when it was merely a warning, but she couldn't help the shiver of fear that went through her.

After that they all grew quiet, and the silence wore on with the day. Tiarnan never left her side and she was painfully conscious of his eyes watching her. She was afraid, but she didn't ask him to stop or comfort her. It was enough that he'd come. Now that she was in the thick of these malevolent woods, she couldn't fathom being there alone.

Chapter Twelve

They'd been walking for over an hour, oppressed by the quiet and the shifting shadows. Shealy's worries tangled with her fear of this dark and dangerous forest, leaving her feeling knotted and too frustrated to think clearly. She'd yet to reach a decision on what she should tell Tiarnan and what she shouldn't. The experience by the river, seeing her dad, traveling not only to the *other* world, but to another time . . . She couldn't sort out what the best next step would be and so she trudged on beside Tiarnan, afraid to do anything more than put one foot in front of the other.

Tiarnan's silence added another layer of anxiety to her troubled mind. He moved beside her with fluid grace, hacking at branches and vines that tried to hold them back. He hadn't touched her since they'd left the boats, but Shealy was as aware of his presence as she was of the danger that stalked them. She could see Liam up ahead, but not Jamie. Behind them, Zac and Reyes had faded into the trees. She knew the other men were still out there, but not seeing them made her feel exposed and excluded at the same time.

She glanced at Tiarnan's serious face and wondered what occupied his mind. Was it her? Ridiculous to be worried about such a thing when their lives were in danger, yet she couldn't seem to think of anything *but* him. At some point in her life, she'd come to believe she'd never have a *normal* relationship with a man and now having Tiarnan fill her thoughts so completely felt wrong. She realized the trauma of the accident had left more than her face and body shattered; it had broken the trusting person who'd once lived inside and made her cynical and fearful of anyone who tried to get too close.

Tiarnan glanced at her pensively.

"What are y' thinking?" he asked, and she felt her face heat.

No way would she tell him she was thinking of how his hands felt against her body, how his mouth had seduced every thought from her mind. How she wished he would kiss her again. Kiss her until she forgot where she was and why she was here . . .

"I was worried the others might get lost," she mumbled.

His golden brown eyes narrowed and his mouth tilted in a hint of a smile—as if he'd heard her thoughts as well as her words. There was something agonizingly intimate in the idea of it, in the eloquent look he trailed lazily over her. The man was a walking invitation to sin.

"Jamie and the others know these woods better than anyone," he said at last. "They will not lose their way."

"But Jamie said something was brewing and that you felt it, too. If that's true, who knows what's going on in this forest."

"Is that what yer really thinking about, Shealy? The forest?"

She felt the flush heat her chest and race up her throat, knew her face had turned the color of beets by now. It was one of the many disadvantages of being fair skinned—sunburns, freckles, and excruciating blushes.

"Because I am not thinking of that at all."

She willed herself not to ask, but those were her lips forming the words. "What are you thinking about?"

"You," he said, drawing out the word. "It is y' on my mind."

And again those whiskey eyes made a slow and thorough sweep over her. There was sex in that look—hot, needy, and oh so wonderful sex—but there was more to it. The complex message embedded within the fleeting glance made her yearn to know more about him at the same time it urged her to back away and flee.

"I heard the men talking about y'," he said, and the words felt like a splash of icy river water against her hot skin.

She felt the familiar sting of censure though she knew it was in her head, not his voice. Men had been talking about Shealy O'Leary for years. She didn't bother to ask what he'd heard. She could guess.

Tiarnan caught his bottom lip with his teeth, watching her as she braced herself for what he might say next. She felt her mask slip into place and faced him with distant curiosity.

"They talk about y' as if they know y'," he said. "But I don't think y' met one another before Inis Brandubh."

Shealy glanced down, remembering how they'd stared at her when they'd realized who she was. She knew she had only herself to blame—no one had held a gun to her head when she'd posed for those pictures. But the look in their eyes as they'd gazed at her made her want to pull a bag over her head and tie it at her ankles. She took a breath and hesitated before saying, "Where I come from, I'm something of a celebrity."

Tiarnan chopped at a thorny branch and then held another thicker bough up so she could slip under.

"What does it mean, *celebrity*?" he asked when they were both through.

She shrugged, not wanting to go into it more than that. Not wanting to talk about the circumstances that had made her famous. Tiarnan carried the weight of his wrong decisions, and so did

Shealy. There was a reason why the men looked at her like she was a delectable dessert on an all-you-can-eat menu.

"I'm known," she said.

"By men?"

"By everyone. They recognize me." Then, under her breath, "But they don't *know* me."

"They look at y' as if they do."

She glanced up then, met his eyes, and knew she couldn't hide the uncertainty in her own. "They know my face, my body, but that's all they know."

She watched the tension pull at the corners of his mouth and knew he was thinking of her body even now. The gleam in his eyes was full of possessive heat. It should have irritated her. From any other man, it would have. But Tiarnan was not like any other man in *any* way, shape, or form.

"They know yer body?" he asked, his voice dark.

"They've seen pictures of me, Tiarnan. I'm on television. In magazines. I do commercials, I'm in the news." At his confusion, she sighed. There was no way to explain without actually *explaining*. This man had put himself between her and the three-headed monsters, and she owed him at least that. "I told you about the car accident that I thought killed my mother. I told you it almost killed me, too. Our car went off the cliffs at sixty-five kilometers an hour. It hit every rock going down before ending up in the sea."

He frowned as her words spun the visual. "How did y' survive?"

She laughed, but not with humor. "I shouldn't have. That's the honest truth. I had critical injuries, and it took a team of surgeons to put me back together again. But the worst thing was my face."

She swallowed, hating this part, though she'd told the story over and over and she should be immune to the pain it caused by now.

"I looked just like my mom before the accident. A younger version, but just as pretty."

It seemed like he wanted to comment, to tell her that she looked beautiful now, but something in her expression or inside Tiarnan himself stopped him. The hard knot in Shealy's chest eased. For all the times she'd recited the facts of her accident, she'd never felt like the listeners *got it*. They didn't understand what had made her bitter and sad.

"They used to tell me I looked like my father," Tiarnan said softly. "Yet I cannot remember his face. I remember only his grief. He lost everything he loved before he died."

They stared at one another for a long moment, words unnecessary as they shared that common, if painful ground.

"Go on," Tiarnan said. "What happened?"

She shrugged, always overwhelmed when she spoke this part. "I guess I had a guardian angel looking out for me. I didn't die, and it just so happened a world-renowned plastic surgeon was visiting Ireland at the time of the accident. He'd been trying to pull in funding for a cause he felt passionate about—helping children with correctable deformities."

At Tiarnan's quizzical glance, she explained, "Kids who are born with birth defects that can be fixed. Or kids like me who are injured in accidents. He saw me as an opportunity to launch his cause."

"I still do not understand."

"He used me to promote his cause. A *great* cause and I'm happy to be used for it. It's the only good thing that came out of the tragedy. But it made me famous in a wrong sort of way. I'm the shining example of how perfection can be achieved—except of course, it wasn't achieved as you can see. When people meet me, they're usually looking for the flaws, you know? Trying to find the cracks in the crystal."

"Ah," he said, and she heard a wealth of meaning in that sound. "That is why y' do this." And he mimed pulling his hair over his throat.

If possible, she felt herself blushing harder as she nodded.

"Y' do not need to hide the cracks in the crystal from me, lass," he murmured.

The words felt like honey, hot and sweet, filling those fractures inside her. She cleared her throat, uncomfortable with the feeling, with the power he had in his soft words, his deep voice.

"Half the time I don't even realize I'm doing it."

"Now who is telling lies?" he said. "Y' do it with defiance. I've seen the lightning strike in those stormy eyes of yers when y' catch me looking."

Feeling raw, exposed, she glanced away. "Anyway, that's why they recognize me."

She felt the weight of his gaze, the questions he still meant to ask hanging in it. She walked on, refusing to look up, to give him an in. She was vulnerable enough without letting him turn that perceptive stare into the window of her soul.

"Y' know I will not let it go at that, Shealy. Tell me the rest."

Despite the seriousness of the topic, despite the pain it caused, she felt her lips twitch in a smile. No, Tiarnan would not let her squirm out of telling all.

She took a deep breath and went on. "They put me back together. But not the way I was before the accident."

"What does that mean?"

She wished she could give Tiarnan her canned answers. *She was grateful for the second chance at a normal life. She was happy with how she looked. She owed a debt of gratitude to the doctors who'd given her a second chance at life. . . .* But Tiarnan would not accept anything less than the truth.

"My parents were fighting when the accident happened," she said softly. She swallowed hard and kept her gaze on her feet. "About dad's obsession with the Book of Fennore. It had been a great day up until then, and I was so mad at myself for bringing it up—I hadn't realized that Dad had orchestrated the whole day—taken us to the Isle of Fennore as part of his quest until I blurted out how odd it was that an island had been named after Dad's book. As soon as I spoke, I knew my mistake, but it was too late. My mom went into orbit, ranting and raving at my dad. My parents were on the verge of splitting up, and I was so upset about it that I started shouting, too. I said horrible, unforgivable things to my mother that day. Things I can never take back, never say I'm sorry for."

Tiarnan nodded, his silent understanding opening a floodgate within her. She felt tears burning in her eyes—tears that she'd sworn would never be shed. Deep down she felt that she deserved to carry those tears locked away inside. They were her burden, her cross. And she'd welcomed the pain their holding brought. It was her fault her mother died. She'd escalated the age-old argument into a shouting match. Because of Shealy, her dad had taken his attention from the winding road. . . . She *should* suffer.

She knew that children always felt responsible when tragedy struck. But she couldn't stop the feeling of blame, the sense that in her case that feeling was well deserved.

"When the doctors were done with me, I didn't even recognize myself," she said with a brittle laugh. "They didn't just fix me. They changed me. They made me better. The new and improved Shealy O'Leary."

Tiarnan said nothing. He just waited for her to go on. She tried to summon some anger about that—tried to twist his silence into a verdict and use it as a wall between them. Already he'd managed to bring her to new thresholds and entice her over without any awareness of his manipulation. He hadn't breached her barriers—he'd simply ignored them and they'd crumbled into the useless dust they were.

"They would have done more for me. Fixed the last of the scars—erased all evidence of what had happened, but they couldn't."

Her voice broke and she took a deep, shuddering breath, forcing herself to go on. Feeling like it was a test of courage now, with Tiarnan the judge. But that wasn't fair—he demanded nothing with his quiet presence.

He took her hand in his, letting the hard pad of his thumb trill along her pounding pulse. That small gesture, that subdued caress, nearly stopped her. Her voice sounded strained, the words disconnected, but somehow speaking them kept her grounded and able to focus beyond his touch.

"My body couldn't tolerate the anesthesia—the medicine they had to give me in order to do the surgery. So they had to stop."

They'd realized then that they couldn't fix everything unless they were willing to kill her to do it. And secretly, she thought they might have considered it.

"By then it wasn't about fixing me anymore. I'd become, I don't know, their 'masterpiece' and leaving me flawed went against the grain. I felt like they blamed me. Like it was my fault I couldn't tolerate the anesthesia long enough to allow them to finish. And you know, maybe they were right."

"Why would they be right, Shealy?"

"Because I didn't want them to finish. I mean, who wants to be perfect?"

He smiled gently at that, and again she felt that throbbing need to cry. Why, after all this time, had she dredged this up? Why did it feel like it had all happened just yesterday?

"People used to look at me," Tiarnan said in that deep voice that felt like fur against her senses. "They'd see my father. They'd want me to be him. *I* wanted me to be him. I tried so hard to do what he would have done, but he was a great man. I could never stand as tall as he did."

Shealy looked at Tiarnan, saw the shame he couldn't quite conceal. "I never met your dad—and don't get me wrong, I know what you're saying. I've experienced it myself, that . . . feeling like you'll never be good enough no matter what you do. But I think you are a great man, Tiarnan. You *are* an amazing man."

He looked startled by the throbbing emotion in her declaration. In honesty, she was surprised by it as well. It rattled her already crumbling composure.

After a moment that felt endless to Shealy, Tiarnan asked, "After they called y' *done*, what happened then?"

"They applauded each other. Said with enough makeup no one would be able to see my imperfections and then they paraded me around town. Even with all the time the surgeons donated, there were bills, and my dad didn't make enough money to pay them." She shook her head, thinking of the mountains of debt. "I was approached by a modeling agency. A cosmetic line wanted me to endorse their products. They figured I was a novelty, and if they could cover my scars, they could defeat any old wrinkle." The humor was lost on Tiarnan, but it wasn't really that funny anyway.

"The pay was good and Dad and I needed the money, so I took it. The ad campaign was very successful and the more famous I became, the more money the New Smile Foundation received from donors. It was a win-win situation."

"That is good," he said, but she caught the question in his tone. She knew that he'd heard at least some of what she hadn't said, and it made her defensive now.

"Of course it is," she said sharply.

"But it hurts y'?" he asked.

How did he know that? "No. Bringing in the funds the foundation so desperately needs—it's given my life purpose."

It was the truth and she stared at him until she was sure he understood that.

"It's just that in order to make people open their wallets, they have to see results. So there's always the before and after."

He waited, silent. She forced herself to go on.

"They show my face after the accident and then they show me now. Only it's not really me. Not the real *me* anyway. There's always a pound of makeup and then the image is touched up before it's shown. Look at my face."

She turned to him, knowing she wore that defiant look he'd commented about. A part of her wanted him to recoil. Wanted him to be disappointed that she wasn't as perfect as everyone thought she was. That reaction she knew. She'd lived with it for years, and it didn't bother her.

"I can tell there's something yer braced and waiting for." Those warm, callus-roughened hands moved up her shoulders to her throat, his thumb grazing the sickle-shaped scar on her neck. He cupped her face, forcing her to look at him. "I see it in yer eyes."

She blinked, surprised and angry to find moisture building there again, trying to become tears she refused to shed.

"I think y' are beautiful. Did y' not hear me before?"

She clenched her jaw, steeled her heart against the soft words. She'd heard this before, from other men who'd been as perplexed as Tiarnan by her savage insistence that the scars were horrible, repelling.

Shealy knew that the scars had nothing to do with what she felt deep down. She didn't really care about them—knew that if she let them be forgotten, they would be.

But they'd become her blockade, her defense. Her excuse.

Because there was something wrong with Shealy. Perhaps inside she'd always known.

Gently, he touched the side of her face, running his fingers up to the damaged shell of her ear. The skin there was at once hypersensitive and numb, and the heated caresses seemed to glance off each alternating point in a jumble of sensation.

Before she could think of a cutting response, of a way to stop his foray into her most vulnerable core, he pressed his lips to her cheek, flicked his tongue over the mottled scarring, brought his mouth to her ear, and said softly, "There is not an inch of y' that I would not taste."

The words sent a trembling shudder down from the very top of her head to the tips of her toes. In the shivering wake, she felt hot and cold, her skin tight and fluid. Every nuance of the night before flooded her senses, reminding her of that heated pool he'd made burn within her.

She wanted to step closer, to press her body against his heat, let him do whatever he might want. But she felt so completely exposed—so completely out of her depth with him. There was no shield, no mask. He saw through it all, made the idea of either completely ridiculous. If she let him in any deeper, there would be no secrets, no place to hide.

She took a jerky step back and then turned away and quickly started walking again.

After a moment, he fell in step beside her. She prayed he'd changed the subject, let it drop completely. But of course he didn't.

"So it's yer image the men talked about?"

She almost spun and snarled "*What men?*" before she remembered that Tiarnan had said he'd heard the others talking about her.

"I suppose."

He said nothing for a moment, and she glanced at him to find that he looked embarrassed.

"What exactly did they say, Tiarnan?" she asked, wishing she could swallow the question whole. Wishing that it didn't have to be asked.

He didn't answer, and she knew if she let it drop, so would he. And that's what she wanted, but the very shame she felt in thinking it stopped her.

"Did they talk about a blindfold?" she asked.

Scowling, he nodded.

"I did a spread in a magazine—a book of pictures. In it I was wearing a red blindfold and . . ." She swallowed, feeling her face burn. "And nothing else above the waist. Just my hands, strategically placed."

They'd wanted her to wear a gag instead of the blindfold, but she couldn't tolerate having something over her mouth. It was too much like the equipment that had kept her alive after the accident. The blindfold had been hard enough.

The photo spread had been disturbing, compelling, artistic. It had gone on the cover of *Vogue* and been their number-one-selling issue for the year.

"Y' let someone take yer likeness when y' were wearing nothing but a blindfold?"

"I had pants on," she said defensively. "It was only the waist up."

But that wasn't the point, and they both knew it.

"I don't understand," he said, and his expression mirrored his bewilderment. "I can see on yer face that it's not something yer proud of. Why did y' do it?"

She lifted a hand to the scars and then dropped it. "It's difficult to explain," she said.

"Try."

There was something hard in that single word and yet something beseeching. She saw that he could not reconcile the image in his head with what he knew of Shealy. She understood—even her father had been mystified by her decision to be photographed in such a way.

"Have you ever been faced with something that scares you so badly, you just want to run?"

Tiarnan raised his brows and looked around them, and she realized how foolish her question was. Tiarnan's world was one of absolute danger. He would have to be dead not to fear it.

"I mean, something here," she said and tapped her fingers to the hard, slabbed muscle of his chest.

He looked down at her hand then took it in his and flattened her fingers over his heart. She felt the warm beat, the steady pulse.

"Aye," he said softly. "I have."

"I felt that every time I opened my eyes. I was always afraid I'd be caught for being such a fraud."

"Fraud?"

"Here I was walking around with this face that everyone thought was so perfect. But if they saw me in the morning, like this"—she shrugged—"the show would be over. It was like walking on a tightrope."

She could see that he didn't quite get her terminology, but the gist came through. "One of the photographers who'd seen me before and after suggested it—a photo with no makeup, showing the scars. I said no at first. I couldn't think of exposing myself that way. But then I decided I had to do it. I had to be fearless."

He waited, listening intently. She realized that in her whole life, no one had ever listened to her with such focus. It unnerved her.

"I didn't tell anyone what I planned. He took the pictures—"

"A man?"

"Yes. Would it help to know he was gay?"

The baffled expression answered her.

"He wasn't interested in me that way. He only saw me through his camera. In the pictures I didn't wear makeup. And I didn't wear a top so the scars wouldn't be hidden. It was just me, with my hair pulled back in a ponytail, a red blindfold, and the scars on my face and this one." Her finger went to the slashing wound on her neck. "It was symbolic for me. I'd almost died and this was me . . . reborn."

He pushed her hand away and traced the scar with his fingertips. Shealy shivered, and it seemed he felt the movement inside himself. His glittering brown eyes met hers and held.

"It felt honest. I guess I needed that."

His warm palm spread over the slashing scar at her throat, covering it, heating it. His long fingers pressed against the hollow behind her ear, the vulnerable dip beneath her chin.

"What they see," she went on, her voice thick with emotion, "what the men talk about . . . what they think they know . . . it doesn't exist."

"What I see is real," he said softly. "I see *you*."

He drew out the last word instead of clipping it short as he usually did, and despite her determination to turn away, to not show him how deep he cut with that simple statement, she didn't. What she saw in his eyes undermined her resolve, shook her foundation. She thought that maybe he was right—maybe he did see her. And it terrified her.

"I guess I sound pretty crazy, huh?" she said, meaning to add a sharp edge of sarcasm, managing only a whisper of uncertainty.

Staring into Tiarnan's eyes was like looking into a pool of molten amber. And then he smiled and his whole face transformed, from the fine lines that crinkled at the corners of his eyes to the hint of a dimple in his cheek. He was beautiful—carved masculinity that evoked such a feminine response in her that she wanted to arch her back and rub against him.

Stunned by the visceral reaction, she tried to step away, but Tiarnan's hands cupped her face and his mouth came down over hers, hot, demanding. She gave without hesitation, opening to his gentle onslaught, falling into the thrill that burned down low inside her.

"I do think yer crazy," he muttered against her lips. "But it seems to be working for y' and it's doing the job on me as well."

He leaned back, winked, and started walking again.

Mouth open, she followed. But before she could say anything else, before he could clarify just what he meant by his statement, a strange whistle broke the silence. Tiarnan stopped, grabbing her arm and jerking her to a halt as well. He put his finger to his lips and hushed her before she could speak. From nowhere, Liam and Ellie reappeared. Silent, Liam handed the child to Shealy and pulled a short-handled ax from the leather loop holding it at his belt.

Tiarnan had his sword in one hand and ax in the other. Like ghosts, Reyes and Zac stepped silently from the trees behind them. Tiarnan gave them a quick shake of his head, answering the silent question that passed between. *What was out there?*

Fear tightening every muscle, Shealy waited to meet the next monster of Inis Brandubh.

Chapter Thirteen

TIARNAN stepped protectively in front of Shealy. Liam fell into place beside him.

Ahead Jamie motioned with his hands to get their attention and then gave one of his signals to alert them about what he'd seen. Two fingers at his eyes then to the forest at his left. Five fingers. Eyes again, forest to his right, four fingers. Whatever was coming, Jamie could see nine of them.

"Stay close," he said to Shealy. He took her hand and hooked her fingers into the leather at his waist. She nodded and followed like a shadow.

Liam turned and flashed Jamie's hand signal back to Reyes and Zac, who moved up in silent unity. As they neared, Jamie closed in and crouched down. The others did the same, keeping voices low and heads down.

"What did y' see?" Tiarnan asked, afraid to even think of facing nine *ellén trechend*.

"Men," Jamie said. "Nine of them. And a wolf."

"Hunting them?"

Jamie shook his head. "Like a pet."

"Fuck that," Zac said.

Tiarnan stared at the others, confounded. The only men they'd seen on Inis Brandubh were here with them now or had been killed by the *ellén trechend* that morning. "Who are they?" Tiarnan asked.

"No clue. They look dangerous, though. They're armed."

Nine men and a wolf to their five, a woman, and a child. Men who'd never shown their faces in all the time Tiarnan and the others had been here. In the beginning, they'd scouted, searching for others, banding together, and even recently, there'd been exploration teams sent out each day to monitor the shifting world they lived in. The possibility existed that chance had kept them from meeting this group, but Tiarnan didn't like the odds, nor did he like the timing. These men appearing *now*, after Shealy's father had opened the door between the worlds, did not sit well.

He looked at Jamie's face, seeing the hard look in his eyes. Jamie shared his misgivings and, knowing the other man as he did, Tiarnan was certain he'd want to take the offense.

He'd seen the man at battle too many times not to understand the way his mind worked, but Jamie wouldn't think of Shealy and Ellie. He'd want to leave them behind, hidden. Alone. Perhaps that was the best plan. Certainly Tiarnan didn't want them in the thick of a fight, and with the odds at almost two to one. But what if they were defeated? That would leave Shealy and Ellie unprotected.

"It looked like two parties," Jamie was saying. "Moving fast and parallel to each other. I think they're tracking us, but it was hard to tell from the angle they took."

There would be only one reason for the strangers to be tracking them. They must be working for Cathán. Somehow, Cathán had found these men, recruited them, and sent them out in search of Shealy and her father. If that was true, he could assume they would be ruthless. Tiarnan had fought Cathán before. He knew the man had no conscience, no qualm about slaughtering innocents to get what he wanted.

Tiarnan glanced at his brother, who watched him with steady eyes. Liam would do what he asked, no matter what he asked. But how many times had Tiarnan been in just such a situation? How many times had he made the wrong choice? Seen the wrong options? Led his people to destruction?

In his head, he heard Shealy's soft voice. *If you made some wrong decisions, then it's probably because there weren't any right ones.* But she hadn't been there. She didn't know the full extent of his mistakes.

At his right, Shealy knelt close beside him, waiting. Her eyes shone with intelligence, and he knew she'd seen the options ahead of them as clearly as he. Her fingers were still tucked into his belt, and he felt her hand clench over it, trying to hold on to him. He wanted nothing more than to keep her beside him, keep her safe.

Tiarnan sensed Jamie testing him, seeking an answer that would determine what came next. If Tiarnan chose Shealy now, he might do so again, and that could put the others in danger. He respected Jamie, was proud to fight beside the man, but he lived by inflexible standards that didn't always fit the situation.

"Can we avoid them?" Tiarnan asked.

Jamie shook his head. "They're too close. Besides, if they're looking for her, they'll just keep coming. We need to know who these guys are. We could get away, but next time the odds may be worse."

He was right and Tiarnan knew it, though he wished the situation could be sidestepped altogether.

"I think they're trying to get behind us, maybe circle us," Jamie went on. "We're not going to let them." To Reyes and Zac, he said, "You two go around and flank them." The two men moved out without question, but Tiarnan stopped them.

"Wait. What about Shealy and the child?"

"They stay here and hide," Jamie replied.

"Not alone," Tiarnan said.

"We've got two to one odds, T. We can't leave anyone back. Besides, chances are they're coming for her. We need to keep her out of sight."

"All the more reason not to leave them alone," he insisted.

"You're not running the show. I am. Liam, get someplace high where you've got a clean shot."

Liam didn't move and Reyes and Zac both hesitated, waiting for the orders to be cleared. Tiarnan kept his gaze steady, his voice low.

"Not alone," Tiarnan said once more.

"Fuck me," Jamie said under his breath. "You picked now for this? Really? You think this is the time or place for a pissing contest?"

"It doesn't have to be a contest. Leave Liam with Shealy and Ellie," Tiarnan said. "Y', Reyes, and Zac circle around. I'll meet them in the middle."

Jamie looked stunned. "You'll meet them in the middle," he repeated. "What? You're just going to saunter out and make friends? There's nine of them that I saw, probably more that I didn't. You hearing me?"

Tiarnan didn't answer, afraid his voice would betray how uncertain he felt. Put in black-and-white terms, it sounded ridiculous. The kind of *plan* that was doomed to fail. He'd helmed more of them in his lifetime then he wanted to own. But the choices were few, and if the enemy was strong enough to take on Tiarnan, Jamie, Zac, and Reyes, then leaving Liam behind wouldn't make that much difference to the outcome, but it might save Shealy and Ellie. Liam would be there to help the females survive if the rest of them died.

And in his mind, Shealy spoke again. *You were unbelievable. You were like five men.*

Once before he'd heard the same thing said of him. When in battle, Tiarnan lost all sense of himself, so he could only guess at what they'd meant, what he'd done, what they'd seen in him as he fought. But he could hope to be so strong again, now, when it was needed.

He held Jamie's eyes, unwavering. Inside his heart thumped hard and he felt hot and cold at the same time. He'd sworn that he would never try to take charge again, that he had learned from the past that he was not made to lead others. He was *happy* to follow, he'd assured himself. But he didn't back down now.

Shealy pressed closer as if in silent support.

Jamie shook his head and cursed. "Okay. Okay, we'll play your way. I just hope you know what you're doing."

So did he. Tiarnan let out a shaky breath, his chest locked tight. If he got them all killed, well, he'd probably deserve it.

"Liam," Tiarnan said, glancing at Shealy and away. Every time he looked at her, he had the strange feeling that she knew what was going on inside his head. If she was a seer, then she probably did, and he liked that not at all. Bad enough to be wracked with indecision, but to have this woman witness it was torture. "Take Shealy and Ellie back through the trees. Ye'll come to the rock hills. Y' can wait there by the three balancing stones. Y' know the place?"

Liam nodded without question, hefted the weight of his ax, and adjusted his quiver and bow so that he could reach it quickly. Without a word, he signaled to Shealy and her sister.

Shealy eased her fingers out of Tiarnan's belt, leaving a cold wash where the heat of her touch had been.

"I'll be back for y'," he said.

She shifted her gaze to Jamie's face, met impassive eyes that couldn't have told her much, and then looked back to Tiarnan. Her chin came up. Holding her sister tightly, she brushed her fingers against his heart and softly said, "I know. Be careful," before she turned away.

Without even knowing what he meant to do, he caught her trailing fingers and tugged her back. His hands cupped her face and he kissed her, right there in front of the others. Kissed her like it was the first time . . . the last time. She held herself still for a moment, and the bitter bite of rejection cut him deep, but then she was leaning into him, into the kiss, and the sweetness of it flooded him with heat and passion. Ellie was still in her arms, the only reason he didn't gather her closer and print his body with hers. He yearned to hold her so tight that they'd become one. He pulled away reluctantly, lips clinging for a charged second.

"I will come for y'," he murmured against her mouth.

Her thunder-and-lightning eyes flashed at him, and he caught a glimmer of hope, the rumble of fear in the storm brewing within them.

"I will," he said again.

"You better," was all she said in return.

Watching her go, he found his throat closed tight with dread and he couldn't have spoken if he'd wanted to. It divided him, having Liam moving away with Shealy. Tiarnan had always fought side by side with his brother, there to defend him, there to keep him from falling. Now he had Shealy and her sister to protect as well. The looming moment when he might be forced to choose between them taunted him like the approaching enemy.

Tiarnan gave the remaining three men a nod and watched them move off, intent on circling the invaders they'd seen. Jamie cut through the foliage at a distance. He'd be watching, ready to attack.

Tiarnan waited another moment, giving Liam a chance to find shelter for Shealy, Ellie, and himself. Then he faced the dark, shadowed trees and moved ahead, aiming for the place where Jamie had seen the others. Wherever they'd gone from there, he'd be able to track them.

The forest grew very quiet, and Tiarnan felt as if it watched him with invisible eyes. Maybe it did. Everything on Inis Brandubh was alive right down to the dirt, the weather, the plants. He didn't know what he would meet in this wooded battleground. It could be Cathán's men, it could be the Druid's minions, it could be another beast that defied the imagination.

He took some strength from thinking that Liam and Shealy were safe and refused to let himself consider that they might not be.

To his right he heard a low whistle. Jamie, letting him know he was in place. Tiarnan didn't glance his way in case he was being watched. He paused now, straining to hear movement. Nine men had to make some noise. And what about the wolf Jamie had seen? Surely he'd mistaken its behavior—no wolf of Inis Brandubh had ever been tamed.

Ahead a twig snapped and Tiarnan turned to meet his enemy.

Chapter Fourteen

As the words *spread out* reached Tiarnan, he felt his heartbeat accelerate, his skin grow tight. He tested the weight of his ax, rested his palm against the knife still in the scabbard at his waist, and crouched down low.

The shout came sudden and fierce, and then it seemed that the forest was alive. He saw five men bolt from cover. Dressed in the mismatched clothing of all those who lived here, they seemed intent on something hidden in the bushes. From the other side, two more pounced out, flushing a seventh from hiding. Still more spilled from the trees. Jamie had counted nine, but Tiarnan's quick assessment put it closer to twenty. *Twenty.*

The loosely formed theory that these men belonged to Cathán solidified as he saw familiar faces mixed in with those of strangers. Some of these men had fought against Tiarnan before Inis Brandubh. Tiarnan's shock mixed with rage, but there was no time to dwell on it.

The lone man they'd chased from hiding ran toward him, and

Tiarnan formed a plan of action. The other men still hadn't seen him, but soon they would. There was no way for him to get out of this unnoticed. Running wasn't an option, and even if it had been, he didn't think he could stomach fleeing from Cathán's vermin, no matter what the odds.

Through the branches, he caught sight of the one they chased and had a flashing impression of a big man—nearly as tall as himself and broad, though not so heavy through the shoulders. A fit man, but not one who depended on his strength for survival. He wore a white tunic with short sleeves and buttons down the front. A queer black inset at the collar rode tight to his neck, and torn black trews covered his legs. He carried a satchel slung across his chest, and it flopped at his back as he ran.

"Just kill the bastard and be done with it," one of Cathán's men shouted as he led a pack of eight to cut off the fleeing man's escape. "We've got the girl. We don't need him."

"And if Cathán disagrees?" another answered just before he came to a skidding stop and stared in shock at Tiarnan.

Tiarnan only heard *We've got the girl*, and that was enough to turn his dread into a harsh inferno. He couldn't reason out how they'd found Shealy so fast, but their meaning was clear. As the man in black and white dodged to his left, another man came straight at him with a long, shining sword raised over his head, and Tiarnan's rage wiped all else from his mind.

These men had Shealy.

Tiarnan feinted to the side and then caught the man hard in the gut with his shoulder, plowing him back until he rammed into a tree trunk. Without hesitation, Tiarnan spun, slamming his body against the pinned man and using the man's own arm to lift his sword and impale a second man who'd charged. There were more coming now, attacking from all sides at once. One gnarled face with mean eyes caught in Tiarnan's sights and froze him for an instant.

Tiarnan recognized him. His name was Paidric, and he'd once been of Tiarnan's people before he'd turned traitor with Tiarnan's brother Eamonn.

Savage fury filled Tiarnan and blazed within his belly. He saw nothing but Paidric's twisted face as he hurled his ax. In the same swift move, he wrenched the sword from the grasp of the man pinned behind him, flipped the angle, and brought it hard and back, impaling the man against the tree. The sound of the blade piercing flesh, *thunking* into the hard wood on the other side, fanned the flames in Tiarnan until it seemed they lifted him, bringing him higher, skewing his perspective. He yanked the blade free and faced his attackers with a howl of vengeance.

The ax had found its mark and stuck, handle still quivering from Paidric's skull. Running at the clot of Cathán's soldiers, Tiarnan wrenched his ax free and started swinging, weapon in each hand. He'd mowed down five men before they'd had the chance to see what was coming. Their blood sprayed in a wild storm as severed heads and chopped limbs littered the ground. Those who'd been chasing the stranger with his satchel and queer collar stopped at the screams of their comrades and came to their aid. Tiarnan welcomed them into his wrath.

He seemed to tower over them, his ire lifting him higher. The others tilted their heads back, mouths open as they stared at him in horror. He didn't give them the chance to act on the impulse to run. No sooner had their terror made its way to their feet than Tiarnan was on them, blades flashing as he leaped over corpses to hunt them down. His sword became an extension of his arm, his ax a part of his hand. He swung both with all his might and zeal, heedless of the glancing blows the lucky ones managed before he killed them. He took down men with one swipe, killing them before their screams could leave their lips. Their blood showered him and he reveled in it, each drop a tribute to his own slain people.

He fought tirelessly, indomitably, violently until finally he reached the last enemy, whom he trapped on the forest floor with a pounce and a triumphant shout that echoed among the trees, sending birds to flight in a burst of black wings.

"Tiarnan!"

He heard his name, but the white-hot frenzy in his brain would not respond. The man beneath him was screaming, and the sound flowed with Tiarnan's blood, making it faster, hotter, more potent. He wanted more screams. He wanted more terror. He wanted to take this man apart piece by piece until his agony matched that which lived in Tiarnan's heart every day.

"Tiarnan!"

His name again, called more urgently as men crashed through the bushes and at him.

Tiarnan clamped his hand around his prey's throat and then rose, dragging the man to his feet as he choked and gasped for air. Tiarnan swung, ready to slash his blade at the newcomers, ready to cut them to pieces and bathe in their blood. He swiped at his eyes, knowing he was already red with the gore of his victims. Wanting more of it.

He threw back his head and bellowed to the sky, to the gods, to the cursed land.

"TIARNAN!"

This time his name pushed against some sense of awareness buried so deep within him that it now struggled to surface. There were three men standing in a semicircle in front of him, each with his hands out in a placating gesture. They were armed, but not brandishing weapons. Tiarnan snarled, snapping his teeth as he looked down on them. They seemed so small, so puny. So ready to die.

The man whose throat he gripped struggled, holding on to Tiarnan's arm with both of his hands as his feet scuttled above the ground.

"Tiarnan, that's it, look at me," the dark-skinned man standing in front of him was saying, and a tickle of recognition hit Tiarnan's thoughts. "That's right, T. It's me, Jamie."

The man took a step forward as he spoke, and Tiarnan snarled again ready to leap. It felt as if every hair on his body stood on end and the air around him shivered with the storm of his passion.

The man named Jamie froze, hands still raised with palms out. "It's me, T. You know me. You know me."

He said it over and over until finally the voice penetrated the thick and vicious storm that held him. *Jamie.* The dark man was Jamie. Tiarnan shifted his gaze to the one next to him.

"That's right," Jamie went on in that crooning, soothing tone. "That's Reyes. You know Reyes. He's your friend. Zac is your friend. I'm your friend."

Tiarnan sucked in a harsh breath, suddenly enraged once more. He had no friends. No people. Nothing but this bloodlust that enveloped him.

He jerked the hand that still held his captive. Roared into the man's terrified and purpling face.

"We need him, T," Jamie said. "We need to question him. Don't kill him."

But Tiarnan couldn't process so many words. All he knew was that this man had threatened him. Threatened someone else . . . someone . . . The image of a woman filled his head, her skin golden in the firelight, stripped and beautiful beyond anything he'd ever beheld as she straddled his hips, wrapped him in the blistering tight heat of her body. This man had threatened *her*.

It filled him, eviscerated him, devoured the last human thought until all he felt was threat and the need to destroy it. The ax hit the dirt at his feet as he spiraled down to something more primitive than weapons and how to use them. With his hands, he brought the man up and around until he held him eye to eye.

The purpling face screamed at him, but Tiarnan couldn't hear it. He covered the face with one hand, crushing the bones with his fingers as the other hand tightened until he felt the cartilage splinter and the last breath cease.

Only then did he drop the ruined body. Only then did he draw a breath that didn't sear his throat. The hazy feral wave eased just a bit and Tiarnan saw his hands, enormous and bloody. He held them up to his face, seeing the familiar scars, the lines of his palm, the shape of his fingers. Yes, they were his hands and yet . . .

"Fuck," Jamie said. He turned to the man standing beside him and asked, "Did you see any others? Did any get away?"

"No man, I don't think anyone could. . . ."

They all looked at Tiarnan again. He stared back at them through his spread fingers, now truly recognizing who they were. *Jamie, Reyes, and Zac.* He felt a dull ache in his skull, a throbbing that seemed to come from a great distance as he stared down at them. They seemed so far away.

"T, you with us?" Reyes was asking. He took a step forward.

"Stay back, Reyes. He'll kill you."

Kill Reyes? Why would he do that? He cocked his head, looking at the three of them. They were closer now and that relieved him, but he couldn't say why. The throbbing increased, pounding like a hammer in his head.

"Nah, check out his eyes. He's coming back."

Coming back. From where? He turned to Jamie again, finding that he didn't have to look down anymore. The other man stood at eye level, but his face was set into a mask that Tiarnan couldn't read. Scattered on the ground all around them were bloody bodies, some hacked to pieces, others cleanly killed. Something had happened here. Something had . . .

A movement came from behind the three men, and Tiarnan tensed, felt that savage beast inside him rear, but it no longer had the strength to bare its teeth. Zac reacted first, pulling his weapon and spinning to find the man dressed in black and white with his satchel standing behind him. He had his hands clasped on top of his head and he went to his knees in instant submission. He fastened his terrified gaze on Tiarnan and something in his expression rocked Tiarnan back. Did he know this man?

"Who are y'?" Tiarnan managed to ask, but his voice sounded gruff, pitched so deep it barely seemed human. His vision swam, and he braced himself against a tree and then tried again. "Who are y'?"

"My name's Mahon. I'm Kyle Mahon," the man answered. "And you would be Tiarnan of the Favored Lands."

The old title from a time and place that seemed another lifetime wiped the last vestiges of rage from Tiarnan's mind. But before he could form a response, before he could ask this Kyle Mahon any of the tumult of questions he had, there came a scream that split the forest like a scythe.

It was Shealy, and before the echo ended, Tiarnan began to run toward the terrified sound.

Chapter Fifteen

L IAM carried Ellie as he set a brisk pace through the tangle of woods and away from the men and whatever conflict awaited them. She knew the young man would rather be back fighting at his brother's side than escorting a woman and a child, but he didn't say it. Only the tension that stiffened his shoulders when a shout echoed in the thick foliage betrayed him. Both of them strained to hear something more, to know what was happening with Tiarnan, but the farther they moved away, the quieter it became.

Shealy did her best to keep up with Liam or at least to not slow him down, but it was hard to focus on what was ahead when she didn't know exactly what she'd left behind. Who had Jamie seen in the woods? There were too many enemies to count in this place, and it could have been anyone from Cathán himself to the mysterious Druid that Tiarnan had told her about. At least Jamie said he'd seen men approaching and not another creature. She couldn't imagine facing one of those again. Still, even if it was *only* men, they'd be greatly outnumbered. She couldn't help but be afraid for them.

"Yer all right there, Leary?" Liam asked as he began to climb.

She shook her head at his teasing tone and use of Leary—a nickname that seemed to be sticking.

"I'm okay," she answered, but her legs cramped and she had a hitch in her side that felt deadly. She was hopelessly out of shape and all the running and the climbing she'd done in the past two days made every muscle and joint ache.

The trees had thinned without her noticing and Shealy saw that they'd entered a rocky area that rose steadily up. Were they near the cliffs where the wolves had caught them? The landscape appeared similar, and yet the hills didn't peak so high and she couldn't hear the sea. The air had a different feel to it, more arid and scented of rich dust and earth, not fish and salt. Up ahead she saw three stones balanced one on top of the other.

Liam skimmed across the treacherous terrain without thought to where he should put each foot, but Shealy had to focus on every step or risk slipping and ending up flat on her ass . . . or her face. Neither scenario held much appeal. They'd just reached the balanced stones when suddenly Liam stopped and held out a hand to steady her as she drew up beside him.

He hushed her with a finger to his lips in a gesture that made him look exactly like his brother even though their physical resemblances were few. His expression, his bearing, his intensity had Tiarnan written all over them.

He pointed to an area below, and Shealy crept up to the boulder blocking the way and looked down. A man on horseback appeared to be giving orders to others she couldn't see from her position.

Two men held a woman between them who kicked and fought as they kept her prisoner.

Instinctively, Shealy moved forward, thinking only that the woman needed help. That if not for Tiarnan, she herself might have been in the same situation. *Captive.* Liam jerked her down just as the men below glanced up. Heart pounding, she waited in silence, wondering if they'd seen her, waiting to be discovered. The moments stretched, cranking the tension in the air into something unbearable, but no one investigated, no sound of footsteps climbing reached them.

After what seemed ages, she whispered to Liam, "Do you think it's safe now?"

Cautiously he inched up and looked. "They're leaving," he murmured.

Shealy peered over the rocks again just in time to see the men riding away, taking their prisoner with them. The sun was in her eyes and she couldn't tell much about the riders, but if they were Cathán's men . . .

"Aren't we going to do something?" Shealy asked.

"What would y' have us do? I want to help the girl, too, but Tiarnan told me to watch over y'. I'd be putting all of y' in danger if I charged down there."

"I know, but . . ."

"As soon as the others join us, we'll go," Liam said.

"Maybe we should follow them, though. Maybe they'll lead us to my dad."

Liam nodded, seeing the logic in what she said, and she could see the argument waging behind his eyes. Then he looked from Shealy to her sister, who sat quietly between. "We cannot risk it. If something were to happen to either of y' . . ."

Shealy wouldn't win this fight. Looking at Ellie, she knew Liam was right. If something happened to them, both Tiarnan and Liam would hold themselves responsible. She'd seen the heavy weight Tiarnan already carried. Adding to it was not an option.

Quietly, Liam led them to a spot close to the trio of balanced stones, where a smooth platform offered a place to wait, concealed from anyone below. He lowered himself down and Shealy sat next to him, taking Ellie from his arms once she'd settled. He'd carried her a long way and his fingers must be all but numb by now, but like his older brother, Liam didn't complain.

"How you doing, sweetheart?" she asked Ellie.

Her little sister hadn't spoken a single word since shouting "*No*" at the monsters when Shealy had scooped her up from the carnage, but her bright eyes followed every movement. Shealy was certain that she understood what went on around her.

"She'll come around and start talking again," Liam said, reaching into his pack and pulling out some dried meat and a hunk of bread. Unwrapping the offerings, he shared them with Ellie and Shealy before taking some himself.

"I wasn't sure if she knew how yet. I don't know how old she is . . . if she's too young."

"Well, half the time y' have to guess what she's saying, but she talks. Yer mother used to tell her stories. Tell us all, truth be told. She had a gift."

Shealy swallowed hard, remembering that about her mother. She could weave a trip to the market into a tale of excitement and intrigue.

"I miss her," Shealy said. "Every day." Eyes blurred with pointless tears, she looked down into Ellie's face. "You miss her, too, don't you?"

Solemnly, Ellie nodded.

"Well, we have each other now. And we'll have to remember her by telling our own stories." The barest hint of a smile tilted Ellie's lips. "And when we find Dad, we'll make him tell us stories as well."

Ellie heaved a great sigh and leaned back against her. Shealy pressed a kiss to her head and held her.

They all fell silent for a while as they ate their sparse meal. Shealy found herself looking back at the way they'd come, praying that soon

Tiarnan would stride from the forest, big, strong, and unharmed. She could no longer hear the shouts or cries, and the worst fears began to crowd in. He'd said he'd come for her. . . . but what if he didn't? What if he was hurt, mortally wounded, dying. . . .

To stop the morbid thoughts, she looked back at Liam.

"Tiarnan told me you'd been at war with Cathán for most of your life."

"Aye. It will be a good day when Tiarnan puts an end to that vermin."

"Why were you at war?"

"The bloody Book of Fennore. He thought we had it. Ha. Little did he know that fighting for it would land his sorry arse dead in its center."

There was a certain poetic justice to it.

"Tiarnan said he damaged the Book and that's how you all ended up here."

"Aye, and that's true as well. But Tiarnan . . . he feels responsible for everything, y' see?"

She nodded, thinking of the torment she'd seen in his golden brown eyes so many times. "He does seem to carry a lot of baggage."

"Y've no idea. He was our leader, and he was a good one. But even a good leader must lose when winning is impossible. Cathán never relented and his numbers grew because each time he conquered, he made new subjects. Our people died, if not from battle then from the cold or hunger. There was hardly anything left of us when Tiarnan made a match between our sister and a man we thought an enemy. I did not agree with it, but I trusted Tiarnan, and in the end he was right, wasn't he?"

Shealy didn't know, but Liam's voice had grown wistful and his eyes took on a shine that might have been tears. He was too proud to shed them, though. Instead he went on in that soft and solemn voice.

"Everything might have been good after that if we hadn't been betrayed."

"By Eamonn?"

Liam shot her a startled glance. "He told y' about Eamonn?"

She nodded, and Liam's gaze became thoughtful. Evidently Tiarnan did not talk about his deceitful brother much. She couldn't blame him.

She wanted to ask Liam more about this traitorous brother, but Liam's closed expression made her hold her questions in. Speaking Eamonn's name had obviously brought to the surface all the emotional upheaval that went with his betrayal.

"It destroyed what was left of the leader Tiarnan once was," Liam said at last, his voice low and distant. "He hasn't the heart for it anymore. When we first came, I worried that he'd give up altogether."

Shealy thought about this for a moment. What Liam said seemed to explain much about the serious man who'd set her blood on fire. She sensed his reluctance to take charge and yet . . . yet he'd agreed to come with Shealy to find her father.

Liam looked at her, as if he'd heard her thoughts. "It's a good thing, y' coming. Y've given him something."

She blushed as memories of the night before and just what and how much she'd given to Tiarnan filled her thoughts in aching detail.

"I don't think it's me," she mumbled.

"Aye, it is," Liam said with certainty. "Tiarnan was younger than I am when Cathán killed our father. After that, he became chieftain. Chieftain, at war, and younger than me. Yet sometimes he still treats me like I'm a child. It's not right, not for either of us. But today . . ." He looked at her with raised brows. "Today he tells me to go with Shealy. Not stay beside him so he can watch over me, but go so I can take care of this woman who's come from nowhere and changed him."

"I think you're reading more into it than there is, Liam."

He shook his head. "There are few things I know, Leary. But Tiarnan is one of them."

He grew quiet again, and Shealy knew that inside he turned this new revelation over and analyzed each side of it. He might know Tiarnan, but even after so short a time, so did Shealy. And Liam was very much like his brother. Letting him mull his conclusions, Shealy looked down at her little sister. Ellie dozed fitfully in her arms, startling with a gasp or small cry before slipping back into uneasy sleep. Shealy worried about her. Children were resilient, but Ellie had been through too much. She was too young, her language not yet developed enough to talk about the brutal murder of their mother that both of them had witnessed. How would she cope? How could Shealy help her through this?

A roaring bellow echoed across the land, interrupting her thoughts. It sounded like a bear or a lion and yet nothing like either. It rumbled with bone-chilling dimensions, at once piercing and earth shaking.

"What was that?" Liam asked, rising to his haunches and peering over the boulders.

Easing the child into a firmer grip, Shealy inched up beside him and did the same. Nothing moved as far as they could see, but the roar came again, louder, more riveting. The sound was so primeval that it struck them with instinctive terror—the kind that made a person bolt blindly into peril just to escape.

In the distance the treetops shuddered and Shealy's heart thumped with fear at what might be out there, strong enough to shake a tree that size. More of the three-headed creatures? Something worse? They were both so gripped with horror by the predatory roar that echoed again and the ominous shudder of branches that followed, that neither one of them heard the intruders approaching from behind until it was too late.

Liam spun, reaching for his weapons even as a blade flashed out and the point pressed against the soft flesh of his throat. Caught squatting, there was no way he could fend it off. Beside him, Shealy kept her body angled so that Ellie was protected, but she glanced back, taking in the group of men that surrounded them.

"Drop it," the one holding the sword said to Liam.

For a moment, Liam shifted his weight, and Shealy knew he was gauging his odds, playing his next move in his head.

"Try it," the man with the sword said. "You'll get a few of us, but not all, and we'll make sure you live long enough to see her and the child gutted."

Whether it was a bluff or not, the visual was there and reluctantly, Liam let his sword and ax clatter to the rocks. He glanced at Shealy with a look of misery and she knew that he thought of Tiarnan and how disappointed he'd be to find Liam had failed in his one task to protect her and Ellie. She wanted to reassure him, to tell him that this wasn't his fault, but even if she'd been able to say it, he wouldn't believe her. She could see that.

A new man shouldered through to the front of the group, and the others fell back to let him pass. When he reached the one holding the blade to Liam's throat, he motioned with his head to move away. It was obvious the sword wielder didn't agree, but he followed orders and stepped to the side.

At this new man's feet, an enormous wolf waited, tongue lolling, teeth bared. Shealy couldn't tolerate being on the same level as those sharp teeth. Cautiously, she stood. Liam, looking like he'd been carved from stone, stood as well and stared at the newcomer with an expression of revulsion and hatred that seemed oddly personal. Did he know this man?

Shealy shifted her attention from Liam, glancing over at the wolf, who'd calmly sat, and then back to the newcomer. His face was in shadow, but she glimpsed an intricate pattern of tattoos that circled his throat, disappearing beneath his shirt to reemerge at his arms, where they snaked down to his wrists. *Chains*, she realized. The tattoos were of chains, binding him at the throat, the wrists. . . . She glanced down, taking in the muscled legs that showed where the short pants ended. The chains were there as well. She would bet they went all the way down, inside his boots, to loop around his ankles. The chains, though only an illusion, gave him a look of dishonor, but she couldn't pinpoint just how she'd come to that. From head to toe, he was fearsome with a sinister air that went above and beyond the weapons and aggression they all wore like second skins.

He was tall and broad, though not as big as Tiarnan or Jamie. Still, muscle and brawn packed his frame, and the menace in his eyes added another two feet and fifty pounds to his appearance. Beside him, the huge wolf shifted, watching her with pale eyes and a curled lip. The fixed stare made her feel like a slab of ground beef with a slice of cheese on top. The wolf let out a low growl and the man clicked his tongue sharply at it. Dutifully the animal dropped its frigid gaze to her feet. Still, she could almost see the cartoon bubble over its head as it contemplated her toes and compared them to little sausages.

Her heart thumped painfully in her chest, forcing sluggish blood through veins that had narrowed from fear. Her pulse drummed in her ears. She curled her fingers into her palms, trying to stay calm, trying to control the fight-or-flight instinct that screamed *run, run, run* in her head. She wanted to cower, but she stayed put, Ellie held tight in her arms. The child had awakened, but she didn't squirm or make a sound.

Something told Shealy that this man would view passivity as a weakness, and weakness as a request to be dominated, so she fought her own compulsion to shy away. Stiffening her back, Shealy said, "Who are you? What do you want?"

Her voice wobbled, betraying her, but she managed to get enough steel in the questions that it caught the man off guard. Behind him, the others murmured at her audacity. She raised her chin and waited for an answer.

The man didn't give her one. He stared at her silently for a moment and behind him the others fanned out like cards from the bottom of a deck. Warriors, armed to the teeth, battle-scarred with hard eyes and harder bodies. She counted four, but suspected there were others waiting in the soundless twilight.

The men wore the strange mixture of modern clothes and the hides and fur ensemble that their leader sported, that all the men here on Testosterone Island donned. Some had jeans beneath their tunics, some had T-shirts with their crudely made pants. They all carried spears or swords, axes and arrows. *Like a bizarre caveman convention*, she thought with a dark twist of humor. If a T-Rex burst through the crowd, she wouldn't even be surprised.

The tattooed man with the wolf—the one she suspected was the leader—took a step closer and now she could see a scar on the side of his face that ripped three parallel lines through his short hair at the temple. The tattoos on his throat stood out more clearly. Even tempered by the shadowed murk, the heavy chain links made him look savage and pitiless, more frightening than all the wicked blades combined.

Without lowering her gaze from the watching men, she took a tentative step back. The wolf growled in warning a moment before she bumped into something hard behind her. She couldn't stop her gasp when hands came up, pinning her in place.

"And where is it you think you'll be off to?" the man holding her said in her ear. He had a deep voice with a lilting accent.

The leader of this motley army stepped forward, boxing her in. She wanted to struggle against the hands that pinned her, but feared she'd drop Ellie if he jerked on her arms. The child clung to her, crying mutely. Perhaps it was the very silence of her distress that gave Shealy courage. No child should ever be so afraid, and it enraged her that these men had brought tears to her sister's eyes after all she'd endured already.

"Do you get off on scaring little girls?" she asked the man holding her. "Does that make you feel like a big man, to make them cry?"

Her captor said nothing, but he eased his tight hold and she felt a small measure of relief.

The leader turned to Liam and stared at him with an unfathomable expression. Liam glared back with hatred. It was definitely personal. *Very* personal.

"I thought never to see y' again," the leader said to Liam in a voice that throbbed with some unidentifiable emotion. It made his words thick and guttural.

Liam responded to that by spitting in the leader's face. Shealy sucked in her shock as the soldiers behind him moved up angrily, but the leader held his hand out, stopping them. He wiped the spittle away and said nothing, but the taut silence rippled with anger and restrained aggression.

"Who are you?" she demanded again.

His cold eyes shifted to her and he smiled, the baring of teeth as intimidating as the wolf's.

She amused him. But not in a good way.

He grabbed her chin in a hard clamp and turned it, inspecting her scars with narrowed eyes. His wolf took advantage of his distraction and inched forward to sniff at her feet. Shealy bit back a whimper as memories of his pack mates trying to eat her alive surfaced. The leader made another noise with his tongue and the wolf backed off.

"I am Eamonn," he said finally, still smiling with such chilling cruelty that Shealy shrank back against the man holding her.

"Eamonn the Traitor," Liam said, ire giving his words a hostile edge that made the others take another step closer, hemming them in.

Shealy stared at the man numbly as she put the pieces together. This was the brother who had betrayed Tiarnan?

"I swore one day I'd kill y'," Liam said. "I hope that day has come."

The men behind Eamonn grumbled warnings, but Liam didn't flinch and Eamonn stood stiffly, a mask of malice hiding his thoughts. But so close, Shealy saw the flash of pain in his eyes and realized that no matter what he'd done in the past, no matter what he planned to do in the very near future, Liam's hatred wounded him. The black markings on his throat moved as he swallowed, but he didn't respond to Liam's threat. Instead, he looked back at Shealy.

"And who would y' be?" he asked in a silky voice.

"I am Shealy O'Leary," she said, tilting her head to glare at him even though her knees were banging and she was sure the man holding her knew it.

"Leary," Eamonn snarled in a tone similar to the one that Tiarnan and Liam had used when she'd first told them her name. At least now she had some clue as to why. Her ancestor must have pissed this guy off, too.

"O'Leary," she said, trying to tug her arms free. "What do you want from us?"

"It is y' who've wandered into my territory. I would ask y' the same."

She lowered her gaze as she tried to form the best response. If she told them they'd been attacked and had come here to hide while the others fought their foe, she'd be revealing that there were more of them. If she said nothing, Eamonn would think she and Liam were alone and defenseless. Which was best, given the situation? Either one seemed a dangerous admission. Better to keep silent than to reveal their situation.

Eamonn leaned in, intimidating her with his size and obvious irritation. It took all her will not to show just how afraid he made her.

"Are y' a spy then?" he accused.

"No and she's no traitor either," Liam said. "So let her go."

Eamonn ignored Liam's demand and instead asked, "How long have y' been here, brother?"

"I am not yer brother. Not anymore. And I've been here long enough to learn to fight y' like a man. To kill y' with my bare hands."

Eamonn's smile never faltered, but for one unguarded instant Shealy saw how deeply Liam's words cut him. Had she not seen the mirror of that pain in Tiarnan's eyes that morning, she might have felt sorry for Eamonn.

Coldly, he said, "I can scarce believe y've survived alone in a land such as this and I'm equally amazed y've managed it without me seeing y'. I thought I knew everything that went on in this world."

"No one could ever know everything. Least of all y'. 'Twas yer problem all along, wasn't it, though? Y' always thought y' knew it all."

Eamonn's jaw clenched tighter, as if he had to bite back his response. Any fool could see he wanted to explain himself, but knew the danger in such a thing. He ruled a motley group in an outland of horror. Explaining himself might be perceived as a weakness; even now his men shifted restlessly. Shealy caught more than one look exchanged between them, and she realized in that instant that Liam's angry accusation had struck a chord in the tangled harmony of the men. Eamonn's position as leader was not as secure as he would like.

Eamonn looked back at Shealy. "If y' are a spy, I will slit y' from throat to gullet. Do y' hear me?"

Silent, she nodded.

He watched her for another long moment, searching her face

for answers that he seemed sure she had. She was glad for all the years she'd practiced keeping her expression impassive and gazed calmly back, but inside she quaked. This man had turned on his own brother. She'd be a fool to think he'd be anything less than cruel to a stranger.

"Bring them," Eamonn ordered the man holding her. "And keep her quiet."

Shealy saw the man reach for something and knew he planned to gag her. Two panicked thoughts collided with her fear as he pulled free a tattered rag. After the accident, her jaw had been wired shut and her face wrapped, mummylike. She'd been in a coma when they'd done it, but she'd awakened to find herself trapped in bandages, unable to speak, to move, to call for help. Her terror had spiked her heartbeat, which finally brought the nurse to see her. By then she was hysterical, unable to talk or see, a high-pitched squeal the only call for help she could make.

Since then, she couldn't stand to have anything covering her face—not a scarf, not a veil, nothing. It was one of the many reasons why the blindfolded photo in the magazine had been so symbolic for her. It represented a monumental conquering of fear to Shealy.

There was no way she'd tolerate a gag. But she knew she didn't stand a chance of fighting it if they were intent on her wearing it.

I will come for y' . . .

Tiarnan's words whispered through her mind, offering her an anchor in her panic. She had to believe that he was out there, looking for them by now. This might be her only chance to call for help, to warn him of danger. But if she took it, if she screamed, they'd make sure she didn't do it again.

Always before she'd known that her screams would only bring more pain and disappointment. No one really wanted to know the messed-up woman behind the porcelain visage. No one but her father would try to reach into the blackened pits of her suffering and help her out. But now . . . She knew, *she knew*, Tiarnan would come if she called.

Shealy screamed.

Loud and clear, her voice rising out of the dark. She screamed until the man clapped a hand over her mouth and shook her. Ellie let loose a wail, too, and wrapped her arms tighter around Shealy's neck, her hot tears running in rivulets, scalding Shealy's throat, reproachful and heartbreaking. Holding her sister tight, she caught her last pealing scream in her throat and swallowed it before it reached the muffling hand, hoping the echoes still rebounding in the rocky hills would be enough. Praying that wherever he was now, Tiarnan had heard and he would come.

Eamonn charged forward until they were nose to nose. She tried to say something, to deflect the rage that shrouded him like a razor suit, but the other man's hand still covered her mouth and the residue of alarm whipped through her like a torrential storm. She squirmed and fought, hearing Liam's agonized shout for them to let her go as if his voice came from some great distance.

She stared into Eamonn's hateful eyes as she tried to breathe, but the hand over her face sealed her mouth and nose and she couldn't draw in air. Her head felt heavy, thick with blackness that rolled like fog off the sea.

"Let her breathe," Eamonn ordered as her eyes began to flutter and her knees to give.

She felt the reluctance in the man who removed his hand at last, leaving her gasping for air through her constricted throat. Black spots danced in her vision as she sucked in great draughts of oxygen, hearing as if from a distance far away a keening sound that she realized must be coming from her.

Eamonn slapped her face with a cruel swiftness. The sting burning her cheek cut through the blinding terror that still dominated her and slammed her back into the moment and the terrifying consequences of her actions.

"Scream again, lass, and I'll have yer tongue cut out. Do y' understand?" he said.

Slowly she nodded, eyes rolling to the gag the man still held. "Don't . . ." She couldn't even say the words. "Don't use that. I can't tolerate having things over my face."

There was no shielding the raw fear in her eyes and Eamonn studied it with clinical detachment. She hoped she hadn't just provided the handbook for her torture, but it was too late to retract the words or swallow the screams. She lifted her chin, trying to look brave, suspecting she probably managed foolish instead. She'd never know what swayed him—her fear or the control over it she'd just given him, but finally, with a curt shake of his head, Eamonn signaled to the man holding her and he shoved the filthy gag back into his pocket.

"Do not think to test me," he said softly to Shealy.

"I won't. Just no gag. Please."

She nearly fell as her captor jerked her arm forward and pulled her along behind the others, showing no leniency as they moved down the rocky slope like sure-footed mountain goats. Still holding Ellie, Shealy struggled to keep her balance on the uneven terrain. Her arms ached with Ellie's weight, but she held her tight, trying to soothe her sister's anxiety with a show of calm.

"Don't worry, Ellie," she whispered against her silky hair. "I won't let go. I won't leave you here in this terrible place."

"Where are we going?" she asked Eamonn after a while, afraid to incite him more but unable to keep the question inside.

Eamonn shot her an icy glare and then surprised her with an answer. "We are on the trail of Cathán. We saw some of his men this way. If we find them, it will be bloody."

He said the last with grim satisfaction.

"Cathán," she whispered. "You saw him here?"

"What do you know of Cathán?" the man holding her arm asked suspiciously. She now saw that he was dark eyed with dark skin, possibly from India by the sound of him.

Liam gave her a warning glance as he walked at her side, alert and furious to have been captured without a fight. For her part, if she had to be a prisoner, she was just as happy to skip the bloodshed.

"Nothing," she said, keeping her voice low, giving the man no reason to use that gag that still poked from his pocket like a taunting flag. "I know nothing about Cathán."

Eamonn signaled to his men as they neared the tree line. Night had fallen completely and they were mere shadows moving in the darkness. Taking over for the man who held her, Eamonn towed her toward the forest. She felt a moment of relief. They'd moved closer to where Tiarnan was the last time she'd seen him. Any minute now, he might burst into the open and rescue them.

But something was going on. Shealy felt the shifting tension in the band of warriors surrounding them. Eamonn gave another signal, this one with more force and a black scowl. The men obeyed, and yet Shealy had caught the surge in the dynamic that held the group together.

They did what he wanted, but not wholeheartedly. She couldn't explain how she knew or even if she had it right, but something told her that these men didn't trust Eamonn. As she watched surreptitiously, she saw that each command Eamonn gave prompted a veiled look between the others—a sanity check to make sure they all agreed.

From the corner of her eye, she watched Liam note it as well. She filed the knowledge away, wondering what would happen if these men found issue with the orders Eamonn gave. Would they revolt?

There was no time to question, though. Eamonn crossed into

the trees, keeping his hand firmly wrapped around her arm. Liam's *escort* gave him a push and the boy stumbled forward. As they walked, Shealy searched for a sign of Tiarnan, of Jamie, Zac, and Reyes. What if the creature they'd heard had attacked them? What if it had killed them?

She tried to keep her imagination from going berserk, but she was scared and it had grown very dark now. The moon broke through the branches at rare intervals, keeping the night from becoming all consuming, but just barely. The treacherous forest floor had been difficult to navigate in daylight; now it was nearly impossible. Eamonn and the others seemed undeterred by the same groping vines and treacherous shadows that tried to trip Shealy. They moved silent and sure-footed, but Shealy stumbled, making a racket that drew icy glares.

Eamonn pressed his lips to her ear and hissed, "Quiet or y'll find more than yer mouth bound."

She nodded jerkily and focused harder on her footing, no longer scanning the trees for a sign of Tiarnan. Though it was hard to determine just where they were, it seemed they tromped through the forest forever, and she could only guess that they'd circumvented the direct route that she and Liam had taken when they'd left Tiarnan behind in the thick of it and headed to the rocks to wait. She was looking down when the first man gasped in shock, and by the time she'd jerked her gaze up, they were in the gruesome center of a circle of blood and bodies.

It was impossible to tell how many bodies. They were strewn in pieces and parts and gory chunks all through the small clearing they'd entered. Here the moon shone bright and left nothing to the imagination but the horror that was all too real. Eamonn's soldiers spread out, walking through the corpses with dazed, aghast expressions but alert eyes. Silent, they scanned the forest as they took in the mass destruction and brutality of the attack. Even these seasoned warriors looked shaken by what they saw. Eamonn's wolf, she noted, would not enter the blood-soaked ring. It sat at the edge and whined. She didn't blame it. The stench was everywhere.

"What did this?" Shealy breathed, keeping Ellie's face turned away from the carnage.

No one answered her.

Was Tiarnan's one of the broken and mutilated bodies littering the ground? The thought clenched her insides and made her want to scream again. Eamonn told the man guarding Liam to watch Shealy as well and he moved into the clearing, squatting to examine the remains with that indifferent manner that sent a shudder through her. She didn't know what had done this. It could be human, it could be a monster. The fact that there were still bodies told her it wasn't the same three-headed creature that had attacked the village that morning, though.

After what seemed forever, standing at the edge of the bloodbath, trying not to swoon from the reek of so much death, Eamonn and the others returned to where Liam and Shealy waited with the guards.

"Did you see the footprints?" the Indian man asked.

Stone-faced, Eamonn nodded but did not explain. Shealy and Liam exchanged wary glances, thinking of the roar that had echoed through the forest and those shuddering treetops. Eamonn had come upon them just after. Had he heard it, too? How could he not have?

"These were the men we were tracking," he said. "There's no point in going deeper into the woods. Whatever did this is best not met in the dark."

This, at least, the others did not question. As one they nodded.

With more enthusiasm than when they'd arrived, they changed direction and quickly made their way through the woods, emerging at a sheltered copse.

Protected on two sides by rising stones, the clearing occupied a tight corner between forest and foothills. There were tents arranged around a cold fire pit and a pair of lean-to structures that opened on three sides with a sloping wall that met an overhang. Shealy imagined the sentries used them for shelter when it rained while still having the advantage of an unobstructed view and one defensive wall if an attack should come.

She looked up and around, thinking the location perfectly shielded from outsiders with its natural barriers and secluded location.

Tiarnan would never find them here unless by chance, and on Inis Brandubh, chance seemed as much the enemy as the men who held her captive.

Chapter Sixteen

TIARNAN was so weak he could barely put one foot in front of the other. He'd followed the sound of Shealy's scream through the forest, running like one of the vicious wolves on the scent of prey. Behind him, Jamie, Reyes, Zac, and the new one—Mahon—struggled to keep up, but he didn't slow for them. He'd reached the three balancing rocks where Liam and Shealy should have been waiting. Frantically he searched the surrounding boulders and the nooks, calling their names, uncaring who else might hear him, knowing he wouldn't find them yet unable to cease in his search. No one answered. Nothing moved.

They were gone. The realization thundered through him. *Gone.*

Why would Liam have left this place? Why would he have disobeyed Tiarnan's orders to stay? The answer crouched in his cloudy brain, a beast he couldn't face. Only one thing would have compelled Liam to strike out on his own with Shealy and a child in tow, and that was danger.

There were no tracks on the rocks, no sand to capture a footprint, only stone stretching on rising levels. Sick with fear, with self-recriminations for having sent them off on their own, Tiarnan slowly made his way down to where the others waited.

"Spread out," he said. "Look for signs of where they went."

In the shadowed gloom, it was hard to see more than a foot ahead yet after a few moments, Reyes gave a low whistle. There, on the edge of the forest, they spotted tracks.

The four men squatted around them, noting the different prints. Mahon stood off to the side, watching with a stillness that Tiarnan had rarely seen in a man. *Mahon*. Another name he could trace back to the three men who'd told the tale of the Book of Fennore. It could not be coincidence that he was here. Nor could it be chance that men who reported to Cathán had been hunting him. "There were nine—no, eleven," Jamie said, pointing at the tracks. "And the wolf. I told you there was a wolf."

"So this is who you saw?" Zac asked what Tiarnan was thinking. "Not the ones in the clearing? Not the ones T killed?"

Jamie shook his head, casting Tiarnan another of those complicated glances that he couldn't decipher. His brain felt like a primitive beast inside his skull, roaring with fury, snarling with frustration, searching for one thing and one thing only . . . Shealy.

Jamie said, "That's my guess. And look here." He pointed to a smaller set of tracks. "This is Shealy. I'd bet on it."

That was all Tiarnan needed to hear. He charged through the trees, not heeding Jamie's order to wait. The other man's curses followed him as he forced his shaking legs to run.

Liam would not have left the rocks unless he'd been forced, and the scattered footprints told Tiarnan that he and Shealy had been led from this place. That meant led against their will. Led as prisoners.

The rage that simmered in his gut flared.

Jamie caught up and tried again to slow Tiarnan down, to talk sense to him, but finally stopped. Tiarnan was glad. The constant flow of words still hit him with jarring uncertainty. He couldn't quite grasp what Jamie said and that wild jam of confusion in his head made him want to snarl with frustration. He pushed himself harder when he didn't feel like he could take another step, leaving the others behind again as he crashed through branches and bushes, leaping over logs and racing flat out through the treachery that was the forest of Fennore. The tracks he followed were easy to see, now. They hadn't attempted to cover them, and Tiarnan's vision seemed to have sharpened until he could spot every broken twig, every disturbed leaf. They hadn't expected him to hunt them down like the vermin they were. *Fools.*

When the trail led him back to the clearing where he'd begun, where the mangled bodies lay strewn in horrific bits and pieces, he slowed, approaching with caution and stealth. His muscles quivered and he felt like his legs might give at any moment as he ducked low and peered through the branches.

Flashes of what had happened here peppered his thoughts as he stared at all the blood and gore soaking the ground, but none of them made sense. He remembered the wrath, the searing ferocity, when he realized that these men threatened Shealy and Liam. He'd always felt protective of his brother, but the molten ire that had welled up inside him—it was like nothing he'd ever experienced. It had frightened him even as it took control, dominating him, filling him with power and strength. He'd killed them all—twenty men, struck down before Jamie and the others had even reached the clearing. But he remembered only two. There'd been the first, who'd drawn his weapon and advanced without a clue about what waited for him behind Tiarnan's eyes. And then Paidric, the cowardly traitor. After that . . . only seething anger.

He wanted that cruel anger now as he followed the tracks away, gaining on them until he could see the branches moving up ahead. They stopped, and he heard voices. They were striking camp.

He inched closer, peering through the trees until his gaze finally found who he'd come for. There they were, Shealy, Ellie, and Liam. Alive.

It was all he saw. All he *could* see.

Behind him, Jamie and the others quietly crept to where he crouched.

"What's the plan, T?" Jamie whispered.

Tiarnan was beyond an answer. He simply moved forward, silent as a stalking panther. Fast and agile, though his limbs felt rubbery. He managed to evade Jamie and Reyes's reach as they tried to hold him back. Weapon clenched in each hand, he came to a stop directly behind the man who held on to Shealy's arm before anyone even noticed he'd breached their guard. The wolf startled and backed away without a sound, its tail curled between its legs and its ears flattened.

"What the—" the man he'd stalked mumbled, and in a corner of his mind, Tiarnan felt something familiar jolt him, but he cared only about Shealy and his brother.

The rest of them would die as easily as the others for daring to take what belonged to him. This man's death had arrived in the form of a furious warrior and his first clue to his fate was Tiarnan's blade, tight against his throat.

"Move and I'll cut yer head clean off," Tiarnan growled in the man's ear. His voice sounded rough and gravely, feral even to himself. The wolf crouched low in submission.

"*Tiarnan*," Shealy mouthed his name on a breath as the captured man raised his hands, shouting, "*No!*" when his soldiers spun with weapons drawn.

Liam didn't hesitate. With a chop to the throat and then a jab to the gut, he disarmed a second man who'd been guarding him. The man was twice Liam's size, but he found himself on the ground with his own sword pointed hard into his chest before he knew what had hit him. Pride swelled within Tiarnan's chest.

"Get behind me, Shealy," Tiarnan said softly, trying to gentle the growl of his voice. She did as he asked without hesitation and that savage beast that seemed to be clawing his insides roared with satisfaction.

"Yer wondering what killed all those men in that clearing," he said, making sure they all saw him now, making certain they all heard him, all felt the violence in his abraded voice. Knowing he was covered in blood from his hair to his boots, he smiled. "Well, yer looking at it."

Flashes of disbelief crossed their faces, but never truly took hold. He could only imagine what manner of monster he appeared to them. He was glad for it.

Smile stretching wider, he said, "I've no war with y' unless y' fight for Cathán. Y' can go yer way or y' can die. It matters not to me. The choice is yers."

And he hoped they'd make it quickly, because his vision now faded in and out of focus and he felt himself sway as blackness tried to creep into his consciousness and take control. Only then did it occur to him that he must have been wounded in the fight, that perhaps all the blood was his own. This rescue of his might end in his death before the deed was done. He braced himself and fought back the swirl of darkness. He would not fail Shealy, Ellie, and his brother. If it took his dying breath, he would do what he came to do.

"What if we want to fight with y', Tiarnan of the Favored Lands?" the man Tiarnan held with a blade at his throat asked.

As always, the old title caught him off guard, but now the familiar voice gave it a weight that brought a crashing pain and throbbing ache. He knew that voice and suddenly, he knew whose life dangled at the end of his sword. He listed to the side, his legs unsteady. It felt as if he'd been hit in the gut with a giant stone that had pulverized his insides.

"Who calls me this?" he demanded—or tried to demand, but his voice broke and the rough gravel of it turned the words into a guttural slur. He didn't want the answer. He knew it already.

For a moment no one spoke and then Liam, his words as cold as the icy waters of Wolf River, said, "'Tis Eamonn. The traitor."

Hearing it spoken, confirmed, shattered something deep within him. Disbelief warred with acceptance as the echo followed the collapse of his control. *Eamonn.* His brother. His enemy. He grasped the man by the hair, turning him against the point of his blade, not piercing skin, but grazing it in a manner that left no doubt that he would kill.

When he looked upon his brother's face, the wash of black that had been fading in and out became fiery red and his wrath ignited a blaze inside him that burned out what was left of his strength. He felt his knees give, realized he would fall an instant before he toppled like the ancient giant brought down by the pebble in his shoe. The hard earth rushed up at him as he fell what seemed an impossibly long way down. Shealy called his name and the sound of her fear chased him as he plummeted to the ground. Then there was nothing but the burn of betrayal chasing him into the dark.

Chapter Seventeen

WHEN Tiarnan opened his eyes to the sound of rain, night had crept to its velvety pinnacle.

He lay flat on his back in a crude tent with hide sloping from a short peaked crest to pinioned walls to the ground where it met another stretch of hide that kept the damp earth from soaking through to the furs beneath him. He didn't know where he was.

Frowning, he turned his head, wincing as even this small shift wracked his body with pain. It felt as if every joint had been ripped apart and then reseated improperly. Breathing was excruciating. Even thinking brought its own brand of torment. What happened to him? Why did it feel like some hulking terror waited just out of sight, ready to pounce as soon as he showed signs of life?

His eyes focused on Shealy next to him and something eased in his chest at the same time it tightened everywhere else. She was safe. Shealy was safe.

She slept on her side, face pillowed on her bent arm. Her lashes made lacy shadows on her cheeks, their gold tips fluttering as her eyes moved behind closed lids. What did she dream about, he wondered with a sudden and consuming desire that it be him. He wanted to touch her and found his fingertips brushing the silk of her face before he could stop himself. He knew very little about this woman, and yet in that moment, he felt like he knew everything he'd ever need to know.

Reluctantly he pulled his gaze and fingers away and looked beyond her soft form to the shadows clustered all around them.

They were alone.

He turned, seeking Liam, but didn't see his brother anywhere. Where was he? And where was Shealy's sister—where was Ellie?

Gingerly he sat up, scowling at the pain that shot through him. What had he done to himself? Was he wounded? He moved his hands over his body while a hazy image of himself drenched in blood crowded into his head. Was it a dream or a memory?

He must have washed, because his skin was clean and he smelled of soap, but he had no recollection of bathing. He realized that beneath the furs covering him warmly, he'd been stripped. Where were his clothes? His sword? His ax?

Perhaps Liam had his weapons. Likely his brother sat outside this tent keeping guard with Jamie and the others nearby. Ellie might be dozing beside him. The girl liked his brother.

But something about that scenario felt too wished for to be right. A flask sat beside him and he lifted it, drank the cool water inside, and tried to put the pieces of what had happened together.

A sound drew his attention, and he looked back at Shealy to find her eyes open and watching him. The strange silvery light of them glowed in the darkness, pulling him closer. He lay down again, turning on his side to face her.

"How do you feel?" she asked softly.

"Like I've been trampled by a herd of cattle. Where is Liam?"

"Gone."

The word froze him. "Gone . . . where?" he said, keeping his voice calm. Had something happened to his brother while Tiarnan slept like a pathetic babe?

"To find Jamie and the others. He slipped away when it started to rain. He took my sister with him." She said it calmly yet he saw the anxiety in her eyes, her worry for the little girl.

"Why?"

"We thought it better that he get her out of this camp in case . . ." She gave a small shrug. "You passed out after you found us. We didn't see Jamie, but we guessed he was close by. Liam went to find him."

His brain stuttered and sputtered as it tried to churn that information into sense. "Where are we?"

"With Eamonn. Don't you remember?"

It all came crashing down on him, wave after wave rolling over his head, stinging his eyes with the salt and brine of bitter memory, scouring his skin with the sand and grit of violence.

"Y' should have stopped Liam from leaving."

"Really? Stopped Liam?" She smiled wryly and raised her brows. "I'm sorry, have you met your brother? I'd have better luck stopping the rain."

Even as he cursed himself for not being there to keep Liam from venturing out on his own, Tiarnan felt a flash of pride at his little brother's determination. No, Shealy would not have been able to stop him if he'd made up his mind to go. But why would he leave? He had to know that Tiarnan wouldn't have wanted that.

Shealy reached out and placed a soft hand against the wall of his chest, silencing his thoughts. It seemed his heart jumped at that touch and then beat madly against it. "Tiarnan, what happened to you? You told Eamonn that you killed all those men. You looked . . . different. Bigger, fiercer. Did you? Kill them?"

Yes. He saw it all now, images jerking, falling, sliding through his mind. Horrifying, satisfying, condemning pictures that painted a scene of bloody vengeance like nothing he'd ever imagined.

"I cleaned you up," she said, and he felt the heat of her blush even if he couldn't see it. "I thought you must be wounded, there was so much blood. But after I washed it all away . . . there was nothing. A few scratches, that's it."

She was still touching him, her palm hot against his chest, her words featherlight in the dark. Their whispers created a cocoon that surrounded them as completely as the tent, sealed by the soft patter of rain against the hide. It was warm and dry where they lay, as secluded as a curtained bed.

"When I saw those men," he said, and his voice still held a deep, raspy tone, as if he'd screamed himself hoarse. "When I saw *him* with his filthy hands on y' . . ."

He stared into her eyes, unable to put words around what he'd felt. But it seemed she didn't need him to explain. The hand on his chest moved up until it rested at the base of his throat, her touch light and tentative over the pulse that surged there. It was as if she held in her palm everything that made him alive, every reason, every sadness, every hope.

With a soft groan, he circled her with his arms, pulling her yielding body tight against his, finding that nothing felt close enough. She was soft and pliant beneath the heavy tunic she wore, but it was a barrier he couldn't tolerate. The first time they'd come together it had tasted of desperation and desire born of denial. Before that, it had been years since Tiarnan had last known a woman's touch. A lifetime since he'd wanted to lose himself in the intoxicating flavor and scent of a female. But he wanted Shealy now.

He gripped the hem of the too large tunic and pulled it up and over her head in one movement, leaving her as nude as him beneath the furs. His muscles still ached, his joints still burned, but none of it compared to the throb of need that swelled and consumed him.

He'd fought to protect this woman and now here she was in his arms, making every misery worth enduring. He might not have conquered the foe, but he hadn't failed her either, and for that he was grateful in ways that couldn't be explained with mere words.

The soft rub of fur against his back contrasted with the hot burn of Shealy's flesh against his chest, and the dissimilar sensations merged into one overwhelming pleasure that whipped his arousal until it became all he was. All he'd ever be again.

Was it only last night that they'd come together in a frenzy of heat and passion? It felt like a lifetime ago. Then he hadn't been able to slow himself enough to simply *feel*, to experience the lush softness of her skin, the sweet spice of her scent, the seductive brush of her fingers against his body. He'd been too consumed with the *needing* to indulge in the wants of his senses, but now he wanted to stroke every inch of her. Her hands had slipped into his hair and he let his do the same to hers, reveling in the silken feel of each strand against his hard and callused fingers. Cupping her scalp, he looked into her eyes as his pain merged with his pleasure, making his blood run faster, hotter, wilder.

He still couldn't say just who this strange and powerful woman really was, but he knew one thing. He wanted her to belong to him and he would do whatever it took to have her. He would protect her with his life, open his own veins if it meant saving her pain.

These thoughts took hold and grew, rampant as Fennore's dark forests, single-minded as its violent predators.

He wanted her to be his. His to hold. His to love. His to protect.

She murmured his name, arching beneath him with a slight shift that wrenched a moan from somewhere deep in his throat. Her skin glowed in the darkness like a luminescent pool spilling with moonlight. Against his burnished tone, she seemed ethereal and too fragile to touch and yet so much a temptation that he knew he'd never pull away. Carefully he eased his weight and freed one hand so he could trail his fingers down the damaged shell of her ear, finding beauty even in her flaws, stirred by the shivers that traveled through her at his gentle touch.

He knew now just how vulnerable those tiny blemishes made her feel. That she bared herself for him was a gift like none he'd ever been given.

He felt the muscles in her neck flex when she swallowed, and then he followed the silky pucker of that slashing scar that might have ended her life. Thanking the fates that had spared her, he pressed his mouth to the old wound, to the hollow at the base of her throat, the fine bones of her collar, the delicately rounded shoulders. Each dip and curve of her body became a fascination he couldn't pull himself away from.

And then he was moving down, letting his hand cup the satin weight of her breast. Her nipple pebbled as he thumbed it, and he couldn't have kept his lips away from that seductive invitation if he'd been risking death in kissing it.

She made a small, sharp sound in her throat, so alluring and feminine that it hardened every muscle in his body until it felt like his skin could no longer contain him. The friction of that flesh beneath his tongue, the song of her ragged breathing expanding her lungs, the scent of her filling him up . . . it all conspired to turn him into a flame teased across a dry meadow until every parched blade and stalk went up in a blaze. Never had he felt so much the master and so desperately enslaved at the same time, and he gave himself over to it, at once challenging and obeying each warring instinct.

She pulled him away from his sweet torture and captured his mouth with her own, tasting his lips with the stroke of her tongue before urging him into a silken dance that consumed him. The kiss was more than passion, more than sensation and gratification. It demanded something very personal from him, and even as a deep-seated sense of preservation tried to shy away, he surrendered and allowed the stroke and slide to center his world.

She stole his breath, returned it with the murmur of his name. Filled him with a sense of power that had been missing for so long that he barely remembered what it had felt like. In her arms, he was strong and *capable* and though it shouldn't have been such a monumental thing, it was. It was.

He'd thought that piece of himself dead. For so long he'd blundered through fault, chasing error, always taking the wrong turn, forever making the wrong decision. But with this woman in his arms, he could do no wrong. Each silent caress of her hands, every wordless brush of her tongue against his told him this.

His reactions and responses made him dizzy and for a moment he stilled, half afraid she would vanish like a dream in the morning light. But Shealy seemed to read his mind and she took over without taking control, leaving him his strength and purging his weakness. A silken thigh slid between his as she arched against him, centering the hard length of him against the soft dip of her belly, using her whole body to caress and fondle him. He could smell the soft fragrance of her arousal, knew that he wasn't alone in any part of this dance.

He slid his fingers down the valley between her breasts to the hollow beneath her ribs, to the cradle of her hips, and then deep into the folds between her legs. She bucked against him and sank her teeth gently into his shoulder, muffling her cry of passion, imbuing him with that heady feeling of power.

The need to be quiet and not alert anyone who might be outside spiced their passion with an erotic flavor that turned his brain to putty and the hard weight of him trapped between their bodies became a painful rapture. He sank his fingers into the slick wet of her and used his thumb to tease her, feeling her body tense and tighten around him, the grip of her fingers against his back, hearing her breath in his ear. In that moment, he felt invincible, and when she sucked in a soft cry and clenched around his fingers, he wanted to shout with triumph at her release, wanted to savor the contractions that rode her. But he needed more and she gave it, pulling him down, wrapping her legs around him as he slipped between her thighs.

The moment he entered her felt like it stretched an eternity. She was so hot she burned him to the core, but like everything else, the pain was a joy that he'd thought never to experience. He buried himself deep inside her, losing his identity, freely surrendering his sense of reason and control, his awareness of anything but the slick, tight hold she had on him. If Cathán stormed the tent at that very moment, Tiarnan would die, but die a happy man.

But no, that wasn't true, because now that he'd felt this unbelievable oneness, he never wanted to be without it. He would die to protect Shealy O'Leary, but he didn't think he'd ever be able to let her go.

"Tiarnan," she breathed in his ear. "Get out of your head. Feel me."

Oh he was, he did. He felt nothing *but* Shealy. He moved, finding a rhythm that had her sucking in air, gripping his back, and lifting her hips to meet him. He heard the sawing rasp of his breath, felt his muscles bunch and quiver as she drove him to the edge where he balanced for just a moment before she caught his lips with hers, cried his name into his mouth, and then came with a great wash of wet heat that undulated around him until he plummeted into pleasure so intense that all else ceased to exist. He was blind and deaf, a creature of sensation and nothing more. His heart pounded in his chest, his blood burned beneath his skin, and his muscles went hard, then lax as slowly, like a rising sun, awareness came back.

He realized he must be crushing her and tried to pull away, but she wrapped her legs tighter and kept him where he was, where he always wanted to be, mated to her heat. At last he lifted his head from where he'd buried it in the crook of her shoulder and looked into Shealy's eyes. They were wide and silvery, shining with satisfaction that made him hard all over again.

"Wow," she whispered. "We're definitely going to have to do more of that."

He found he was smiling. *Smiling*. He'd never thought he'd feel again the bliss that settled through him as he looked into her face. Here he was—in the camp of his traitorous brother, disconnected from Liam and his responsibility, separated from his men, holding a woman who might be his enemy's greatest weapon.

And he was smiling.

Chapter Eighteen

BRANDUBH the Druid stood behind bars, his memory clouded. Uncertain how he'd come to be there . . . only minutes had passed since he'd opened his eyes and found himself stripped and shivering in the dark, dank dungeon. But it was long enough to grow cold. Long enough to feel something he hadn't felt in thousands of years.

Fear.

He paced the cell, eyeing the dead man in the corner distastefully. The rot of decay had not yet descended, perhaps because of the chill penetrating the stone walls and pouring through the barred window, thick with damp and winter. But it disturbed him, this corpse in his space, an unpleasant reminder of the mortality he'd not thought of for millennia. He shivered, naked and exposed to every gust that found its way in.

He was a man of flesh and blood—something else he hadn't been for centuries unending. Rubbing his arms, he moved to the corpse, scowling his revulsion. The man wore a faded blue garment that covered his legs and circled his pelvis. It fastened in front of his groin with hard silver discs. Brandubh had never seen the likes of such clothing. On the man's feet were bright white shoes with strange, colorful symbols on the sides and laces on the top. Brandubh removed them and the short white stockings beneath. He fumbled with the fasteners at the dead man's hips and finally managed to strip him of the queer leggings. Beneath he wore a tight white loincloth, but he left that alone.

The soft and flexible leggings fit him snugly. The stockings were warm but the shoes too tight. He couldn't get the stretchy tunic over his shoulders. Still cold, but feeling less vulnerable now with at least some covering for his nudity, he pulled the lacings from one of the shoes and tied his hair back with it. Then he paced again, trying to fit the pieces together of how he'd come to be there.

Voices carried from the dark passage leading up to the uneven steps and the dungeon door. A moment later the heavy door swung open and a woman's voice carried down.

"Get your fecking hands off me, you fecking moron."

There was a clatter and thump and the sound of a man groaning followed an instant later by the crack of a hand striking against flesh and a woman's sharp cry of pain.

"Cathán said not to kill you, didn't he?" a man shouted. "But he didn't say nothing about hurting you. Didn't say nothing about shutting that mouth of yours, did he?"

"No, he didn't say nothing about that," another male voice agreed.

Cathán. Brandubh felt his anger rise. Of course it would be Cathán.

The footsteps descended and Brandubh could see feet, then legs. Two men dressed in deerskin clothing carried a woman wearing leggings almost identical to the ones Brandubh had stripped from the corpse. The small, short tunic she wore looked as soft and stretchy as the one he'd taken from the dead man, but again, the picture on the front was different and hers molded to womanly curves. The two men hauled her up to the cell where Brandubh stood and unlocked the door.

As soon as it swung open, he charged, throwing his weight against the bars, intent on pinning one man in the opening while reaching through to impale the other with his own sword. The cell door jerked out of the smaller man's hands, but not with the force Brandubh had intended. Instead he merely jarred it, and he couldn't reach the second man to disarm him.

"Whot you do that for?" the smaller man demanded of the bigger.

"I didn't do nothing, did I?" the first snarled back.

Undeterred, the two men pushed the woman forward, and Brandubh tried again, filled with rising anger now. The woman screamed as he came toward her, reaching for the bigger of the two men who held her captive. He hit the solid mass hard enough to knock the breath out of himself, but the big man simply grunted and the other jumped in surprise, staring at the woman with accusing eyes.

"Whot you scream for?" he demanded, giving her a shove into the cell. She was looking at Brandubh over her shoulder, her eyes huge and horrified. But the two men didn't spare him a glance. Furious, he launched himself at them again. Once more, he went for the bigger of the two, thinking it best to bring that one down while his strength was fresh. He rammed the man in the back, hoping to bowl him over and get the advantage before he knew what hit him, but the other man spun, weapon drawn as he pulled the woman in front of him and put the point of his blade to the soft flesh beneath her chin. Brandubh skidded to a stop. He didn't care about the woman, but he had no desire to find himself run through by the sword.

The woman still stared at him, her mouth open, her eyes wide. But the man stared past Brandubh and scanned the cell with jerky motions.

"Whot?" asked the smaller man. "Whot's wrong?"

"Nothing. I thought I heard something."

He lowered his sword, and the woman touched her chin with a wince. Brandubh saw a smear of blood on her fingers.

"Whot you hear?"

The big man shook his head with a scowl. "Nothing. I never liked it down here. Rats, you know. Can't abide rats."

The woman made a noise in her throat and then said, "Who is he?" using her injured chin to point at Brandubh.

Her captors turned their heads, following her fixed stare. They looked right through Brandubh to the corpse that lay on the floor behind him.

"Oh," said the smaller one. "Forgot about him, didn't I?"

"Is he dead, then?" the other one said.

"Looks like. Whot you suppose he took off his clothes for?"

"How the bloody hell should I know?"

"Not him!" the woman said angrily. When the two looked at her, she pointed at Brandubh. *"Him."*

They stared at the place where Brandubh stood with furrowed brows and open mouths.

"Did you hit her on the head?" the big one asked the other.

"Nah, just clipped her smart mouth. That's all. Just a clip."

"Go over there," the big one ordered the woman. "Sit down and shut it."

When she didn't move right away, he raised a fist at her and the smaller one brandished a short, lethal-looking knife. Her lip was bleeding and her cheek chaffed and bruised, the swelling rising to puff up the skin beneath her eye. Swallowing thickly, she gave a jerky nod. Still, her eyes held defiance, even as she obeyed. She squatted with her back to the wall of the corner, wrapping her arms around her knees as she silently watched them.

Quietly, Brandubh moved around behind the smaller man and threw an elbow into his kidneys while reaching for his knife hand. He clamped his fingers around the man's wrist, squeezing tight but unable to get him to release his hold. Far from it, the man wrenched free with barely any effort.

"Something had me there!" he said, voice squeaking with panic.

"Had you? Whot're you talking about?"

The smaller man looked from his wrist to the air to his wrist again.

"Nothing. Don't like it down here."

"Rats," the other agreed. "Suppose we get his sorry arse out and quit the place," he said, looking uneasily at the dead body on the floor.

"Suppose," the other agreed.

"Still don't know why he took off his clothes. Whot you think he done with his pants?"

The bigger man looked around, perplexed. "Dunno. His socks is gone, too, aren't they?"

Now they both looked like they were attempting to solve the mysteries of the world. Brandubh tried one last time to get hold of a weapon, but if anything he'd grown weaker and now he could barely stand. The girl watched him with a wary expression as she divided her attention between the two men and Brandubh.

"Well, that's a shame," the small man said after he looked around for the *pants* and *socks* as he'd called them. "I coulda used a new pair of jeans. Mine fell apart they's so worn."

"Eh, they wouldn'ta fit your skinny shanks anyway, would they?"

Seeing his one opportunity to leave vanishing, Brandubh lurched toward the open gate. He couldn't overwhelm the guards but he could, at least, escape the prison. But when he tried to cross the threshold, an invisible force slammed him back. He skidded across the floor in shock, breath knocked out of him.

The two guards hoisted the corpse, one at either end, and waddled out of the cell. Quickly Brandubh scrambled to his feet and followed. The two men and their cargo walked through without a problem, but again Brandubh hit something hard, unseen, and impenetrable. He sprawled on the ground once more, cursing as he saw them swing the bars shut and lock them as they went. Neither man spared him so much as a glance, but the woman watched his every move. Why could she see him when the others could not?

"Where are you going?" she asked as the men moved down the dark passage. "You're just leaving me here? With the rats and the . . . and . . . why am I a prisoner? I have rights, you know. I'm Irish for the love of Jesus."

The two men seemed to find this very funny, and the smaller dropped his end of the corpse as he laughed.

"That's a good one. Irish. Ha. You're not Irish anymore, girl. You're cursed. Get that through your head, the sooner the better."

They fumbled the body up the stairs and out the door. Stunned, the woman threw herself at the bars, gripping them in white knuckles as she shook them. The clanking sound echoed down the empty passageway.

"What do you mean?" she shouted. "What do you mean I'm *cursed*?"

She let loose a stream of words, some Brandubh knew, others he only recognized by the tone and the way she hurled them at the retreating footsteps. At last she took a deep breath and rested her head against the bars before turning around.

She eyed Brandubh crossly and then demanded, "Who the feck *are you*?"

Her tone of disrespect irked him, but he answered. "I am Brandubh. I am the Black Raven."

She snorted and rolled her eyes. "Are you, now? And that's what people call you?"

They called him Druid. They called him Brandubh. They called him fearsome.

"That's what your mother named you when you were born?" the insolent girl demanded.

No, he'd been named Áedán after his father, a tribal king. His future had been set on the day of his birth—he'd been meant to rule when his father could no longer carry on. But then the Northmen had come and slaughtered everyone in their way. His mother had lived only long enough to escape with her son. Áedán had been raised by the Druids and given the new name Brandubh, which meant Black Raven.

The girl watched him with a look of unease, waiting for a response.

"Áedán," he said, and the name felt like chalk in his mouth. It rippled through him, filled with memory and loss and the taint of humanity. Long ago, another female had called him Áedán, and he'd loved her right up until the moment she'd condemned him.

The girl repeated his name. Although the guards had looked right through him, she did not.

"You can see me," he said.

"I'm fecking talking to you, aren't I?"

Torn between offense at her tone and wonder that she could see him when the other two hadn't, he asked, "Who are you?"

"Meaghan. Meaghan Ballagh."

The name meant nothing to him. "Why can you see me?"

"Feck if I know. How did you get here?"

He shook his head. "I'm not sure."

"Not sure? You just opened your eyes and here you were?" As the words left her mouth in a snide tone, her eyes widened and her face paled. She shook her head. "Don't answer that. I believe you."

"Why?"

"Because that's how I ended up here, too," she said. "Although who the feck knows where *here* is?"

"Fennore, I would guess."

"I live on the Isle of Fennore," she told him coldly. "And this is hell and gone from there."

"Exactly," he agreed, ignoring the narrow-eyed look she gave him. "Why do they want you?"

"I don't know," she said. "I was out there—God knows where—talking to the old man and then they just swarmed the place and grabbed me."

"What old man?"

"Donnell. I don't know where they took him. I think to see this Cathán they mentioned."

"Who was this old man? This Donnell?"

"Don't know. Just met him."

She began pacing the cell as he'd been doing just moments before.

"So Áedán . . . what are you, then? A ghost?"

She looked like it embarrassed her to ask such a question, but again he saw that angry defiance in her eyes, as if she dared him to laugh. She needn't have worried. There was nothing about being a ghost that he found remotely humorous. For thousands of years, he'd been a god. An entity of power. He'd been beyond flesh, beyond cold and fear.

But now he was here, reduced. Diminished by Cathán.

She was eyeing him again. He could feel the heat of her assessing gaze as it moved from his hair to his face, down his bare chest to the *pants* that covered his hips and legs. His body was much as he'd remembered it, hard and lean. He'd been a person of influence in his remembered life. He'd carved the pillars of their temple with his own two hands, hammering from stone the images he saw in his mind, in his heart. He flexed his arms, recalling how it felt to strike stone with a mallet, to hone it down in the hot sun.

And then had come Elan, the White Fennore, the woman who'd stolen his heart and soul and then condemned him to a life interred in the Book he'd created for her. For more than a thousand years he'd raged, punished, and victimized all that came into contact with him. For a thousand more, he'd retreated, hiding away, mimicking death. And then he'd emerged, remembering what she'd said before she condemned him. She'd banished him *like a vile creature*," to suffer for the greed of men, to be used and abused. She'd told him that if he survived, she would see him again. It was that promise that lured him from retreat. He would see her again and when he did, he would pull her into his purgatory and trap her as she had trapped him.

He'd begun his pilgrimage again, searching for those who could give him strength. Seeking those he could use. And he'd found Cathán MacGrath, pathetic, needy, but powerful. Powerful in ways he didn't know.

"Yo, Áedán," Meaghan said with an exasperated glance.

"You use my name freely," he said coldly.

"Would you rather I called you Black Raven?" she asked with raised brows.

He glared, to show his dislike of the ridicule in her tone, but ignored her question.

"What do you know of Cathán MacGrath?" he demanded instead.

"He was married to my mother, once upon a time," she said matter-of-factly, stunning Brandubh into silence. And then, as if it had just occurred to her. "Cathán—that's who they've brought me to see? Bollocks. He can't be the same person, can he?"

"Cathán is your father?"

"Feck no. He disappeared and my mum remarried." She paused and said, "You don't think that's who they're talking about? Those men, when they mentioned Cathán?"

"It is," he said.

"But he disappeared before I was born."

"Time has no significance in the Book of Fennore."

"*In* the Book of Fennore?" she repeated incredulously. "And what does that mean?"

"Are you a twin?"

"No. Why? What does that have to do with anything?"

Disappointed, he didn't answer.

"My sister—half sister and brother, they're twins."

"Who?"

"Danni and Ror—"

"Ruairi," he snarled. "Yes, of course. Who else would it be?"

She glared at him now. "You're a bit nutters, aren't you, Áedán?"

He wasn't certain what *nutters* meant, but he could guess and probably he was more than a bit. Now he looked at Meaghan again, eyeing her from head to toe. If she was related to Ruairi and his sister, then perhaps she wasn't without use.

"Why are you looking at me like that?" she asked warily.

He stepped closer. The men had barely flinched when he'd thrown all his weight at them. But this woman who could see him . . . He reached out and took her face between his hands.

"What are you doing?" she demanded, trying to slap him away. "Let go of me."

She shoved at his chest and squirmed as she fought to break free. He held her, not letting her loose. She scratched his face and kicked out with her strange shoes, startling him into releasing her. As soon as he dropped his hands, she slammed her knee into his groin and when he bent over with breathless pain, she brought it up again and whammed it into his nose. He fell, clutching his groin, feeling blood spill over his face and chest.

"Keep your hands to yourself, you fecking . . . fecking *ghost*."

She went back to her corner and slid down the wall, curling into a tight ball. He thought he heard her crying, but he was in too much pain to care. He didn't know if she was a powerful witch or just a mean woman. But he would use her, no matter what. He would drain her of her life, her power, her very essence. And then he would move on to Cathán.

Just as soon as he could stand.

Chapter Nineteen

THE rain had stopped when Tiarnan woke again, his body curled around Shealy's, her spine pressed to his chest, his arms holding her tight even in sleep. He looked around in the pitch-black that came before dawn. Beside them, Ellie sat on their furs, blinking owlishly and shivering. He stared at her for one confused moment, as his brain woke up. If Ellie was here, Liam must have returned. He raised himself and glanced around the dark tent, but didn't see his brother.

Had he smuggled Ellie back into camp? Returned her to the tent? Obviously, yes. But why? The only reason he could think of was to leave a sign. Liam had found Jamie and he wanted Tiarnan to know. He'd risked much, if this was what he'd done, and yet Tiarnan couldn't help but admire the sheer genius of it. Liam was no longer a helpless boy and as hard as it was to accept, accept it he must.

Ellie stared at him and he smiled, finding the gesture came easily now, as if Shealy had unlocked some great door within him that had kept his smile imprisoned.

Ellie didn't smile back, but she scooted a little closer, looking lost and forlorn. He reached for her, tugging her arm and settling her down in front of Shealy. He pulled the furs up and covered her chilled little body. Ellie gave a contented sigh when he put his arm around them both and she fell asleep in moments. Tiarnan lay awake, though, thinking of all that had happened since he'd first seen Shealy through the shredded darkness. He felt like a different man now—a new man. A man who might offer this woman a future. If only they could find her father and escape this hell.

After a while, the sun began to rise, casting a bright splinter of light across the hide tent, and in his arms Shealy stirred, waking Ellie, too. Together the two females pushed to a sit and turned to face him.

"How—where did Ellie . . ." Shealy let the question trail away as she drew the same conclusions Tiarnan had.

"He must have found the others and wanted us to know."

Shealy nodded, pulling furs up over her chest. When she looked at him, he braced himself. Last night she hadn't made him breach her barriers. She'd lowered them. She'd given herself to him in a way that still made his heart ache and his blood heat. Now she stared back. She still looked wary. She still looked defiant. But withdrawn . . . no, she didn't even try for that. He smiled—again he smiled, some wondering part of his brain acknowledged— and brushed a stray lock of hair behind her ear. For a moment he indulged himself in the fantasy that Shealy was really his woman, Ellie their child, and that the morning would bring a day of meals spent together and moments shared.

The utter foolishness of it wiped the smile from his face. It was easy to deceive himself inside this tent, but outside waited Eamonn.

Eamonn . . . The memory of the day his brother had conspired against him came back with a jolt that caused him physical pain. Eamonn was *here*, here on Inis Brandubh. He'd made Shealy and

Liam his prisoners. What else had he done? How long had she been at his mercy?

"Did he hurt y', Shealy?" Tiarnan asked, suddenly horrified that he hadn't asked before.

She didn't ask who. Instead she gazed solemnly back. "No. He didn't hurt us."

"Does he think to make us hostages?"

"I don't know." She scooted closer, until they were almost touching. Ellie crawled into her lap, and lovingly Shealy stroked the child's head. "His men wanted to kill you, Tiarnan," she said softly, as if they might be lurking outside the tent, listening. For all he knew they were . . . had been all night. "But Eamonn stopped them. He made them bring you here. There are guards standing watch, but they didn't tie us up and that's what the men wanted."

"Do they know Liam is gone?"

She shook her head. "No. Once they put us in here, they didn't come back. I watched when Liam slipped away. They were guarding us, but they didn't see him. You'd have been proud of him. He moved like a shadow."

He was proud, but he wished Liam hadn't risked so much.

"You could have been killed bursting out of the woods like you did when you found us. Why did you do it, Tiarnan?"

He looked at her worried eyes, remembering those moments before he'd taken Eamonn by the throat. He'd had no concern for himself or his own safety. He'd only thought of Shealy and Liam and poor little Ellie. He lifted a hand, noting that the aches and pains from last night still lingered, but none were as severe as they'd been earlier. It was as if joining with Shealy had eased whatever ailed him. Gently she took his hand in hers and that small touch felt like an anchor, an anchor he'd been desperate to have for so many years.

He swallowed hard and said, "Jamie and Reyes tried to hold me back, but I saw y' and . . ."

He felt his face grow hot and wanted to look away, but she'd trapped him with her storm-cloud eyes and wouldn't allow it. Her soft fingers stroked the split skin over his knuckles, her touch so gentle it soothed.

"I couldn't stand to see his hands on y', Shealy," he confessed at last, blushing more at his own weakness.

She stared at him with her mouth slightly open and then she grinned.

"It's not funny," he said.

But her expression was so surprised and pleased that he found himself smiling back at her. With a shake of his head, he leaned in and pressed his lips to hers. The kiss was hard, possessive, and binding. He knew it even if she did not.

When he pulled away, she lowered her lashes, hiding whatever she might be feeling. A part of him was glad, but another part wanted to demand she raise her eyes and show him all of her secrets.

"We should dress and see what waits for us outside," he said softly. "If Eamonn plans to kill me, I'd just as soon face him now."

She gave a jerky nod. "Your pack is in the corner. I hope you brought a change of clothes because your others were . . . well you won't want to wear them again until they've been washed and even then . . ."

She trailed off and he remembered the blood. He'd been covered in it.

"My sword and ax?"

"Eamonn took them."

That made his jaw tighten with anger, though he'd already assumed as much.

Shealy moved Ellie from her lap and still holding the fur, reached out to snag his pack, giving Tiarnan a glimpse of the long line of her spine and the round softness of her hips before she settled down again. Turning her back to him, she told Ellie to cover her eyes so they could both pull on their tunics. He pressed a kiss to the sensitive skin of her shoulder before she clothed it and was rewarded with a small shiver and deep breath that pulled something tight inside him. He was rock hard as he eased his trews up over his hips, glad his tunic hung low. When he glanced up, he caught Shealy watching him, her eyes shining and bottomless. Her cheeks pinked and she tilted her head, hiding the scars on her left side as she shoved her feet into a pair of Liam's old boots. When she looked up again, he squatted beside her and tucked her hair back once more. She gave him that defiant look he'd come to expect, and yet another smile curved his lips as he pressed them to her ear.

"Y' are beautiful. Every bit of y'," he whispered.

She didn't flip her hair out again when he moved away, and that pleased him more than it should have.

Shealy talked to her wee sister as she straightened her clothing and finger-combed her hair into a braid. She'd coaxed a smile from the child before she'd finished, and Tiarnan's heart clenched as he watched them. Thoughts of Eamonn stoked his fear that he would not be able to protect these two females that had become the center of his world.

"Give me a hug," she told Ellie, and the child threw her arms around Shealy's neck. "I love you, Ellie. I'm so glad I found you."

Once Tiarnan had felt that much love for his sister and each of his brothers, thought nothing could ever test that emotion. He still loved them all, but Eamonn had broken his heart. To be betrayed by a brother he would have died for was a blow that no words could ever describe.

He'd been enraged when he'd first seen Eamonn, but now he felt something closer to resignation. The time had come to confront him. When at last Shealy stood at his side holding Ellie's hand, he was almost ready to face his traitor brother.

They stepped from the tent into the harsh dawning light, startling the man who'd dozed off nearby—close enough to see them if they emerged but not so close, he noted with relief, to have heard them. Tiarnan scanned the crude camp, spotting a second and third guard positioned around them. A small fire with a spit over it burned in the center of a few scattered tents that, like theirs, had been constructed of hide and rope strung between trees. He counted nine men in the group. There might be more in the tents, but they weren't big enough to hold many. The men he could see stared balefully back at him, weapons ready.

Eamonn stood beside the fire, watching Tiarnan warily. He should. If it hadn't been for Shealy and Ellie, he might well have ripped his brother in two with his bare hands. Eamonn, it seemed, knew it. He hung his head in something that looked surprisingly like defeat before taking a deep breath and squaring his shoulders. With the manner of a man going to his execution, Eamonn crossed the camp and came to a stop in front of him. The wolf followed placidly but halted before he reached Tiarnan. With a low growl, it sat and watched with shifting eyes. Eamonn's men all surveyed the happenings with an alertness that told Tiarnan that they knew which way the wind blew for Tiarnan, knew he hated his brother.

Eamonn had aged since Tiarnan had last seen him. His face was drawn, thinner than it had been. Gone was the boyish roundness and in its place was a hardened and scarred man. The black chains around his throat and wrists were new as well. They gave Eamonn a sinister look that went with the black heart that Tiarnan had never noticed until the day Eamonn turned on him and left his own heart in shreds. Beside him, Shealy watched uncomfortably as the two men stared at one another. There'd been a time when another woman had stood between them, and Tiarnan had chosen to protect his brother over her. He would not make that mistake again.

Eamonn motioned to one of his men, who brought him a large

basin filled with water. Silently he handed it to Eamonn, gave Tiarnan a dark look, and then retreated.

"Ye'll want to wash before y' eat," Eamonn said, setting the basin on the ground in front of their tent in a gesture that screamed servitude and confounded Tiarnan.

"I'd rather starve then eat yer food," Tiarnan shot back, his voice cold and calm. It didn't match the churn of rage and pain inside him.

"I know that," Eamonn said softly, and there was an edge of regret to his voice that almost penetrated the haze of Tiarnan's anger. *Almost.*

"Do y' plan to keep me prisoner, Eamonn? Because I'll tell y' now it'll be the last plan y' make."

"Yer not my prisoner. Y' can go anytime."

Tiarnan laughed harshly. "Do they know that?" he asked, gesturing with his chin at the guards set around the camp.

"No one will stop y'," Eamonn said, before turning and walking back to his men, wolf at his heels.

With disbelief, Tiarnan saw the others lowering their weapons. Did he mean it, then? Why would he capture them only to set them free?

Bewildered, Tiarnan stayed where he was, trying to sort out just what this meant. Something roasting on a spit nearby tantalized Tiarnan, distracting him. He couldn't remember when last he'd eaten, and his stomach growled, protesting his decision to forgo what had been offered. He felt hollowed out and depleted of every ounce of strength. He glanced back at Shealy and the child, knowing they hadn't eaten either, yet neither complained.

Shealy moved to the basin Eamonn had left and dipped her hands in it. There was a cloth for washing and a hunk of crude soap that smelled strongly of tallow. She rubbed the gritty clump into the cloth, washed her face and hands then Ellie's before cautiously looking at Tiarnan. Biting back a groan, he followed her actions and scrubbed the crusted blood from his nails where it lingered as a reminder of the violence he'd inflicted yesterday. Once his hands and face were clean, he couldn't seem to stop. He pulled his tunic off and washed his arms and chest. Shealy had already cleaned away the blood, but the memory of it made him want to scour his skin from his body. Draped over a rope were the clothes he'd worn yesterday. The rain had rinsed much of the blood away, but still it crusted the tunic, ground into the creases of his trews. The puddles below were thick with it.

He already felt defenseless, missing his weapons and aching like an old man, but the cold water had revived him and he felt better for it. Should he test them now? Demand his weapons and march away from this camp? But if Liam had gone for help, he would return. What if they attacked him? What if Tiarnan couldn't find him first?

While he debated the next step he should take, a dark-skinned man brought over a platter of roasted meat and hard, coarse bread. He glanced at Tiarnan and then away as he handed it to Shealy.

"Thank you," Shealy said softly, taking it from him.

He gave a short bow and took a step back.

"What is your name?" she asked, surprising them all.

Why did she want to know his name? What did it matter what this filth called himself?

He gave her a startled glance then looked warily at Tiarnan. "I am called Nanda," he answered.

"Thank you, Nanda."

Nanda gave her a quick nod, then a formal bow. He took the bowl of water and returned to Eamonn's side. The two men spoke for a moment, and then Eamonn stared at his brother once more. Deliberately Tiarnan turned his back.

He said nothing as Shealy and Ellie sat down on a fallen log with the platter of food in front of them. Ellie looked from the food to Tiarnan and back again several times. It took her about a half a second to work out that Tiarnan had refused to eat. Ellie sat back and crossed her arms, shunning the offering as well. Tiarnan felt a reluctant grin on his face. She was a smart one, this child. She knew to wait for the adults to taste something and deem it safe before she would try it.

"Tiarnan," Shealy said, "may I have a word, please?"

Startled by the exasperated tone, he nodded and stood, moving a few steps away. Shealy followed and Ellie watched with barely suppressed trepidation.

"I understand that you have *issues* with Eamonn," she began.

"I've more than issues," he interrupted.

"But if you refuse to eat, so will Ellie. What good will anyone be if they're starved half to death and too weak to stand? Look at her, Tiarnan. She's just a little girl. She needs to eat."

He grimaced, looking back at the little girl who sat with a mutinous expression, arms crossed over her small chest, glaring at the platter of food.

"I'm not hungry."

"Oh," Shealy said. "Of course. I should have known. You probably don't need food, big strong warrior that you are. I suppose you'll just want to wait until you faint again before you decide it's time to eat."

Tiarnan's mouth fell open. "I did *not* faint."

She just raised her brows and turned away. "Whatever," she muttered as she went.

His face grew hot with humiliation. "I was wounded," he insisted.

"Uh, no. You weren't."

The certainty in her voice shocked him.

"I checked you out, Tiarnan. I thought you must be bleeding to death when you collapsed. But you barely have a scratch on your body."

He tried to think of a response to that, but he'd just washed and knew it was true. A few bruises covered his ribs, but there were no wounds on him.

"I don't know what happened to you," Shealy went on. "But I do know you're weak right now."

He stiffened his spine and glared at her. "I am not weak."

With a roll of her eyes, she said, "Okay, *weakened*. Is that easier on the ego?"

"I didn't notice y' complaining about my weakness last night," he said.

Her face turned pink but her gaze remained steady. "Yes, you were Superman last night. I'll not deny it. But unless you want to destroy your hero status in my eyes, you'd better eat something. Please. For Ellie's sake."

She was right, and he knew it just as he knew it was childish to refuse food when who knew when the next meal would come. But Shealy didn't understand what it meant to him to eat food that Eamonn served.

Silently she waited, and with a sigh, he lifted a piece of bread and shoved it in his mouth before he could talk himself out of it. "Eat," he barked at the little girl.

The child moved closer and began cramming food in her mouth like it might be snatched away the next second.

"Easy sweetheart," Shealy said, sitting on the other side of the child. "You're going to choke."

Ellie slowed down when she saw Shealy take a bite and began to eat like a human instead of a ravenous wolf cub. Tiarnan's anger drained as he chewed. Shealy was right. For all he knew, Eamonn meant to kill them soon and Tiarnan would need all the strength he could muster to protect them.

But even as he thought it, he knew that wasn't Eamonn's intention. He didn't know what Eamonn had in mind, but if it had been to murder them, he'd had ample opportunity to do it already.

A chilling thought occurred to him then. Could he know about Shealy's father?

"What did y' tell him?" he asked quietly as they ate.

"Tell him? Who? Eamonn?"

Tiarnan nodded.

"Nothing—well, last night after you collapsed—"

Tiarnan made a sound in his throat at that but bit back the denial. He *had* collapsed, as much as he wished he hadn't.

Shealy went on, "I told Eamonn that we were searching for my father and that Cathán might be holding him prisoner."

"Did he ask why?"

"Of course not. Why wouldn't I search—"

"No, Shealy. Did he ask why Cathán wanted yer father?"

"Oh. Yes. I told him I didn't know."

The fist in Tiarnan's stomach eased a bit. "Did he believe y'?"

"I think so."

Once the food was gone, the three of them better for having shared it, Eamonn approached once more. Tiarnan rose to face him, eyeing him suspiciously, but Eamonn only thrust out Tiarnan's sword and ax, both still anchored in his belt.

Cautiously, Tiarnan took them.

"When Liam awakes and breaks his fast, y' can go."

"Liam isn't here," Tiarnan said with satisfaction.

Eamonn glowered at him. "What do y' mean, not here? I brought him here myself last night."

"Well yer guard is not so good, is it then, because he left."

"Why?"

"Because he wanted nothing to do with his traitor brother I suppose."

Eamonn blanched but spoke boldly, as if the words hadn't cut him deeply. "Y' always did let him behave like a wild boy."

"No more than y' did, as I recall. Why are y' letting us go?"

"I will not be yer jailer."

"That's exactly what y' were trying to be when y' sided with Cathán," Tiarnan said coldly. "Or have y' now turned on him as well?"

"I was wrong about Cathán," he confessed in a low, shamed voice. "I believed his lies."

"Why?" Tiarnan asked before he could stop himself. And in that one word was a wealth of other questions. Why had he chosen Cathán over his own flesh and blood? Why had he turned on his people? Why had he taken the last thing they had, their unity, their brotherhood? *Why?*

Eamonn shook his head, perhaps hearing all of those other questions. Perhaps simply refusing to answer.

"I will not rest until Cathán is dead," he said. "Whether y' call that another betrayal or justice, it matters not."

Tiarnan looked at the men in the camp. The faces that turned to him held a desperate edge. Eamonn was their leader, and yet Tiarnan could see that these men didn't fight *for* him. It was there in their hollow eyes, in the twitchy glances that they cast between them. Tiarnan could tell from the way they watched his brother with a bleak mixture of contempt and fear. Perhaps Eamonn had won some fight for dominance, but he did not have their loyalty. They would turn on him without compunction and they didn't bother to hide it.

"Y' still fight alone, Tiarnan?" Eamonn asked, distracting him.

"Alone?"

"It's how it always was. Y' made the decisions. Y' chose our fate. Always alone."

His accusing tone bewildered Tiarnan. "'Twas my place to do that."

"Not just yer place. All of ours. But y' made yer bloody pacts without asking one of us what we thought."

As much as he hated to admit it, Eamonn was right. He'd never consulted anyone before he chose the path they would take. The arrogance in such a thing astounded him now, but at the time it had seemed the only way, his only option.

Perhaps, though, Eamonn had seen his actions in the same tainted light that Tiarnan saw Eamonn's treachery. Eamonn had made decisions of his own, based on what *he* thought was right.

"Yes, I made the wrong choices. But y' betrayed us all, Eamonn."

"I tried to save what was left of us," Eamonn answered with an angry step forward. "Y' could no longer see what was coming. Y' could only see what y'd lost already, what lay in ruins behind y'."

That it was true only served to make Tiarnan angrier. "And what about y', Eamonn? Were yer choices so much better? Y' fight alone as well, don't y'? Tell me it's not true."

Eamonn hung his head. "No, my decisions were no better. My actions were those of a coward. I've no pride in the role I played. I am cursed and disgraced, and I have no one but myself to blame. Go, Tiarnan. May y' find a way to live with yer choices as I will never find the way to live with what I have done."

Tiarnan's throat was tight as he stared into his brother's haunted eyes. After all that had happened, after Eamonn had turned on him and taken arms with the enemy, he still responded to the pain he saw in his eyes. He still wanted to banish the shadows. To make the world right. None of them had ever known a real life or lived in a time of peace, devoid of pain and loss and suffering.

He might have reached out then. He might have taken his brother's hand in farewell if not forgiveness, but a call of warning split the chilled morning air and suddenly the weapons flew from their sheaths and pointed at a lone figure that appeared.

Looking as if he hadn't a care in the world, Liam strolled into camp.

Behind him came Jamie and Reyes, each holding a man that

Tiarnan did not recognize by a twisted arm and pointed knife. Following them was another who had his arm wrapped around Zac's waist, Zac's arm around his shoulders. Tiarnan stared, knowing he'd seen the man before.

He wore a strange collar and carried a satchel slung over his neck.

Mahon.

Zac leaned heavily on him as he clutched at a wound in his gut that spilled blood between his fingers. His head lolled and his skin was pasty.

"Let them pass," Tiarnan barked as Eamonn's men moved to block them. Eamonn turned, giving him an angry look.

"Y' are not my prisoner, but I say who enters this place."

Tiarnan glanced over Eamonn's head to the guards at the perimeter of camp. "Let them through."

The guards hesitated for a moment, and then the one named Nanda said, "It's James and Cooley with them. Let them in."

Eamonn's face reddened but he turned back as the small group staggered forward. Tiarnan had never been so happy to see someone as he was to see Liam, cocky and unharmed, and Jamie, steady and indomitable as he marched into the camp with his prisoner in his grasp. Beside him, Reyes did the same.

"Y' can let him go, Reyes," Tiarnan said, nodding at the prisoners. "These men are Cathán's enemies. Not ours."

Jamie raised his brow in question, but at Tiarnan's nod, Reyes gave his prisoner a push and the man scrambled away.

"What happened to Zac?" Tiarnan asked, looking at the wounded man.

"He killed Farmsworth, that's what happened," the man Reyes had just let loose shouted.

"He gave as good as he got," Jamie said. "And he attacked first."

Eamonn looked at his man. "Is that the truth?"

The "*yes*" came reluctantly. Tiarnan looked at the men standing around the camp, still armed and ready. "We can fight y' here and now, or y' can lower yer weapons. Y've seen what I can do. Y' don't want to test these men either."

"Lower yer weapons," Eamonn said a fraction too late. The men had already listened to Tiarnan.

Jamie stepped forward. "You good, T?"

Tiarnan nodded, nearly grinning. "I'm good."

"Shealy?" Jamie asked.

"Thank you, Jamie," Shealy said from behind Tiarnan. "We're fine. All of us. But Zac should get some help."

The man called Nanda stepped forward. "Bring him to the fire," he said.

For a moment, distrustful glances moved between the two groups of men, and then Mahon stepped forward and Zac limped along beside him. As soon as they passed, Liam approached, cupped the back of Tiarnan's neck, and pulled him into an embrace. Even as he held his brother, Tiarnan thought that somehow the two of them had changed places. Liam had been worried about Tiarnan's safety and though Tiarnan had been concerned, he realized with a start that he hadn't doubted for a moment that his brother would return.

"Good to see y' looking so fit, brother," Liam teased. "Our Shealy took care of y', did she?"

Our Shealy. When had she become that? And why were Liam's eyes sparkling with laughter, as if he knew just how completely Shealy had *taken care* of his brother? Tiarnan grinned back as he stepped away, seeing the knowing smiles on some of the faces surrounding him. Others had expressions of hunger—not only for the physical relationship he had with Shealy, but for the brotherhood that Tiarnan shared with Liam. They were family, blood. Nothing could take that away from them.

Eamonn gazed at them with the same pained yearning, and

Tiarnan wanted more than anything to pull him into their circle. Right and wrong were not so black-and-white as he'd thought just days ago. Only the cold rage in Liam's eyes when he glanced at Eamonn kept Tiarnan from acting on the impulse.

Liam scooped Ellie out of Shealy's arms, saying, "How's my favorite girl?" as he made gobble noises at her throat. Ellie wrapped her arms tightly around him and pressed her cheek against his.

Watching the two of them, Tiarnan almost missed Shealy stepping forward. She'd gotten in front of him before he realized it, placing herself in danger if anyone decided to attack. He reached out to stop her, but she stared beyond him to Mahon, her expression so shocked that it made Tiarnan pause, cutting his eyes between the man and Shealy.

"Father Mahon?" she said, her voice shaking, her brow furrowed with confusion. "What are you doing here?"

The man called Mahon let loose a strange, strangled laugh and said, "Now isn't that a question. Evidently, you brought me, Shealy."

Chapter Twenty

SHEALY shook off Tiarnan's restraining hold and stepped closer to Father Mahon, still not quite believing it was really him.

Father Mahon.

A man so attractive that his pledge to God seemed like a gauntlet thrown down to challenge every female on the planet. He'd come to her dad's aid after the accident, offering prayer and support in those long weeks when Donnell had mourned Shealy's mother and Shealy had still balanced between life and death. When she'd finally stabilized, he'd visited her often, praying and reading from the Bible until she'd finally told him to go find someone else to bother. Her faith had been shattered by her mother's death. Later, her dad told her Father Mahon had been training to be a priest but had left the church without taking his vows, that he'd gone away because he'd questioned his faith. She'd always regretted that she'd been so cold and rude.

Donnell had taken Shealy and moved to Arizona without a backward glance after that, and Shealy had forgotten about Father Mahon.

Now as she stared at him, she realized he was the man she'd seen standing in her dad's study when she'd gone from the river banks of Inis Brandubh to the real world and back. . . .

Tall, with golden brown hair, he was dressed in a plain white button-down shirt and the same black trousers he'd been wearing then. Both were torn and dirty, but a clergy collar circled his neck. Had he reconnected with his faith, then? Had he gone on to take his vows?

"What are you doing here, Father Mahon?" she asked again, and it seemed that her question called back a million memories. The pain she'd thought unending after the accident. The way Donnell and Father Mahon would go off into his den together and close the door, locking her out. Not that she'd wanted to pray with them, but some part of her knew that more than God had been discussed in that sanctuary, and with equal power she'd wanted to know and feared the knowledge that they shared, the realizations they unearthed. . . .

Her head began to swim and she felt that same weightless sensation of sinking into a thick layer of gel that she'd felt in the parking lot and then again beside the river with Ellie after the attack of the three-headed creatures. Now it seemed to rise up from the ground, that thickness. She felt it immobilize her, casting her in a yielding shell from which she could not break free. She had a moment to reach out, and Tiarnan gripped her hand in his, staring at her with confusion and alarm. At the same time, Father Mahon rushed forward and took her other hand, concern in his eyes. Caught between the two, she could do nothing but hold on.

The strange and terrifying inertia spread so quickly that they were consumed by it in an instant, trapping both men in its foggy sphere with her. The world went white and spinning, rushing by in a soft misty blur, and then suddenly there was nothing but the heat of their bodies beside her and the whirling white of oblivion.

The scent of ocean, cold and foaming, came to her first, and she immediately thought she must be back on the cliffs, but the roaring sound of the tide didn't come with the tar and brine smell of the sea. Now she sensed a dankness to the odor, a caged and decaying layer that told her she might be near the water, but not close enough to feel the spray, not outdoors.

She opened her eyes and saw Tiarnan beside her doing the same, his expression stunned. On her left, Father Mahon let out a small gasp.

"Where are we?" Father Mahon asked.

"I don't know," Tiarnan and Shealy said at the same time.

"It was like before, though," Tiarnan said. "Did yer dad do it again? Did he bring us . . ."

Shealy shook her head. *No.* It wasn't her dad, not this time. But she didn't say it aloud.

It seemed they were in a tunnel made of gray, moldy stones that snaked back into dark shadows. The air felt old and drafty. Behind them, a rough stairway led to a door with a heavy lock on it. A barred window stared out from its center.

Silently Tiarnan climbed the stairs and tested it. The door would not budge and the lock was secure. He peered through the window but shook his head after a moment and came back to where Shealy and Father Mahon waited.

"Looks the same on the other side. Just a long hallway leading into the dark."

"It's a dungeon," Father Mahon said.

"Are we still on Inis Brandubh?" she asked.

"I cannot say, lass. I've never seen a place with stone walls or bars here. But there is only one person I can think of who'd have a dungeon."

"And who is that?" Father Mahon asked.

"Cathán," he said.

"By God," Father Mahon muttered. "To think I doubted him."

That caught Shealy's attention. "Doubted who?"

"Donnell. He told me. He showed me the prophecy, but I didn't believe him. I scoffed at his tales."

She wanted to ask more, but their precarious position in this unknown point of the mysterious dungeon discouraged them from talking. The echo of their lowered voices seemed unnaturally loud. They had no idea who might lurk outside that locked door or beyond the corridor on the other side.

By silent consent, they began to walk down the only avenue they could. After a moment, the stone wall on their right opened up and they could see cells, small and crude, with bolts hammered into the walls and chains hanging from them. The floor had bits of straw and debris, and there were windows high up with bars over them. Shealy suspected they looked out at ground level, which meant when it rained, the water would pour in. Stains beneath the barred windows seemed to confirm that guess.

The first cell was empty and so was the second, but as the three of them approached the last cell they saw something move. Tiarnan put a hand out, holding Shealy back as he inched up and peered in. Someone gave a small yelp of surprise, and instantly Shealy knew who that voice belonged to.

"Daddy!" she cried and rushed forward.

Donnell O'Leary looked small and weak, trapped behind the bars. His clothes were torn and dirty and he had a black eye. Until that moment, she hadn't realized that a part of her feared she'd never see him again, or, like her mother, she'd find him too late. Now relief flooded her, making her legs weak. She ran to her dad like she had when she was a little girl with a scrape that needed kissing.

She threw her arms around him through the bars just as, from behind her, Father Mahon exclaimed, "Lord in heaven, Donnell. What happened to you?"

"Kyle?" Donnell said, staring at the priest in shock. "Is that really you, Kyle? I thought I'd seen you earlier, captured, but then I convinced myself I was wrong, that you couldn't really be here. Even now I can't believe it. You haven't changed. Not a bit."

Father Mahon glanced at Shealy, his expression mirroring the confusion on her father's face. "It was only yesterday that I saw you last. In your study," he said, but in each word Shealy heard doubt.

Father Mahon stared at Donnell like he was a ghost, and the way her dad gazed back wasn't much different. She remembered when she'd seen them together yesterday—when she and Ellie had somehow gone through a door into the past. Her dad had been young and hale, hardly gray at all. Now he looked withered and aged beyond his years. But Father Mahon still appeared as attractive and strong as ever. In fact, he looked *exactly* the same. He even had the same book bag slung over his shoulder.

"It was longer than yesterday, Kyle," her dad said softly. "It's been so long I thought never to see you again."

"What do you mean?" Father Mahon asked.

"Seven years have passed."

Father Mahon laughed, but the sound had a hollow ring and the eyes that shifted between Shealy and her dad held the glitter of panic. He couldn't believe what he saw—the changes that time had wrought on both Shealy and Donnell—and yet he couldn't deny it when the two of them stood solidly before him, each of them seven years older.

"Did you hit your head?" he insisted. "It's only been a day or two at the most. Though I will confess, it's been hard to keep track of those since I came."

No one joined him in the laughter and when Donnell only gazed at him with tired and troubled eyes, Father Mahon took a deep breath and began shaking his head. "It couldn't be . . ."

"It is, Kyle. Think about it. Look at me."

It was the last that did the trick.

Staring at Donnell, Father Mahon shook his head. "Jesus God, you're serious, aren't you? Seven years? *Seven years?* I don't understand it?"

"What are y' talking about?" Tiarnan demanded with a scowl. "What happened seven years ago?"

Father Mahon looked at Tiarnan and said, "I was visiting Donnell. I'd come to tell him that I'd decided to leave the church. I thought it only yesterday. . . ." He trailed off, shaking his head. "I should have realized it when I saw you, Shealy. You were all grown up. Healed . . . Like you are now."

Disconcerted, Donnell moved away, pacing between the cell walls.

Shealy said, as if to herself. "You went away and then we moved to the States. When I asked after you, Dad told me you'd left—us, the priesthood. I thought it was because of the things I said to you, about God."

"Not that you wouldn't tempt a saint, Shealy O'Leary, but my questioning my faith had nothing to do with you. It got so that all I did was question it. And it's Kyle now. He was right about that—I'm not a priest. I never will be. That's why I was at your house yesterday. . . ." He paused, looking anxious. "Whenever it was. Why I'm still dressed this way. I'd come straight from talking to the Bishop to tell Donnell that I'd done what he asked. I'd left the church."

Shealy's jaw dropped. "You asked him to leave, Daddy? Why? You love God. You love the church."

Donnell shook his head, looking guilt ridden at what Father—Kyle—had revealed.

"He only gave me the push I needed, Shealy. I wasn't made for the priesthood."

Her dad reached for her through the bars, distracting her from the thoughts gathering in her head. There was something here, something big that skimmed the surface of her consciousness without delving deep enough for her to examine. Something about Fath—*Kyle* being here now. About yesterday.

Still in shock, Shealy let her dad pull her closer. "Come here, sweetheart. Let me look at you. I've been so worried. Are you all right? Are you harmed? Did *he* hurt you?"

He directed the last at Tiarnan, who stiffened in surprise at the rancor in Donnell's voice. Confused, Tiarnan stepped forward as if to present himself. He looked as nervous as any suitor meeting a father for the first time, and Shealy might have laughed about it under different circumstances. But this was no parlor and Tiarnan wouldn't be taking her out to dinner afterwards.

Awkwardly, Shealy performed the introductions. Tiarnan reached out his hand to her father. Reluctantly, Donnell shook it.

"And to answer your question, Daddy, Tiarnan didn't hurt me. He'd never hurt me. He saved my life. More than once."

Her father narrowed his eyes at her like he used to do when she was a child and he'd caught her lying.

"I mean it. He's been helping find you so we can go home."

"Is that what he told you?"

Frowning, she looked between her father and Tiarnan, bewildered by her dad's hostility. Obviously, he didn't understand their situation. Perhaps he didn't even realize where he was.

"Daddy, what happened to you after Cathán attacked us in the parking lot? I thought he had . . . Did he bring you here?"

Donnell eyed her guardedly and shook his head. "No. We fought but when you and . . ." He glared at Tiarnan. "When you went with *him*, the doorway began to close on us. It sucked us apart. The next thing I knew I was alone, stranded in this strange land. What is this place anyway?"

"They call it Inis Brandubh. You were right about the Book of

Fennore," she said, drawing his attention away from Tiarnan and back to her. "It is real and powerful. And this place—it's part of it."

"'Tis what I feared," he replied wearily. "When I saw you that day in my study, I knew you'd come to harm."

Tiarnan moved closer, settling a warm hand at the small of her back. She glanced at him, saw the frustration in his eyes as he tried to follow their conversation. He sensed the undercurrents to her father's statement, but couldn't begin to comprehend what it all meant. Now that the time had come, she regretted that she hadn't told him what happened to her and Ellie by the river. She should have trusted him.

"What day is he talking about?" Tiarnan asked her.

"Shealy," her dad said, interrupting before she could form an answer. "You need to get away from here. This place is too dangerous for you. Don't you be worrying about me."

"But it is y' who can open the door," Tiarnan said to him.

"Me?" Donnell exclaimed and then snapped his mouth shut. Suddenly a feeling of malaise went through Shealy. Dark and insidious, it pulsed in her blood and solidified in her heart.

"You know about me?" she whispered, shocked by the revelation. "You know that I . . ."

"Know what, lass?" Tiarnan asked.

She shook her head, trying to deny the realizations that exploded like fireworks in her mind. And suddenly the pieces fell into place, one by one, and she began to see the terrible, unforgivable picture.

Yesterday, she and Ellie had stepped through a door, passed through time and place, and ended up in her father's study seven years ago.

"You saw me. You spoke to me," she said softly, the hurt running through her like a rampant disease, eating away at the heart of her.

"Shealy, you have to understand," her father pleaded. "You have to—"

"And you," she said to Kyle, cutting her father off. Turning her eyes from his pain. She couldn't bear to see it, not when her own was so great. "You touched my shoulder just as I felt the door closing."

Kyle nodded. "That's right. That's when it felt like I'd been trapped in a bubble I couldn't get out of."

"I came back to the river. And you . . ." The terrible truth flooded her senses. "Oh my God. I brought you with me, didn't I? I yanked you out of time."

Her dad had lied all those years ago when he'd said the priest had gone away because he'd decided not to become a priest. That's not what happened at all. He'd gone away all right, but only because Shealy had wrenched him into another world.

"Shealy," her father said urgently. "Listen to me."

"And you *knew*," she said, spinning to stare at him with horrified eyes. "You knew what I could do."

Tiarnan had been looking from one man to another then back to her, trying to make sense of what they said. Now he demanded, "What are y' talking about, the three of y'? What happened seven years ago? What happened yesterday? What can y' do, Shealy?"

She wanted to answer him, but her brain had seized as the ramifications rolled over her.

Kyle said, "You had the little girl with you. You said she was your sister."

Her father made a strangled noise and turned his back.

"Yes. Her name is Ellie. She was living here with Mom . . ."

She spoke the words and a feeling of vertigo shook her and tried to bring her down. Her mother, living here . . . The accident . . . Yesterday, in the study . . .

Kyle and her father were both talking at once, but Shealy couldn't hear anything but the chaos in her head as everything she'd thought she'd known about her father and the accident that had almost killed her exploded.

"What are y' talking about?" Tiarnan repeated angrily. "What is going on?"

"You knew," she breathed again. "You knew she was here, because I *told* you. I told you I saw her. I told you Ellie was your daughter. You sent Mommy to this place and you *left her.*"

"No, Shealy. Sweetheart, no. That's not—"

"What. Is. Going. ON?" Tiarnan shouted, startling them all into silence. They turned their stunned gazes to him. "Tell me. Now."

Chapter Twenty-one

MEAGHAN shivered in the cold, eyeing the man who sat with his back against the wall, watching her with equal focus. Áedán could sit very still for long periods of time. Meaghan envied that even as she stood and began pacing again.

Stripped but for the fancy jeans that rode dangerously low on his hips, Áedán looked like a model in an advertisement for sex. A five o'clock shadow covered his jaw, setting off the glittering green of his eyes, framed by long, spiky lashes that any woman would covet. His hair was black and long enough to tie back, which he'd done with a shoelace. He had a broad and muscled chest, smooth and without hair, tapering down to abs so tight they looked painted on. His large hands dangled between his bent knees, scarred in many places. The hands of a working man. Her father had hands like that.

His skin was burnished, whether by sun or by heritage, she couldn't tell. It seemed he had no ethnic markers—no traits that defined his genetic makeup. He might be from anywhere and every-where, all trace of his race somehow melded into one sculpted form.

Meaghan had been able to sense the emotions of others since she was a child, but here—*wherever here was*—her gift had been snuffed out. She couldn't pick up anything that Áedán might be feeling. It rattled her, making her realize just how much she depended upon her ability and how much she missed it now.

"Why are you Cathán's prisoner?" she asked.

He gave her a dismissive look. "He wants what I have."

"You're not even wearing a shirt or shoes. What could you have that he'd want?"

She saw the flash of white teeth in the murky darkness before he answered. "Power."

"Power?" she repeated. "If you're so powerful, how'd he catch you?"

He stood, as lithe as a big cat. Through the small window high up on the other side of the bars, a rising sun slanted a few weak rays into their cell, making his bare skin glow. She couldn't help watching him as he paced. He was a truly gorgeous man if somewhat strange and more than a bit scary. His eyes were very cold. When he'd gripped her face, she'd felt the chill of them.

A door opened at the top of the stairs, interrupting before he could answer—if he'd intended to answer at all. Hard to tell with this guy. Meaghan moved to the bars. Beside her, Áedán did the same, making her feel very small as he towered over her in his sock feet.

She expected the guards who'd brought her down to appear, but the man who descended was obviously someone of importance. He carried himself with an authority that seemed second nature. He was heavyset and solid, clothed not in furs or modern jeans like Áedán, but in a bright blue and purple tunic with a spiraled image woven into the front. She recognized the symbol, of course. It was ancient and prevalent in Ireland, and it was also duplicated on the ceiling of the great room in the renovated castle where her family lived.

Over his shoulders hung a massive fur cloak that was white and amazingly bright in the shadowed dungeon. It looked very soft, rabbit perhaps, and Meaghan found herself wondering how many bunnies had died for the making of it. A gold chain held it in place, and it didn't surprise her in the least that the clasp was yet another jeweled triple spiral.

A very big guard walked beside him, armed to the teeth. As the first man moved closer, the shadows concealing his features shifted, and Meaghan caught her breath. His hair glinted golden and red, and a neatly trimmed mustache and goatee covered his lower face. He looked youthful with the only wrinkles in his sun-browned skin coming from the laugh lines that seemed somehow incongruous on the chilling face.

She knew who it was instantly. *Cathán MacGrath.*

She'd never met him of course. Cathán had been married to her mother when he vanished, and though her mom was pregnant with Meaghan at the time, Cathán wasn't Meaghan's father. Meaghan resembled her mother's second husband too much to ever doubt her parentage. From the dimples to the stubborn chin, she was Niall Ballagh's daughter through and through. But she might have been this man's child or raised as such, had he not become abusive and twisted. If he hadn't disappeared all those years ago.

He stopped in front of the bars and stared at Meaghan for a long moment. His eyes were a clear and frosty blue and they glittered in a hard, flat way that made her want to step back. She forced herself not to move. Beside her, Áedán stiffened and she could feel the hostility rolling off of him in waves.

"Is she the one?" Cathán's guard asked.

"No idea," Cathán said, still studying Meaghan.

"Who does he think you are?" Áedán asked in a low voice.

Cathán had not looked at Áedán since coming down and he didn't react to Áedán's question.

"I'm no one," Meaghan said.

This made Cathán smile. "I think you're lying. How did you get here?"

"I don't know. I was searching for my brother."

"Your brother?"

"Rory MacGrath. I think you know him."

Cathán froze at that and his cruel features took on a predatory edge. "Rory is your brother?" he said softly.

"Half brother."

As soon as she said it, she wanted to call the words back. Cathán's expression went from cold to frigid, and she realized a moment too late that he'd mistakenly thought she was his daughter, and as distasteful as the idea was to Meaghan, it might have kept him from hurting her.

Now his cold eyes glittered, making her think of a reptile eyeing a tasty morsel.

"Who is your father?" he said in that same, deadly quiet voice.

Meaghan swallowed. "Why?" she asked, trying to match the steely tone. Trying and failing.

Cathán leaned forward, the movement nearly imperceptible but the menace exponentially huge until Meaghan wanted to scuttle back and hide.

"Who. Is. He?"

Meaghan did step back. She couldn't stop herself. The violence in Cathán MacGrath hummed around him, vibrating the air between them until it settled deep in her gut like a sickness. When she looked into his eyes, it wasn't a sociopath she saw. It was an animal, a predator that didn't care if its prey was scared or hurt. It didn't thrill to the kill, desire the terror, gain satisfaction from the conquest.

It just did what it needed to do to get what it wanted. Nothing else mattered to it.

If Meaghan didn't answer Cathán, he would have no qualms about taking her apart piece by piece. And he would do it with the same passion he might have when cutting the meat from the bone of a chicken.

Meaghan lowered her eyes and mumbled, "My father is Niall Ballagh."

She was not prepared for the rage that suffused his face, making him for a split second once again human . . . and even more terrifying.

"Niall Ballagh," he repeated. "The *filthy fisherman*?"

"A good man," Meaghan said and then, because she couldn't stop herself, "Clearly the better man."

Beside her, Áedán snorted softly. "Have you a death wish, beauty?"

He'd been so silent, she'd forgotten he was there. Now both his words and the casual way he called her *beauty* startled her.

She glanced at him, finding herself momentarily distracted by all that bare skin so close to her. His eyes glowed jewel bright in the gloom and his teeth flashed.

Cathán scanned the cell again and Meaghan saw a small crack in his composure when he didn't discern whatever it was pinging against his inner alarms. But the moment was there and gone so quickly she might have imagined it.

"Niall Ballagh." Cathán shook his head. His disbelief would have been humorous if it didn't feel so malignant. He paused, eyeing Meaghan for another long moment. "She went from me to a filthy fisherman. Your mother was a whore."

"Go fuck yourself."

The words were foolish, but they felt good on her lips and powerful in the air between them.

Cathán lunged at her, reaching through the bars for her throat, but before he could touch her, Áedán moved, coming between them and shoving Cathán back. She saw the power in Áedán's action, the force of his feat, but cause and effect seemed inconsequential here. The hard push deterred Cathán, but it didn't send him back as it should have.

Luck was with her, though, and Cathán's guard moved up just as Áedán thrust out, and Cathán stumbled over him and went sliding hard on the stone floor. He was up in an instant, rage turning his eyes into flinty points of malice. He scanned the cell, searching, Meaghan knew, for the force that he had felt.

"How did you do that?" he demanded.

"Don't tell him anything," Áedán warned.

She didn't like Áedán ordering her around, but it was good advice and as much as it rankled to back down, she took it. Silently she gazed back at Cathán. She couldn't help the hard smile that she knew had curled her lip. For a moment, they stood locked in one another's sights.

"Don't challenge him," Áedán said. "Look away. Damn you, look away."

Quit telling me what to do, she wanted to snarl. Instead, she raised her brows and continued to look calmly back at Cathán until he gave a low laugh that made all the hair at the back of her neck stand on end.

She'd hated this man her entire life. He'd been the anonymous face that could be blamed for everything that had ever gone wrong in Ballyfionúir, in Meaghan's world. And now that she'd met him, that hatred was justified. He'd beat her mother when she was his to love and cherish, wounded her big brother in a way he'd never recovered from. Meaghan had heard the talk, the whispered rumors. And now she saw the truth of who and what he was.

"She's the one then," the guard said to Cathán.

"Not the one I thought, but she is important. I'm sure of it." Cathán leaned closer, pinning her with those inhuman eyes. "Beautiful, too. An added bonus."

"The only bonus you're getting—"

But Áedán had grabbed her arms from behind, yanking her hard against his chest. His lips hovered over her ear. "Do not antagonize him, Meaghan. He will kill you."

She knew that, but in those few minutes she'd realized that nothing she did would affect the outcome of Cathán's actions. He would kill her no matter what—perhaps today, perhaps tomorrow, perhaps next year. All she could do was decide how that end would come about.

"There is a prophecy," Áedán said darkly. His mouth brushed the sensitive skin of her ear as he spoke. "About a woman who has great power. She is *idir eatarthu*—of two realms. She can move between this world and the real world. You do not want him to think this woman is you."

"You were saying?" Cathán asked, eyes narrowed.

He sensed Áedán there, guiding her, but he couldn't see Áedán. Another chink broke from the brittle façade he presented. Cathán thought himself all-prevailing in this twisted place, but somewhere deep within, he must know there was a higher power and he feared it. Was that power Áedán?

"Hold your tongue," Áedán breathed.

Against her back, she felt the rise and fall of his chest, the heat of his skin, the brute strength of him. Yet when he'd attacked Cathán, that power had been muted, just as his presence was undetected.

It cost her every ounce of her dubious self-control to do as he asked, but slowly she took in a deep breath and exhaled before answering Cathán. "I didn't say anything," she told him.

That sharp, glittering stare cut through her, dissecting her belligerent silence, trying to dismember her thoughts. She felt the slice and dice of his probe and the terror that she'd managed to hold at bay became a spinning blade, whirling deep in her gut. She wasn't afraid of dying—no that wasn't true—of course she feared death.

But more petrifying was the idea of being at this man's mercy, because she saw that her first assessment was truer than she could have imagined.

Cathán MacGrath was not human. Not anymore.

"I'm not the one you're looking for," she said, her voice sounding thick and unstable.

Cathán stared back, nonplussed, but behind his impassive face she saw the calculations running, a ticker tape of scenarios he would devise to find the truth. A shudder crept through her. Áedán loosened his hold on her arms, let his warm hands travel down to her wrists and up in a soothing caress. But nothing could calm the dread fanning from inside, teasing the edges of hysteria in her mind. She was suddenly grateful for the cell, for the bars that separated her from Cathán.

"Did your mother ever tell you how we met?" Cathán asked, his voice a soft threat in the dank quiet.

She didn't answer. She couldn't answer.

"I knew she was a stupid, pliable woman. And her mother was just as ignorant. But she had the Book of Fennore."

Something flickered in those brittle eyes and then was gone. Behind her, Áedán tensed, as if he feared what Cathán would say next.

"The Book called to me," Cathán went on. "It *chose* me."

"It's a book. How could it choose?"

The question sounded harsh, defiant. But inside, Meaghan quaked.

"It's true. I chose him," Áedán said, startling her, adding to the spinning fall of her courage.

"What does that mean?" she asked before she could stop herself.

It was Cathán who answered. "The Book of Fennore is not just a book. It's not a *thing*. Not anymore."

Meaghan shook her head. There were no words to explain what she thought, what she needed to ask. At her back she felt the rapid rise and fall of Áedán's chest. Something she or Cathán said had agitated him, but Meaghan couldn't understand what.

"What is it then?" she whispered.

"Power. Freed, that power would know no limits. It is all-controlling, all-conceiving, all-mighty."

"You're talking about God."

His smile was like ice shards, shoved beneath her skin. "Yes."

"No," Áedán said, his breath a hot burst against her temple.

"All of that power was trapped within the Book of Fennore. But now the lock has been sprung, and the power is within me."

That did it. That chilling statement tipped the balances, and Meaghan careened over into a calmness that was as much a façade as the monster's eyes that stared from the human face.

"You're no God."

"Not yet. But once I step from this world back to my own . . ."

He paused, waiting for her to follow that sticky trail. "Back to your own?"

"I will return, Meaghan Ballagh, and I will have justice. I will see your mother begging for mercy. I will feed your father to the fish he so loves. I will bathe in my children's blood. And you, lovely Meaghan, will help me. You will take me to my destiny and I will reward you."

"I don't want your fecking reward."

"Which will make it all the sweeter. I will be worshiped. I will be obeyed."

The dark tone reverberated like a gong echoing in her soul. Áedán had gone very still, but she could feel the hard beat of his heart against her spine.

"Ask him about the Druid," he said softly. "Ask him."

"What about the Druid?"

Cathán's eyes narrowed, and once again, he seemed to scan the cell for something he felt sure he'd find.

"He is weakened. I will take his power and leave him bound to wither and die in his own nightmares."

Áedán released her arms and stepped back. The cold that washed down her spine made her want to cry out. She felt abandoned, though it was foolish. She focused on remaining erect, keeping her chin up and her eyes dry.

Cathán turned to his guard. "Have her cleaned up and brought to the hall. And for the love of God, be careful. Death will seem a blessing if she escapes."

Without another word, he left, climbing the stairs alone while his guard moved to the cell.

Chapter Twenty-two

"TELL me now," Tiarnan repeated, his eyes narrowed, his expression tense. "What is it y' can do? What is it y' think y've done?"

Shealy shook her head, not wanting to speak it. But Tiarnan deserved to know. He had saved her from the wolves, from monsters. He'd come for her when Eamonn had taken her captive. More than that, he'd touched her heart. He'd cracked the shell she'd built around herself and he'd filled her with warmth. With passion . . . with love. Tiarnan deserved so much more than she'd given him. He'd be hurt when he found out she'd kept the truth from him, but that was no excuse to continue to do so. Taking a deep breath, she told him what happened yesterday by the river, detailing the surprise, the shock, the speed with which it had taken place.

"I saw my dad and Kyle in the study—Ellie and I did."

"*You* did this? *You* opened the door."

She nodded, noting that in his shock, he drew out the vowels, pronouncing them instead of clipping them as he usually did.

"I guess it runs in the family. My dad's not the only one who can do it. I can, too. I didn't want to tell you because I was afraid you'd change your mind about helping me find my dad."

His mouth opened and he cocked his head, as if maybe he'd misunderstood. But his eyes darkened and his brows pulled low. He'd heard her all right.

"It was stupid of me, Tiarnan," she said in a rush. "I don't know what I was thinking."

"Y' were thinking y' couldn't trust me," he said, and in his tone she heard how much that wounded him. "Y' were thinking I wouldn't care enough to help y'. That I'd just use y'. Is that the right of it?"

Miserable, she nodded. "I was afraid. You have to understand that."

"Do I?" he said. Then he lowered his lashes, shielding those beautiful eyes from her. "Go on. What happened next?"

Throat aching with the emotions she refused to let loose, she said, "I just realized as we were talking that seven years ago my dad saw me in his study. I mean, of course I realized it then, but I didn't get the importance. It was yesterday for me, but for him"—she cast a betrayed look at her father—"for him it was right after the accident. I told him about Ellie—I told him he had another daughter. He would have known that my mother had to be alive—would be alive long enough to give birth and raise Ellie to a toddler. He would have known that if he'd opened the door right then he could save her. Don't you see? He could have come for her before . . . before the monster killed her."

She couldn't hold the tears back any longer. They spilled over her lashes and down her cheeks, hot and salty, and filled with her agony. She wanted to throw herself in Tiarnan's arms. She'd come to think of them as her haven. She'd come to think of him as the one person who would always be there for her. And yet she hadn't trusted him with the simple truth.

She brushed her tears away with an angry swipe and glared at her father.

"Why, Daddy? Why did you leave her here?"

Donnell stared at his feet, slowly shaking his head. "I didn't," he said sadly. "I couldn't go back for her."

"Why not?"

"Because I had you to think of, Shealy. You were in the hospital, barely hanging on to life."

"So you traded mine for hers? You could have saved her. The doctors were taking care of me, but you *left her*. Alone. Here. Pregnant. She had her baby, Daddy. She had Ellie *here*."

"Try to understand," he begged in a broken voice.

"No, *you* try to understand. I've been carrying this weight around with me for all this time. I thought it was my fault that she died. *Mine*. If I hadn't brought up the Book of Fennore, she wouldn't have snapped at you about being obsessed, you two wouldn't have fought, and you wouldn't have driven off that cliff. But now I know that you sent her here. You opened the door and then you didn't come back for her."

"That's not how it happened," her dad insisted, anger flaring in his eyes.

"No?" she cried. "It's not? Then why don't you set the record straight. Tell me what *really* happened. Tell me why you lied to me for *SEVEN YEARS*!"

Her voice echoed in the chamber. She had a moment to worry that someone might hear it, but she didn't care. Not anymore. Her whole world had fallen apart. She wanted answers. She wanted reasons. Beside her, Tiarnan took an automatic step, his hands outstretched, but he stopped before he touched her. Her tears fell faster.

"I couldn't tell you the truth," her father said, tears in his eyes, too.

"Why? Because you were afraid I would hate you?"

"No. Not because I thought you would hate me. I didn't tell you, Shealy, because I was afraid you would hate *you*."

His words settled around her, alien, incomprehensible. She shook her head, trying to make sense of them, but she couldn't. What did he mean? Tiarnan moved again and this time his hand settled on her shoulder, moved beneath the length of her hair and curled around her neck. Gently he pulled her to him.

"I cannot open the door between this world and Fennore, Shealy. I don't have that power. I never have."

"What do you mean? I saw you do it the night Cathán attacked us. I *saw it*."

"It wasn't me, Shealy. You did it. Only you can open the passage between the two worlds."

"Me?" she asked softly.

He nodded, eyes so filled with desolation that she knew he spoke the truth. "I didn't know you could do it before the accident. I only knew that you had a sensitivity to the Book, and even that I discovered by chance."

"What do y' mean?" Tiarnan asked.

"Maggie, Shealy's mother, she didn't believe, so I had to be sneaky about my search for it. It was a bone of contention between us, the Book was. So I would tell little fibs when I went out and I would take Shealy with me. We'd visit places where rumors abounded. And when we did, Shealy would tell me things. Like if it had been there or where it had gone."

Shealy listened, her head resting against Tiarnan's strong chest, his scent soothing her. Bringing her comfort she didn't deserve. She wrapped her arms around him tightly and pulled him closer, and he pressed a kiss to the top of her head.

"She knew where the Book was?" he asked her father.

"Only if it had used where we were as its jumping point. She could say, 'From here it went south, Daddy. With a woman.' And so

I could narrow my search to the south and look for tales of women who'd suddenly become wealthy but then gone mad. Or children healed from fatal diseases only to have their mommy shoot herself later. Miracles followed by tragedies. That is the wake of the Book of Fennore."

"I remember," Shealy whispered. "I remember us doing that. It was our secret."

"Yes. But then you started growing up and you weren't so interested in day trips with your crazy dad. You started thinking like your mum. That I was obsessed."

He sighed, glanced at Kyle and then away. "I thought I was being quite clever taking the two of you to the Isle of Fennore for the day. Maggie, she loved the quiet towns, the little pubs. She never took to Dublin, you know. I told her I'd looked from shore to shore on the island long ago and never caught a hint of the Book that was named for it, and I suppose she believed me because surely if the Book had been on that island I would have found it long ago. It was the only reason she agreed to go that day—because she thought I'd eliminated it from my . . . quest."

"But then I brought up how we used to search for it and I asked if that's why you'd brought me to the place named for it," Shealy murmured, her voice cracking.

"Don't blame yourself for the fight, sweetheart. She planned to leave me no matter what. I loved her like I've never loved another woman, and she loved me, too, but not enough to believe in my mission."

Tiarnan asked, "So Shealy opened the door while y' were driving on the island?"

"I don't know exactly," her dad answered, eyeing the tender way he held Shealy. "We saw a blinding white light and it was like we fell through. Not like the other night at all."

"Ah," Tiarnan said. He reached down, took Shealy's chin in his hand, and tilted her face up so he could look in her eyes. "It was not yer fault, then. It was mine. For each of the persons who came to Inis Brandubh the story is the same. Y' were in yer cart when I was trying to destroy the Book. I brought yer mother here. Not y', lass."

She stared deeply into his eyes, expecting to see pity. Expecting that he said it only to make her feel better, not because it was the truth. But what she saw there told her what she should have known. Tiarnan was not a man of deception. Not ever.

"I concur with that," her dad said. "The experience was not the same."

Shealy looked at him. "What do you mean? How could you know?"

"We went with her, Shealy. All of us. But you and I landed together. There was a creature—I can't even describe it. It saw us and charged. You screamed and I wrapped myself around you to protect you. The next thing I knew, we were back in the car, sailing over the cliff. I thought for certain that thing had killed your mother right then. I didn't know where we'd gone or how we'd gotten there and back. I didn't know it had anything to do with you, Shealy, until the day you appeared in the study with the child."

"Ellie."

He nodded. "It was then I realized the danger you were in. I thought it was the proximity to the Book that had caused the accident. My only thought was to get you away from it all. I sold everything and moved us to Arizona—a place as opposite and as far from Ireland as I could get."

"But if you'd told me, I could have gone back. I could have saved her."

"Or you could have died just as she did. I didn't dare risk the daughter I loved more than life itself for 'could haves.'"

Shealy shook her head sadly, seeing the twisted dilemma her

father had faced, knowing that it wasn't fair to judge him for the choices he'd made.

Tiarnan lowered his head and said softly in her ear, "A wise woman once told me that if I'd made some wrong decisions, probably there weren't any right ones."

"She's not so wise," Shealy whispered back.

Before Tiarnan could answer her, that feeling of gathering, of the air thickening around her, began to fill up the wretched spaces of hollowness that ached deep inside.

"I think we're out of time," she murmured, her voice strained by the feeling, the words hard to form. But Kyle spoke over her and no one heard.

"What triggered this *door* opening in Arizona?" he asked.

"I don't know for certain," her dad said. "But it seemed like Cathán was searching for something. For Shealy. He came after her."

"That's right," Tiarnan said, frowning. "It was like he knew that she could pull him out. But how would he know?"

"The prophecy," her dad and Kyle said at once.

"What prophecy?"

Kyle and Donnell exchanged a solemn glance, and then Kyle pulled his shoulder bag open. He lifted a bundle wrapped in oilcloth from inside, held it for a moment, and then carefully unwrapped it. Inside was a small, thin book.

Donnell let out his breath in a rush as soon as he saw it. "I thought it lost," he murmured. He glanced at Shealy. "Kyle was holding it the night he vanished and it went with him."

"Is that the Book of Fennore, then?" she asked with a combination of fear and anticlimax. She didn't know what she'd expected, but this seemed too mild, too *ordinary* to be the Book of Fennore.

"No," Donnell said with a grim smile. "Not the Book of Fennore. But a very old journal. Old, Shealy. Older than either you or

I can even imagine. It belonged to our ancestors' ancestors, and it plots the journey of the Book of Fennore. It tells the history of when it was created, who has used it, where it has been. It has been passed from generation to generation, from Keeper to Keeper. It came to me from my father and to him from his father."

Shealy stared at it. She'd seen her father with this journal before, but she'd never known its importance. She was beginning to think she'd never known anything.

As if sensing her feelings, Tiarnan moved his hand to her nape in a gentle caress. His touch was so warm that it melted some of the icy dread growing inside of her. Her father gave Tiarnan a thinly veiled look Shealy struggled to understand. He had a problem with Tiarnan, but she had no idea why. If not for Tiarnan, she wouldn't have survived five minutes in this hellish place.

"Look, Shealy," her dad said, pulling her attention to the journal. It boggled the mind to think this was a chronicle of the Book of Fennore, penned by Keepers over the ages. The pages were withered and browned, the red leather cover cracked and creased with age and grime. Kyle held it gingerly, as if he feared it might disintegrate in his very hands.

With utmost care, Kyle settled the journal in his palm and opened it to a page he had marked with a small slip of paper. He sent Shealy a cryptic glance before he turned the journal to face her. Tiarnan leaned close so he could see as well.

"Here is the prophecy. It tells of a woman who will have the power to release the Druid—the entity that has been the power of the Book for all of time."

"Not anymore," Shealy said. "Tiarnan told me it's Cathán who runs the show now."

"That remains to be seen," her father answered. "However it is, this woman is *idir eatarthu*. That means she can walk between worlds. She can take others with her."

He turned a page, and there was a picture of a woman straddling two land masses. One rippled with green fields and crops. Cattle roamed and people harvested grain. In the other, dragons filled the sky and wolves howled at a dark moon. Shadows hid the woman's features but she had golden blonde hair.

"The prophecy says that if this woman should open the door between the worlds, the Druid will escape, and if he does, he will rain evil on the earth we love."

Another page, another picture. This one showed the same two worlds, only now no cattle, no crops, no green fields existed. The people all lay dead in a wasted land.

"Only one man can stop this from happening," her father went on in a strained voice. "A warrior who is part beast himself. To protect the world he loves, he must stop the woman from releasing the Druid."

"How does he do that?" she asked, knowing the answer would not be good. Knowing the apprehension building inside her had its roots in this prophecy. Overwhelmed by exhaustion, by the emotional roller coaster that had brought her here, she braced for the worst. As if sensing her weakness, the thickening air became sticky and weighted. She fought the gelatinous feeling but still it crept in from every shadow.

"I think we're running out of time," she said again, but the viscous atmosphere seemed to gobble her words and no one heard.

"Turn the page," her dad said.

This picture had been penned with quick, bold strokes. The image was clear, though. The woman who'd straddled the two worlds lay in a pool of blackened blood. Her eyes stared sightlessly, her face deathly pale.

"He kills her?" Shealy asked, though she didn't want an answer. She took the journal from Kyle so she could see the details in the image. A man towered over the woman, larger than life, his clothes in tatters. She thought of that old American television show, *The Incredible Hulk*. This man wasn't green, but he bulged with muscles, appeared ten feet tall, and his eyes glowed like amber.

She sucked in a breath. *Those eyes . . .*

Shealy's knees felt watery, her legs useless. How she managed to keep standing, she didn't know, but that feeling of the room closing in on her grew.

Her gaze went back to the dead woman, and now she saw something that made her blood run cold. Low on the side of her face, a crisscross of fine pinkish white lines covered her skin. Lower still, a crescent-shaped scar hooked from just below a burned and damaged ear to her throat.

"That's me," she said, her voice no more than a whisper.

"And the warrior," her dad said in a angry voice. "That would be Tiarnan."

She turned her widened eyes to the man standing beside her. "Tiarnan?"

"Do not believe these lies, Shealy. I would take the blade myself before I put it to y'."

"But look at these pictures. That's us. This was written hundreds of years ago, and they drew us. *Us.*"

"I do not care what they drew," he said, his voice deep and harsh. "I know y' do not trust me, but I give y' my word. I swear to y', nothing would make me hurt y', lass."

"Show him the next page," her father said coldly.

Kyle took the journal from Shealy's unresisting fingers and turned the page to another sketch. This one showed five people on a desolate stretch of beach, running as they looked over their shoulders at dragons, swooping down on them. Most of the faces Shealy didn't recognize, but she saw Liam's clear enough. Eamonn's, too.

Tiarnan sucked in a rasping breath and took a step back.

"You know these people, Tiarnan?" Kyle asked.

He nodded. "My brothers. My sister. Her husband."

All the color had drained from his face. When he looked at her, his eyes burned with thoughts he would not express. She moved to him, put her hands against his chest.

"Read them the sonnet," her father commanded.

The thickened air surged around her, filling the room like water poured into a tank. Shealy knew she wouldn't be able to stop the suction that even now pulled at her skin.

"We don't have time," Shealy managed to say, louder this time. She tried to push away from Tiarnan, but her knees gave and he caught her just before she fell. Kyle hurried to her side as Tiarnan swung her into his arms. He took her hand, and reached out to touch her father as well, but she knew it was too late. That gel-like sensation that she'd come to know too well rushed in at her, overwhelmed her. It filled all the dark corners and pressed tight to her chest, blocking the air in her lungs. The world turned to a thick fog that swirled and obscured everything from sight. Only the sound of Tiarnan's heart beating, the feel of his arms kept her anchored. But even that wasn't enough. She couldn't see her father anymore, couldn't find him in the static world of white.

There was only Shealy, Tiarnan, and Kyle locked in the swirling melee that held her tight. Then suddenly she was falling, falling. She felt Tiarnan's arms tighten around her, curled herself into him. And then her body struck something hard and unyielding. It knocked the breath from her lungs, and blackness swam behind her eyes.

Chapter Twenty-three

TIARNAN hit the ground hard, disoriented and confused. His head felt heavy and his stomach sick. He eased to his hands and knees, clammy and queasy. Cathán's dungeon, the old man who was Shealy's father, the cold dark—all of it was gone.

Beside him, Shealy rolled onto her back and stared at the sky. He reached for her, turned her face to his. Her eyes were clear, but her pupils were huge and her skin very pale. She focused on him and for a moment something warm moved through those stormy depths, and then a guarded look pushed in and replaced it.

Tiarnan pulled back, hurt and angry. She didn't trust him—after all they'd been through together, she'd still kept secrets. And now . . . now, it appeared that she believed the lies she'd just been told . . .

Abruptly he stood and took a step away. They'd returned to Eamonn's makeshift camp. The sun had been rising on a bright morning when they'd stood in front of Jamie, when Shealy had taken Tiarnan and Mahon to the dungeons and her father. Now the sun tumbled from the sky in a violent blaze of color. It would be dark soon. He turned in a circle, searching for Mahon, and spotted him on hands and knees a few yards away. Donnell O'Leary was nowhere in sight. Either he'd been left behind in that dungeon or Shealy had flung him somewhere else.

Shealy. How could she have kept secrets from him? How could she believe that after holding her, after loving her, he could ever hurt her?

"They're back," someone shouted from near the fire and suddenly the camp came alive with activity, but in the center neither Tiarnan nor Shealy moved.

Jamie rushed toward him with Reyes on his heels. They helped Mahon stand and then gathered round. From the other side, Eamonn strode angrily forward with four of his men behind him. One he recognized as Nanda, the Indian man who'd brought them food and water.

Jamie's steps slowed as he came nearer, and Tiarnan felt the burn of curiosity and wariness in the gaze that raked him from head to toe.

"Where you been, T?" he asked, looking at Tiarnan like he was a stranger—a dangerous stranger. That shadowed caution was too close to what he'd seen in Shealy's eyes, and it infuriated him. He'd fought beside Jamie time and again, yet now his friend had doubt in his troubled gaze. Would he turn on Tiarnan as Eamonn had? Would they all?

"T?" Jamie repeated. "Where you been?"

Tiarnan didn't know how to answer the question. He didn't know where he'd been, how he'd come to be there, or why he was back now. It seemed best to say nothing at all.

Frowning, Jamie glanced at Shealy, studying her grief-ravaged expression, her averted gaze.

"You, Shealy. You're all right?"

She stood unsteadily and gave him a tight nod.

Eamonn stopped just in front of Tiarnan, so close his presence became a challenge that matched the rage on his face. Jaw tight, he demanded, "Where were y', brother? How did y' do it?"

Tiarnan could only imagine what they'd seen. He, Shealy, and Mahon must have disappeared right in front of them.

"It was the girl, wasn't it?" Eamonn demanded. "Her." And he pointed at Shealy.

It took all of Tiarnan's control not to slap his brother's hand down. His mind worked quickly as he tried to find an explanation that didn't involve the truth, for even now, even knowing how little faith Shealy had in him, Tiarnan would protect her. He would show her that his heart was true or he would die trying. He didn't know how these men would react when they learned that Shealy could open the door between the worlds—when they learned that she'd known she had that power and had kept it from them—but he figured that the fewer people who knew, the better. Still, he would have to explain at least some of what had happened. They'd all seen Tiarnan, Shealy, and Mahon disappear. There was no hiding that.

"We must talk," Tiarnan said to Jamie, ignoring Eamonn and his questions. "We found Shealy's father."

Jamie stared from Shealy to Tiarnan with shock and silent consideration. Eamonn was not so composed.

"Y' found her father? *Y' must talk?* I'll hear what y' have to say."

Tiarnan rounded on him. "Y' would hear what I have to say?" he snarled. "Y' would have me trust y'? Is that it? Well I don't. So either we battle it out or y' step away."

Eamonn clenched his fists tightly and for a moment Tiarnan thought that at last they would fight, but then he let out a tight breath and shook his head. Disappointment and relief made bitter companions in Tiarnan's gut.

Shealy gave Eamonn a look of disdain and defiance. Tiarnan

might have smiled at the daunting front the small woman presented, but there was nothing to laugh about now.

"It doesn't pertain to you anyway," Shealy told Eamonn. To Tiarnan, she said in a brittle voice, "I'm sorry, but I think it would be best if our paths parted now. I'm going back for my dad and then I'll find a way to . . ."

She paused and he felt the anguish of her thoughts as they tangled with her words.

"I don't want you to have to choose between me and the ones you love." Her eyes filled with tears and she brushed them away with a trembling hand. "I can't do that to you. To either one of us. I don't think—"

Tiarnan didn't let her get any further.

"How many times, Shealy O'Leary, do I have to tell y'? *Don't think*. Our paths do not part. Not now. Not ever."

"Not even in death, Tiarnan?" she asked softly. "Not even when you're forced to kill me or watch your brothers and sister die?"

"Kill y'?" Eamonn said. "What are y' talking about woman?"

Shealy's chin trembled, but she stiffened her back. "Evidently, there's trouble brewing here on Inis Brandubh, and Tiarnan and I may not be able to stop it from escaping unless Tiarnan stops *me*. There's a prophecy that says he will murder me to save all the people he loves."

The horror of the words coming from her lips overwhelmed him. He wanted to grab her, shake her, demand that she forget the lies that journal had told. He wanted to make the words she'd spoken, the pictures they'd seen, vanish. Make it so they never existed at all.

As the silence drew in around them, he felt everything inside him spilling out, the muck and mess that made him the man he was. It was all there, exposed and rotting in the dwindling light, unworthy of the bond that kept the pieces whole. Now Eamonn would tell Shealy about another time when Tiarnan had been forced to choose between his brothers and a woman he'd cared for . . . and Shealy would be convinced that the prophecy was right.

"Again, Tiarnan?" Eamonn demanded as if prompted by the rampant thoughts in Tiarnan's head, and the question drew Shealy's frowning gaze.

Before she could ask, before she could question what Eamonn meant, Jamie interrupted, "Kill you? *Murder* you, Shealy?" He gave a harsh laugh. "I don't believe it."

The pain in Shealy's eyes made them glow silver gray. "It's true. Ask him."

Tiarnan braced for the question. For Jamie's dark and intense gaze to swing to his face, analyze the tumult of emotion he'd read there. Jamie was good at that. He'd see the lies and he'd see the truth. But to have his honor questioned by a man he admired would take the legs out from under him. It was already more than he could bear to have Shealy look at him with that fatalistic shine to her tear-drenched eyes.

But Jamie didn't even spare Tiarnan a fleeting look.

"I don't need to ask him. You fight with a man, you learn a few things about him. He'd cut off his own hand before he'd use it against a woman and he'd probably chop off both before he'd hurt you, Shealy. You didn't see what he did when he thought you were being threatened. You didn't see him fight to protect you. He'd never hurt you. Ever."

Stunned, Tiarnan watched Zac and Reyes nodding in agreement, and their faith humbled him. He didn't deserve it, yet he wanted to fall to his knees and thank them.

"If you want to tell me how Tiarnan ran in front of a firing squad to save your pretty ass, that I'll believe. But he'd never harm one of his own." Jamie leaned forward until Shealy was forced to meet his eyes. "And you, Shealy O'Leary, like it or not, are one of his own."

Those words were spoken so softly that they might have been a velvety breeze on the twilight air, but Tiarnan felt them reverberating down to his soul. In his entire life, no one had ever spoken up for him in this way. His brothers, Michael and Liam, followed him, yes. But no one had ever stood for him with such certainty and conviction. Eamonn, even before he'd turned, was ever the devil's advocate, fighting each decision Tiarnan made, questioning every choice. Tiarnan had begun to think he didn't deserve the loyalty that he'd been given.

Jamie turned to Tiarnan and asked, "Tell me how? How did you go . . . wherever it is you went? How did you find Shealy's father?"

"It was me," Shealy said before he could stop her. "I did it. It's what I do, apparently."

"It's what y' do," Eamonn repeated, his voice as soft as the shuddering breath she released, as hot as the popping embers of their campfire.

Tiarnan braced himself, seeing the catastrophe that loomed just ahead.

"And how is it that y' do this thing that makes a man vanish before my very eyes?" Eamonn asked.

"I don't know how I do it," she said sharply. "It just happens."

"It just happens? Y' just *happened* to leave this place?" he went on, incredulous. "And y' just *happened* to take Tiarnan and this man, Mahon, with y'? And where is yer father if y' found him?"

"We don't know," Tiarnan answered.

"Well that's bloody brilliant!" Eamonn shouted. "Y' *don't know*. What *do* y' know?"

"I know that I do not answer to y'. Nor does Shealy."

"That's where yer wrong, brother."

Tiarnan took a half step forward, placing his body in front of Shealy's. Glad to have some action to channel his confusion, pain, and fear. "Y' said we weren't yer prisoners. It shouldn't surprise me that y' have gone back on yer word."

Eamonn flinched, but he didn't back down. "I've not gone back on it. Y' can leave anytime y' want, Tiarnan. But the woman, she stays."

"The woman stays with *me*," Tiarnan corrected.

"The woman has a name," Shealy said, her temper restored. "And she has a mind of her own. I'll do what I choose to do and neither of you have a say in it."

"Time out," Jamie said. "Everybody just take a step back and breathe."

Jamie's deep voice commanded attention, but the tension spiraled higher. Just when it looked like his calming words would have the effect of grease on a fire, Liam came out of a tent with Ellie in his arms. The little girl spotted them and gave a sharp cry, wiggled out of his hold like a wet seal, and then darted across the camp to Shealy. Her distress was so real, so raw that it whipped them, and no one could say a word as they watched Shealy scoop her up and hold her tight. Shealy rocked her sister side to side with soft hushing sounds.

"I'm sorry, Ellie," she murmured into her ear. "I didn't mean to leave. I didn't do it on purpose. I'm sorry."

Tears streaking her face, Ellie jammed a thumb in her mouth and held on tightly. Then after a moment, she lifted her head from Shealy's shoulder and said, "Yiam," around her thumb.

"I'm here, little one," Liam said, smoothing the silky hair on her golden head. She reached for his hand, pulled it from her head, and tucked it tight against her chest, pinning his fingers in place between her body and Shealy's with her small, firm grip. Smiling gently, his little brother didn't try to break away. Instead he moved closer until he stood just behind Shealy.

Ellie was not satisfied yet, though. With an expression of obvious distress she looked at Tiarnan. It was clear in her expression what dilemma she fought. She wanted to pull him nearer as well, but to do so she'd either have to give up the tight clutch she had on Liam's hand or take her thumb out of her mouth. Finally, with a look of grim determination, she yanked her thumb out, leaned so far over that she nearly unbalanced Shealy, grabbed a fistful of his tunic in her tiny hand, and pulled him into the circle she'd created around herself. Tiarnan could not have denied her anything and especially the very thing his own heart craved.

Eyes on Shealy's face, he stepped in close, blocking out the others, the rest of the world, as he captured her hurt gaze and held it tight. He wrapped his arms around them all, one hand settling at the dip of Shealy's waist. The other hand went to Liam's shoulder where he gave his brother a gentle squeeze, closing a circle with Shealy in the middle. Satisfied that they were all connected now, Ellie gave a heartfelt sigh and laid her head under Shealy's chin.

"She's been crying since y' disappeared," Liam said softly.

She looked up into Tiarnan's face and he touched her forehead with his, closing his eyes to the pain he saw in her eyes.

"I didn't mean to leave you," Shealy whispered again to her sister.

As Tiarnan held the huddle of people that were his world, he was filled with such a violent need to protect, to keep this unit whole, that it nearly buckled his knees. He didn't care what the others thought; he clung to those he loved like the desperate man he was.

"Why don't we all move over to the fire?" Jamie said, breaking the solidified silence.

No one argued, and Tiarnan heard them breaking up, moving toward the campfire. Slowly Liam stepped back. He placed his hand on Tiarnan's shoulder and said, "Y' do what is in yer heart, brother. I will follow."

The pledge was spoken so simply, so calmly, but the words filled him until it felt like he would burst. Liam walked away, leaving only Tiarnan with Shealy and Ellie in his arms. The child stayed quiet, head tucked beneath Shealy's chin, eyes closed. He wanted to say something to Shealy, something that would make everything right, but there were no magic words that would do such a thing. There was only this moment, strung like pearls to the next.

He would do as his baby brother instructed. He would follow his heart, and that meant follow this woman. No matter where she led him, no matter what she demanded of him.

Without a word, he took her hand, not letting her resist, but when he would have moved to the fire, she stopped him.

"What did he mean, Tiarnan?" she asked.

Tiarnan froze, wishing he could pretend not to know what she wanted. Wishing he could lie and tell her some untruth that would satisfy that entreaty.

"Eamonn," she went on. "He said 'again'. What did he mean by that?"

With a deep breath, Tiarnan faced her. Faced his own misery. "There are many reasons why my brother betrayed me," he said softly. "One of them involved a woman."

She looked startled by that, and he imagined she pictured a lover's triangle wedging the brothers apart. Oh that it had only been that.

"We were under attack," he said, "and I used this woman, who trusted me, as a hostage to save my brothers."

He couldn't look at Shealy. Couldn't breathe through the weight of his shame. "I thought in doing this I would save all of us, but I miscalculated and she was wounded. Because of me."

"You hurt her?" Shealy asked incredulously.

"I did not throw the knife, but it was my fault the blade found her."

Shealy absorbed that in stoic silence, but he could not look up. Could not face the disgust that would turn those stormy eyes dark.

"Did she . . . die?"

"No. But she blamed me, as she should. When she was well, she left with Eamonn. Every day since, I have seen her blood on my hands. I have relived those moments and wished I could change how they'd passed."

She shifted and he felt the weight of her stare on his face. "Would you do it again?" she asked. "Same circumstances, same odds. Would you do it again?"

He swallowed hard, but he did not have to think twice. "No. I was a fool not to trust my brothers to defend themselves. Eamonn was right—I fought alone, always thinking that only I could control the outcome. Had I believed in them, none of them would have been hurt."

"You don't know that, Tiarnan," she said softly.

No, he didn't. "It doesn't matter. I brought shame on myself and on my family with my actions. Better for all of us to have died than what I did."

"Is that what you really think, Tiarnan?"

"Yes. I was wrong that day, but I will not be wrong again. I did not mean for her to be hurt, I would not have hurt her myself, but I endangered her. It is not a mistake I will ever forget."

"Look at me," she said, and when he brought his eyes up, she searched them for the truth. He could do nothing more than gaze back, open and exposed for the treacherous fool he was.

"The prophecy," she began. "It said you would have to choose—"

"The choice is made. If y' believe nothing else of me, believe that, Shealy. I will never be a danger to y'. Never."

The declaration hovered between them, fragile but fierce. Tiarnan's heart turned to stone as he watched her consider it. It would crumble like granite beneath a hammer if she turned away. *Please*, he begged silently. *Please do not turn away.*

After a long, painful moment, she nodded. "I believe you."

The breath he released felt like it had been locked inside his chest for a million years.

There was so much more he wanted to say to her, but Jamie cut him off. "T? You coming?"

Then Shealy turned and moved away without another word and the moment was lost. He caught her before she took her seat by the fire and took her hand again, braced for her rejection. When she didn't pull away, he found a place to sit with a log behind him to lean against and pulled Shealy down between his legs so that her back rested against his chest, Ellie tight in her arms. Liam sat to his right and wrapped his big hand around the child's small foot, letting her know he was there, too.

After Jamie and Reyes settled beside Zac, Eamonn and his men filled in the spaces in between. Mahon hovered at the fringes, silent even now as he gauged the mood and the possible outcomes of this meeting. Wariness canvassed the air between them, reinforced by the suspicious glances they all exchanged.

At last, Jamie said, "Let's start with the clearing."

"The clearing?" Eamonn demanded. "What fooking clearing?"

Jamie gave him a cold look. "The one with a hundred body parts in it."

That shut Eamonn's mouth, but Tiarnan didn't feel any satisfaction from it. For reasons he couldn't explain, he didn't want to talk about the clearing. He didn't want to discuss the bodies.

"What about it?" Eamonn said.

"Tiarnan here killed about twenty men in just under five minutes. Granted he's not my brother"—and Jamie shot him a look that seemed to contradict that statement—"but I know the man, and I've never seen him do anything like that before."

Tiarnan opened his mouth to deny that he'd done anything out of the ordinary, but no words came out. Suddenly a flashing assault of images filled his head. Men, charging him with their weapons drawn. Tiarnan, looking down on them from what seemed a great distance. Blood. Everywhere, blood.

"I always thought he had a wee bit of the *riastradh* in him," Liam said in a very calm tone.

Riastradh. It was said to transform a man into something that wasn't quite human, something that knew only death and destruction. A creature that would battle until no blood was left to spill. A man-beast that probably resembled the drawing he'd just seen. Tiarnan swallowed hard, feeling Shealy tense against him. Every damning image in that journal seemed to confirm that the prophecy was true, but he knew his own heart. He'd betrayed it once. He would not do so again.

Encircled by his arms, settled between his spread knees, Shealy was remembering the image in the journal as well, he knew. Her words echoed silently between them. *You were like five men and ten feet tall.* . . . He prayed she wouldn't turn and look at his face, wouldn't see the horror lurking in his eyes.

"What does that mean, *reeastr. . . ?*" Reyes asked.

"It's the frenzy that comes over a man in battle," Eamonn answered in a choked voice.

"It's more than that," Liam said, giving Eamonn a dirty look. "Tiarnan, y' remember the night of our sister's wedding, when y' fought a dozen of Cathán's men at once?"

"Not only Tiarnan fought," Eamonn said. "I was with him. Y' weren't."

"I was a boy," Liam answered coldly. "And y' all forced me to stay behind. But even there I was fighting *with* my brothers. Y' were fighting for the other side."

"I didn't," Eamonn snarled, paling so that his angry eyes seemed to burn in his white face.

Liam turned back to Shealy. "My brother Michael told me later. The odds were twelve to three."

"I killed my share," Eamonn insisted stubbornly, but there was a pleading note in his voice that Tiarnan could not help but hear.

"It was an ugly situation," Liam went on. "But in the end, Tiarnan brought down eight men in the time it took Eamonn and Michael to kill four."

A hushed silence followed and Tiarnan felt the curious eyes of all upon him.

"When we came on you, T," Jamie said. "You were . . ."

While he searched for the right words, Reyes blurted, "You were a fucking giant, man. Like eight feet tall, like a killing machine."

Zac nodded and said, "You were ripping them apart with your bare hands. I thought Jamie was dead when you turned on him. I thought you were going to kill him, too."

Tiarnan could feel his face growing hot with disgust. Was it true? Had he become *riastradh*? A mindless monster? He remembered looking down on his victims. He remembered the red-hot fury, the feeling that they'd threatened him. Threatened those who were his to protect. More than that . . .

"Is that what happened before?" Jamie asked Liam. "When he fought those other men, did he . . . grow?"

Liam looked at Eamonn. "I thought it was my imagination that changed him," Eamonn said. "It was dark and it happened so fast . . . I couldn't be sure that my eyes hadn't tricked me. I convinced myself they had and I never mentioned it. Michael never said a word either, but I don't think he saw—he was too busy trying to stay alive." Eamonn made a small, choked sound. "To him y' were always stronger than any other man could be. If he'd seen, it would have only confirmed what he believed."

In the confession there was bitter truthfulness, the admission of jealousy, the shame of being the one who harbored it against his own brother.

"Do you remember what happened, T?" Jamie said. "Today, in the clearing?"

"No. Not really. Just bits. Pieces." *Blood. Gore. Violence.* "If y' say it's true, then I believe y', but do not expect me to explain because I can't."

Jamie nodded calmly. "Not looking for an explanation, my friend. Just want you to be aware that it happened. You saved all of our asses and so we'll just tell you thanks, and be done with it. But the next time you feel that power coming on, you need to recognize it, you understand? I've served with some of the baddest mother-fuckers to take a breath and I know there's a fine line between being the best fighter and the most dangerous one. You just remember who your friends are." Jamie paused. "And we'll do the same. We got your back."

The lecture might have sat irritably on his shoulders if he hadn't sensed the sincerity and the honest compassion in Jamie's tone. They weren't afraid of him, though he thought that Reyes was right and he might have easily murdered Jamie when they'd come upon him.

Moved by that pledge of friendship, Tiarnan nodded. In his arms, Shealy sat less stiffly. Ellie was looking at him over Shealy's shoulder. The thumb was still in her mouth and her eyes were solemn. He brushed a finger over the soft petal of her cheek and she sighed, the small sound anchoring him to this moment, stripping him of any defense he might have once possessed. These two females were his ballast, and if being *riastradh* enabled him to protect them, then he would embrace it.

"I will not forget who fights with me," Tiarnan said softly. "I will not forget who I fight for. And I will not forget my friends."

"Excellent," Jamie said. "Now, let's talk about the other thing. Let's talk about where you went and how we save Shealy's father."

And with those simple words, Jamie made clear his position. No matter that Tiarnan was a creature, not unlike those of Inis Brandubh, Jamie would follow him into battle. Tiarnan couldn't fathom what he'd ever done to deserve such a friend, but that is what Jamie was. A friend. A comrade.

"So tell us what you're thinking, T. You know what we're up against better than any of us. How do you want this to play?"

Still overwhelmed by the myriad of emotions tightening his chest, Tiarnan looked over each of their faces and saw the absolute trust in the eyes that looked back. In that moment, he saw his vow to remain in the background, to avoid stepping forward and taking charge for what it was—an act not of wisdom, but of weakness. If he was ever to be the man that Shealy needed, he must move beyond the fears that had crippled him for so long. He must shed that weakness like the stained and tattered rag it was and be strong.

And he must do it now.

Decision made, Tiarnan took a deep breath and did what he'd been born to do.

He led.

Chapter Twenty-four

CATHÁN stood on the balcony overlooking his *kingdom* and glared at what he saw. He'd thought nothing could be worse than the hell he'd been thrust into all those years ago when his own children had cheated him. He'd thought the life he'd been condemned to live a nightmare beyond imagination. Still he'd thought it would all be temporary.

He'd been wrong.

He recognized now that in those days, there'd still been enough man, enough *humanity* inside him to hope. But that, too, was gone now. He could see it clearly, like watching a film of someone else's life, where the steps and missteps could be appraised and disparaged from afar.

He didn't know what was left of the man he'd once been. A man like any other, with dreams and desires. With fears and cares. Did enough of that person exist to return to the real world? Or would they recognize that he'd become *Other* and shun him?

He could pinpoint exactly when the change that had transformed him from man to *Other* happened. He'd been fleeing the battlefield on horseback, flying across the open land when an explosion had shaken the earth, knocked him from his horse. He'd seen a wall of blinding white rushing at him. A mushroom cloud stretching out before it rose above and then he was inside the white, being sucked into the aftermath of the detonation. Spinning and falling and screaming. He was alone. Stranded . . .

He'd felt the brush of another in that thickened mist. He'd recoiled, floundering as he tried to understand what was happening. But it had curled around him, sucked him down, and he'd heard that voice, so compelling, so seductive. It called him closer, as it had years ago when he'd been a young man searching for his way.

Disobeying it was not an option.

He recognized the voice and knew it belonged to the Druid Brandubh, the entity that controlled the Book of Fennore. Even as he feared it, he felt something change in that swirling white miasma. He knew that the Druid shared this strange fogged space with him and he'd felt a give and take, an exchange of consciousness. For a moment, he'd seen the Druid's thoughts as if they were his own. He realized then that he'd been wrong. Yes, Brandubh had control, he worked from within the boundaries of the Book of Fennore, powerful and awe inspiring. But in the end, he was little more than a prisoner. The Book of Fennore controlled Brandubh as much as he controlled it.

And Brandubh was tired of being imprisoned. The Druid wanted out just as much as Cathán wanted to go home.

The knowledge was stunning. It blew away all of Cathán's preconceived ideas. That the Druid might want for something had never occurred to him before. But now . . .

In those thoughts he'd seen images spanning years, decades, centuries. He'd absorbed the knowledge like a sponge. It was only later that he realized that while he'd been soaking up the Druid's memories, the Druid had been sucking Cathán dry of the last of his humanity.

They'd emerged from that white mist together, for one moment facing each other, man to man. Then the moment was gone, and Cathán was alone in this hell that Tiarnan had named Inis Brandubh. He didn't know where the Druid went. Had he escaped? Left Cathán behind to serve his life sentence?

After that, the changes began.

It was as if a siphon had come through with him, a siphon that tapped the power that was once the Book of Fennore and fed it directly into Cathán's bloodstream. At first it was a high, a rush that had him shouting, elated, joyous. And then, by degrees, the rush began to wane. The high began to ebb, the thrill ceased. He'd leveled off somewhere between needing it and hating it—an addict in the constant throes of craving.

But oh, the things he could do.

He created the beasts of Inis Brandubh. He heard their voices, felt their needs. Slowly those voices became clearer until Cathán not only heard them, but he could speak to them as well. He could command them. He could call them out of nothingness and shape them. Now, when he called, they came.

That was not all he commanded.

If the Druid was still here, still somewhere in this twisted hell, he wasn't running the show. Not anymore. Cathán was.

He stood in his temple, a creation that defied explanation. Made of stone and marble, it perched high between two rocky mountains, balanced precariously by massive boulders on each side. Disc shaped, one entire half opened onto a balcony that looked out over the endless miles of Inis Brandubh. It had no doors, no stairs leading up. Cathán could not recall how he entered or how he exited. He wasn't sure that he'd ever left this place. Time and place had become a meaningless blur—a traffic jam of moments that collided and left wreckage behind without reason.

He moved to the wide balcony and looked out at the fields below, at the creatures waiting for his next order. There were *alkonosts*—enormous birds with the heads and breasts of women. Vicious and cruel, they laid their eggs on the shore and awaited his command. At the birth of their offspring would come storms that carried the strength to rip up trees from the earth and fling them into the sea. Darting through the shadows were the evil *rakshasas*, man-eating godlike atrocities with wicked, venomous nails and a hunger for human flesh, especially spoiled. *Chimeras*, fire-breathing monstrosities that looked like a nightmare from a sick mind, lounged nonchalantly, occasionally snapping at an unsuspecting passerby and killing it with a powerful chomp of jaws. They had more teeth than any of the rest.

And of course there was the *bahamut* that lurked out in the dark depths of the sea. A creature of water so immense that the sight of it alone was enough to terrify a man into death. The *bahamut* simply waited to appease its own hunger. There were other creatures out there, waiting for his call. Others that defied description or comprehension scuttling in the darkness, waiting.

And then there were the dragons . . .

All he had to do was call them, send them. But he'd nearly made a fatal mistake dispatching the *ellén trechend* to find the girl. He might command them, but control was another matter entirely. They'd almost killed her—might have if she hadn't changed the game.

Pensive, he turned away and faced the chamber with its pure white walls and calming silence. To his right stood the pedestal where the Book of Fennore waited, looking like any other book in the world. Except this one had pages ripped from the center. And this one was evil.

He stared at it for a long moment before turning again to face the balcony. He'd learned about the girl, Shealy O'Leary, from that brief brush with the Druid's consciousness. The Druid had been looking for her for an eternity. With his new power, Cathán had found a way to search on his own. That other world appeared to him like he was looking out a window. He could see it, but he couldn't touch it.

He'd backtracked, revisiting the key moments in his life after the Book of Fennore had found him. And then he'd caught sight of Shealy O'Leary and he'd known . . . *known* that he'd found what he'd been looking for, had felt the power humming in the girl. As soon as he got near, the door had opened, like the electric doors in the market. And he had stepped out, but only for a moment. He didn't know if it was Shealy, Donnell, or Tiarnan who had shoved him back in, but it didn't matter. When he found her again, he would succeed. He would escape.

Angry with the knot his thoughts had become, he called to his guard.

"Bring me Meaghan Ballagh and the old man."

He knew how Shealy O'Leary had come to this world, but she wasn't the woman he had in his dungeon. The question was—why and how had Meaghan Ballagh come to Inis Brandubh and, more importantly, how could she be used? What gift did she bring with her?

Chapter Twenty-five

IT would be dangerous leaving at dark, moving through the treacherous forest with nothing but dim moonlight to guide them. But as Tiarnan had told Shealy once, what *wasn't* dangerous on Inis Brandubh? As she stood to the side and watched the men packing up the camp, she felt cold to her very bones. Liam sat next to Ellie beside the fire, checking supplies and stuffing them into his bag. He sang to her sister and she almost smiled as she rocked back and forth in tune. They would be ready to leave soon.

Tiarnan stood nearby, watching Shealy with those enigmatic eyes. She was aware of his every breath, his every move. She knew he wanted to talk to her, just as she wanted to hear whatever it was he wanted to say. But the sketched drawing they'd seen felt like it was burned on her retinas. There'd been so many details that had been correct. Her face, her scars, her burned ear. And Tiarnan, puffed up like an action hero . . . How could they have all of those details right if the prophecy was a lie?

And what about the confession Tiarnan had made earlier? He'd chosen his loved ones over a woman once before . . .

Her gaze shifted to Jamie and the others.

Jamie didn't care what the journal foretold. He didn't believe it. He believed in Tiarnan and the heart and soul that made him the man he was.

So what did Shealy believe? What truth did she see when she looked into Tiarnan's eyes?

How could she think that the man who touched her like she was a precious gift would ever hurt her?

He held his body still, his back straight as if braced for the heavy burden he was determined not to drop. His eyes glowed amber in the gloom. From the first moment she'd seen him, she'd thought he carried the weight of the world on his shoulders. She could see it there now, precariously balanced. Too much for any man and she knew *she* had added to its weight.

He moved away until he stood on the edge of the camp where the forest crowded up to the clearing. Then he looked back, beseeching without words. He waited to see if Shealy would join him. She hesitated for only a moment. Life was short—hers might be very short. No matter what the outcome, she didn't want to waste this minute with him.

Before she followed him, she knelt beside her sister. "I'm going to talk to Tiarnan for just a minute. You stay with Liam, all right? I promise I'll be right back."

Ellie didn't look happy about it, but after a long, serious perusal, the little girl nodded.

He'd waited just beyond the trees. Silently she fell in step with him and they walked without speaking for a few feet until the trees concealed them and their voices would not be overheard. Only then did Tiarnan stop and face her.

"Why did y' not trust me when y' realized what y' could do?" he asked softly.

She glanced at him, seeing the hurt that still darkened his eyes.

"Do y' not think I'm worthy of it? Yer trust, I mean."

"It's not that. It was never that. It's not you I don't trust, Tiarnan. It's me. What happened to me—the accident, everything that came after—it made me feel like I had one purpose. That was to be what everyone else wanted me to be—useful, used. I guess I started thinking that no one would ever want me for the person I am. Only what I could do for them. I stopped trusting people."

"And now?"

"Tiarnan," she said softly. "Now I see I was wrong and I'm sorry I hurt you. I don't know what that prophecy meant. I don't know if we should believe it. If we should be running away from one another and screaming at anyone who gets in our way. I only know that's not what I want to do. Whatever happens, I want it to happen with you."

His hand hovered in the air between them and she knew he wanted to touch her. To bind himself to her. And she wanted that, too. Crazy as it was, she needed to feel his heat. His life. His heart.

"I'm glad you told me about that woman, Tiarnan. I know it must have been . . ." She swallowed. "What happened to her shouldn't have happened. But Tiarnan, none of it should have. You shouldn't have been backed into that corner, you shouldn't have had to make those choices. I believe you tried to do the right thing, because I believe in you. You, the human man who isn't perfect. You made a mistake—I trust you not to do it again."

Silent, he watched her but she couldn't tell what went on behind those whiskey eyes.

"What are you thinking?" she asked when the moment stretched.

"I think I would rather have my limbs torn from my body than see yer eyes fill with loathing when y' look at me."

The statement was spoken so softly that it might have been a wish. But Shealy felt the words down to the very core of her being.

He stared at her, and she saw in those whiskey depths the pain of a man nearly destroyed by betrayal and futility. A man who'd been forced to lead at too young an age. A man who'd been haunted by decisions he should never have had to make. A man fighting odds stacked so high against him that he never had a chance to win.

But she had seen him fight to protect his brother, to protect Ellie, to protect his friends. To protect *her*. Jamie was right. There was not an untrustworthy bone in Tiarnan's body. He was just a good man who'd never been dealt anything but a losing hand.

She took a deep breath and said gently, "I think I love you, Tiarnan."

He went so still that at first she thought he must not have heard her. Then his eyes filled. He looked away, tried to hide his tears from her, but Shealy wouldn't let him. She took his face in her hands and kissed each salty trail, then she led him deeper into the dubious shelter of trees where they were hidden completely. His arms gripped her tight, holding her so close she couldn't breathe. He backed her against an enormous tree trunk and then buried his face in the crook of her shoulder and neck while he cried, shuddering gasps wracking his body as the pain flowed with his tears.

Shealy cried with him and soothed him with nonsensical words, smoothing his hair, his nape, pressing kisses to his face and throat. She wondered if there'd ever been someone to dry his tears before, when he was a child. It didn't sound like Tiarnan had ever had the luxury of being comforted.

After a while he quieted, his arms still steel bands around her. He raised his face, showing her his grief and the oath that she saw glowing within them. "I pledge myself to y', Shealy. I will honor y' and I will protect y' with my dying breath."

In answer, she kissed his mouth, chin, cheeks—tasting the salt of his anguish and the spice of his need. He groaned and cupped her head with his big hands, holding her still so that his mouth could settle over hers and take what he so desperately wanted.

Tiarnan kissed her like she was his last draught of water, his last breath of air. His lips were soft and demanding at the same time, parting hers so that he could taste every inch of her mouth. His tongue was hot and velvety, the feel of it sliding against hers seduction in motion. Suddenly it didn't matter where they were, whether they would live or die. There were only these last moments of now and everything they meant.

For her entire life she'd looked for a connection like she had with Tiarnan. She'd searched for that link to another. Someone who understood who and what she was beneath the skin, beneath the makeup, beneath the exterior that she'd turned into armor, but she'd never thought to find that special person. She'd walled herself up, eliminating even the possibility. But Tiarnan had forged right through her barriers to the soft and broken center of her soul. He'd healed her and he didn't even know it.

He was a man who tried to do the right thing when right was often impossible. How could she blame him for circumstances that were not his to control? How could she do anything but love him for what he tried so hard to be?

They might both die here on this very day, but Shealy would not die denying what she felt for him. In the quiet isolation of the trees, they fumbled with clothing, needing to be closer, needing to join in this bond that they'd both declared for one another. Back pressed to the rough bark of the tree behind her, she hooked her leg at his hip and felt the hard slide of him inside her body, focused every thought on this act, this instant, this man. She'd never been in love before, but if the white-hot feeling that consumed her now wasn't love, she supposed she'd never know what it was. The strength and size of Tiarnan seemed a perfect complement to every inch of her body. He held her, rocking in and out in that slow, sensuous rhythm, bringing her to a pitch that felt like ice and fire, pain and pleasure all mixed with deliverance and redemption. The emotions conflicted even as their passion mated into something greater than either of them.

As he brought her to the edge, she pressed her mouth against his shoulder, muffling the scream that ripped through her, burning and forging until it cleansed her and changed her, making her someone stronger, more beautiful, more loved.

Tiarnan bit back his own shout of release and she felt the savage waves of it rolling through him, creating a new path in him as well. As their hearts slowed, she found they were both trembling.

"I pledge my heart to y', Shealy O'Leary," he said, his forehead resting against hers. "I pledge my life."

Inside her something shifted, cracked and from within it sprang new life. She felt it welling up around her, felt it filling her with strength and determination. She'd come a long way to find Tiarnan. She'd sacrificed so much since she'd lost her mother. She'd carried the burden of guilt, tried to shut out who she really was. But no more. She'd be damned if she'd let anyone take him away from her.

"I pledge my life to you, Tiarnan. And I plan to make it a long one."

Chapter Twenty-six

THEY were ready to go but as they stood in a loose circle, they hesitated. All around them the forest seemed to wait with an evil sort of glee. For the past hour they'd heard rumblings coming from deep within the shadowed woods. Sounds unlike any they'd heard before.

"Cathán is unleashing his monsters," Eamonn said, and there was fear in his voice.

With his body tattooed by the heavy chain links, it was easy to forget how young he was. Shealy thought he couldn't be much older than her.

"More like the three-headed thing?" she asked.

"Worse," Tiarnan said softly.

The small group of men stared from one to another. Beside her, Tiarnan stood straight and strong. The others had given them curious glances when they'd returned from the woods earlier, but no one challenged Tiarnan's right to be by her side. Liam stood next to Nanda with Ellie suspended between as they swung her back and forth by her arms. The sight was so incongruous that Shealy almost laughed. Almost.

Kyle said, "We can't do anything about the monsters. We need to think about the prophecy and how it can help us."

"Help us?" Jamie said. "How would it help us?"

"Shealy can walk between the worlds and open the door to let others escape. Well, we are the others. Once we find her dad, we get the hell out of here. We just need to make sure we don't have any hitchhikers. If we go in knowing that, there's no reason why we can't get out of this mess alive. All of us."

"Works for me," Jamie said.

"The journal also talks of three Keepers. Mahon"—he tapped his chest—"Leary—that's Shealy's dad. And I've got a feeling, you, Jamie, are number three. Shealy told me your dad was a Keeper."

"That might be," Jamie said, "but I don't know jack shit about the Book of Fennore."

"That's not true," Kyle said. "Anyone who's lived in it is an automatic expert. Besides, Donnell knows enough for both of us. We just have to find him, break him free, and then stick to the plan."

"Get out without taking any excess baggage," Jamie said.

"That's right."

"But if we're inside the Book of Fennore, Kyle, how does that work?" Shealy asked.

He smiled. "I'm going to have to rely on faith for that answer. But I'm hoping that being inside it means that we might have some control over this world, over Inis Brandubh."

"I heard that," Jamie muttered.

"Not even Donnell remembers a time when the three came together and used this power we're supposed to have, but it is documented in the journal. And honestly, where does doubt have a place in any of this? We are *inside* the unbelievable. We must fill our hearts with faith and focus only on what we want."

"What do y' want?" Eamonn asked. It seemed he'd meant the question to be belligerent. She could see the anger that still lurked in his eyes, yet his voice was filled with uncertainty and apprehension. His wolf lay forlornly at his feet and Eamonn reached down to stroke it.

"I want to go back to the real world," Kyle said simply. "But not if it means any of the monsters of Fennore can follow me out."

The men standing in the loose circle nodded in agreement. Absently, Nanda reached down and scooped up little Ellie. She looked hesitant for just a moment and then she wrapped a trusting arm around his neck.

At Shealy's surprised glance, he said, "I have a daughter back home. She's Ellie's age. At least she was when I left."

The idea of it, of Nanda being a father wrenched from his child, brought another sense of heartbreak to this mess that had become their lives.

Kyle went on. "Shealy, we need you to take us to your father—or we need you to bring your father to us. With the three united, we might be able to hold the Druid—if he even exists anymore—and Cathán back long enough for you to get us all out of here."

It seemed pointless to mention again that she had no idea how to do any of that.

"How can we hold the Druid back when we don't even know who he is?" Eamonn asked, shifting nervously.

Liam made a derisive sound. "Were y' always a coward, brother, and I just never saw it?"

Eamonn lunged at Liam, and though they were nearly the same height, he outweighed his adolescent brother. But Liam did not back down. He was not so muscular, but he was quick and he was strong. In moments, he had Eamonn pinned to the dirt with an arm across his throat and a blade in his other hand.

"I would spill yer blood and walk away without a care," Liam said. "It is only the knowledge that doing so would hurt a man worth twelve of y' that stops me now. Y've caused him too much pain already."

With that, Liam spat in the dirt and stood and walked away. For a moment, no one spoke. No one moved. And then slowly, as if each step cost him a pint of blood, Tiarnan went to Eamonn and offered him a hand. There were tears in Eamonn's eyes as he took it and Tiarnan helped him to his feet. Eamonn's deep breath shuddered through him, but he didn't let those tears fall. Shealy thought better of him for it—not because she didn't think he had a right to cry— Lord knew they all did. But because she felt his refusal of them was, perhaps, a turning point. When Tiarnan would have moved away, Eamonn would not let him. He grabbed his brother in a desperate embrace and held him.

"My actions have made my words empty," he said in a thick voice. "And so I cannot even ask for forgiveness. But know that I would earn it if I could. It is a cold place, the land of the wrong. I've been there so long I no longer know my way back. But I will try."

Liam hesitated, looking over his shoulder at his brothers with such raw pain that Shealy wished she could do something to breach the bloody chasm that separated them. Eamonn released Tiarnan and stepped away without another word.

It wasn't time for reconciliation if, in fact, such a thing could even be had. But the three brothers standing at opposite points seemed to have formed a bridge that whipped and creaked in the winds of doubt but linked them all the same.

"Okay. We go for Shealy's dad. We all on the same page?" Jamie asked.

The men nodded, though some of Eamonn's looked skeptical and others hostile.

"Let's break it down, Shealy," Kyle said. "We need to figure out how you do this traveling thing you can do. Yesterday—or whenever it was—when I saw you in your dad's study. How did you get there?"

"I don't know. I told you—"

"Stop," he said, holding up a hand. "Think. What were you doing just before?"

"Bathing. Ellie and I were washing away the blood. And I was worrying about Dad. I felt this . . . I don't know . . . spark between me and Ellie and then everything went . . . *thick*. And the next thing I knew I was there."

"Right," Kyle said, with a look of triumph. "You were thinking of him and you went to him."

"But I wasn't thinking of you. Why did I bring you back when you hadn't even crossed my mind?"

"When I saw you, Shealy, I couldn't believe my own eyes. I remember reaching out to touch your shoulder right as you disappeared."

"That's right, you touched me. In the dungeon, too—that's what you were doing. You were trying to reach Dad while you held my hand."

He nodded.

"But Kyle," she said, "I wasn't thinking about Tiarnan when we were attacked and I certainly wasn't thinking about Cathán."

"Maybe Cathán was thinking of you," he said simply. "You already know he was looking for you. And Tiarnan, well, let's just call that destiny."

He winked at them both and moved away. Tiarnan came to stand beside her again and his fingers twined with hers, anchoring her to him and giving her the strength to believe that she might be able to do this crazy thing they had planned.

Kyle went on. "Earlier today, right before you did your thing and took us to the dungeons. You saw me—"

"And thought of my father again. I was thinking of the study and seeing you with him. I thought if you were here, he must be near."

Kyle nodded. "So maybe it's as easy as that, Shealy. Maybe all you need to do is focus."

Could it be? Could it seriously be as simple as putting her mind into it? Was this why she'd shied away from exploring her ability for so long? Why her father had kept so many secrets from her?

Frowning, she closed her eyes, thinking to test the theory, but Tiarnan stopped her.

"Wait," he said, giving her a slight shake. "Not yet. If this works, we want to go together, yes?"

He looked up at each man in turn. His own people, Jamie, Zac, Reyes, and Liam, didn't need the sharp nod they gave him. Eamonn did not hesitate to join, though he looked as anxious as a man could. Each of his men made their own decision and not one of them looked to Eamonn first. All but Nanda bowed out and stepped away.

Tiarnan put his hand in the middle of their circle as he'd done when they left the banks of the small islet where they'd lived. Jamie's hand went next, then the others added theirs until the entire group was clustered close, shoulder to shoulder, hand on hand. Eamonn's wolf nudged his nose into the group, and Eamonn curled his fingers into the soft fur, connecting the canine to the circle. Nanda still held Ellie, and Shealy wished there were some way to leave her little sister somewhere safe, but she knew there was no such place. Shealy squeezed forward and put her hand on the top of the pile.

Jamie looked back at the group of men who'd opted to sit this one out.

"Last call," he said.

But they'd made their decisions, and with resigned glances, they faded into the forest.

"Think of yer father, Shealy," Tiarnan said. "Take us to him. Now. Take us now."

That soft voice had whispered pledges of loyalty, words of love. Those lips had covered her body with kisses, had opened her heart to a world beyond her own selfish pain. She wanted to answer that voice. She wanted to please the man who used it. She wanted to do something right for once in her life.

But she was afraid.

Her father needed her. These people here needed her. They were trapped, and she might be the key to get them out. She'd been a coward for so much of her life, hiding behind her makeup, her injuries, her guilt. Now was the time to be more. If she really was *idir eatarthu*, then damn it to hell, she needed to embrace that.

She stared deeply into Tiarnan's eyes, seeing within the golden brown a faith in her she'd never had in herself. He had pledged his heart to her. She would show him that he hadn't made a mistake.

"The dungeons again?" she asked.

"No," Kyle said. "Not the place. The person. We want your father, wherever he is."

She closed her eyes once more and pictured her father. In her head, she heard his voice calling her name. As she had before, she felt a small spark against her skin, a sense that now, like the first time, something amplified it and made it bigger, more powerful, and she knew that was Ellie, reaching out with a bond that surpassed sisterhood. It boosted the tight coil of power inside of Shealy. The misted gel world closed in on her so quickly she was disoriented, but beneath her hand she felt Tiarnan's and the others, locked in the oath to come, to help. To save . . .

She cast herself out and felt a vortex suctioning the air, pulling her through, and she held on as they flew through the thickness.

Chapter Twenty-seven

THEY hit the ground like missiles, scattered among trees that towered impossibly high. For a moment Shealy thought they must have only blacked out and were still in the forest where Eamonn had been camped. But no, these trees were different and the air . . . A strange, zoolike stench filled the night and covered them in a new kind of dread.

"Holy fucking Jesus," Shealy heard Jamie say.

Beside her, Tiarnan took her hand. "Are you all right?"

She nodded, glancing around quickly, searching for her sister. She saw Ellie with Nanda and Liam.

"Y' all right, honey?" she asked. Ellie looked dazed but she nodded. The others stumbled to their feet and shook off their confusion, doing a quick inventory of body parts and weapons. Shealy looked from one to another. They were all here—even Eamonn's wolf had made it. Somehow she'd managed to move them but it still seemed impossible, and she had no idea where, exactly, she'd brought them.

Liam waited at Tiarnan's side, now holding Ellie as Nanda brushed the dirt and leaves from his clothes. Her sister looked pale but strangely determined. She met Shealy's eyes with a sparkle that seemed to speak to something deep in Shealy's mind and she felt a hum of energy surging toward her. The same she'd felt before, when they'd been attacked by the three-headed monsters and later, when Shealy and Ellie had traveled to her dad's study, and yet indefinably different. What was it?

Ellie leaned forward, put her hand over Shealy's eyes, forcing Shealy to close them. Then her small palm moved up to rest against Shealy's forehead. An image formed in Shealy's mind of darkness so great and vast that it was terrifying and unending. In that black tapestry there was no glimmer of light, no sound, no scent, and then suddenly, like a bright star, a light gleamed, radiating possibility with its silver bright glow. The pulsing glitter of it seemed to wink at Shealy, to coax her forward. It urged her to reach for it.

Ellie removed her hand, and Shealy opened her eyes. She didn't understand what had just happened, but there wasn't time to figure it out because the men were moving. Ellie gazed at Shealy for another moment and then laid her head down again on Liam's shoulder.

They inched to where the others had begun to gather and looked out to a clearing that stretched from the edge of the forest to the rocky cliffs above the sea. Mulling around as if trapped by invisible cages were creatures more bizarre than anything Shealy could even imagine. An enormous lionlike animal seemed to be sprouting a vicious-looking goat from its spine and its tail flicked with a fanged snake hissing at the end. There were the three-headed monsters they'd fought just yesterday, snapping and droning among the others. A huge boar standing on its hind legs roared and swiped bear claws at a lizard the size of a hippopotamus.

"Salamanders," Nanda said with a shudder.

She'd thought salamanders to be quick and harmless little reptiles, but the creature she stared at was far from that. It reared and spat at the boar, which screamed with rage. Flitting at the circumference of the field was something else that moved so fast she couldn't make out what it was. In the distance she could see the sea, and bathed in the silver moonlight there seemed to be a dark shadow wading in the waves—something too big to comprehend.

"Don't look at it," Tiarnan warned. "It's too terrible to behold."

Shealy pulled her gaze from the undulating shadow and looked at Tiarnan. "What is it?"

"Nothing y' want to know more of."

On three sides the looming forest towered around the clearing and the creatures. No visible cage confined them, but the tree line acted like a natural enclosure and they seemed to have no desire to leave it. Straight ahead were two rocky hills that rose like mountains and held balanced between them a stone structure—a temple shaped like a spaceship. It seemed to hover in the sky, rising like something created in the time of myth, a horribly twisted bird's nest of polished marble that shone like bone in the moonlight. A balcony ran the entire half, open like a twisted grin to the field below. The structure was neither man-made nor nature's creation. It was ghastly and terrifying.

And that was where her father would be. She knew it.

Tiarnan motioned to the others and they gathered round. "We can reach the balcony if we approach from there—" He pointed to the spill of boulders and rocks that made up one side of the eerie, elevated structure, leading to a point where the edge of the opening nudged the hillside. "Once we get there, we find Shealy's father and then . . ."

He faltered for a moment.

"And then we pray," Kyle said simply.

They nodded in consent. It was as good a plan as any.

Quietly they cut through the trees, keeping low and silent to avoid the attention of the creatures, and then they moved to the rough hillside rising above them. Jamie, Zac, and Reyes went first, climbing with agility and confidence. Ellie scrambled onto a rock and then onto Liam's back, clinging like a monkey as he ascended. Nanda was a few steps behind, watching the child with concern, looking like he'd be ready if she should lose her grip and fall. Eamonn and his wolf followed, though the canine kept stopping and looking back at the monsters milling below with a cross between alarm and glee.

Tiarnan and Kyle both stared at Shealy for a moment.

"Are y' ready?" Tiarnan asked when she knew what he really wanted to say was "stay here and wait." She saw the fear in his anxious expression—not fear for himself, but fear for her.

"As ready as I'll ever be."

Without waiting for him to help, she followed the others, finding handholds in the boulders and clambering steadily up. Behind her, she heard Tiarnan and Kyle following.

They reached the point where the bright balcony seemed to hover in midair. Zac was in the lead now and as soon as they'd all gathered, he made a graceful, silent leap over the chasm and onto the side. Bracing himself, he reached back, and Reyes went next, then Jamie. Liam handed Ellie over before making the jump himself. Moments later they were all safely on the smooth surface. Below them the creatures paced and roared, unaware their fortress had been breached. To their left the balcony opened onto what appeared to be a large circular chamber. Huge tiles made a shiny patchwork on the ground and climbed the walls to the ceiling, making the room like an optical illusion. There were voices coming from inside.

"Where is your daughter?" a man asked with disdain. His voice had a strange, musical quality that enticed. Shealy took a step forward without even realizing.

"'Tis Cathán," Tiarnan said with revulsion, holding her back.

"Safe in her bed, dreaming of a bright future," came the answer from another man. Shealy recognized that voice. She bit her lip, fighting the instinct to charge forward.

"That's my dad," she breathed.

Beside her, Tiarnan took her hand, as if he'd heard her thoughts and wanted to be sure to restrain her.

"I will find her," Cathán said, "and you will see how futile it is to defy me."

Her dad didn't reply to this and the quiet stretched for a long moment. Zac inched closer to the door and peered around it. When he looked back, he held up five fingers and then made a motion that indicated two people waited on either side of the entrance and the other three were in the middle.

"My men are out searching for her. I will find her. Make no mistake."

The satisfaction in Cathán's tone was ironic. He should have left his men behind to watch the back door.

"It sounds too good to be true," Tiarnan breathed. "We outnumber them."

From the chamber, Cathán raised his voice again. "And you, Meaghan Ballagh. Who brought you here?"

Meaghan Ballagh? Shealy looked around to see if any of the others recognized that name. Kyle stepped forward and said in a low voice, "When I escaped Cathán's men, I saw a woman. She was captured."

Shealy suddenly remembered the woman she and Liam had seen. She'd wanted to help her but there'd been no chance of a rescue.

Shealy heard another man speaking now, and his voice was deep and soft, as seductive as Cathán's but somehow more . . . human. He said, "When you answer, tell him *he* brought you."

"You brought me," Meaghan parroted.

Shealy frowned. That was strange. Surely Cathán had heard that deep voice prompting Meaghan. But when Cathán spoke, it was with breathless awe.

"How?" he said. "How did I bring you?"

"Tell him you cannot begin to comprehend his powers," the silky deep voice murmured.

"How the feck should I know how?" Meaghan said. "You did it. You figure it out."

"Get ready, Shealy," Tiarnan whispered.

Before Shealy could begin to understand what went on in the chamber beyond them, Zac and Reyes moved like the fighting unit they were. They whipped around the corner as one, blades at the ready, and charged. Liam shucked Ellie from his back, ordered her to stay with Shealy, and then he, Jamie, and Nanda disappeared. She felt Tiarnan's fingers trail over her shoulder and then he rounded the corner with Kyle on his heels.

For a moment, Shealy and Ellie just stared at one another in shock and fear. She didn't know what she had expected, but it had begun so quickly. Then Shealy took the child's hand and pulled her tight to the wall, inching closer so they could see. Two men lay dead at either side of the entrance. In the center stood Cathán, her father, and a woman who looked to be somewhere in her twenties, dressed in a T-shirt, blue jeans, and scuffed sneakers. She stood with her chin raised, jaw set defiantly. At her side stood a tall, shirtless man who watched with intense, hooded eyes. He had no weapon, but Shealy sensed he was dangerous in his own right. Yet no one gave him a second glance.

Cautiously, she pulled Ellie into the chamber with her, hugging the wall and trying to keep back. The men had circled Cathán, but he seemed blithely unconcerned. He glanced beyond them and spotted Shealy. His eyes widened, and the shirtless man took a lunging step forward.

"It is you," Cathán breathed, and Shealy felt a bolt of fear drive through her. That voice, the power that seemed to vibrate off of him.

"Who is she, Áedán?" the woman Shealy guessed to be Meaghan whispered to the man no one else seemed to see.

Áedán. Shealy didn't know the name, but this man . . . Her thoughts stumbled, scrambling to find order. Who was he?

"I knew you would come," Cathán said calmly.

Her dad had been staring at Kyle and Jamie with a combination of horror and hope, but now he swung those faded eyes her way. "Shealy!" he exclaimed, distraught that she was there. "For the love of God, why didn't you listen when I told you to go back home?"

Tugging Ellie along with her, Shealy rushed to her father's side and threw her arms around him. "Are you okay, Daddy?"

"Yes, child. But this is no place for you. And you brought the little one." His eyes grew damp as he touched his child for the first time. "Oh and isn't she the very image of your mother. You must leave, though. Go home. Please, Shealy, take her and go home."

"Not without you, Daddy. I won't leave you here."

The shirtless man took an apprehensive step toward Meaghan, pulling Shealy's attention away from her father. He cut his eyes between Cathán, Shealy, and Meaghan in alarm, and suddenly Shealy knew who he was.

The Druid. Invisible to everyone but her and Meaghan. The entity the prophecy said she would unleash on the world. Shealy couldn't say why she was so certain, but deep within her, she *knew*. She *knew* she was right.

She felt a strange vibration in the air and with horror she realized it was coming from Cathán. "What's he doing?" she demanded. The men had all spread out and only Tiarnan stood guard over Cathán.

Shealy pointed. "Stop him," she said. "Whatever he's doing, we've got to sto—"

But it was too late. Even as she spoke they felt the rumble, the quake of the earth. Smooth stones began to careen down from the mountains outside and slam against the strange temple. Inside, cracks spiraled down from the arched ceiling and chunks of tile separated and fell.

"Oh Christ," Zac said, peering out at the field below. "They're coming. They're coming!"

. Shealy knew without being told what he meant.

The creatures. The beasts, confined without a cage, were coming to kill them.

That Cathán had called them was clear. He raised his hands and smiled as they charged up the sides of the mountain. Those with wings flew straight through the entrance. Terrified, Shealy saw dragons among them.

Dragons.

Hysteria rose with that acknowledgment. Of all the unbelievable she'd survived, *dragons* seemed to be the edge that could not be crossed.

She felt Cathán's power surging through the chamber, and from the corner of her eye, she saw the shirtless man who'd spoken to Meaghan sway and then collapse at her feet like a puppet whose strings had suddenly been cut.

"Áedán!" Meaghan shouted, but there was nothing she could do because the beasts from below had found their way in.

It was chaos and terror, mixed into a churning cauldron of violence. Tiarnan leaped in front of Shealy and Ellie, shielding them with his body. Her father and Meaghan huddled close, defenseless against the beasts that stamped, snarling and snapping as they charged. Jamie and the others attacked the creatures with courage that made Shealy want to cry out. She had a moment of relief when she realized the dragons could not find a way through the opening, but the breath of their fire scorched the floors and tried to devour the people beyond their reach.

All around them, energy sparked like a live wire bouncing between puddles of water. She felt it building, like a shock of static electricity seeking an outlet and Shealy focused on it with all her might. Kyle had said being *inside* the Book of Fennore might mean that they had some control over it. Shealy decided this was the time to test that. With a deep breath, she reached out to that growing force and using her mind, she pulled.

Tiarnan gave her a glance over his shoulder, eyes wide as if he'd felt what she was doing. Then suddenly Ellie gripped her hand tight and that energy arrowed into the child, lighting her up with an unearthly glow. Shealy tried to shout, tried to break the connection, but Ellie held on as tightly as she could, and then with her other hand she reached for Meaghan.

The two women faced each other and suddenly everything else fell away until there was only the triumvirate they made. As if controlled by some force beyond them, Shealy held her free hand out, palm up, and Meaghan, as dazed and fearful as Shealy, placed her hand against it.

The moment they touched, the instant the triangle sealed, a high-pitched squeal hit the room like a wave. For that second, Tiarnan, Liam, and the others all glanced back, as if called by the females. Only Cathán remained unaware of what was about to come. The monsters poured through the open door with snapping jaws, driven by violence so that they turned on one another even as they attacked. The men fought valiantly, but more and more of the creatures came and it would be a slaughter in seconds.

Hurry.

Whatever it was that they were doing, they needed to hurry.

Tiarnan fought bravely, swinging his sword and cutting through the creatures. Afraid to look, afraid to turn away, Shealy watched a great and terrible shudder go through him and then suddenly he seemed to jolt and expand into an enraged giant.

Riastradh.

That's what they'd called it.

Suddenly she knew what they needed to do. She pictured it, sent the image through the current flowing between them. From the center of the small, female trine, a spark rose like a star and found its way to Tiarnan, went through him like a meteor, changing colors as it emerged. She felt Tiarnan's power like a blast of heat and she pulled it in and shot it back out. The light hovered for a moment and then it slammed into Jamie, then Liam, then Zac and on it went until all of the men had been touched by it and each of them began to glow.

Liam turned next, followed by Eamonn and Zac. *Riastradh.* All of them. In an instant every man but Jamie, Kyle, and her father transformed into an unconquerable army.

Each of them fought like a dozen men, finding weakness in their foe, finding victory in each blow. In a blink, the tide turned and the creatures were beaten back, heads severed, bodies dismembered. Cathán opened his eyes to find that the carnage of this battle was not what he'd expected.

Her father looked terrified, and yet his eyes scanned the room and landed on a pedestal.

"Kyle," he shouted. "And you—Jamie!"

Kyle heard him, though how she'd never know. He stumbled back, calling to Jamie at the same time. Shealy felt the power ebbing, feared that they would lose control. She held as tightly as she could, but it was no use. The burst had come and gone.

Cathán spun on them, and raising his hands, he muttered words she did not understand in a voice that seemed to coax and seduce. It made her want to break away from the others and go to him.

All but a few of the creatures lay dead in bloody heaps, and the sparking force that had joined the men waned. One by one they turned back into themselves, pale and weakened, blood-soaked and exhausted. As she watched, they collapsed around her as Tiarnan had last night. Only Tiarnan remained *riastradh*, still bringing his blade down against the boarlike creature with the long bear claws.

Cathán advanced on Shealy with fury in his eyes, but with each step he took, the earth shook, and pieces of the ceiling, walls, and floor broke away and clattered down, down to the quarry below them. The ground tilted, breaking the three females apart, making them stagger back. The instant the connection severed the entire temple pulsed from within and then the walls, the ceiling—all of it—exploded outward, leaving the people standing on a vacillating platform that was crumbling before their eyes.

Shealy screamed as the explosion took the tiles around her, leaving her suspended on a floating dais no bigger than a tabletop. A few feet away Meaghan balanced on another dangerous section, and little Ellie stood on a piece even smaller. Shealy's father had moved to someplace behind her, but she couldn't see him and didn't dare turn and risk unbalancing the unstable surface beneath her.

"Tiarnan, where are you?" she cried.

The voice that answered her was guttural and fierce, but she knew it was him. Cathán was just a few feet away, trapped himself by the unhinged flooring. But he didn't look fearful. No, the look in his eyes was calculating.

"We will all die unless you do something, Shealy," Cathán said. "You can stop this. Can't you?"

Behind her, Tiarnan roared like one of the beasts he'd slaughtered and at last she dared a look over her shoulder. He was sprawled over two separated platforms, clinging as they bucked and swiveled beneath him.

Beyond Tiarnan she could see her father, Jamie, and Kyle, gripping the edges of the pedestal with the Book of Fennore between them. What were they doing?

"Stop it!" she shouted at Cathán.

"Only you can stop it, Shealy. You can get us all out of here. Help me and I will help you. Set me free and I will give you whatever your heart desires."

The voice coaxed and lured, and she could see the reason in his words. She felt all will to resist drain away until she wanted to do as he asked. Tiarnan roared again, breaking the spell, pulling her back from a trap she couldn't see.

She couldn't speak, couldn't shout a denial when that was what she wanted to do. As if hearing her defiance, Cathán smiled and shot a look at Liam, where he lay collapsed on a small plane. Cathán cocked his head, held his hand out flat, and then tilted it. Liam began to slide down the surface, knocking Nanda from his shaky position as he went.

Shealy heard Tiarnan's agonized cry and felt her own terror building and building, begging for release. She screamed, and the sound hit the air like an explosion. She saw Cathán recoil, heard now her father's voice raised and chanting, felt the last of the hovering floor fall away.

The screams echoed as they all plummeted down, down faster and faster. Shealy scrambled to pull her thoughts together, focusing on the clouds, pulling them together, meshing the world into something thick and gelatinous. She felt herself slow, searched through the chaos for the others and felt them there with her as the world spun, faster and faster until she was sick with dizziness. The air became so thick it had texture and she had to drag it away, seeking the way out. She remembered a carnival ride that spun so fast it pinned her to the caged walls. She felt that sick plunging feeling now but she fought it, imagining a door that only she could open. As she groped through blank oppression she saw it at last.

A world beyond the small opening that she stretched and held in place by the will of her thoughts. On the other side she saw the now familiar cliffs, the sea surrounding the Isle of Fennore. A man stood on the precipice, a woman at his side. They both turned and looked at her with disbelief. From somewhere in the fog she heard Meaghan shouting, *"Rory!"* but Shealy knew this was not where Meaghan belonged.

She reached through the mist and found Liam, dangling in space. She pulled him to her and then found Ellie, put her sister in his arms, and shoved them out of the mist and into the real world. She sensed Cathán trying to reach her, trying to go through as well, but Tiarnan was there, holding him back.

The door slammed shut and Shealy was spinning, faster, harder. She groped for another door, found the small opening and pried it wider. This world was not familiar, not to her, but she knew instinctively who belonged there. Nanda, with his deep dark eyes and kindness, went through with a shout.

Cathán was closer now, and Tiarnan's strength ebbed. She didn't know how much longer he'd be able to hold Cathán back.

Now she sought her father, probing through the white wash of sound and perception. She found him, linked with Jamie and Kyle as his strange chant rose in the miasma. Suddenly she understood what they were doing.

The Book of Fennore.

It lay open and spread on its dais, pages inside fanning back and forth, their color a strange and unearthly pale. In the center, several stood straight with jagged, torn edges that looked like ghastly wounds. Three cords of silver connected in a mystifying lock that dangled over the edge, sprung open. Suddenly, the pages stopped and the Book remained spread in a vulgar, sexual invitation. Blood filled the bindings, inched across the pages, and embedded in the spiral symbols before welling up and over the edges to drop off into nothingness.

In the fog she heard Cathán shouting, felt him coming closer, sensed his panic. Whatever her father was doing to the Book of Fennore, Cathán did not like it. She had to get them out of here, but how could she do it? How could she leave without knowing if Cathán would find a way to once again bring her back? Or to follow?

And where was the Druid?

The mist began to clear, and Shealy knew she was coming to the end. She couldn't hold them without the blanketing white. She could see Zac and Reyes, coming back into themselves, drained from the battle with the monsters of Inis Brandubh, and with a last burst of strength she reached deep inside and found another doorway she could pry open. She didn't know where it led, but it was away from here. Away from danger. The men jerked as they realized that they hung suspended over a chasm that would kill them if they fell and then again as Shealy swept them up. She forced Zac and Reyes to go through, not knowing where they would land, praying that it was somewhere safe.

The two men wanted to stay with Jamie, they were trained to be the last to go, but there was no time for any of that. Exhausted, she drew in a deep breath.

"Shealy?"

It was Tiarnan, and she turned to find the man she loved, no longer a giant, no longer her avenger. He was pale and gray, exhausted beyond any man's endurance. She reached for him, and he wrapped those strong arms around her.

"Y' saved Liam," he said.

"Yes. He's with your sister now. Ellie, too."

"Ah, I thank y', my Shealy. And what do we do now?"

In his question she saw that he'd given her the choice of what would happen to both of them. She knew it was a monumental thing for a man who'd tried to control even the wind.

"I don't know," she whispered. "He's coming for me."

"Then y' must send him somewhere he cannot escape. You must not let him loose."

"The Druid, Tiarnan. He is here, too. I saw him, with Meaghan. Where can I send them?" she asked, but then she knew.

She looked back at the Book of Fennore. Her father and the others were trying to close it. Seal it with the strange chant her father muttered over and over.

The damage that Tiarnan had done must be mended so that no one else was ever sucked into this terrifying place again. In her gut, she knew there was only one place to send them.

As old as the earth and sky, the Book radiated a hum in a see-sawing rhythm that stroked her in the thick, vaporous white. As she watched the pages begin to fan once more, she saw the ancient symbols move in a blur that was mesmerizing. Her father's voice rose and with it a swirling storm began to grow around them. Shealy wouldn't have much time.

Thunder exploded above them, chasing sizzling spears of lightning that threatened to impale the frail humans. A great, tearing sound ripped through the air, and like wallpaper being stripped, fissures appeared in the sky above and the earth beneath them. That great suctioning force pulled them all closer to the Book. Only Cathán seemed able to fight it.

Shealy looked at her father, Jamie, and Kyle, a front line around the terrible Book. Behind them, Eamonn looked young and terrified, arms wrapped around his panting wolf. And there . . . there was Meaghan and the unconscious man with the velvet voice. Áedán, she'd called him, but Shealy knew who he really was. The Druid. She had to get Meaghan away from him and then somehow bind him to Cathán and trap them here.

Sure. And then maybe she could sprout wings and fly them all out of here.

Closing her eyes, she forced herself to pull the storm and vapor in tight around them, then she focused on Cathán, found him in the wind and rain that pelted the disintegrating world. Next she sent out a line for the Druid, wrapping tight around him.

"You will not have your way," she breathed, and her voice became a tempest, her will a cyclone that hauled them closer. "You will not win."

Meaghan was screaming, reaching for the man she called Áedán. She didn't understand who he was, and Shealy couldn't stop and tell her. They fought for control as the storm rose.

Shealy pictured another doorway, opened it, and looked through to the fanning pages of spiral symbols, runes of a time so long ago they were as mystical as their meaning. She pried that door open, crying as it fought to keep her out. And then she shoved Cathán, the man who'd ruined so many lives, into that small opening. With a deep breath she tried to jerk the Druid free of Meaghan's grasp and hurl him through as well, but the door was smaller and a great blast knocked her back.

"Let him go," Shealy shouted at Meaghan. Around her the men stared, shocked, trying to figure out what she was talking about. They couldn't see the unconscious man, but Meaghan held him tight.

"He's evil, Meaghan. He's the Druid."

It was obvious the other woman couldn't understand Shealy's words over the deafening noise.

"He's a prisoner like me," she shouted.

There was no time to explain. "Let him go or I can't help you."

That seemed to get through to her. Meaghan was still shaking her head, but reluctantly she released the man.

The howling storm unleashed like a demon. The rain became acid, the lightning, blades that sliced through them. Her father's voice rose above all, chanting, chanting, and then suddenly the Book slammed shut with a bang that resounded like a bomb and the spiraled knots of the lock charged forward, forged into one, mating with a primeval violence that ended with a final metallic grind. The door she'd pried open shut with a resounding *boom*. Cathán was on the other side, but not the Druid. . . .

"No," Shealy cried. They'd only imprisoned Cathán. The Druid was still free. . . .

Chapter Twenty-eight

B UT there was nothing she could do. The world of Inis Brandubh
no longer existed, and they were caught in the evolution of its
demise.

The screams of the world shattering around her crowded into her
head, scattering her thoughts. Perhaps it wouldn't matter that the
Druid had not been trapped in the Book, because there wouldn't
be anything left of him either. They were going to die, here in this
nonexistence.

No, a voice from within said. Not if she could help it.

Once more Shealy searched for an opening she could force into a
door, focusing on the only place that she could bring to mind—that
stark cliff where their car had plunged to the rocks and sea. She saw
the hint of a doorway at the edge of her sight, focused, bringing it
closer. There it was, just at the tip of her fingers.

She struggled to pry it open, to create a passage wide enough to
escape, but the opening fought back, trying to collapse in on them. At
last she managed to grasp it with her mind, to force it to open wider.

The fearsome cliffs, the angry sea waited, but night and day seemed to be blinking like a strobe light over them and Shealy understood that time was moving at lightning speed. Eamonn reached for his brother even as Shealy tried to shove Tiarnan through as well, but there were some things even Shealy couldn't accomplish. Moving Tiarnan, evidently, was one of them. Eamonn, arm still looped around his wolf, was sucked into the beyond, but Tiarnan would not budge.

Frustrated, she wasted no time turning to Meaghan, gathering her up and shoving her through the closing door. At the last moment, Meaghan reached for the Druid as she sailed through. It happened so fast, Shealy could do nothing to stop it. He'd escaped, just as the prophecy had warned. Meaghan had taken him, but it was Shealy who had set him free.

There wasn't time to think of the repercussions or dwell on her failure, not with the crush of doom rolling down on her.

She turned her power on her father, Jamie, and Kyle. Still holding the passage to the rocky shores of Fennore open, she shoved the two men through. Then she pictured Ellie, and the scenery of that opening changed, and for an instant she glimpsed her sister, held in Liam's strong arms. Her father tried to tell her something, but the door was collapsing and there was only time for her to shout "I love you, Daddy," as she managed to hurl him through just as the door slammed shut and the mist vanished completely.

She was alone in the black with Tiarnan.

They clung to one another, neither falling nor floating. The torrential storm had devoured the hellish world of Inis Brandubh and nothing was left but the cold. The desolation. The nothingness. There were no more doors to find and pry open. There was no escape.

"I don't know how to get us out," Shealy said.

Tiarnan held her tight and pressed his lips to her temple. "Y've done enough, Shealy."

"No. Tiarnan, the Druid escaped. He went with Meaghan. Wherever I sent her, he went, too."

She was crying and Tiarnan soothed her. "Y' did what y' could. Y' were brave as any warrior."

She shook her head. "But—"

"What will be will be. Destiny has its own path. We've learned that. *I* have learned that."

She realized there were tears on Tiarnan's face. Or maybe it was her own tears she felt.

"Y' saved yer father and yer sister. 'Tis what y' came to do. And y' saved my brothers, my friends. If not for y', lass . . ."

Yes, she'd done what she came to do. But now she was scared. How long would they survive in this void? Seconds? Hours? Forever?

"If I'm going to meet my maker, Tiarnan, I'm glad to be doing it with you."

"And I with y', Shealy O'Leary. Y've made me be more than I ever hoped to be. Y' gave me a purpose and for the first time in my life, I fulfilled it. I wish I could save y' now. That is my regret."

"No regrets, Tiarnan. I have none where you are concerned."

He smiled at her. It was too dark to see those whiskey eyes or the flash of teeth. But she felt the smile.

The black closed in, binding them tighter. A howling sound came from nowhere and everywhere at once; it whipped them and sealed their desolation. Shealy clung tighter to Tiarnan, and he sheltered her in those strong arms. No matter what came next, she knew he'd never let her go.

Then suddenly there was a light, pale and ethereal, floating just overhead like a pinpoint star in a tapestry of velvet. Shealy and Tiarnan watched it as it flickered, went out, and then appeared again, brighter this time.

"What is it?" he asked, his voice but a breath in her ear.

"I don't know."

But as she watched she felt something inside awaken and lift its head. The star flickered again and that awareness blossomed, greeting the small arc of energy.

"Oh my God," Shealy breathed.

"What?" Tiarnan asked.

"Ellie."

As if speaking the child's name gave the star power, it flared, lighting up the area where she and Tiarnan waited. Shealy reached up for it, with her mind, her senses, her heart. She felt the warmth of the connection, the bond that went beyond sisterhood.

A passageway. And here was Ellie showing her where the other side was.

This was no doorway. It was no tear in the fabric of the world through which they could slip. This was a lifeline and it was up to Shealy to grasp it.

"Tiarnan," she said softly. "I think we're going home."

"Home?" he said, staring at the pulsing light. "Is there such a place?"

She peered at him, making out his features in the glow. Then she smiled and pressed her mouth tight to his. "There is for us. I love you, Tiarnan."

He kissed her then, softly, sweetly. "And I love y', Shealy."

She wrapped her arms tightly around his neck, made sure his hands were firmly anchored at her waist, and then she closed her eyes and pictured that light as a tunnel, leading them through to the other side.

She heard Tiarnan suck in a deep breath, and then they were falling, falling, falling.

They hit the ground like stones, hard enough to make colors dance in her head. She groaned with pain, but when she opened her eyes, there was sun on her face and she could hear the sea in the distance. Tiarnan's arms were still wrapped around her, his heart a steady beat in her ear.

"Tiarnan," she whispered. "We made it."

He rolled to his back and looked up at the sky for a dazed moment, and then he laughed and so did she. They lay on the rocky beach, drenched in the fresh chill of salt water, and they laughed.

"Do you mind telling me what's so funny?" a deep voice asked.

Shealy thought her heart might burst with the joy of being alive. Of being here—*wherever here was*. She turned to the voice and saw a huge blond man with the bluest eyes she'd ever seen standing in the froth of the surf.

"Ruairi?" she heard Tiarnan breath.

The man's eyes widened as he saw Tiarnan, and an instant later a pregnant woman skidded to a stop behind him. The man held out a hand to steady her. "Easy, Saraid," he said.

"Is it true?" she cried. "Is it Tiarnan?"

Tiarnan stood, reaching down to help Shealy while the pregnant woman threw her arms around him. Shealy recognized her now from the picture she'd seen in the journal—his sister, and the blond man must be her husband. Before she could process it all, she saw Liam and Ellie racing toward them and behind the two came her father, slower but with no less joy in his face. Then she was in the center of a group hug filled with laughter and tears and knowledge that this moment was a miracle.

She held tight to Tiarnan, felt his strong arms around her, and she thanked a God she'd thought she no longer believed in for giving her this man and this day to love him.

And she prayed for those she'd sent out on their own with the prophecy of the Druid a hot breath behind them. She and Tiarnan had managed to overcome one of the journal's dire predictions. Perhaps it could be done again.

She, Tiarnan, her father, and the others had done all they could, though. They'd fought, and she had to believe they'd won the battle if not the war.

Safely within Tiarnan's arms, she held her little sister tight and gazed with love at her father. As Tiarnan's sister jabbered about a thousand different things at once, Shealy tilted back her head and smiled at the sun.

"Ah, Shealy," Tiarnan said softly. "Y' are more lovely to me now than y've ever been."

After all they'd been through, she knew that couldn't be true, but it was hard to argue with those amazing eyes and that crooked grin that made her knees feel weak.

"Do you know what I think—" she began, but Tiarnan only laughed.

"How many times do I need to tell y', lass. Don't think."

Turn the page for a preview of Erin Quinn's
next book in the Mists of Ireland series...

Haunting Embrace

Coming soon from Berkley Sensation!

FROM the deck of the small fishing vessel, Áedán could see the dark opening of the sea cavern at the base of the jagged shoreline. From here, it looked smaller than he knew it to be, but it called to him, a black hole that was at once ancient, threatening, and expectant. So many turning points of his life had played out in that cavern that in his mind it had become a great, yawning beast waiting to devour what was left of him.

High above it, castle ruins teetered in crumbled disgrace, the desolate remains adding another layer to the menace that shrouded the cliffs. Slowly, he scanned their stark solitude before his gaze returned unerringly to the arched opening at sea level where the icy tide surged in and out, in and out. Each suck and pull begged Áedán to come closer and impelled him to flee until he felt mad from the conflicting urges.

He'd been too long without emotions, without the trappings of humanity. Now the influx of so many disagreeing reactions left him feeling bound and burdened.

He forced himself to look away and focus on the fishing net in his hands. Since they'd docked in the bay an hour ago, he'd been cutting away the rotted sections and replacing them. It was a tedious, loathsome task—something he'd never imagined one such as he would be reduced to. He refused to consider that his present circumstances might be anything but temporary, though.

"You're looking peaked, Mr. Brady," Mickey said, stepping out of the cabin to eye Áedán critically. "Are you under the weather, then?"

Mr. Brady. Áedán hadn't known where he was and—at first—couldn't remember how he'd come to be there when Mickey had found him five days ago, washed up on the rocky beach. Mickey had asked his name, and Áedán almost answered without thought. For too long he'd been known only as Brandubh, the Black Raven, the Druid, but it would be foolish to announce to this stranger that he was the powerful entity of the ancient Book of Fennore—the being that had been feared by humans for thousands of years.

"Bra—I mean, Áedán," he'd amended quickly. "My name is Áedán."

Mickey had stared at him with narrowed eyes. "And would that be Brady, you were about to say?" he asked, knowing he hadn't gotten it right but inadvertently offering Áedán the cover he needed.

Áedán nodded. "Yes. Brady."

"You're a tad south, aren't you?"

Áedán shrugged, not sure what was meant by that.

"Ah, well. What's it matter? You speak a bit odd, but I won't be hiring you for your elocution, will I now?"

To that, Áedán said nothing. Mickey had put him to work on the *The Angel* and questioned him no more. From that point on, he became Áedán Brady, and for the privilege of sleeping in the surprisingly tidy berth below deck and taking meals with Mickey and his lovely, pregnant wife, Colleen, and his infant son, Niall, Áedán had toiled like a slave every day since.

It was incomprehensible that this had become his reality. That he, *Brandubh*, had come to this miserable existence.

"I am fine, Mr. Ballagh," Áedán answered Mickey's question now, looking into the fisherman's concerned face. "Just a bit seasick, I suppose."

"Aye?" Mickey frowned. Mickey was more at home at sea than on land.

The waves that had been gently lapping the hull of *The Angel* surged suddenly, tilting the boat to a dangerous angle, halting any other comments as Mickey hurried to check the lines securing her. "I can't say I've ever seen the bay like this," he said, eyeing it distrustfully before cutting his gaze to the man-made barricade that usually subdued the fierce tides enough to create a safe harbor. "Would you look at how fast that storm is moving in? Best batten the hatches else it will be on us before we've a hint of what's in store."

It was much more than a storm approaching, but Áedán didn't say it. He didn't know what came under its guise, even though it rasped against his senses like the scales of a serpent slithering through the night.

He picked up the knife he'd been using, intending to sheath it so he could help Mickey, just as a more violent surge slammed the boat. The knife jerked across his other hand, cutting it deeply. Immediately blood began to spill from a long slice on his palm and drip to the deck beneath his feet. It caught him by surprise, the sight of his own blood. He could not recall the last time he'd seen it.

His involuntary curse had Mickey hurrying to his side. "Ach, looks bad, lad," Mickey said, whipping a handkerchief from his pocket. He gave it a dubious glance and then wrapped it around Áedán's hand anyway. "You best go on to the house and tell the missus to patch you up. She's not worth much, that woman, but she can stitch as well as any doctor."

Áedán looked at the sky and then the ship that still needed to be readied before the storm.

"Don't worry on that," Mickey said. "I'll finish it up, and you'll have your meal and your bed just as if I'd had a full day's labor from you. It will all come out right in the end."

Áedán held to that thought. Yes, it would all come out right in the end. When he was restored, when he was once again as powerful as he'd been, Áedán would remember Mickey's act of kindness.

Gratitude. He frowned in disgust. *Another* emotion.

With a nod, Áedán stepped onto the weathered dock and strode away in the direction of Mickey's small house. But the lure of the cavern intensified with each step until he found himself turning toward it. Denying it seemed pointless and too cowardly—*too human.*

No matter that he answered to the name of Áedán Brady now, inside he was still Brandubh. The Black Raven. The most powerful Druid to ever draw breath.

As soon as he crested the first hill and was out of Mickey's sight, he veered off, his feet moving faster of their own accord as he headed to the ruins that landmarked the place to descend. The sky darkened and lightning split it into a thousand gray-white pieces as rain began to pelt him with fury.

Filled with urgency, he fought down the pervasive dread that battered him like the sea against the cliffs. He did not know what waited in the cavern, what new turning point it had in store. But he refused to let fear control him. Never again would he allow anything—*anyone*—to rule him.

By the time he reached the point where he could see the ruined castle, he was drenched and out of breath. For a moment he stilled, quaking inside as thunder exploded above. Emotions he couldn't begin to comprehend churned into foam and flotsam, miring any logic that might have surfaced.

Mindless, he raced to the stairs, pausing at the top as his eyes followed their deteriorated slope to the rocky beach below. He knew it had been millennia since he'd hacked them out of the granite cliff, and yet seeing the eroded decay solidified the sense of an eternity come and gone that was his life. Yet he could remember clearly the feeling of dangling over that abyss, of laughing at the danger, the peril of a fall as he'd carved each step. The stone had sparkled with hidden crystals and the sun had favored them, favored him. He'd been Brandubh, the bold Druid. Powerful. Feared.

Betrayed.

The steps were nearly worn away and caked with moss and slime. Treacherous in this storm and still he made his way down, trying to convince himself that his actions were his own. That he came because he was ready, not because he was compelled. The throbbing pain in his wounded hand kept him alert, kept him here and now when it felt like a thousand hooks had embedded in his skin with the lines attaching them stretched taut and towing him forward.

The storm had arrived with all the stealth and vehemence of his perdition. It whipped the sea into a tempest, and huge waves slammed against the beach, trying to shuck him out from between the rocks. They did not dissuade him. He was set now—determined to reach the cavern and face whatever it was that made a Druid fear.

He breached the point where giant boulders made rebellious sentries to the entrance, withstanding the rage of the tides. Then at last he stood in the small passageway that led into the cavern.

A shudder shook him from inside out, like the thunderous storm unleashed. He crossed the threshold into its blackness like a lamb to its slaughter.

The shadows inside heaved and lulled with the fearsome waves, splashing a black tide pool up against the guard stones that surrounded it. For a moment, he took it all in, comparing every detail to his memory of them—the rough walls, the uneven floor, the oily pool that glittered like a thousand mirrors reflecting and refracting the waning light from outside. But it was the runes on the walls— endless spiral symbols that had burned into the stone—that struck him to the core.

Those symbols covered the Book of Fennore, had flowed over each of its sacred pages. Those symbols were embedded in his soul like scars upon scars.

Breathing deep of the wet salty spray, he forced himself to advance into the cavern, laboriously separating shadow from shape. He felt the humming power that had once been his, felt the presence of the Book of Fennore, though he could not see it. So intent was he that he almost stumbled over the woman.

Stunned, he looked down at her crumpled body, and recognition caught him as unaware as this sudden storm, as his presence here in a place he'd vowed never to return to.

He'd seen her before, met her in the nightmare world called Inis Brandubh—a prison named ironically for the prisoner. They'd been allies of sorts, if such a thing could be had by one such as he.

Meaghan . . . her name was Meaghan.

Was she the reason he'd felt compelled to come here? A mere human? A woman?

She wore the same clothes she'd had on when last he'd seen her, though they were decidedly worse for the wear. Sprawled on the hard cold rocks as if she'd been flung there by a greater power, her skin was pale and unblemished, her hair damp and clinging to her head. She looked frail and defenseless, yet he knew better than to forget that beneath that pallor lurked a feisty woman who'd almost broken his nose the first time he'd met her.

He stood over her now, taking in the full curves, the soft slope of her belly, bared where the T-shirt rucked up around her ribs. Dark, greenish bruises covered her arms, and a particularly nasty one spread upward from her hip bone, black and purple above the waist of her jeans. For a moment the sight of her battered flesh touched off something inside of him. Sympathy? Compassion? Concern?

The alien emotions jeered at him. He did not care about others, especially those who weren't of some use to him. For *eons* he'd been an entity, a thing that did not experience, did not rejoice, did not mourn. He'd lived to siphon the emotions of others, to drain them dry, make them so empty that they'd choose death over their hollow existence. But he'd *felt* nothing for them, for their plight, for their demise.

And he felt nothing for this woman either.

She stirred, her eyes opening in the darkness, the palest of blue. She looked frightened, and with a groan she tried to lift her head. It seemed the effort took more than she had, but after a moment's struggle, she sat. She hadn't seen him yet, but her hands moved to tug her T-shirt back in place and smooth her hair in a self-conscious manner so unguarded that it made him pause.

Then she turned that clear, bewildered gaze to his face.

"Áedán," she breathed, and in the moment it took for the sound to whisper over his skin, he saw her expression change from puzzlement to recognition and then something darker, sweeter. It surprised him even as it shocked a reaction from him.

How long had it been since he'd known a woman as a man was meant to?

The stark answer filled his head. An eternity without end.

"What are you doing here?" he demanded, his confusion making his voice harsh, his infuriating fear still riding him without revealing its source.

The blue eyes darkened, wounded, and like a fool he felt another wave of compassion. *Feck*, he thought, using one of Mickey Ballagh's words.

He hunkered down beside her and she flinched, the small reaction like a flame held to his bare skin. "I'm not going to hurt you," he snapped, his anger feeding itself. "How did you get here?"

She shook her head, and Áedán noted that her eyes seemed glazed and unfocused as she searched his features. Instead of answering his question, she placed one palm against the roughened stubble on his cheek and the other over his pounding heart. He found his own hands against the soft, rounded curves of her shoulders and told himself he meant to push her away.

He didn't, though. Instead he stood, gently pulling her to her feet with him.

When he would have stepped back, Meaghan held on to him and rose to tiptoes, leaning into his body and brushing her lips against his in a caress as fleeting as it was riveting. Áedán froze, unprepared for the heat that licked his nerves and burned with his blood. A beast within him lifted its head and growled with satisfaction at the hot thoughts that filled his head. Perhaps this woman did have use.

But he didn't understand what motivated her to touch him, kiss him. When they'd met before, she'd been combative, berating him with little care for what he might do in retaliation. She'd had a wicked tongue that she'd used to lash out at her enemies. He'd expected that behavior from her now, but instead her mouth moved over his again in a silken heat.

What game did she play?

He wanted to ask, but his brain had locked down, refusing any distraction from the sensuous slide of her skin against his. The hand on his cheek trailed to the base of his skull, and she pulled his head down, teasing his lips with her tongue—which was velvety soft, not wicked, not cruel—until he gave in and opened for her, pulling her body against the hard planes of his in the same single act of surrender. Her taste hit his senses like a whisper of hallowed memories, evoking the sultry languor of summer nights, the fragrant spice of misted fields, the perfume of female, aroused under a pale moon . . .

Her soft curves molded perfectly against him, vanquishing any thought but keeping her there, yielding, responding, filling some hollow he hadn't known existed. She made a sound in her throat that set him on fire, made his hands hungry, his lips needy, his body parched.

It was his total capitulation that pierced the fog of want and made him hesitate.

This was not right. *She* was not right.

The Meaghan he'd known so briefly had been fire and hellion. She hadn't yielded to anyone, for anyone.

She opened her eyes slowly, confused as she tried to pull him back into her embrace. Her gaze was unfocused, her pupils so huge they'd swallowed all but a thin strip of blue at the edge. None of that fierce spirit he'd come to grudgingly respect glowed within them.

Entranced, he thought. *Bespelled.*

She fought his efforts to set her away from him, her movements sluggish, not quick and able. This woman had brought him to his knees with two quick blows within minutes of meeting him but now she seemed barely capable of standing.

"Meaghan," he said sharply, holding her at arm's length as she struggled to reach him. "*Meaghan!*"

He gave her a hard shake and then withdrew, needing space from her heat, from her soft scent, from her closeness. His body disagreed with his decision and urged him to take her—no matter what the terms. Have her, use her. She was only human, after all.

He scowled at his own surprising reluctance, but before he could decide what he meant to do about her, she stumbled over an uneven stone and lost her balance. He lurched toward her, trying to halt her momentum, but his reach was not long enough and his reactions too slow. Her shriek joined the echoes of his inner turmoil as she plunged into the icy tide pool.

She burst back to the surface and stared at him in shock. Her eyes were blue again, wide and snapping with anger.

"What the feck is wrong with you?" she shouted in a shaking voice. "You fecking pushed me!"

That was the Meaghan he knew.

"I did not push you, fool. You fell all on your own." He quickly moved to the side and reached out to her. "Here. Take my hand," he ordered.

She flashed him a furious glare and swam to the side, ignoring his outstretched hand. "I don't need your fecking help," she said, the damp and cold framing her words in a vaporous cloud that hovered at her lips.

The injustice of the moment hit his fury and perplexity like oil-soaked kindling. To think, he'd taken *her* feelings into consideration instead of simply taking what he wanted and leaving her to deal with her own circumstances.

"I didn't push you in and you know it," he said, still reaching for her, still confounded by the fact that he hadn't already stormed from the cavern.

Her eyes held defiance and fear. Her body shook with the cold. "Don't be stupid," he said. "You'll freeze to death if you don't get out."

"I-I k-know."

Meaghan, back to her familiar stubborn and irritable self, tried to haul her body from the pool, but the freezing temperature had already made her muscles stiff and her reactions slow. She hefted herself halfway and then slipped again.

Ignoring her feeble protest, Áedán gripped Meaghan by her arms and heaved her out of the freezing waters. Cursing beneath his breath, he looked at the pathetic and bedraggled female and again he felt that alien tug of compassion swiping the feet out from under him.

She didn't want his help. He should leave her and call it a good riddance.

He hunkered down beside her, shrugging out of his coat and wrapping it around her as he began to rub her icy hands with his.

"How did you get here?" he asked as he worked.

"Wh-wh-whe," she answered.

"Where? We are on the Isle of Fennore."

At the panicked look in her eyes, he shook his head. "No, not Inis Brandubh." Not the place where they'd met, where nightmares had been the only reality available. "I believe we have arrived in the year of nineteen hundred and fifty-six. I got here five days ago."

She absorbed this in silence, still shaking from head to toes. "Oth-oth—"

"No, I haven't seen any of the others." He searched her face, looking for hints of what had happened since those last, terrifying moments when they were together. "What happened to you, Meaghan? Where have you been since—"

The sound of a rock scuttling into the cavern behind him drew his attention and silenced the rest of his question. He stood and faced the passageway just as Colleen Ballagh—Mickey's young wife—stepped from the shadows into the cavern, a satchel in one hand, her baby in another.

She wore a shapeless brown dress with a black shawl over her shoulders and serviceable shoes on her feet. Her hair and clothing dripped wetly from the storm outside, which unleashed its fury in time with his own storming rage. She paused as she crossed the threshold to let her eyes adjust to the dark.

"What are you doing here?" he demanded, too shocked by the sight of her to temper his tone or words. *With a baby in her arms at that?*

Colleen ignored him as she peered through the gloom, anxiously hefting the baby up on her hip, making a soothing noise in her throat. Then her eyes fixed on Meaghan, and she let out a gasp.

"Jesus in heaven," she exclaimed, staring at the shivering woman. "Were you in the water? But why? It's nigh on winter, girl. You'll freeze to death!"

As if the two of them couldn't have discerned that without her help, Áedán thought. Not even a brash woman like Meaghan would have chosen to dip into the icy tide pool fully clothed.

"She slipped," Áedán said. "We need to get her warm."

Colleen didn't even glance his way. Instead she gaped at Meaghan as if she'd never seen a wet female before. Granted, Meaghan was a sight. The jeans she wore clung to her legs, and the T-shirt had become a second skin, outlining something lacy over her breasts, communicating just how cold she really was, reminding him how hot she'd felt just moments before in his arms. That traitorous feeling inside him protested at the sight of her body wracked with cold, but he steeled himself against his own baffling reactions.

Bending—for Colleen's benefit he told himself—he took Meaghan's hands between his again and continued to rub. Meaghan's breath plumed in front of her. Outside their shelter, thunder boomed ominously and all three of them startled. Colleen tucked the infant closer to her body, adjusting the blanket over his head to keep him warm.

What could have possessed her to come to this cavern in such a storm?

"What are you doing here, Mrs. Ballagh?" he asked again.

"Sure and didn't she tell me I'd find you here and to bring clothes, but I didn't know why, did I now?" Colleen said, still staring at Meaghan.

And with a trickle of unease, Áedán realized that she had yet to answer him. Was it deliberate? Was she angry about something? Colleen had never been anything but kind and thoughtful to Áedán since her husband had brought him to their door and commanded that she feed him.

"Who told you she'd be here?" Áedán asked. When Colleen still didn't respond to his question, he glanced at Meaghan, glad to see that spark still glinting in her eyes and the vacant look gone. "What is she talking about?"

Teeth chattering, Meaghan shook her head.

"It's the truth," Colleen went on, as if Meaghan had denied her claim. "She told me that I'm to go to the cavern this afternoon. 'Bring clothes,' she says. 'They might be needed.' She said I would find a girl and she might be as naked as Eve in the garden. Instead I find one near turned to ice, but I've no doubt it was you she meant."

"Who?" Áedán barked again. "Who told you?"

He stood and stalked to Colleen's side, feeling once again that dread coil tight and fear tripping over his skin. But with each step, a new kind of horror overtook him. Colleen's gaze never flickered from Meaghan. Even the baby in her arms gazed right through him as he stopped in front of them both.

"I don't suppose I even need to ask if your name would be Meaghan, do I?" Colleen went on, shaking her head even as she confirmed her suspicions. "What other young miss would be down here in the cold, shivering like an ice maiden?"

"Mrs. Ballagh," Áedán said, reaching out to take her arms in his hands and shake her. He watched a shiver go through her body at his touch, but she didn't look his way, didn't acknowledge that he was there. Instead she moved forward toward Meaghan with an air of purpose.

"I don't know how you got here, missy, or who you might be, but I'm here to help you. Let's get you out of those wet clothes and into the dry ones I brought."

And Áedán realized that his instinctive dread of this place had been well founded. He'd let his own vanity guide him, tell him that he was above such petty things as *fear*. He'd let this woman lure him into a trap.

After five days of taking meals across the table from Colleen, of working with her husband from dawn to dusk, of doing whatever menial task would help her, suddenly she couldn't see him . . . Why? What had happened? What had changed?

Slowly, horrified, he turned his eyes to Meaghan.

Only one thing.

From the minute he'd understood that he'd returned to the real world, he'd scorned his return to humanity, his loss of power. But now he realized there was something worse than being human.

Colleen hadn't answered him because she couldn't hear him, couldn't see him. He'd been wrong to think he was once again a man. Now he was less than even that. It wasn't this cavern that had caused his foreboding.

It was the woman.

Meaghan.

Whatever was happening now, he knew, somehow Meaghan was responsible.